"Rising star Maggie Shayne proves that she has what it takes to shine with a work that combines elements of gothic melodrama and romantic suspense and turns the mixture into something rare and precious."   —*Affaire de Coeur*

"Just when you think there's nothing new under the sun, Maggie Shayne reinvents romance!"   —*The Literary Times*

"Maggie Shayne makes it very easy for her audience to willingly suspend disbelief and partake in a delightful fantasy adventure."   —*The Talisman*

"Ms. Shayne has delivered another knockout read. Once again she serves up another erotic vampire tale, filled with dark secrets and powerful longings, with surprising twists and turns."   —*The Belles and Beaux of Romance*

"Maggie Shayne has the ability and the know-how to create suspense, action, and intimacy that will keep you on the edge of your seat, whether it is vampires or covert agents. I love reading Maggie Shayne!"
      —*GEnie Romance and Women's Fiction Exchange*

INFINITY

"[A] dark, enthralling brew of love, danger, and perilous fate."
—Jayne Ann Krentz

"A superb fantasy romance . . . The story line, especially the historical segment, is stupendous. . . . Nicodimus is a wonderful hero and the supporting cast adds dimension while propelling the tale forward to its exciting climax. . . . Ms. Shayne augments her growing reputation for some of the best fantasies on the market today." —*Painted Rock Reviews*

"A heartfelt and believable love story . . . Maggie Shayne's gift is that she creates believable characters who react very humanly to unbelievable situations . . . If you like lush romances set in well-conceived fantasy environments, don't miss *Infinity*." —*All About Romance*

ETERNITY

"A rich, sensual, and bewitching adventure of good vs. evil, with love as the prize." —*Publishers Weekly*

"A hauntingly beautiful story of love that endures through time itself." —Kay Hooper

"Maggie Shayne's gift for melding the mystical and the magical into her novels has made her one of the preeminent voices in paranormal romance today. *Eternity* is an awesome start to a series that promises to be richly textured and powerfully rewarding." —*Romantic Times*

"Ms. Shayne's talent knows no bounds when it comes to romantic fantasy; her latest is a hauntingly exquisite tale . . . lush . . . heart-stopping suspense, spellbinding romance, and enchanting characters. *Eternity* is to be treasured like the precious gem it is." —*Rendezvous*

"[*Eternity*] is one of the best books of the decade as the magnificent Ms. Shayne demonstrates why she is ranked among the top writers of any genre." –*Affaire de Coeur*

continued on next page . . .

DESTINY

Maggie Shayne

JOVE BOOKS, NEW YORK

This is a work of fiction. Names, characters, places, and incidents are either the product of the author's imagination or are used fictitiously, and any resemblance to actual persons, living or dead, business establishments, events, or locales is entirely coincidental.

DESTINY

A Jove Book / published by arrangement with the author

PRINTING HISTORY
Jove edition / February 2001

The Penguin Putnam Inc. World Wide Web site address is
http://www.penguinputnam.com

ISBN: 0-515-13013-3

A JOVE BOOK®
Jove Books are published by The Berkley Publishing Group,
a division of Penguin Putnam Inc.,
375 Hudson Street, New York, New York 10014.
JOVE and the "J" design
are trademarks belonging to Penguin Putnam Inc.

PRINTED IN THE UNITED STATES OF AMERICA

10 9 8 7 6 5 4 3 2 1

This book could not have happened without the help of some special people: My friends. They didn't help me with the research, or the plotting or the character development. They did something far more important than that. They came through for me when I was in trouble. They were there for me when I needed them. With kindness and wisdom they reached out when I was drowning and pulled me onto the shore.

It shouldn't surprise me. They always do.
So here's to you, dear ones: RomEx Rules!

Special thanks to Justine Davis, Anne Stuart,
and Gayle Callen

It also couldn't have happened without the support of my personal hero, who put up with my whining, tears, and hysterics over this project, and stepped in as he always does to take care of everything in the known universe so I could do what needed to be done. (And who dragged me off into the wilderness for a mental health weekend afterward.) Thank you, hon. You're my rock.

Author's Note

Research on the civilization known as Sumer has been a hobby of mine for almost a decade now. I knew that one of these days I'd find the right time to use it in a book, and now I have. The culture, the customs, and the religion of the time are accurately portrayed here, right down to the manner of greeting a respected friend, the clothing, the names, and even the description of the queen's headdress.

However, as happens in fiction, sometimes the author has to take a few liberties, and I want to be clear about those. First of all, two of the characters you meet in this novel, King Eannatum and Queen Puabi, were real Sumerian rulers. She was the Queen of a city-state called Ur, and he was the King of Lagash, and later all of Sumer. They both ruled around the same time—2500 BCE, and Eannatum truly was credited with unifying Sumer and ending threats from the nearby land of Umma. However, there is no historical record of Eannatum and Puabi ever meeting, much less having the relationship depicted here.

The other bit of poetic license I took was in stating that a priestess of the temple had to remain unmarried and chaste until and unless she was chosen to perform the Sacred Marriage Rite with the king. I have no way of knowing if that was the case. No source yet has said one way or the other, and indications are that the Sumerians saw sex as normal, healthy, and even sacred, so they may not have forbidden their holy women to engage in it, married or otherwise. However, the Sacred Marriage Rite itself was very real, and was common practice in Sumer.

The observations I've made in this book about the changing roles of women during this pivotal time in history are absolutely true. Women are still struggling to regain the status and power they had prior to 2500 BCE.

I've sprinkled a few Sumerian phrases through this book. These are guesswork at best, as pronunciations and meanings change with every new research book that comes out. Translating the old cuneiform tablets is one thing—trying to figure out how the language sounded is a great deal more difficult. Even the name "Nidaba" has been given as "Nisaba" in some sources. So nothing is certain.

All that said, I will add that any mistakes you may find in the research were obviously put there by evil typesetters intent on ruining my credibility. <grin>

Maggie Shayne

Prologue

When she opened her eyes, there was a sheet over her face.

She sucked in her next breath, her *first* breath, the breath of life itself, and it rushed into her lungs with a force powerful enough to burst an ordinary set. The power jolted through her, arching her back, electrifying her every cell for just an instant. Then she went limp again and released the air in a slow, shuddering sigh. Slowly, awareness returned.

She was in a vehicle that moved wildly and wailed like a hyena. An ambulance, she realized dully. Disoriented still, she tried to clear her mind, to recall what had preceded this latest death and revival, and found only vague memories; a struggle on a rooftop, a gun, the sense of plummeting downward, and the shattering impact at the bottom. She lifted a hand, to push the sheet away from her face. But her hand moved mere inches, and no more. She was strapped down.

Strapped down!

The emotional dam she had so carefully built broke

open wide to let ice-water panic flood her veins. A pulse beat in her temple and repeated itself, magnified, against her chest. Memories she had long ago buried clawed their way out of their graves, deep inside her mind, and a few gnarled fingers emerged to scratch at her hard-won sanity until they drew blood.

She had been strapped to a contraption like this one before. No details came just then, thank the Gods. Her control had been too hard won for that. Only sensations, feelings and emotions. Pain. Rage. Despair. Pain. Rage. And a tormentor who had savored her suffering.

"Release me."

The voice she heard was her own. It was deep, and low, and bore a tone of command, even though it shook with the force of the emotion it sought to conceal.

"What the hell . . ." someone said. And her mind heard: *Young. Male. Confused. Afraid.*

"Release me," she said again, louder this time, more firmly.

The sheet was yanked away from her face, and the wide brown eyes of a young man blinked down at her. "My God, she's alive!" he called, apparently to whoever was driving the screaming vehicle. He wore a uniform, a badge like a policeman might wear. Lights flashed from without, but the vehicle never slowed. "For the love of Christ, she's . . ."

"Loose the straps!" She commanded, twisting and tugging at the bindings that held her down.

"Easy, now," he said, hands to her shoulders, voice lowering to a soothing tone. "Take it easy. The straps are just to keep you from falling off. You need to lie still. You've been—"

She tugged harder, and one of the restraints snapped in two, lashing backward like a whip and slapping the young man's face even as he jumped away. He pressed a hand to his cheek, and his eyes widened. She could taste his fear but cared nothing about it. Reaching to the strap at her other arm, she ripped it free as well. Then the young paramedic found his courage and leaned over her again, grabbed her shoulders, pressed her body down.

"Calm down!" he ordered. "You'll hurt yourself!"

She shoved him away from her with so much force that he flew off his feet, and his back smashed into the paraphernalia lining one side of the vehicle. He was shouting now. The ambulance skidded to a stop even as she tore at the one remaining strap at her waist, snapped it easily, and surged to her feet. She couldn't stand upright in the vehicle. Bent over, she lunged toward the back of the ambulance, wanting only escape. Freedom.

All her life, it seemed, she had been made to fight for her freedom. She valued it above all else, in a way she imagined few others ever had.

The second man clambered in from the front and came rushing at her even as she reached for the doors. Escape was so close! He grabbed her shoulders. Turning on him like a cyclone, she flung him away. Items crashed and broke and spilled. Both men swore and grappled for her.

She lunged toward the doors again, but the younger one was right behind her now, having recovered himself. He jabbed her hard with something before she could fling him away, and the stab of the needle's fang pierced her flesh. She felt her eyes widen as she looked down at the hypodermic in her arm.

Drugs, her memory whispered.

Experiments.

Living death, mired in inky blackness with no hope of escape.

She would not go back to that place! She *must* not!

Yet she felt it creeping up on her even now. Reaching for her. Coming to pull her back into its cold embrace. "No . . ." she whispered.

She whirled on the young man, but dizziness made her sway. The man caught her in his arms. "Easy."

"Gods, what have you done to me?" She pressed a hand to her head as if she could slow the dizziness, the weakness, push it away somehow. "The drugs . . . you mustn't . . . give me drugs . . ." Her knees bent against her will. Her legs turned to water.

"It's just a sedative," he said, bearing her weight now, cradling her carefully. He was cut, bleeding in several places. The other one behind him held his arm oddly. Vaguely, she realized it was broken. He shouldn't have tried to stop her. He should have just let her go.

"You're going to be fine, I promise you," said the one who held her. "Come on, now." He eased her down onto the stretcher and she tried to push his hands off her, to resist, but she had no strength. Darkness closed in around the edges of her vision. Her body was slowly going numb. "Lie down, now," he said. "Relax."

"I . . . cannot . . ."

She moved her mouth, but no further words emerged. Hazy outlines now, the two men leaned over her, shaking their heads. One ran his hands over her legs, her arms. "I don't understand it," he was saying. "She was as bent and broken as—"

"Broken, hell," said the other, still clutching his arm to his chest. "She was *dead*. We were going through the motions, but we both knew we'd lost her."

"It was a mistake. We messed up—"

"She was dead, Jerry. You know it and I know it."

"That's not possible."

Her vision faded even as she saw the man shaking his

head. He said, "Damn, I think she broke my freaking arm."

"Can you drive one-handed?"

"Yeah. Yeah, I can manage it. Can you handle her?"

"I can *now*."

She heard the driver move away while the other man remained beside her, checking her for injuries. She felt the vehicle lurch into motion again, heard the siren begin to wail once more . . . but then it, too, faded into nothingness. She felt herself slipping away as well, and she fought to cling to her soul.

"I cannot let go," she whispered, sensing that if she did, she might never find her way out of the darkness again.

She needed something . . . something to cling to. Something to keep her anchored.

It came to her slowly, like a gentle, loving hand curling around her own. Her memories. Not the horrible memories she had buried so deeply, but the better ones. The real ones . . . of the life before.

"Yes," she said, though she never knew if she had spoken the word or only thought it. Four thousand, five hundred years and more had come and gone . . . but though the ages in between faded like morning mists, that *before-time* was as clear to her as if she were living it still. It was *her* time. She had known nothing of what she truly was then. She was a child, innocent, young, with so much ahead . . .

More than she ever could have guessed.

2501 B.C.E.
City-State of Lagash, Kingdom of Sumer

Her little *kaunake* dress was white and made of fine linen, just like the ones the grown-up priestesses wore.

It reached to mid-calf. Her feet were bare, at the moment. She wore the fringed shawl that was reserved for sacred occasions, and in her tiny hands she carried a large pottery bowl brimming with lush ripe fruits. The priestess beside her was dressed in the same manner, except that she also wore a golden band about her head, in deference to her station. Her arms were bare, save for the gleaming gold and silver bands wrapped around her coppery skin like vipers. Her hair was dark as night, and long and gleaming. The little girl thought the priestess Lia was the most beautiful woman in all the world.

Soberly, the two entered the *cella*, the room at the very top of the ziggurat tower. The little girl tried to concentrate on being serious and appropriately solemn as they crossed the dim room that was lined with stone statues, all winking their lapis lazuli eyes in the flickering torchlight. But the entire never-ending rite seemed so silly to her that she battled a smile, and finally a giggle emerged despite her best efforts.

The priestess looked down at her, a frown etched in her dark brows. "Hush, Nidaba! This is the most sacred room in the temple, the home of the Gods themselves! Show some respect."

Biting her lip, Nidaba stopped giggling. Instead she spoke. "The home of the Gods is in the heavens, is it not, Lia?"

"You know it is."

"Then how can they also live here, in these figures?"

"The Gods are everywhere, child. Now, come, we must attend them."

Nidaba sighed, but obeyed. The two walked forward, side by side, their feet whispering through the dried rushes that lined the floor and filled the *cella* with their green fragrance. They passed by all the smaller stone figures, which represented worshippers, for the Ancient

Ones must never be left unattended. At the front of the room were statues created to house the essence of several deities. Enlil Lord of Air, Enki Lord of the Fresh Waters and the *Abzu*, Nidaba, Goddess of the Sacred Script, for whom the little girl had been named. And standing in the center, larger and more beautiful than any, was the Queen of Heaven, Inanna.

Bowing deeply, the priestess Lia held her bowl of fruit before the Great Goddess, and chanted, *"Inanna me en, Inanna me en. Inanna duna agruna ka me en."* She placed the bowl of fruit at the feet of the statue.

"She won't eat it, you know," Nidaba said, eyeing the statue. "She *never* eats it."

"The offering is only symbolic," Lia said, obviously struggling now to keep the impatience from her tone. "You'll understand when you're older."

Nidaba sniffed. "The High Priest will eat what he wants of it, and we will get his scraps."

"That's enough, child. Now, go. Place your offering."

With a sigh, Nidaba walked to the statue depicting her namesake, held up her bowl of sweet-smelling fruits, and heard her stomach growl as she chanted the sacred words. Then she set the bowl at the feet of the Goddess, licked her lips, and snatched a plum, taking a big, juicy bite before Lia could stop her.

"Nidaba, you *mustn't*!" Lia pressed her hands to her mouth as Nidaba chewed and swallowed, smiling all the while. The priestess's wide-eyed gaze darted into every corner of the room around them, as if fearing witnesses to such blasphemy.

Nidaba only shrugged and took another bite, then wiped the luscious juice from her chin with one hand. "Why mustn't I? There is more of the Goddess in me than in this statue. And I am named for her, am I not? I will learn the sacred script one day soon. And then I will fill a thousand tablets with the reasons why it is wasteful and silly to feed delicious fruit to stone statues." Crossing her arms over her chest, she nodded once for emphasis. Her long, dark hair fell into her eyes, ruining her powerful declaration, she thought, but she simply stuck out her lower lip and blew the hair aside.

The priestess Lia seemed to stifle a smile, but it was a sad one. Kneeling, she gripped the little girl's shoulders. "You know that only boys are allowed to attend the *edubba* school and learn the sacred script."

"It's not fair, and you know it," Nidaba said, her chin coming up higher. "The Goddess never made that rule! I'll bet some . . . some *boy* did!"

Lia lowered her head a bit, conceding the point, but not aloud. Never aloud. "It is the way of things," she said. "It was not always so . . . but . . . well, it is today, and there is nothing to be done. I'm sorry, Nidaba."

"It was the Goddess Nidaba who gave us the script," the girl said slowly. "And *she* is not a boy."

"No, she is not."

"And it was Nidaba who gave me to you, as well, and gave me her name," the child went on.

The priestess nodded. "That is what some believe. You were found in a basket on the doorstep of the temple, with only your pendant, and the Goddess's name was etched in its face."

Remembering the tale she loved best, Nidaba softened her stance and her tone. "And you were the one who found me there," she said.

"Yes. There was a terrible storm that night. I found you howling with rage, your little face just red with fury. I brought you inside, and all the priestesses gathered round to see you. We wrapped you in dry clothes, fed you warm goat's milk sweetened with honey, sang to you until your wrath seemed to ease. And as it did, so did the storm. With your first smile, the clouds skittered away and the full moon beamed down on the city of Lagash. And that is why some believe you to be the daughter of the Goddess herself."

Nodding slowly, Nidaba smiled. But then she recalled the beginning of the conversation, and her smile became a frown. "Then . . . who would *dare* forbid me from attending the *edubba* school?" she asked.

Lia sighed. "It is as it is, Nidaba. We can only accept and be content."

"I will *not* be content. I want to go! I want to learn! I want to go to *edubba*!" Nidaba made fists of her hands, stomped her foot, and grated her teeth as a flood of rage washed through her. Her face heated and her heart pounded.

The floor beneath her bare feet began to tremble as she ranted and raged. The shaking intensified; the entire room, perched high atop the ziggurat tower quaked and shuddered violently. The stone images themselves rocked back and forth, some of the smaller ones tumbling onto their frozen faces.

Screaming in fear, Lia fell to her knees, prostrating herself before the image of the Goddess Nidaba, even as the tremors faded. "Forgive me!" she cried. "The child *will* learn the sacred script! I vow I will make it so!"

The rumbling stopped. There remained only silence as the little girl stared at the bowed form of her beloved priestess and felt sorry for her outburst. Quietly, Nidaba went to where Lia still knelt trembling, her face damp with tears. The child touched the priestess's shoulder. "Don't be afraid," she said softly.

"I have angered the Goddess!"

"But . . . you didn't," Nidaba whispered. Moving in front of Lia, she cupped the priestess's cheeks in her

small palms and looked right into her dark eyes. "The
Goddess didn't make all that fuss, Lia. *I* did."

Lia sat up slowly, looking at the child with eyes as
wide as the sky over all of Sumer. "You . . . *you* did?"

Nidaba gnawed her lip. "Sometimes . . . when I get
very angry, things . . . *happen*." She sighed and bent her
head. "I'll try not to do it again."

•

1

Of all the men he'd ever been, he thought he liked Nathan Ian King best.

He sat on the veranda, sipping strong Nepalese tea as the sun rose. Orange with a pink hue, its upper curve licked at the sky over the Atlantic. This veranda, on the back of his house, looked out over the sea from on high. It was the view that had made him choose this place . . . had made him want to stay. All that water . . .

It still seemed incomprehensible to him.

Nathan King was a collector and dealer in antiquities. He was an expert in his field, though few would venture to guess how he had come by his expertise. Even fewer would believe he had acquired most of the pieces in his personal collection long before they'd been considered old.

Nathan was at ease and content with his life. And why shouldn't he be? He had established his gallery in a "historic"—the term made him smile—two-story brick building on the narrow, cobbled streets of old Boston. Then he had purchased this estate, an hour's drive from the city. The house was a sprawling one, built of red brick in the Victorian style: flat roof, tall, narrow windows, endless rooms lining long hallways, all of it set on fifty acres of lush meadows and secluded woods against the backdrop of the mighty sea.

He had created Nathan King, and his *kingdom*, some ten years ago. He'd been tired, then, of caution, tired of living in anonymity, of keeping to himself, of moving around so frequently. Enter Nathan, who in a very short time had become known and loved by hundreds. Nathan, who contributed yearly to homeless shelters and scholarship funds. Nathan, who had even been known to speak to local students about various historical periods, at the requests of their teachers.

Nathan Ian King was a model citizen. He never so much as ran a red light. His life was so perfectly ordinary that it was almost boring.

Almost.

Too good to last, this persona. Already he knew his time as Nathan King would eventually come to an end. In ten years he hadn't aged a day. In ten more people would begin to wonder about that. And while he had cut off all contact with others of his kind, they were bound to find him out as soon as tales of a man who did not age began to surface.

Then again, he thought, lifting the porcelain cup to his smiling lips, there was always makeup. A drastic measure, perhaps, but possible. He was really going to hate to give up his mundane life as Nathan King. It had been peaceful, tranquil . . . and not a single immortal Witch, Dark or Light, had tracked him down in all the time he'd been living it. The past decade had healed some of his oldest wounds, he thought. Like an overworked laborer after a long vacation, he felt renewed. Almost . . . reborn. Which was a miracle in itself.

"Got the mornin' paper for you, Nathan."

Nathan inclined his head without taking his eyes off the spectacular sunrise in progress over the ocean. So much water. The abundance of so precious an element still amazed him, even after so much time. You could take the man out of the desert, he mused . . .

"Come, George. Watch this with me. It's incredible."

"Aw, you say that *every* mornin'," George said, obviously unimpressed but with a touch of humor in his childlike voice. He closed the French doors behind him and lumbered onto the veranda to take a seat at the round glass-topped table. He tossed the newspaper down in front of Nathan, but Nathan didn't so much as glance at it. Not yet.

The sun rose still higher, its neon-orange glow spreading now over the face of the water, reflected in a million glowing ripples. And higher still, beaming warmth onto Nathan's face, spilling light and heat over his body. "It's glorious," Nathan whispered.

A deep, booming laugh escaped George. "You say *that* every mornin', too."

"I do, don't I?" Nathan finally dragged his gaze away to look at George. As always, his right-hand man was dressed . . . interestingly. Today he wore a stylish brown suit from the Big and Tall Shop over a pink tie-dyed T-shirt that he must have picked up at a garage sale. Glancing down, Nathan saw the ever-present Air Jordans on George's size 12 feet. He managed not to smile. He wouldn't hurt the big man's feelings for the world.

"So tell me what's on the schedule for you today, George," Nathan began.

But before George could answer, there was a thump on the French doors. Nathan looked up to see Sheila, her pudgy arms weighed down by a cluttered tray, stand-

ing on the other side of them. Nathan jumped up and
flung the doors open.

"About time, too!" Sheila huffed, handing him the
tray. "A lady could die of old age by the time you two
gentlemen got around to opening a door for her."

Nathan smiled at her. He knew full well her name
wasn't Sheila. Not really. She used to wait tables at a
diner where he liked the tea. Until they caught her steal-
ing leftovers to feed the pigeons outside and fired her.
Just an excuse, really. She was getting on in years, and
maybe someone had learned, as well, that she hadn't
given them her real name and that her green card was a
fake.

If you asked her who she was, where she was from,
her reply was always the same. "Just a sheila from Down
Under. Born in the bush and raised with the joeys."

She sank into a chair at the table and fanned her face
with one hand for dramatic effect. "I swear, you two
will work me to death one of these days."

She was kidding. It was a running joke how hard the
two men of the house tried to *keep* her from overdoing.
When Nathan thought about the way she had been living
when he'd met her—the condition she had been in . . .
ah, but that was over now. She was part of his own, odd
little family. She kept pigeons of her own up on the flat
roof of Nathan's house.

"Breakfast smells fantastic," he told her, carrying the
laden tray to the table and scrutinizing her weathered
face, as he did every morning. She would never say a
word if she was feeling poorly. She couldn't know it,
of course, but Nathan would pick up on it anyway. His
gift was empathy. He tended to pick up on and often-
times internalize the pain—physical or otherwise—of
others. He'd had to learn to shield himself, block it out,
for the most part, or live in misery. But he often lowered

his guard to experience the feelings of those closest to him. It was probably why, when he loved at all, he loved so much.

Today Sheila was well. Her cheeks were pink and plump and freckled, eyes bright and blue. Her carrot hair, just starting to line itself with silver strands, was pulled into a 1950s-style ponytail high atop her head.

"My breakfasts *always* smell fantastic!" she declared with a wink. She reached for his newspaper, moving it out of the way as Nathan deposited the tray in the middle of the table. Then she said, "Oh, my, now, is this a sorry-looking beauty!" She turned the paper toward him, and Nathan glanced down with feigned interest as he took his own seat.

Then he went still, staring at the small photo in the sidebar on the front page. The caption read, "Do You Know This Woman? (Story on page 10)"

Nathan's throat went dry. His eyes seemed to burn and his vision blurred. Even as he stared, trying to make sense of something he knew to be impossible, George and Sheila were taking their plates from the tray, removing the shiny stainless-steel lids, and digging in.

"Today we'll get those new bulbs planted in the front garden, won't we, Georgie?" Sheila was saying. "It's gonna be turnin' cold before we know it. We'll soon be fresh out of time for fall gardening."

"I like to plant things," George said with a smile.

"Will you have time to pick us up some more mulch on your way home from the shop tonight, Nathan?" Sheila asked.

Nathan didn't reply. He was lifting the newspaper now, staring down at the photo, unable to look away, even to read the story that went with the hauntingly familiar face in the photograph.

"Nathan?" Sheila asked.

He finally tore his gaze away from the photo and turned to Sheila. "I . . . Sorry, I . . ."

"Say, now! Is it the unknown beauty who's got you so dumbstruck?" She was using her motherly tone. From time to time she tended to do so. More often with George than with Nathan, however.

She leaned closer, looking over his shoulder, and Nathan smelled the ever present scent of Ben-Gay on her shoulders. "She's a looker, she is. All that long, dark hair. Do you know her, then?"

"I . . . No, I don't believe so."

"Couldn't tell from the look on your face, love. Crimey, you've gone chalk white."

He shook his head in denial, because, of course, it was not possible. "She resembles someone I knew once."

It was George's turn to become curious. He got to his feet and limped around the table to lean over and stare as well. "I know who she is," he announced, as if it should be obvious to them all.

His words made both Nathan and Sheila stare up at him.

George smiled. "She's the lady in the picture," he said, looking toward the French doors with a nod. "The one in the front parlor, over the fireplace."

Nathan closed his eyes. Neither of them could know he'd painted the piece himself. Neither of them ever would, if he had his way. His secrets were his own. And knowing them . . . could be dangerous. Fatal.

"Well, now, you know, George, you're right. She *does* look a good deal like the woman in that painting! Isn't that curious?" Sheila asked, and her eyes narrowed on Nathan. "Turn the pages, Nathan, love. Don't keep us in suspense."

He pried his numb fingers loose and managed to turn the pages. He found the article beneath the headline

MIRACLE IN MANHATTAN.

Yanking her bifocals out of her apron pocket, Sheila perched them on her nose and read aloud in her Aussie accent. " 'An unidentified woman survived an apparent suicide attempt in Manhattan last week.' " She clucked her tongue. "Oh my, such foolishness! 'Witnesses claim the woman jumped from the rooftop gardens of the Hotel Tremayne on Wednesday night and fell four hundred feet to the street below. Paramedics at the scene were astounded. The woman, who they said appeared to have been near death, regained consciousness en route to the hospital. She became disoriented, and even violent, breaking the arm of one paramedic in her panic.' "

Tilting her head, Sheila frowned. "My, now, but she don't look strong enough to break a twig, does she?"

Nathan gently took the newspaper from Sheila's hands, and she let him, looking at him with worry in her eyes.

Nathan read on, silently. The woman had been sedated and taken to a nearby hospital. Despite what should have been a lethal plunge, the article reported, she was unharmed but catatonic, and had been moved to a mental hospital in New Jersey.

" 'No identification was found among her personal effects,' " Sheila read, the sound of her voice startling Nathan by coming from so close. She had run out of patience and was now reading over his shoulder. " 'Police are asking for help in establishing her identity and locating her family. She is approximately five feet nine inches tall, of slender build, with black hair and eyes, and an olive complexion, perhaps indicative of Middle-

Eastern descent. The only other possible identifying features, police said, are a pierced left nostril, in which she was wearing a ruby stone—' "

"A ruby stone," Nathan echoed.

" '—and an unusual birthmark,' " Sheila read on. "Odd, they don't say what the birthmark might be."

Nathan swallowed the lump of sandstone that seemed to have lodged in his throat. "They'll keep that quiet. A genuine relative would know. That way they can filter out crackpots."

"Makes sense," she said. "Lord knows, this sorry world has enough of those."

Nathan stared at the story, willing it to tell him more, but the final line was nothing but the number to call should anyone have knowledge of the woman's identity.

He folded the paper closed, staring again at the fuzzy black-and-white photo on the front page—the one that looked so much like a woman who had been dead for well over four thousand years.

She couldn't possibly be the same person.

And he couldn't possibly rest until he knew that for sure.

He gave his head a shake, closed his eyes. Gods, it had been so long. He told himself it was an illusion, a trick of a faulty memory. But he knew better. He could never forget her . . . could never forget the woman she had been, the woman he had loved.

Or the girl he had known first . . .

The young prince removed the royal cloak with its fiery crimson fabric and gold-threaded edging the moment he got beyond the palace doors. It was cool within, but far too hot outside beneath the blazing sun to wear such heavy garments. Besides, the cloak set him apart. When he went to the *edubba* school for his daily lessons in the art of the scribe—as his father insisted he must—he preferred to look more like the other boys.

Not that it did much good. They all knew who he was. And they avoided him as if he were an outcast. No twelve-year-old boy would wish to befriend the son of his king.

And now, Eannatum thought glumly, his father had decided that he needed still more lessons to prepare him for ruling Lagash of Sumer one day. Lessons in *religion*, of all things.

And he had no choice but to obey.

He walked the hot paths from the *edubba* through the center of the city. Grasses grew lush on either side of the well-worn paths of Lagash. Palms and *hashur* trees shaded his way, growing between and around the frond-covered roofs and sun-bleached mudbrick stalls of merchants and tradesmen. He passed countless people, many with bundles on their backs, farmers come to trade and craftspeople of all kinds, some with so many crops or wares that they came with donkeys or oxen pulling laden carts along behind them. Others displayed sculptures and jewelry, pottery vessels and new clay tablets, wrapped in wet leaves to keep them moist. And even more vendors hawked fruits and vegetables and grains, costly fabrics and more. Anything you might desire could be found in his father's kingdom. The city was a thriving one, gleaming like a jewel on the banks of the Euphrates. A lush oasis in the midst of the wild desert. It made young Eannatum lift his chin a bit higher and straighten his spine as he walked.

The path wound further and then, towering before him, was the mighty ziggurat. A huge structure, a man-made mountain, bleached white by the sun and reaching into the very heavens. It was built with a massive square base. Each succeeding level was a smaller square, all the way to the sacred *cella* at the very top. It resembled a giant stairway on all sides, one that might seem to lead to heaven itself.

This was his destination, and he mounted the steps with some trepidation. Learning the ways of the temple priests and priestesses—the ways of magick, divination, healing—was a frightening prospect. Far more difficult, he suspected, than learning to make the symbols of the written language on the moist clay tablets at school. But more than the lessons themselves, Eannatum feared he might disappoint his father. And above all, he did not wish to do that. He often felt burdened by the weight of his father's expectations. He disliked being set apart from the other boys his age. He disliked being held above them, and often wished he could put on a disguise and run away to live the life of a normal boy.

Much as he might fantasize about that, though, he knew his duty. And he took honor seriously. He would do what he should . . . what he must.

He opened the door at the top of the stairs and stepped out of the blazing sun into the cool, dim corridors of the tower's lower levels. The door groaned as it slowly swung closed behind him.

Eannatum swallowed hard, looking around.

Then the flickering of a torch appeared in the distance, and a female voice said, "This way, my prince."

With a nod, he followed that dancing torchlight, barely glimpsing she who carried it. Brief flashes of her white robes, and the gold bracelets adorning her arms were all he was allowed. He was led to a small room, where baked stone tablets lined the shelves on the walls. In the center was a table of wood, with three chairs around it and a rack of unlit candles in its center.

"Sit. Light the candles and wait," the woman said. She

then anchored the torch she carried in a chink in the
wall and vanished like a shadow.

Eannatum sighed, wondering what would become of
him were he to wander off into the depths of this massive structure. He'd been inside before, of course. During ceremonies and on the High Holy Days. But then
he'd been in the company of his father and a dozen
servants. The halls had been alive with people and chanting and alight with candles and torches.

It was different now. Dark. Lonely. So dim and hollow that every step, every breath, echoed a thousand
times. Haunted, he thought. His footsteps in the corridors had bounced from the walls over and over again,
and it had sounded as if he were surrounded by netherworld ghosts.

He took the candlestick to the torch in the wall, lifted
the wicks to the dancing flames, and lit them one by
one. Then he carried the softer candlelight to the table
and replaced it in the center. Waiting had never been his
favorite thing to do. As the son of the king, he rarely
had to tolerate it. But today he must. So to pass the time,
he removed the moist clay tablet from the sack he carried, and took out the stylus reeds as well. He might as
well work on his lessons as sit here wasting time.

He was still bent over the tablet, pressing symbols into
clay with the reed, when the priestess stepped into the
room. At her side was a girl, younger than Eannatum by
two years, at least.

The priestess was beautiful, as was every priestess
Eannatum had ever seen, be she young or old, plump or
poor. There was a kind of emanation from women who
served the Goddess. A glow that seemed to come from
within, making them beautiful to any eye that beheld
them. What they might actually look like seemed to Eannatum to have very little to do with that beauty.

But the girl . . . the girl was different. Stunning. Her eyes were large and round, thickly fringed with extravagantly long, curling lashes and gleaming black in the candlelight with an intensity that took his breath away. Her brows were thick and dark, her lips, lush and red. And there was something else about her . . . something invisible, yet real all the same. It was something that went beyond that inner light that all priestesses possessed. He didn't know what it was, but he was certain it was real. She made his stomach clench tight and his skin heat and tingle. The feelings confused him.

The priestess bowed slightly. "Welcome, my prince," she said. Then she nudged the little girl beside her.

The girl looked startled. "Prince?" she asked. "Are you Prince Eannatum?"

"Yes," he said, smiling slightly when her eyes went wider.

Again the priestess nudged the girl, and this time the girl bowed, but only halfway. She never took her eyes from Eannatum's. And when she straightened, she looked up at the priestess, a question in her eyes. "Lia, what is the prince doing here?"

The priestess smiled at the girl. It was obvious to Eannatum that the woman loved the child very much. He wished yet again that his own mother had lived beyond the day of his birth, that he might have known such love. But regrets were a waste of his thoughts.

To distract himself, he answered the girl's question himself. "My father feels that if I am to be fit to rule one day, I need more education than just that of the *edubba*. He wishes that I learn all the tales of the Gods and of creation. All the rites and divinations mastered by priests and priestesses. And all the secrets of magick."

"Yes," the priestess said. "All the very same things

you are learning here with us, Nidaba," she told the girl.

"The king is very wise," the girl whispered.

Her name was that of a goddess, and Eannatum remembered hearing talk about her, but just then he was too busy watching her to recall it. He had placed all his stylus reeds into a pottery vessel on the table, and the girl's eyes kept darting to them. He saw eagerness and longing unmistakably gleaming from their ebon depths.

"This is my charge," Lia said to him. "Her name is Nidaba."

He nodded, noticing for the first time the onyx pendant the girl wore around her neck. As shiny and black as her eyes. And it came to him what he'd heard of her before.

"You are the one they say is born of a goddess," he said.

"That is what some say, yes." She moved forward without being asked and sat down at the table, her eyes still flicking over the stylus reeds every few seconds and over the clay tablet on which he'd been doing his assignment.

"I was hoping you might allow Nidaba to join us in your lessons, my prince," the priestess Lia said. "She is truly the most gifted student we've ever had here at the temple. She will be a powerful priestess one day."

At the praise the girl smiled, bowing her head slightly but beaming with pride all the same.

"I thought you two might become friends," Lia continued. "Learning is always easier with a friend at your side."

Eannatum looked warily at the girl. "Are you not afraid to be my friend?" he asked.

Her chin came up. "I am not afraid of anything. Why should I be?"

Such a spirited reply surprised him. He tried not to

smile, because he thought it would offend her. But he found her truly amusing. So small, so pretty . . . and yet obviously not the least bit intimidated to be in the presence of her future king. "Not afraid of anything?" he repeated, lifting his brows.

"No."

"I don't believe you. What about a lion? Surely you would be afraid of a lion?"

"What could a lion do to me?" she asked, tilting her head to one side.

"Kill you and eat you, of course!"

Nidaba looked very thoughtful. "Then perhaps I should finally be able to know my mother and my father."

Eannatum fell silent for a moment. He could see the sadness in her eyes, hear it in her voice. His own voice was softer when he said, "They are dead, your parents?"

Nidaba shrugged. "They must be dead. Or else why would they not have kept me to raise for their own?" She looked down at the table. "Unless they simply did not want me."

"No," Eannatum said quickly. "It couldn't have been that." And he meant it, though he barely knew her.

"Why couldn't it?"

He smiled at her, seeing a slight moisture now glistening in her downcast eyes. "You are wise, your priestess says. It's plain that you are brave as well. And you are quite the prettiest girl in all of Lagash. Only a fool would give such a child away."

The girl's head came up quickly, and she presseed her hands to her cheeks. They grew pinker, and she smiled. Eannatum saw the moisture in her eyes vanish and felt extremely pleased with himself.

"Why would you think I might be afraid to be your friend, Prince Eannatum?" she asked at length.

"If we are to be friends, you must call me Natum. I like it far better."

"All right—Natum, then. Surely the other boys at the *edubba* school are your friends. Aren't they?"

"My friends?" he asked, lifting his brows. "They are afraid even to sit too close to me, in case they might make some mistake and offend me, thus incurring my father's wrath."

Nidaba smiled at him. "More likely they're afraid you'll tell your father of the mischief they make." Then she leaned closer over the table. "But I *do* know how it feels, Natum. Girls give me a wide berth when I pass them in the streets."

"And why do you suppose that is?" he asked, fascinated by her even though he was not entirely certain just why.

She shrugged. "I think they fear that I really *am* part deity, and that I can incinerate them with my divine glare." As she said it she narrowed her eyes to slits, demonstrating what she perceived to be a frightening look. It only made him smile wider.

"And can you?"

Her smile was swift and brilliant, and so stunning he had to gasp for his next breath. She crossed her arms over her chest, and settled back into her chair again. "I have never tried. But I promise not to try it on you, so long as you promise not to report my mischief to your father."

"It's a bargain, then."

Reaching across the table, he clasped Nidaba's hand in his, and the feeling that went through him was like none he had known before. A tingling, jolting sensation that made no sense. Her eyes widened and leapt to his, and she drew her hand back quickly, staring down at her palm. So she had felt it too, then. How very odd. It had to be a sign. An omen.

"You will be my first real friend," he said, already sensing that it was true. And he reached out again to take her hand.

Warily she slid her hand into his, and again there was that jolt, but only briefly. It passed in an instant, and he closed his hand around hers, cradling it, and liking the feeling.

"And you will be mine," she told him in return, her hand warming beneath his as their fingers laced and their eyes seemed to lock.

Lia cleared her throat. Eannatum released Nidaba's hand quickly, and they both looked up at the priestess. "Nidaba can be a great help to you in your lessons," she told Eannatum. "She is already far more talented at divination and certain healing rites than many of the priestesses in the temple."

"Than *all* of them, she means," Nidaba whispered behind her hand, her eyes sparkling with mirth.

Lia sent her a quelling look. But the remark only made Natum like the girl more. "I'll be grateful for the help," he said. "My work at the *edubba* takes up most of my time, and for these added studies I will take any help offered. But . . . but I would wish to repay your kindness in some way, Nidaba. Is there anything you would like in return?"

Nidaba's gaze fell again upon the clay tablet, covered with wedge-shaped figures. Then she looked up at Lia. The priestess nodded once. Licking her lips, facing Eannatum once more, Nidaba said, "Yes. There is something. Something I wish for more than anything in all of Sumer." She reached out and gently took the reed stylus from the pottery cup. Staring at it, she whispered, "I wish to learn the script."

For some reason, the declaration seemed perfectly
logical. It didn't surprise him in the least. Though he
supposed it should have, since girls were no longer allowed to learn the script. It had always seemed an odd
law to him, but it had been that way for his entire lifetime. His father said it had not always been so. "Then I
will teach you," he said.

Her eyes widened as she looked from the pen to his
face. "You will? Honestly, you truly will?"

Smiling, he bent down, reached into his pack on the
floor, and pulled out a new tablet, still wrapped in moist
leaves. Unwrapping it, he placed it on the table, took a
fresh reed from the cup, and carefully inscribed the symbols that stood for Nidaba's name into the clay.

Fascinated, the girl came around the table to stand
beside him, leaning over him to see what he had done.
"That . . . that's my name," she whispered. "Just like on
my pendant."

"Yes." He pushed the tablet sideways so it was in
front of her. "Now you make the symbols. Just the way
I did."

She stared at him, blinking, looking doubtful, but he
nodded at her. She bent over the tablet, clutched the
stylus awkwardly, and began. Eannatum watched, oc-
casionally covering her hand with his own to help her
guide the stylus reed. The result was clumsy, sloppy, but
legible.

And her eyes were brighter than any two stars in the
Sumerian night sky. "I did it," she whispered, awestruck.

It amazed him that such a small thing could mean so
much to her. And it amazed him even more that seeing
that light in her eyes, and knowing he was the one who
put it there, could make him feel the way it did.

"Thank you, Natum," she whispered. "You have
given me a gift more precious than anyone ever has. And

I will not forget. Not even if I live forever."

"Don't be silly," Eannatum said with a grin. "No one lives forever."

Folding the newspaper and setting it carefully aside, Nathan looked up at his two dearest friends. He had been living the life of a mortal for a long time. He'd had no contact at all with others like him. He loved this life of his. And he knew—dammit, he knew full well—that he would be risking all he had built if he did what he felt compelled to do.

And yet he had no choice.

"I can't explain this to you . . . but I need to go there."

"Go where, Nathan?" Sheila asked.

He cleared his throat. "To New Jersey. To . . . to this hospital. I need to see her." Lowering his head, fixing his gaze on that fuzzy photo once more, he muttered, "I need to be sure."

2

Masses of raven hair, uncombed, unwashed and tangled, spilled over the shoulders and down the front of her straitjacket. She sat on the floor in the darkest corner of her locked room. Knees drawn up to her chest, eyes focused on nothing and utterly vacant. Onyx eyes. Thick, dark lashes. She never blinked, seemed totally unaware of Nathan, peering at her through the tiny square of double-paned, mesh-lined safety glass in the door.

"So?" Dr. June Sterling asked. "Do you know her?"

There was a tight knot in Nathan's chest. This couldn't be . . . it couldn't be Nidaba. "Can I go inside?" he managed, though his voice came out hoarse and barely audible.

"It's your neck." The short, slender woman with her bobbed auburn hair and gold-rimmed glasses took a jangling key ring from her pocket and unlocked the door. "Just don't get too close."

"I don't imagine she could hurt me if she wanted to," he said, staring at the heavy-lidded eyes veiled by locks of matted hair. "It looks as if she's drugged to the point where she's not even lucid."

"Mild tranquilizers don't make people catatonic, Mr. Smith." Pushing the heavy door open, the doctor stood back to let him pass.

"Not most people, no." He walked into the room, saying nothing more. What could he say? That in immortals, certain drugs could have exaggerated effects? No, of course he couldn't. Not without ending up in the padded room next to this one. So he said nothing at all.

He stood there for a moment, just staring at the woman, torn between hoping she was Nidaba and hoping to the Gods she wasn't. Because he'd known Nidaba. Fiercely proud, stubbornly independent. She would hate the way he'd been living his life, he thought vaguely. She had been the opposite of this boring man he had created. Free. Unashamedly proud to be who and what she was and refusing to tone it down or hide her truest self for anyone. And let those who had a problem with that be damned.

No, the Nidaba he had known wouldn't like Nathan Ian King very much. Not the way she had liked King Eannatum.

And she would rather have been dead than reduced to this . . . this . . . shell of a woman. If she was aware of her surroundings, the confinement alone would have been enough to drive her mad. She had always been a free spirit. The freest he had ever known.

This woman could not be that fierce priestess he had known. She could not be his Nidaba.

His throat painfully tight, Nathan spoke without turning, his eyes on the pathetic piece of humanity curled into the fetal position on the floor in front of him. "Leave me alone with her, will you?"

"I don't think—"

"Just go out and close the door. I'll take full responsibility."

"Mr. Smith, that isn't—"

"For the love of God, *do it*." If he put some small
portion of his power into the command, he couldn't help
it. Manipulative it may be, but, dammit, he needed pri-
vacy. He needed to see her. To touch her.

To *know* . . .

Dr. Sterling said no more. She backed out, her steps
echoing as she left. The door groaned as it closed again.
Good. Nathan braced himself, took a deep breath, told
himself this woman wasn't Nidaba. She couldn't be Nidaba. He crossed the room to where she sat on the floor,
moving slowly so he wouldn't startle her. "Hello," he
whispered, keeping his voice low, filling it with tranquility and calm. Whoever she was, the last thing he
wanted to do was frighten her. "I've come to visit you.
Is that all right?"

The woman didn't move. Didn't blink. Just sat there,
her knees drawn up, arms wrapped around them, head
tipped down against them, hair curtaining her face. Her
hospital gown had bunched around her hips, and her
underpants were showing. He couldn't see her hip. If
she were immortal—and Nidaba or not, he suspected she
must be immortal—the mark would be there. She was
still rocking slightly back and forth, forehead to her
knees. Her tangled hair was wild, and the room smelled
of disinfectant and vaguely, urine.

Nathan moved closer, crouched before her, and very
slowly lifted a hand to her hair. For more than a week
she had been confined here. And he had to wonder if
she had been bathed or properly cared for once in all
that time. Her hair was matted, knotted, and dull. He
touched that hair, pushed it aside and tried to see her
face. But she tipped her head downward even more

sharply, and she hunched her shoulders against him.

"It's all right," he whispered. "I just want to see you."

Her rocking had stopped. She sat rigid, tense. Trembling.

She was afraid of him. And while he was sorry for that, it made him even more certain that she could not be Nidaba, despite the resemblance. Nidaba had never been afraid of anything.

He lifted his hand again. She flinched.

"I'm sorry. I didn't mean to frighten you." Sighing, Nathan lowered his hand, and his gaze with it. And then he saw the edge of a berry-colored birthmark, just peering out from the bottom of the hospital gown, on her right hip. His mouth went dry as he moved his hand to the gown, touching only the fabric, not the woman, watching her the whole time and seeing not a flicker of interest in her unfocused, unblinking eyes. He lifted the edge of the gown. And he saw it—the crescent moon emblazoned on her right hip. His stomach heaved, and his back bowed with the force of it. Nathan bit his lip to keep the shock from taking over, tried to reason with his own mind.

Immortal. Yes, whoever she was, she was that. But he had already suspected that might be the case. For her to have survived the fall from the top of that building, to have revived in the ambulance, to have had the strength to fracture the arm of an attendant—she would have had to be an immortal High Witch. She was one of the Light Ones, obviously—if she were a Dark Witch, the mark of the crescent would be on her left flank rather than the right. But that didn't mean she was his Nidaba. It couldn't mean that.

It mustn't . . .

"Nidaba?" he whispered.

He touched her chin, to tip it up. The jolt sizzled

through him at the contact, as happened whenever one immortal High Witch touched another. Like a static charge, only magnified.

She jerked away so fast that her head slammed into the wall behind her. Had the wall not been padded, he was certain she would have split her skull.

"Easy, easy," he said, his voice low, soft, coaxing. "I need to look at you . . . please . . ." Softly, very gently, he cupped her chin again. She flinched, but not so violently this time. And, finally, he managed to turn her face up so he could see her. Her tangled hair fell away, revealing her fully to him.

Sunken eyes, haloed in gray. Hollow cheeks, jaw too sharply delineated. Despite all of that, he knew this face—knew it well. His eyes drank in every bit of it, but only for a moment. Because his vision became clouded . . . with tears he thought he'd finished shedding long ago. Seeing her hurt—*physically hurt*—like a blow too powerful to withstand. It was a moment before he could even manage words.

"By the Gods, it *is* you," he whispered. "Nidaba . . . what's happened? What's happened to you?" Instinctively, he put his arms around her shoulders, pulled her to his chest, rocked her slowly—but it was like embracing a corpse. There was no response. No reaction. Barely any warmth at all. Nothing even to indicate that she was alive. And yet he held her against him, held her close as he hadn't done in too long . . . and realized he was trembling fiercely.

Finally he withdrew his arms from around her, settling his hands on her shoulders instead. He stared into her expressionless face. "Where are you, Nidaba?" he whispered. "Where have you gone? Can you hear me at all? Do you even know I'm here?"

She didn't blink, didn't flinch. Just curled there

limply, eyelids at half mast, head heavy on a boneless
neck. He had believed her dead. He had mourned her to
the point of madness. He had existed in living anguish
for years before he had even begun to recover from her
loss. And he never had recovered from it—not fully.
Now, his head was spinning—he was reeling with the
realization that she had been alive all this time. And he
had never known. Never . . . but then again, he hadn't
known there *were* such beings as immortal High Witches
when he'd known Nidaba. He hadn't learned any of that
until much, much later. And by then she had been dead
. . . her body burned to ash.

Or so he had been led to believe.

He didn't think Nidaba had known what she was back
then, either. But she had learned all the secrets, in time.
And when she had, she would have realized that he was
immortal as well. Why hadn't she come back to him,
then? Why hadn't she sought him out, found him, told
him she was alive? Why would she have hidden from
him all this time?

The door opened. He felt a cold draft but dismissed
it quickly. "Well?" Dr. Sterling asked from the doorway.
"Is she the woman you thought she was?"

Slowly, Nathan gathered his wits. He couldn't take
his eyes off Nidaba. Sitting there, vacant eyes staring at
nothing, mouth slightly agape and wet. If he took her
from here now, openly, the papers would run the story.
Nidaba had already become fodder for human-interest
stories. The tale of the woman who had survived a fatal
fall would be told, and they would track her down, track
him down, despite his use of a false name. His haven,
his perfect, anonymous life, would be ruined. And he
would have gladly allowed it to be, for her sake. But it
wouldn't end there. If her whereabouts were known, Nidaba would be in danger. She wouldn't be able to defend

herself in this state. He needed to take her away from here, in secret. Protect her. Try to . . . try to reach her again, through that darkness into which she'd fallen.

"Mr. Smith?" Dr. Sterling asked.

"No," he said. "No, she's not the woman I knew. I'm sorry I wasted your time." But with his back to the doctor, he leaned close to Nidaba and whispered into her ear, "I'll be back for you. I promise. I'll take you out of here, Nidaba. I'll make you well again. It won't be long."

He thought there was a hitch in her shallow breathing. Perhaps a flicker in her eyes. But nothing more. From her, at least. The reaction in Nathan was nothing short of catastrophic. He was trembling even harder than before, from somewhere down deep. He felt it right to his bones. He brushed his lips over her cheek and got to his feet, but his knees seemed almost too weak to carry him. His steps were as uneven as a drunkard's when he started toward the door. Everything in him rebelled at the notion of leaving her behind, even for a little while.

"Thank you," he said to Dr. Sterling as she held the door for him.

She closed it, the locks clicked into place, and he thought he was going to vomit.

"It was no trouble at all," Dr. Sterling said. "The exit is that way, just down the stairs and—"

"I know where the exit is."

He walked away in a daze. He didn't know what had happened to Nidaba to bring her to this point. How she had survived this long, or why she had never sought him out. He only knew that when he took her from this place—and he *would*—he must leave no clue as to where she had gone. He wouldn't risk drawing hordes of reporters to his door. Because they would be followed, and in very short order, by hordes of immortals.

Dark Ones. And his quiet existence would come to a violent end. As would Nidaba's life.

He hadn't recognized her!

Dr. Sterling stood in the hall, watching the man who called himself John Smith as he walked away. She waited. He rounded the corner, out of sight, and she heard his feet tapping down the stairs, then the closing of the doors to this wing. She let a few more minutes tick by, ensuring that he'd had time to leave the hospital, get into his car, and drive away. Then, finally, she pressed her palms lightly to the front of her face, heels of her hands curving just beneath her chin, and slid them slowly upward, over the top of her head, through her hair, and down to her nape, wiping out the glamour she had cast.

When she took her hands away, she once again appeared as she truly was. Dark. Small. Ever young.

She almost smiled as she thought that perhaps her most well-honed magickal skill might not even have been necessary. If John Smith—or rather Nathan King, as he called himself these days—hadn't recognized his precious Nidaba, then it wasn't likely he would remember her.

Ahh, but then again, Eannatum was a wise man. His name had gone down in history as one of the greatest leaders Sumer had ever known, and not without reason. His intelligence was legend—as was his cunning. It would not do to underestimate him.

She had been afforded precious little time to plan for this. Always she'd had to keep herself hidden from Eannatum, knowing he would have killed her with his bare hands if he had crossed her path again—*if* he had ever put it all together, realized the truth of what she had done.

Yet she had managed to see him from time to time. Sometimes from a distance. Other times, using her favorite spell—the glamourie. It had become something of a game, seeing just how close she could get without his seeing through the illusion. It was an occasional lark, a way for her to pass the time, all the while laughing at him from behind her borrowed countenance. She'd had conversations with him in one guise or another. She'd shared tea with the man. She'd even toyed with the idea of seducing him. Though if she had acted on the idea, he'd have known her as an immortal at her first touch.

But in all that time, she had never seen the priestess Nidaba. Until recently, the name of Nidaba had been unspoken among immortals. And she had become convinced that the harlot truly had died in that long-ago fire, her body burned to ashes.

She should have known that was a tale too perfect to be true.

Nidaba had been alive. All the while, alive. She had certainly kept her existence a secret. Until a year ago, when that detestable name began being whispered among the Dark Ones. She was old—one of the oldest, they speculated, their tones awed, almost reverent. Her heart would be a prize worth seeking. And many had begun doing just that. Hunting her. For a time, Puabi had convinced herself that was enough. That she could just sit back and wait for one of the other Dark Witches to destroy Nidaba forever.

But it hadn't happened. So Puabi had to take matters into her own hands. If you wanted a task done properly, she had mused, you must see to it yourself. And why should she allow some other Dark Witch to claim a heart with nearly four thousand years of power pounding within its chambers? Why not make it her own?

After hunting Nidaba for months, Puabi had finally

found her in the city. And she'd thought that her lust for vengeance would finally be sated. She'd altered her appearance and followed Nidaba to the rooftop gardens of a hotel, and there, Puabi had attacked. Nidaba was strong—more skilled in battle than Puabi had expected. The bitch nearly defeated her! But the Dark Witch had been prepared for that eventuality. She pulled the gun she had brought along, just in case. She could easily carve out Nidaba's heart before the woman had time to revive from a gunshot wound.

Nidaba saw the weapon, and in the split second before the shot rang out—she jumped.

Jumped.

There had been a crowd. Police. Paramedics. And Puabi thought her chance at ice cold revenge was gone— that Nidaba had outsmarted her yet again

It wasn't until she had seen the article in the newspaper that she'd realized her chance was not lost after all. Her oldest enemy was imprisoned, drugged, helpless . . . all but gift-wrapped. Just waiting for Puabi to come and claim her heart, as she should have done a long, long time ago.

Puabi had arrived here only minutes before Nathan had. She hadn't expected to see him here. She'd planned to slip in, murder the bitch, and leave with her bloody prize beating endlessly in her hands. But Nathan's unexpected appearance had ruined her plans, and she'd had to act quickly.

Just as she would act quickly now—to take the beating heart from her enemy, and claim the wealth of power from the mindless shell where it awaited her blade. It would be easy, like taking a fledgling.

She slipped her hand beneath the draped fabric of the blouse she wore, closed her fingers around the hilt of the dagger at her side, and turned toward the door of Nidaba's padded cell.

"Excuse me?" a voice said.

Puabi let go of the blade, and looked up quickly— only to see the *real* Dr. June Sterling staring at her, her identification badge pinned neatly to her lab coat. "What are you doing here? This is a restricted area."

Too late now to cast a glamour and alter her appearance to the good doctor's myopic mortal eyes. The woman had already seen her. "I . . . seem to have got lost," she said, concocting a smile she hoped looked sincere.

Dr. Sterling peered through the glass at her patient, worry in her eyes, before looking back at her again.

"The doors to this wing are kept locked."

"I guess someone forgot that rule."

"No one forgot," Dr. Sterling said, her eyes narrowing. She lifted a hand toward her side. There was a small electronic box there, clipped to a pocket of the white lab coat. She knew Dr. Sterling would summon help by pressing the button on that box. She knew in an instant, and acted just as quickly. Her blade hissed from its sheath and slid cleanly between the psychiatrist's ribs. Blood bubbled when she drew the razor-edged steel out again, and Dr. Sterling, her mouth working soundlessly, slumped to the floor. Her eyes were wide, wet, but fading.

She started to smile . . . but then she saw the stubborn woman's fingers twitch on that little box in one final effort. *Damn her!*

Some sort of alarm went off, and the formerly silent hallways seemed to come alive with slamming doors, pounding feet. No time now to do what she had come to do.

Puabi, once the most revered queen of all Sumer, leapt

over the fallen doctor, and ran. Nidaba's heart—the trophy she had come here to collect—would have to wait for another time.

The woman sitting on the other side of the mesh lined, locked door, frowned at what was happening inside her mind.

For a moment there had been a ripple in the sky, and the young priestess-in-training looked up, tilting her head to one side.

"What is it?" Natum asked.

Nidaba frowned. "A voice," she said softly. "Did you hear it?"

"No. Was it a man's voice or a woman's?"

She shrugged. "A man's, I think."

"And what did he say?" Natum asked.

"That he was coming to take me out of this place." Nidaba frowned and tipped her head to one side. "But I don't want to go."

"Don't you?"

"No. There is only pain out there. And loss."

Natum tilted his head to one side at that. He was such a beautiful boy. His almond-shaped eyes were fringed with thick lashes. He had such a strong jawline, for a boy, and the nose of a king. Thirteen now, and she'd known him for a year and a day. "How do you know of this pain?" He asked her.

"I've lived it. We both have, Natum. Don't you remember? It is our future."

"How can I remember what hasn't happened yet?"

That question caused more ripples in the fabric of the world around her. She stared harder down into the waters of the Euphrates from where she and Natum sat on its grassy bank, their robes pulled up to their knees and their feet dangling in the muddy water. She searched the blue sky and examined blazing red sun. Then she focused on the palm trees, their fronds swaying slowly in the gentle, searing breeze. Part of the sky seemed to fold away, and beyond it Nidaba saw a door, with a glass window that had wire crisscrossing it and a wall lined with some kind of cushioning.

Don't look there. Don't!

"This isn't right," Nidaba said, averting her eyes from that tear in the world. "We never had this conversation."

"No, we didn't."

She concentrated, and the rippling stopped. The world around her solidified once again. The tear was gone, the sky sealed itself in place again. "That's better," she said. "I know what this is. It's our first rite together. You've been studying for a year and a day, so to celebrate, Natum, we shall conjure a boon from the Gods."

"I was afraid you'd forgotten."

Nidaba lowered her head. "I would never forget. I . . . I even made a gift for you."

Natum smiled broadly, his white teeth gleaming in his copper-skinned face. "You did?"

Nodding, Nidaba shyly opened her pouch and extracted a tiny piece of a clay tablet, already baked hard by the sun. She handed it to him.

Natum held it in his palm, and drew it closer. He looked down at it and read aloud the symbols she had inscribed. " 'Nidaba. Eannatum. Forever Friends.' " He pressed his lips together and closed his hand around the small piece of clay. "Thank you, Nidaba. I will treasure this always."

She tipped her chin up. "Even when you are a great king and your people shower you with gifts of gold and lapis?"

"This bit of clay is more precious than any of that

could ever be." He opened his palm and looked at it again. "And no mistakes!"

"I had a good teacher."

"As did I . . . I hope." He looked a bit nervously toward the area Nidaba had set up. Candles stood in a circle, and a libation of honeyed wine lay at the ready, beside a dish of salt.

"We'll soon find out. Have you decided what your request shall be?"

He licked his lips. "Does the priestess Lia know we are doing this, Nidaba?"

Nidaba shook her head. "The priests and priestesses of the temple are planning a stuffy initiation rite for you, to be held in the temple *cella,* as befits a future king of Lagash," she told him. "It will be very boring, and I assure you nothing of note will happen." She smiled. "I've learned many secrets, the greatest one being that magick works best when practiced outside, beneath the sky, bare feet in the grass. But if I told them I thought so, I would be condemned for heresy."

"So might I, if we're caught," he said.

"Are you afraid?"

Holding her gaze with his, he shook his head slowly.

"Come, then." She took his hand, and again the tingling bolt rushed into her, and into him. This they had taken note of, discussed, but neither could explain it. Nor could they explain what happened next.

"My petition to the Gods should be one made for the good of all the people of Lagash, rather than for my personal good."

"Kingly already, are you?" she teased.

"I am trying to be."

What a wonderful leader he is going to become, Nidaba thought, but she did not say it aloud. She wouldn't wish to fill his head with too much arrogance or pride.

"The fishermen have been complaining of dwindling catches," Natum said. "So I will petition Enki to send an abundance of fish into the waters of the Euphrates."

Nidaba lifted her brows. "It is a good request," she told him.

They walked together to the circle, and while Natum sat down in the center, preparing himself for the rite, Nidaba walked 'round, lighting the candles one by one. Then she moved to the center and sat down, facing Natum. He lifted his palms, and she hers, and the two pressed their hands together. And together they began to chant the incantation.

"*Enki me en. Uta am i i ki Enki* . . . I am of Enki. I conjure thee, Enki."

And the sky darkened, and thunder rumbled in the distance. The waters of the Euphrates began to lap against the shoreline.

"*Ana-am ersetam nara-am!* By Heaven, by Earth, by the river!"

The winds increased, and Nidaba felt a rush of power coursing through her body. She knew Natum felt it too when his fingers laced with hers, clenching tight.

"*Amesh ikiba ul ishu-u!* Water without taboo!"

Lightning flashed, striking so close by that she felt the jolt sizzle up into her body from the ground, and her eyes flew open. They met Natum's, and she nodded once. Together they stood, facing the now roiling black waters. They lifted their joined hands, extended their forefingers side by side to point to the waters, and shouted, "Fill the Euphrates with Fish, Enki! *Akalu!*"

Lightning flashed again, this time striking the water itself and causing a huge spout to arise in its midst. The force made the hairs on Nidaba's nape stand erect, and her skin tingled. Then, slowly, the odd wind died, and the sky cleared. And when it did, she stared, wide-eyed, as fish leapt and jumped amid the now calm waters in numbers she had never seen before.

Nidaba turned to Natum and said, "You must tell no one of our rite, Natum."

"But why?" He was breathless, his brows arched in wonder as he watched the fish bounding and diving about, where before the waters had appeared barren. "We—look what we did, Nidaba! *We* caused this. We *must* tell!"

"No." She shook her head firmly. "What do you suppose the High Priest of the temple would say of a child who could command such powers as we have just done? More powers than anyone in the temple? More powers than the High Priest himself can command?"

"The High Priest is my father's most trusted adviser!"

Nidaba swallowed hard and looked at him intently. "I know more of the man than you, Natum. Please, if you are my friend, you will not speak of this."

He stared hard into her eyes. "Is it so unusual, what we've done here today?"

"Unheard of, Natum. We are a powerful force, you and I."

He nodded once, smiled gently. "Yes. We are that . . . and more. Because you ask it, Nidaba, I will tell no one."

"Thank you, Natum."

Leaning forward, he kissed her cheek very gently. "We are friends," he said. "There are no thanks needed."

When he left her there, alone, she wondered which was the greater miracle. The fish splashing about in the water . . . or the warmth his kiss had left on her cheek.

3

"Now, do you understand what to do?"

George was frowning at Nathan in absolute concentration. "I can do it. Just the way you said."

"I know you can," Nathan told him, patting him hard on the shoulder.

They were sitting in a parked car in a rural part of New Jersey, across the street from a century-old building that still had the words "Brooker Asylum" chiseled into its stony face. It was dark outside. Midnight, and neither the moon nor so much as a single star managed to pierce the gloom. A steady drizzle misted the windshield. And it felt damn cold outside.

In his pocket Nathan had a small bottle of ether and a gauze pad. He hoped he didn't have to use it, but if he did, he figured it was far better than the alternative.

George opened the back door with a gloved hand and got out of the car, bowing his wide back against that cold, misty rain. Nathan glanced beside him at Sheila, who sat behind the wheel. "And you, Sheila? Are sure you want to go through with this?"

She pursed her lips. "If you're determined to do this, then so am I. But that doesn't mean I have to like it. And I don't, you know. I don't like it a bit. This is completely unlike you, Nathan."

"It's more like me than you know." Like the man he'd once been, he thought vaguely. Not the one he'd become. Not the one Sheila thought she knew.

"Ah, you're talkin' in circles again. If you knew the woman in the photograph, Nathan, why didn't you just say so? The authorities would have let you take her— unless she's totally insane." Sheila widened her eyes. "Is that it, Nathan? Are you bringin' a lunatic into the house?"

Nathan took a breath to bolster his waning patience. "It wouldn't be safe for this woman if anyone were to know where she was. I can't explain any more than that, Sheila, and I'd appreciate it if you would stop asking me. Just . . . trust me on this."

"Oh, sure, and suppose you're caught? What then, I ask you? Is this crazy woman worth getting yourself thrown into the pen?"

He stared at the building in the distance, with its barred windows and safety glass, and he thought of the woman he'd seen yesterday, sitting inside, a captive of this place and, perhaps, of her own mind. And he nodded. "Yes, as a matter of fact, she is. She's worth . . . anything."

"They likely have security cameras," Sheila said, continuing the argument she'd waged all the way out here. "I don't suppose you've thought of that."

"As a matter of fact, I have. It's been . . . taken care of." He couldn't tell her that he'd called up a bit of the magick he'd learned from the very woman he was about to rescue. But he had. His magickal skills were rusty, but not forgotten. Some things, once learned, were never truly forgotten. He only wished he'd thought to disable the cameras when he'd visited here yesterday. Perhaps no one would make the connection.

Sheila tipped her head to one side. "I swear, I've never seen you like this, Nathan."

"I haven't *been* like this. Not—not in a long time."

"Maybe you'll explain that remark to me one of these days."

He turned toward her, touched her cheek. "It means a lot to me, you and George standing by me like this. Insisting on coming along when I would have done it alone."

"You couldn't get by without us, and you know it. Go on with you, now. Fetch your woman and let's be away with her." She glanced toward the hospital and shivered. "This place gives me chills."

Nathan nodded, pulled on his gloves, and got out of the car. "Keep it running, Sheila." Then he closed the car door and gave his lapels a tug. Hunching his shoulders against the frigid autumn wind and slashing droplets, he crossed the narrow drive and walked along the winding path up to the old brick building. It was grim, this place. Dead leaves skittered across its lawns and sidewalks. The bricks were uneven, chipped in places, and the bars installed when the structure had been built in the 1890s remained in the arching windows. They had never replaced them with the modern mesh equivalent. The place looked like a prison. Dirty and cold. A Gothic nightmare. No night sounds reached him beyond the rustling of the dead leaves and the whisper of the cold rain. No crickets chirping. No night birds singing. But he could hear, on another level. A deeper level, even though he tried to block his own empathic tendencies. Ghosts of this building's past lingered, howling and shrieking in their madness, their torment too powerful to filter out.

No such sounds pervaded the nights around the building anymore, he supposed. Today, the terror of insanity was drugged into slumberous submission. Just as Nidaba had been when he'd seen her here the day before.

The front doors opened easily, and he walked through a foyer that looked shockingly modern—so much so that he'd been startled by it when he'd first seen it the day before. There were padded chairs and magazine racks, and a reception desk with no one in attendance, since visiting hours were long since over. The main doors stood before him, and they too were unlocked. They led only to an admitting area, a nurses' desk, and a row of administrative offices. The patients were housed on the second through fifth floors, with every stairway and elevator inaccessible without a key. *His* patient, Nathan mused, was in room 419. For a bit longer, anyway.

He nodded toward the fire alarm on the wall in the dim reception area, and George followed his gaze and nodded back. They'd planned this. Rehearsed it. Gone over it. Nathan was as prepared for tonight's adventure as he used to be when leading his army into battle. He'd bought clothes, prepared a room for Nidaba, and researched this building. He'd even studied blueprints. He was ready.

Something stirred inside him. Deep down. Adrenaline, excitement even, surged in his veins, and he thought for a moment that he felt more alive than he had in years.

George backed into a shadowy corner to count silently to one hundred, just the way they'd planned, and Nathan went through the second set of doors. A nurse looked up from a folder at the desk and said, "Visiting hours ended at seven."

"Yes, I know. I wanted to see one of your doctors," he lied. "Dr. Sterling. Is there any chance she's still here?"

"You a friend of hers?"

"A . . . colleague, actually. I was hoping to discuss a case with her."

The woman's expression eased a bit. She had a pinched look about her, even then. Narrow nose, skin a hint too pale. She didn't get a lot of sun. "I guess you didn't hear, did you?"

"Hear?" Nathan's senses went on alert.

"Dr. Sterling's in the hospital—she's critical. One of the patients upstairs attacked her yesterday."

"What?"

Nodding hard, the nurse rose from her chair, smoothed her dress. "Stabbed her," she said. "It's a miracle she didn't bleed to death on the spot."

"I can't believe this." Nathan's mind raced. He pinched the bridge of his nose, fighting the certainty that there was more to this than he was just now hearing. "I just saw her yesterday afternoon. When did this happen?"

The nurse shrugged. "The alarm went off just after four. We found Dr. Sterling outside our Jane Doe's room on the fourth floor, but Jane was still trussed up nice and neat. All the patients were accounted for, in fact. I still can't figure it out." She rubbed her arms, gave a little shiver. "No one saw anything unusual. It's as if a ghost did it. I'll tell you, it makes you want off the night shift in this mausoleum."

The woman had been stabbed—right outside Nidaba's room. By someone who had managed to go undetected. And only minutes after Nathan's own visit. Could all that be coincidence?

"Did they . . . did they find a weapon?" he asked slowly.

"No, actually, they didn't. Whoever it was took it with them. But we searched all the patients' rooms and—I

suppose whoever did it probably hid the weapon somewhere before running back to their room. You know,
some of these psychos are sharper than we give them
credit for. Obviously." She shook her head. "Poor Dr.
Sterling."

Nathan was so shocked to hear all of this that he
nearly forgot his plan. But his nerves were bristling, and
he didn't like the feeling of static dancing up and down
his nape and forearms. Like a storm in the air. Something was very wrong here.

He vowed to get to the bottom of it all later, but now
he steered himself back to the subject at hand. He
glanced at his watch, then pretended to sniff the air. "My
God . . . is that *smoke* I smell?" he asked.

The nurse sniffed, frowning and tipping her head to
one side. "I don't smell anything."

Right on cue, George hit the fire alarm in the waiting
room. A bell went off, and the nurse flew out from behind the desk, her key ring in hand. Others came running. She raced to the stairway doors, to the control
panel there. Inserting her key, she turned it and hit a
button to release the main locks. According to the building's plans and renovations, the individual rooms would
still be locked, and the elevators would go to the bottom
floor and shut down. But now the stairways and all the
exits were unlocked. They would not be that way for
very long.

The nurse ran to the first landing. Nathan headed up,
too, only a few steps behind her. He could hear others
coming behind them, but he knew the staff would be
thin at this time of night. Still, that wouldn't stop them
from questioning his presence, if George didn't hurry up
and . . .

Before he completed the thought, the lights went out.
"Good man," Nathan muttered under his breath. He

shrugged off his overcoat, revealing the white lab coat he wore underneath it, folded his overcoat over one arm, and continued up the stairs. At each landing the head nurse shoved open a stair door and shouted behind her, sending a handful of her staff onto that floor in search of the fire. The emergency lighting finally kicked in, but it was dim.

"Do we evacuate the patients?" someone asked at the first landing.

"Not yet. Let's just make sure this isn't another false alarm first."

Nathan bit back his instinctive response to that. He wanted to chastise the fools. If the fire had been real, their hesitation could have cost lives. But it wasn't real. And he was concerned only about getting one patient safely out of here.

At the fourth floor, he simply went in with the rest as they spread out to check the rooms. His eyes were sharp, even in low light. Years of immortality tended to hone all of the senses to new levels. He chose one nurse, a small blond woman who blinked like a mole at him in the darkness when he said, "I think it's coming from in here" and led her straight to Nidaba's door.

The nurse didn't even hesitate, and the others were racing down the halls, running from room to room, getting further and further away. She unlocked the door, and Nathan gripped her hand, tugged her inside, and closed the door behind them. "Don't you smell it?" he said. "Over there, by the window."

The nurse hurried forward, and he quickly moistened a gauze pad with the chloroform in his pocket, recapped the bottle, and moved up beside her.

A second later, his hand was covering her face, and she was slumping in his arms. He laid her down gently, carefully. "Sorry about this," he said. "I didn't have a choice." Mentally, he willed her to forget this incident, but he had to hurry. He had no idea if the command would take.

But there was just no more time. He hurried to the bed where Nidaba lay still, eyes closed, totally oblivious to the alarm sounding throughout the halls.

At least she wore no straitjacket now. They must put it on her only when forced to be in the room with her. He scooped her into his arms and headed to the door. He looked up and down the hall, but the searchers had moved past this point and the path to the open stair door was clear. Taking a deep breath, he opened the door and he ran. He reached the stairway, raced down it, and emerged at the bottom after three flights.

A burly attendant appeared as Nathan crossed toward the reception area. He hadn't seen Nathan yet, but he would at any second, unless . . .

Even as the attendant started to turn toward Nathan, George's shadow fell over the man. Sensing it, the attendant whirled, but not in time. George picked the man up by the front of his shirt and tossed him aside like yesterday's garbage. Then, even as the man struggled to his feet, stumbling toward the control panel to re-engage the locks, and even as the stampeding of a dozen pairs of feet thundered down the stairs, George ran ahead, opening the doors, and holding them as Nathan carried Nidaba through. Nathan heard the locks engage as he passed. They'd only just made it out in time.

Outside, they sprinted across the lawn for the car. George said, "Let me carry her, Nathan! I'm bigger than you are."

Nathan shook his head. "Can't do that, George," he panted. Nidaba's weight was a warm burden in his arms, and her body pressed to his, even limp like this, was something he had long thought he would never feel again. Silently, he heard a little voice telling him not ever to let anyone take this woman from his arms. Not ever. But he knew better than to think that way. She had changed—even if he *could* reach her and bring her back to him, she would still have changed. And so had he. Lifetimes had come and gone, for both of them.

George opened the back door, and Nathan cradled Nidaba closer to his chest and folded himself into the car. The single attendant stepped outside the madhouse doors, rubbing his head and looking around. He had probably mistaken George for a patient and wondered where he'd gone. But no one had seen Nathan taking Nidaba away. And Nathan hadn't been stupid enough to leave the car in plain sight. He'd had Sheila park it in a well chosen spot, away from any streetlights and with a line of shrubbery between the car and the front door of the hospital. Between those precautions, the moonless night, and the steady drizzling rain, the car was all but invisible to mortal eyes.

Still, he had no doubt that the police were on the way, or would be shortly. George went still, crouching beside the car until the attendant walked back inside, shaking his head. Then George ran around and got into the front seat, and Sheila shouted, "Hold on!" and hit the gas.

The tires spun a little, caught, and the car lurched into motion.

The irony of it all was far from lost on Nathan. Particularly when he could hear the sirens in the distance and when Sheila took a corner too fast and the car rocked up dangerously, flirting with a two-wheeled stunt before gripping the pavement with all fours again.

"It's all right, Sheila," he told her. "They're not chasing us. At least I hope not."

She slowed down, but not by much.

For a decade, Nathan thought, he had cultivated the

most mundane, most placid, staid, uneventful existence any man had ever known. And now he was breaking into a mental hospital to kidnap a patient and then speeding through the night in a getaway car. All because of a single glimpse of Nidaba's face.

She had always had this effect on his life. Always.

He held her now. Her upper body lay across his lap, her shoulder against his belly, her head resting just above his heart. The car swayed and shuddered, even now that he'd told Sheila it would be all right to slow down a bit. Streetlights fought with shadows for the right to bathe Nidaba's pale face. He pushed her hair away.

"I've got you now, Nidaba," he whispered. "Can you hear me?" With one hand he stroked her cheek. "I know you can. If you want to, you can. And I'm going to keep talking to you until you do. You're coming back from wherever it is you've gone, Nidaba. Whether you want to or not. I'll bring you back."

The car slowed a bit, Sheila finally getting the idea that the police had been left far behind them, if they'd ever been after them in the first place, which was doubtful. Or perhaps she was only distracted by listening to Nathan's soft-spoken words.

"How are you goin' to care for her, love?" she asked him.

He glanced up, met her eyes in the rearview mirror. "Take her home, clean her up, put her to bed . . ."

"She needs nourishment, Nathan. She can't eat in that state. She ought to have an IV. She could dehydrate in short order without one. She can't go to the bathroom on her own. She needs a nurse, Nathan, and how you're goin' to hire one without answerin' a lot of uncomfortable questions is beyond me."

He swallowed hard. "I'm not going to hire a nurse. Whatever care she needs . . . I'll do it myself."

"And I can help," George announced, looking anxiously at the woman lying so still in Nathan's arms.

"You've got no clue what you're saying—neither of you."

"Yes, I do." Nathan looked down at Nidaba, at her long lashes, blackest velvet lying against her cheeks. She had always had the thickest, longest lashes . . .

"Besides," he said, forcing the words past the lump in his throat. "It will only be until the drugs have a chance to clear out of her system."

Sheila sighed. "They don't drug mental patients into a state of catatonia, Nathan. She's ill."

"No. No, you don't understand. Nidaba . . . she has a . . . *reaction* to certain drugs. Most tranquilizers have a magnified effect on her. As if she'd been given ten times the normal dose."

Sheila's silence made him look up again to see her frowning ferociously into the mirror. "How do you know all this, Nathan?" Then she blinked. "And didn't I once hear you say something similar about yourself?"

He nodded very slightly, averting his eyes as he did so. "We have the same . . . sensitivity to chemicals," he explained quietly. "For all we know, without all the drugs in her system, Nidaba could be perfectly sane."

"Or completely *in*sane!" Sheila said.

There was silence in the car for a long moment. Then George asked, "Didn't the newspaper say she jumped off a building?"

"They can't know she jumped," Nathan answered quickly. "*She* certainly didn't tell them so. She could have fallen . . . or been pushed." To his own ears his voice sounded defensive and childish.

"But . . . but, Nathan, didn't she break somebody's arm in the ambulance?" George pressed on.

Sheila caught Nathan's eyes again. And he could see

that she was once again suspicious of him. She was not
a foolish woman. She knew he was keeping secrets—
that there was something about him that wasn't quite . . .
normal. He'd seen this look in her eyes before. But she
was also a woman with her own secrets to keep. So she
had never pressed him to reveal his.

This time, though, he might have pushed her too far.

"We're just going to have to wait and see," Nathan
said softly.

George turned around, one big arm anchored on the
back of the front seat as he stared back at Nathan. "I
hope she doesn't break *my* arm, Nathan. That would
hurt."

"I won't let her hurt you, George. You're my friend.
I don't let anyone hurt my friends." He lifted a hand,
gave George's shoulder a squeeze. "You trust me, don't
you?"

Nodding hard, George looked a bit more at ease. "My
arms are pretty big, anyway. It would be awfully hard
for her to break them, I think."

"I'll bet it would."

The remainder of the long ride back passed in relative
silence. George fell asleep, his gentle snoring keeping
an odd rhythm. Sheila stopped asking questions, but Nathan caught her eyes on him every now and then, wide
with worry, and on Nidaba, narrowed in distrust. The
next several days were not going to be easy.

Then again, nothing with Nidaba had *ever* been easy.
Or calm, or boring. He sometimes thought the Gods had
decided to give turmoil a physical body, and his Nidaba
had been the result.

She feared nothing. She dared anything. Consequences be damned.

It had always been that way. Nidaba was . . . chaos.

•   •   •

She learned fast, the littlest novice priestess in the temple of Inanna at Lagash. At first, Prince Eannatum had simply thought her to be unusually brilliant. At first . . . but soon, he, like everyone else in the city-state, began to wonder about her origins. Particularly after witnessing her powers firsthand.

For more than a year after that secret rite they had performed together, fishermen had been hauling more bounty from the Euphrates than they ever had. So many fish that the excess had to be salted, packed in barrels, and shipped upriver to Nippur and Kish and downriver to Ur and Eridu. And Natum wasn't vain enough to believe *he* was responsible for the magick they had wrought that day. No. It had been *her* doing.

There was something *more* to Nidaba. A power that surged through her. Made her somehow . . . more than anyone he'd known before. More alive. More beautiful. More passionate, more inquisitive. Just more. As if she truly were the child of a Goddess.

Though she would have likely punched him in the belly if he said so aloud.

Yes, she would. Despite that he was a prince. That was one of the things he loved about her. She dared *anything*.

They had been studying together for more than three years, and she had become a far more talented scribe than he would ever be, when he one day set aside his tablet and stylus and stared at her across the table. "I am tired of lessons," he said.

"Then what shall we do?" She had seen thirteen seasons by then. He had seen fifteen, but she had already grown nearly as tall as he.

He shrugged. He didn't know what he wanted to do, but he was restless. His father said it was natural for a

boy of his age. That did nothing to ease the feeling,
however.

"Shall we attempt some divinations? Or visit the
cella? We could drop pebbles from the uppermost windows onto the people as they pass below!" Her smile
was as bright as her eyes. And her eyes were brighter
than any he'd ever seen. But even their excited gleam
failed to reach him today.

"We do those things all the time. I want to go outside.
I want to swim in the river and roll in the dirt!"

Her beautiful smile faded, and she tilted her head to
one side. "Perhaps if you ask the guards . . ."

"Pah, they would only tell me I must behave with
dignity at all times!" He shook his head. "Everywhere I
go, they follow. They watch. Soon I will be finished with
the *edubba*, and my father says my lessons here will end
soon as well. It is time for me to move on, now. To
learn the skills of battle, and of war." He heaved a sigh.
"My life is nothing but lessons and responsibilities. I
would give it all to be free, like you."

Nidaba got up from her chair and came round to
where he stood. "I know it is difficult for you, Natum,
but don't assume it is any easier for me. I too have
duties, responsibilities—"

"Oh, come! The priestesses let you do just as you
please! They are too afraid of you to do otherwise!"

She took a step back as if he'd struck her, and he
instantly regretted his words. He reached out for her,
parted his lips to speak the apology he knew he should
give, but she held up a hand to stop him. "So that is
what you think, is it? Let me set your mind to rights,
my prince. They *let* me do nothing, here. I do what I
please because I *dare* do what I please. I am free because
I insist on my freedom. It is too valuable to me to give
it away without a fight. So I do what I want, and I break

their silly rules. When I am caught, I am punished for it, believe me. But the punishment is the price of my freedom, so I take it without complaint."

He crossed his arms over his chest, certain that a slip of a girl such as she would not know punishment if she saw it. "Do you, now?"

"You doubt me?" she asked, eyes going wider.

"I doubt you know what real punishment is," he said. "I would be beaten were I to defy my father. Don't you doubt it. And if you faced such consequences as I, you would understand my frustration far better."

She lifted her brows. Then she turned her back to him, and before he could guess what she was about to do, she pushed the white gown from her shoulders, letting it fall, baring her skin to him and catching the garment again only just above her hips. Her arms, her back, were unclothed, and for an instant he felt an unknown pull in his groin, and a tightening in his belly. But only for an instant. For though her flesh was bared . . . it was also marred.

Natum leaned closer, eyes widening at the strips he saw crisscrossing her slender back. He lifted the candle-rack from the table, and the golden glow fell across her coppery skin, illuminating the angry red welts, and the darker places where the skin had been ripped and the blood had encrusted.

"By the Gods, Nidaba . . ." he said on a breath. Tears stung at his eyes, and his throat went taut, even as an unfamiliar rage rose like fire in his chest. Gently, he reached out, lifted her dress up, and righted it for her. Then, placing his trembling hands on her shoulders, he turned her around. "Who did this to you?" he demanded, surprised at the depth of emotion in his voice, and the churning in his belly. "Tell me and I will have his head on a pike by dawn!"

She smiled at him, very slowly. "Listen to you, already sounding like some mighty king."

He didn't like what he was feeling. The churning in his gut, the pounding in his chest.

"I am but an orphan child, and I belong to the temple—as much as I am capable of *belonging* to anything or any*one*. The priestesses are kind and loving. But you know how stern the old High Priest can be."

"Lathor did this to you?"

"Yes. Your father's most trusted adviser, the High Priest of the temple, has a fondness for the scourge that goes, I believe, beyond what is holy." She shrugged. "He enjoys it, I think. But for the most part, I am able to avoid him."

"And what grave offense brought about such a punishment?" Natum asked, his anger still seething.

She shrugged. "I took a date from the offering plate set before the stone image of a deity in the *cella*. I have done so for years, whenever I please. This time he saw me. And when he asked for an explanation, I replied that the goddess lives in me, and therefore I have every right to eat her dates."

"You *said* that?" He was amazed.

"Lathor called it blasphemy and took the scourge to me." Again, that slight shrug. "He is very lucky that I have learned to control my anger," she said softly. "I wanted to bring the entire tower crashing down upon his hairless head."

And for some reason, as she said it, Eannatum had the feeling she could have done exactly that.

"I still believe I am right and he is wrong," Nidaba went on. "And I told him so, when he finished whipping me."

Lowering his head, shaking it slowly, Natum tried to

quell the nausea in his belly. "Gods, Nidaba, do you fear nothing?"

"What is there to fear?" She shook her head. "I wanted the date, I knew the consequences of taking it— *if* I were to be caught. I usually am not, you know." She shrugged as if it mattered not in the least. "You want to go outside without your guards, and you know the consequences of doing so—*if* you're caught. So tell me, is it worth the risk to you, Natum?"

"How can you even speak of this when your back bears the marks of Lathor's scourge? He must be made to pay!"

She rolled her eyes. "You do tend to change the subject, Natum. I am used to Lathor's scourge. It doesn't hurt so much after the first day or so. And if he deserves to be punished for what he does to me, the Goddess will see to that. Or, I will, when I am grown and no longer under his care."

"You will not have to. And this will not happen again. Mark my words, Nidaba."

She smiled very slowly. "Do you want to go out without your guards, my prince, or don't you?"

Looking into her eyes, he managed to put his anger aside. They glowed, her eyes, with a gleam of excitement, and somehow, despite his fury at the High Priest, he felt an answering excitement well up within him. One that only she seemed able to provoke. "Yes," he said, "I do."

"And do you dare to do as you please, despite the consequences?"

"I do," he repeated.

"Then come with me." She offered her hand. He took it, felt the tingling sensation he always felt when they touched, and let her lead him through the ever-darkening hallways of the ziggurat tower, down sloping passages and hidden stairways, into the very bowels of the place, and lower. He grabbed a torch as they passed. Otherwise, he thought she'd have gone in utter darkness and been content.

Truly, she feared nothing.

"Here," she said at length, pushing hard on a block of stone that was easily larger than she was. It moved a bit in the wall, and Natum joined her, shoving hard at it. To his surprise it gave, moving inward, sliding on its own once they got it started. It revealed a passage to the left and one to the right.

"This way," she said, grabbing his hand once again.

He followed her into the darkness, and the huge stone slid back into place behind them by means of some hidden mechanism. He'd seen similar passages in the palace, but he'd never explored them. She would have, he thought. Nidaba would leave no mystery unexplored.

They walked for a time and soon emerged from what appeared to be a cave, half covered in sandy soil and reeds, into a grove of trees and grasses on the far side of the river. Blinking in the light, Natum looked across the water and saw the pristine white tower and the palace with its jeweled roof gleaming in the sun.

"We crossed beneath the Euphrates!" he said in amazement.

"Yes, and none of your guards are in sight. And look how far away the temple is! They cannot even see what we do here."

No one could see them there, it was true. And that place, that grove of untended lushness on the far banks of the Euphrates, became their hideaway. Where they could run and romp, climb trees and splash in the water, behave as normal children instead of as a future king and a future priestess.

That was, he had thought much later, where he had first fallen in love with her.

They hadn't been caught . . . not that time at least. But he'd decided then and there that it would be worth the consequences even if they were. To him, anyway. As for the so-called punishments Nidaba had suffered. . . . he vowed to see to that as well.

The opportunity came later that same night, in his father's palace. Natum saw the High Priest Lathor exiting his father's throne room, resplendent in robes threaded with gold.

"*Ea* Lathor," Natum said, "might I have a private word?"

Turning, Lathor cupped his right fist in his left palm and bowed slightly, a greeting of deepest respect among Sumerian men. "Of course, my prince," he said. But for all his show of respect, there was none in the man's patronizing eyes. His eyes looked at Natum as a boy, not a man.

But the prince did not *feel* like a boy just then.

He nodded toward a smaller room, and the priest walked into it, taking a chair only after the prince had closed the door and waved a hand toward one. Eannatum himself remained standing.

"What is it, young prince? Do you require counsel of a spiritual nature?"

"No, Lathor. I require an explanation."

Lathor's brows rose. "An explanation? Whatever for, my prince?"

"For the marks of the scourge I saw today, cut into the back of a girl in your care."

Lathor frowned, then gasped, making his eyes wide. "Do you mean Nidaba? But how could you have seen . . . Prince Eannatum! Have you . . . *known* the girl?"

Natum had not realized he was capable of delivering

his father's very well-known glare, but he did it then, and saw the priest pale in reaction. "I owe you no answer to such a question, Lathor. I am your prince, and that you would *dare* ask a question like that one leaves me to doubt your judgment even more than I already did. But for the sake of the young priestess—"

"Nidaba is no priestess, but a foundling and a student," Lathor interrupted. "And an unruly one, at that."

"Nidaba is more priestess than any woman in the temple," Eannatum shot back. And again, the High Priest fell silent. Good. "For the sake of her good name, I will deign to answer your impertinent question, Lathor. No. I have not *known* the girl. But I have seen the marks of your scourge on her tender skin."

The priest seemed relieved. He smoothed his robes. "Punishment well deserved, I assure you. Her upbringing is in my hands, Eannatum. I must see to it as I deem appropriate."

"Just as I will see to running Lagash as I deem appropriate when I take my father's place on the throne one day," Eannatum replied. He walked closer, leaned over the chair in which the High Priest sat, and braced his hands on either arm, framing the man. "And I promise you, Lathor, that should I ever see a mark on Nidaba's flesh again, my first command as king shall be the one I give to your executioner, and I shall word it thusly: '*Use a dull blade, and take all the time you wish.*'" He said the words slowly, drawing them out.

Lathor gasped audibly. "You . . . you *dare* speak to me in such . . ."

"It is only a matter of time, Lathor. My father is not a young man. I warn you, when I am king you will pay dearly for every welt on Nidaba's body. Do not forget."

The door to the room opened, and Lathor looked past Eannatum, his face easing in relief. Natum looked behind him to see his father standing there. And from the look on the king's face, his son deduced he had been listening for some time. Eannatum straightened up away from Lathor and, turning, pressed his right fist into his left palm and inclined his head. Lathor scrambled to his feet to do likewise.

No one said anything for a long moment, as the king looked his son right in the eye. Natum returned the steady gaze, not blinking or looking away. Then finally the king met the eyes of his adviser instead, and he spoke. "Lathor, it seems your prince has issued his first royal command. I would advise you to heed it."

Lathor's eyes widened. He sputtered once or twice, then bit his lip, bowed low, and scurried away. Only when they were alone again did Natum's father turn to him. "She will one day be a High Priestess, my son."

"She's not even an initiated priestess yet," he said.

"No. But if the talk of her talents has even a grain of truth to it, she will excel in her studies and grow into a woman of great power in the temple. And as for you, you will one day be a king. Not just of Lagash, but of all of Sumer."

"Your dreams are bigger than the ziggurat tower, Father," Natum said.

"They are more than dreams. They are strategies, plans that are already unfolding, Eannatum. But you do not need to know of them now. What you do need to know is this: Nidaba must serve her Goddess and you your kingdom. Do you understand this, Eannatum?" he asked.

Natum lowered his head. "She is my only friend, Father."

The king nodded. "She is *only* your friend, Natum. You would do well to remember that it is all she can ever be. With . . . perhaps, the exception of one night—

the night of your coronation, when you must perform the sacred rite with the High Priestess of your temple. If my plans to install you to the throne of all Sumer come to fruition, and if she advances to the rank of High Priestess in time. Do you understand what I am saying?"

Natum felt the blood rush to his face, hotter with every word his father uttered. "I have never thought of Nidaba in . . . in such a way!"

His father smiled, came closer, and tousled his son's hair in an almost playful manner. "Then we'll save this talk for another time, when you have. For you will, Eannatum. You surely will. Already you are becoming a man." He smiled. "A good man. You will be a great leader one day. And you will think of this priestess in exactly such a way."

At the time Eannatum had thought his father could not have been more wrong.

But later . . . oh, later . . . he knew that it had been all but inevitable that he would think of Nidaba in the terms to which his father had alluded. Soon, all too soon, in fact, he found he was able to think of little else.

4

Nathan cradled her in his arms in the back seat of the car as it sped through the rain-glistened night, and he remembered the day everything had changed between them.

She was fifteen. They had been in their secret place, swimming in the waters of the sacred river. The sun blazed in all its fury, baking the city. So they'd slipped away together, to cool themselves in the life-giving waters. They'd been laughing, splashing each other, ducking underneath the waves. And then, breathless and giddy, they got out and stretched themselves out on their backs among the tall, lush grasses along the riverbank, to let the sun dry their skin and their clothes.

"So what did you learn today, little priestess?" he asked her. "Have they taught you any new rites?"

He glanced sideways at her, grinning. It was a running joke between them how the magick they could work together would shock those who claimed to be far more learned about such things. Ironic, he thought, that she spent each day learning about religion and deities and powers when she ought, perhaps, to be teaching her teachers.

She didn't smile back, however. Instead, a frown puckered her brow. "Today I was taught about the Sacred Marriage Rite of the king."

"Oh." He turned his gaze skyward. It was a subject he thought unwise to discuss with her.

"You know of it, don't you?" she asked.

"Well . . . yes, I . . . I know . . . enough."

Her brows rising, she turned on her side to face him, elbow to the earth, her head resting in her palm. "You're embarrassed to talk to me about this, aren't you, Natum?"

"No!"

"You are so."

"Am not." And to prove it, he too turned on his side, facing her, just as she faced him. "I'll be king one day. Why should I be embarrassed about the sacred rite conferring my rulership?"

"Because you have to copulate with the High Priestess of the temple. That's why." She grinned. "I hope it's soon. The current High Priestess is already an old woman. If she gets any older—"

"Maybe you'll be High Priestess by then."

He blurted the words in self-defense. But the moment they were out of his mouth, her eyes shot to his, widened, and remained there. And he couldn't look away. "Maybe I will," she answered, her voice barely a whisper.

His throat was suddenly dry, tight. "I shouldn't have said that," he managed to say. "I'm sorry."

"I don't know why. I've thought of it many times." She closed her eyes, perhaps to find the courage to go on. "Wondered . . . what it would be like to be . . . more than your friend."

His stomach tightened into a knot, and he felt another place tightening, stirring, and pulling as well. His gaze drifted downward while she lay there, eyes closed, awaiting his reply. Soaking wet, her white gown was all but transparent, and plastered to her breasts, so their full, soft shape was clear to him, even to the tiny nubs at their tips. The gown clung to her belly, so he could trace the well of her navel. Sex was normal and healthy, and not something whispered about or forbidden—except if a girl wished to advance to the rank of High Priestess. She must save herself then, for the time when a king would need her. Untouched, she must draw the spirit of the Goddess into her own body. And then offer herself to the new ruler, who could be anointed king only by knowing her. By having her.

And suddenly, he felt as if he were on fire.

"Natum?"

He jerked his gaze upward again, meeting her eyes, which were open now.

"Am I pleasing to you? As . . . as a woman?"

He swallowed hard. "You're the most beautiful woman in all of Sumer. You know you are."

"Then you would not mind so much, if it were me? I mean . . . in the role of High Priestess . . . when the time comes."

He couldn't answer her. His voice fled him. So instead of speaking, he obeyed his body's demands. He leaned a breath closer and pressed his lips to hers. He kissed her slowly, tenderly, and he tasted lips he had dreamed of tasting for many nights. "I pray it will be you," he whispered, and kissed her again.

It was raining. It had been raining a little harder with every mile they had driven, and by the time they got back to Nathan's haven, it was pouring. It didn't look as if it was going to let up anytime soon. The headlights gleamed on wet gravel and shiny fallen leaves, slick with water. Everything bore that unnatural sheen that comes only on rainy, moonless autumn nights. It rained on Nathan when he carried Nidaba up the flagstone path to the house. George raced along beside him, holding an umbrella that did little good, while Sheila ran ahead to open the front doors.

So Nidaba got wet, and maybe chilled too, on such a brisk night as this. If she became ill . . .

"One step at a time," he muttered.

"What, Nathan? I didn't hear you." George started to close the door behind them, then paused. "Nathan! Nathan, look."

"Close the door, George. It's freezing," Sheila chided.

"No!" George darted back outside, and a moment later he returned with a sopping-wet dog slogging in beside him. It stopped halfway through the door, and Nathan tensed with Nidaba in his arms.

"George, that's a Rottweiler. They can be dangerous, you know."

"C'mon, that's a good dog. C'mon, now," George crooned, and the beast, easily weighing 90 pounds on a dry day, slunk inside. George closed the door, and the dog shook, sending a spray of dog-scented droplets throughout the entire foyer.

"Dammit, George!"

"Nathan," Sheila said, her tone firm. And Nathan stopped himself, knowing better than to scold the sensitive and childlike George. "We'll deal with the dog later. Let's see to your new charge now."

Nathan nodded, knowing she was right. "Get some towels and dry that beast off, George. And be careful. If it starts growling at you . . ." He glanced back at the pair. George was on his knees now, his arms around the soaked canine, his cheek resting on its wet fur. It didn't look as if he was in any danger of being bitten.

Nathan carried Nidaba forward, leaving wet footprints on the marble floor of the foyer, and on the plush carpeting of the front parlor, and on every step of the staircase as he carried her up. It was wide, this staircase, but steep. At the second floor, Sheila again ran ahead to open Nathan's bedroom door.

He carried Nidaba through it, and into the adjoining room, as Sheila flicked on lights. Technically a part of the master suite, this smaller room would serve as Nidaba's bedroom. Nathan wanted her close to him. He wanted to be able to watch over her every moment until she was well again.

If . . .

No. She *would be* well again.

Sheila pulled back the covers of the bed they had made ready. Nathan peeled off the now damp blanket he had wrapped around Nidaba in the car. She wore only a thin hospital gown beneath it. But at least it was dry. Gently, Nathan lowered her into the bed and pulled the covers over her, tucking them tight. Swallowing hard, he straightened, staring down at her, pushing a hand through his damp hair.

"Now what?" Sheila asked, sounding skeptical. "You've got her here, Nathan. But just what you intend to do with her is beyond me."

He drew a breath, sighed, and turned to the fireplace. Logs and kindling lay ready, and Nathan drew a long, slender match from the holder, struck it against the brick, and knelt to touch the dancing flames to the tinder. As the tongues of fire licked and spread, he dropped the match but remained kneeling there, watching the fire dance. Fire.

Fire was the hungry beast that had devoured his only

love . . . and her only child, or that was what he had been led to believe lifetimes upon lifetimes ago. But Nidaba lived.

What of the child?

"Nathan?"

"Go on to bed, Sheila," he said, and his voice came out harsh, raspy. "Get warm and dry and get some rest. See to it that George does the same."

"You might follow your own advice, Nathan," Sheila said. "But I know full well you won't do it, so at least change your clothes. They're damp, and you're chilled through."

He felt his lips pull into an affectionate smile. "It's a wonder I ever survived before you came along with your mothering, Sheila." His tone was teasing.

"It's more than a wonder," she replied, in all seriousness. "It's a bloody miracle."

He glanced behind him to see her shrugging and turning to walk away, back through Nathan's bedroom, and toward the hall beyond its door. "Thank you, Sheila," he called. "Good night."

"Good night, Nathan," she called back. "Try and get at least a couple of hours' sleep, will you?"

"I will."

Shaking her head, she stepped into the hall, pulling the door closed behind her, and Nathan heard her mutter, "Liar."

She knew him a little bit too well.

Straightening up from the fire, Nathan went to the windows and parted the curtains to stare out at the falling rain. It beaded like liquid diamonds on the glass, melting and sliding downward in slow motion. Beyond the rain was only blackness. The pattering sound of the droplets on the glass and the low, distant moan of the wind were lulling. Soothing, somehow.

"What will you do to me this time, Nidaba?" he asked softly, letting the curtains fall back into place. He went to the chair beside the bed and sank into it. Hooking a forefinger under his chin, he studied her. "Sleeping Beauty," he murmured. "So peaceful, so tranquil, even if you do look a bit tousled and tangled right now. But you're not those things, Nidaba. You've never been peace or tranquility. You come into my life like a sandstorm in the desert. You rain chaos on my head, and everything inside me responds by joining in the madness. And then you leave me again."

His throat tightened on the final words. Leaning forward, he closed his hand around hers. "My life was turmoil for so long. I raged, Nidaba. For centuries I raged, and I'm not even sure I knew that you were the cause. Not then. But I fought with every Dark challenger I could find. I killed with a vengeance and a taste for blood that chills me now when I think back on it. I loved like a wanton, taking my pleasure wherever and whenever I wished and never letting it mean a thing to me."

He shook his head slowly. "But how long can a man live like that? I was a hurricane, Nidaba, and eventually all that anger, all that grief, blew itself out and left me . . . empty. Drained. It took a long time. A long time to reach that point. And it only heralded a new kind of existence for me. One in which I didn't care, didn't feel . . . anything at all. I killed if I had to. Felt nothing. If sex were offered to me, I would take it, and barely feel the pleasure of release. I was a shell. I closed myself off from every emotion, blocked my mind from the touch of any feelings not my own. But eventually, that too passed."

He ran his thumb over the back of her hand, slowly, in circles, wondering if she could hear him at all—or if she would give a damn about any of this even if she could.

"Finally I settled into this life. Calm. Placid. I learned how to care for people again. To connect. Even to open myself up a little. With George, and with Sheila. They're my family. I love them, but I've never—not in all this time—felt for anyone the way I felt for you. I made a conscious decision not to. Because I couldn't have survived that sandstorm again. The angst. The loss that crippled me for so long. I settled for a life without that kind of passion, that kind of need. And it's been . . . a good life."

He reached out, touched her cheek, smoothed her tangled hair away from her face. "And now you're back. And I have to tell you the truth, Nidaba. I'm scared to death of what's going to happen next. I don't even know if you'll recognize me after all this time. Or if you'll even remember the same things I do . . . like that night . . . the first time I told you I loved you. The first time you broke my heart . . ."

There was a voice.

His voice.

The words were not clear, but she recognized the tone even though he spoke English rather than the ancient Sumerian language he'd used when she had known him. And there was, just once, a touch. A warmth, surrounding her hand.

But her memories called, and they were so warm and good—so much more so than the reality that tried to encroach on her dreamworld—that she willed herself to ignore the interruption and returned to the bliss of her mind.

"I love you, Nidaba."

She had been sixteen when Natum had first said those

words to her. They had been in their favorite place, the lush oasis on the far banks of the river. And she had been secretly dreaming that he would one day say those three sweet words to her. So fervently had she wished for it that she almost thought she must have imagined it.

But he took her hands firmly in his, and he said it again. "Do you hear me? I love you."

Her lips pulled into a tremulous smile, and her eyes grew moist as she stared up into his.

Natum frowned at her. "Have you no reply?"

"I . . . I . . ." She simply could not form words. So she didn't. Instead, she leaned closer to him, tipping her head back, pressing her lips to his.

Natum's arms closed around her at once. He held her close, and he kissed her for a long time. He tangled his fingers in her long hair, pulled her body tight to his, moved against her, and tasted her mouth in ways she had only imagined. And everything inside her seemed to come alive for the very first time.

When he finally lifted his head he said, "Do not attend the initiation rite, Nidaba. Do not take the final step in becoming a true priestess of Inanna. For when you do, marriage between us will be forbidden."

"Marriage?" She whispered the word, shocked to her core.

"Of course! Nidaba, there can be no other woman for me. Don't you know that?"

Blinking, she took two backward steps. "But . . . but Natum, your father has already chosen your bride! You're to marry the princess of Ur."

"A girl I've never so much as set eyes upon," he said, grimacing.

Nidaba's throat tightened. "I have heard tales of her

beauty, Natum. If that is what you fear, then you need not."

"By the wings of Enlil, woman, are you even listening to me? Princess Puabi could be as beautiful as Inanna herself, and it would make no difference. It is you I love, and I will wed no other."

Staring at him in wonder, she felt tears brimming in her eyes. "Oh, Natum. If only it could be—"

"It can be. It will. I will be king of Lagash one day, Nidaba. And when I am, you will be my queen. None other." Then his face clouded slightly, and he searched hers. "That is . . . if you wish it."

"Natum, you know I do!" she cried, flinging herself into his arms, relishing the feel of them tightening around her. "I have loved you for always!"

She felt some of the tension leave him as he held her. He was so precious to her. Reed thin, tall and gangly now. He'd shot up in height so that he stood a hand's length taller than she. And he'd begun to sprout fine, dark hairs upon his face, which he seemed reluctant to scrape away. As if he were proud of the ever thickening whiskers. How she loved him!

"If you only knew," she confessed to him, "the tears I have shed lying alone at night and thinking that you would be married to some other girl one day."

"And yet you said nothing?"

"How could I?" Then she frowned. "How can I now, when wedding Puabi would be better for you, and for the kingdom itself?"

He leaned close, resting his forehead against hers. "It will never be, Nidaba. I vow to you, it will never be. And I will never give you cause to shed a single tear, ever again."

She sighed, and smiled at him as her doubts fled.

"I will speak with my father tonight," Eannatum said. "He will understand, I know he will."

Nidaba's lovely memory faded, and darkness began to creep in around the edges of her vision. She knew, sensed, that she was leaving now, the safe haven of her most precious memories ... sailing into storm-tossed seas, where things she would rather not think about lurked beneath the surface, like sea monsters, with great snapping jaws and razor-edged teeth. She wished then for that voice from without to come for her, to call to her, so that she could cling to it and escape the darkness.

But the voice had fallen silent, and the dream she'd been relishing became the nightmare she had not wished to recall.

The High Priest came to her chamber that night, with Lia, her beloved Lia, at his side. The priestess who had been like a mother to her. Lia's gentle hand woke her, and Nidaba instantly saw the turmoil in the priestess's eyes.

"What is it?" she asked, instantly alarmed.

"You must wake, child. You've been summoned by the king himself."

Blinking in shock, Nidaba tried to quell her fears. But they rose up all the same. The king. What could he want of her? Only one answer came to mind. If Natum had spoken to his father as he had promised he would, then that must be what had instigated this midnight summons.

"Quickly, now," Lia said, handing Nidaba her finest white *kaunake* dress, and her fringed shawl. The High Priest turned his back while Nidaba donned the garments, but he never left the room, which was so odd that Nidaba wondered at it. Did he fear she would run away? Or was it that he did not wish Lia to have a private moment with her?

Her senses prickled. Something was wrong here.

Lia dragged a silver comb through Nidaba's hair and all too soon took her hand and led her down from the level where all the bedchambers were located, to the first level, and into the grand room that was used only for the visits of foreign dignitaries or religious officials. It was very much like a throne room, she thought. Two giant stone lions stood guard at either side of a dais, and golden animals and goblets rested at intervals atop marble stands. A goddess sculpture stood in the room's center, cradling a pottery vase, from which water flowed endlessly into a golden chalice.

The king sat in a thronelike chair upon the dais. Two soldiers stood on his left and two on his right.

Nidaba bowed deeply before the king and remained that way until he said, "You may rise."

She straightened. "Long life and health to you, my king," she said in greeting, and she fisted her hand in her opposite palm, inclining her head.

"And to you," he replied. "Sit down, Nidaba. The matter about which I must speak to you is of grave import to this kingdom. And to my son."

She blinked in surprise, but took the seat the king indicated.

The king looked at her steadily for a long moment. His gaze was powerful, his very visage spoke of authority not to be questioned. "I understand the prince spoke to you today . . . of marriage."

Nidaba lowered her head to hide the heat that rushed into her cheeks. "Y-yes."

"When my son spoke, Nidaba, he was not fully aware of the situation facing our kingdom. Nor of the threats to his rule."

"Threats, my king?" Nidaba's head came up, and her eyes searched the king's face. He was dark, like his son. Thick, dark hair and bushy brows. But his jaw was not so well defined, soft where Natum's was hard. His cheekbones were not as sculpted, and they hid beneath fleshy skin.

"Do you know that Ur and Lagash have long been enemies, vying for rule of all of Sumer?"

"Yes, of course I know this."

"Of course," he said, nodding. "But perhaps you do not know that an allegiance between the two would create the most powerful force in our land. Perhaps you did not know that he who rules over Lagash and Ur would be in a position to declare himself King of Kish, Ruler of all Sumer."

Nidaba said nothing. She knew suddenly why the king had come here. He meant to prevent her from marrying his son. Her throat burned, and her eyes grew hot with tears she refused to shed.

"I have been setting a plan in motion since before my son's birth, Nidaba. We are being threatened by enemies from all sides—particularly by the Ummamites. United under my son's rule, we would be at peace, a land too powerful for even the king of Umma to think of challenging, and Lagash would prosper as never before. When he weds Puabi, princess of Ur, Eannatum's kingship will be sealed. He will be king not just of Lagash, as I am, but of all Sumer."

The lump that rose in her throat was almost too large to speak around. "But he does not *wish* to wed Puabi," she said very softly, in a voice unlike her own.

"Perhaps he *did* not. But now that I have informed my son of what is at stake, he knows where his responsibility lies. And he is eager to accept the title King of Kish and to wear the crown of Sumer. Only one thing stands in his way, Nidaba."

Blinking away tears, she lifted her chin and looked

the king squarely in the eye. "And what is that, my king?"

"Oh, I think you know."

Her voice reduced to little more than a dry rasp, she said, "Me?"

The king nodded. "You. He cannot bring himself to cause you pain. He cannot retract his proposal of marriage, Nidaba. His honor will not allow it. Though it is what he wishes, he will not betray his vow to you."

She nodded slowly, and the first of many tears finally spilled over and rolled down her cheek. "So you have come to me, to ask me to betray my vow to him instead," she murmured, understanding at last.

"Not to ask it," he said, his voice firm. "I am your king. My duty is to my country. As is my son's. Your duty is to obey. You will refuse my son's offer of marriage. It is the only way to free him of this promise."

Licking her dry lips, she battled a soul-deep tremor. "Respectfully, my king, how can I believe this is what Natum truly wants?"

"What he wants is of little consequence. His duty is to Lagash." He slanted a quick glance toward Lia, who stood behind Nidaba. "And what you believe matters very little. But your teacher knows the truth of this. Lia?" the king said. And he lifted a hand toward the priestess.

Nidaba turned and saw her, very pale, and trembling, one of the king's guards at her side, with a hand firmly around her forearm. Her heart raced as Lia, eyes cast downward, said, "The king speaks the truth, Nidaba. I heard it from the prince's own lips. He wishes to wed Puabi . . . for the sake of Lagash, if not for his own."

Every part of Nidaba's body began to quiver. "It's a lie!" She shot to her feet and ran toward the door. But Lathor, the High Priest, stepped into her path and blocked her flight. "You have not been dismissed, Nidaba. This is not finished."

She stood there, trembling, battling the sobs that were tearing at her breast. She squared her shoulders and stared defiantly at Lathor. "I believe none of this! Natum wants me, not some spoiled princess. You force my own priestess to lie to me, and you expect me to believe it?"

"As your king told you, woman, it is of no concern to us what you believe. You will do as we command."

A cry was wrenched from Lia, and when Nidaba spun toward her, it was to see Lia forced to her knees, the king's soldier gripping her shoulder.

"If you don't," Lathor went on, "then it's painfully obvious that you've been taught poorly. A priestess who can't even manage to teach obedience to one orphan girl is not one we would reward."

Nidaba understood suddenly, vividly, clearly. If she did not obey, it would be Lia who would suffer the wrath of the king. Of Lathor. Oh, if the punishment were hers alone, Nidaba would gladly bear it. But she knew too well how cruel Lathor could be. And she couldn't bear the thought of him taking the scourge to Lia. Goddess, if he'd beaten Nidaba bloody so often over the minor offenses she had committed, what would he do to Lia over something this significant?

He might even kill her.

Lia's eyes met Nidaba's. And Nidaba saw the plea in them. The priestess was afraid. Bowing her head in despair, Nidaba sighed. "What must I do?"

"Ahh, much better. Perhaps you've learned something from us here in the temple after all," Lathor said. "It is very simple, really. Since you have been so eager to break the law and learn the script, you must compose a message to the prince. Tell him you have decided that your promise to the Goddess is more sacred than your promise to him, and that you intend to take your initiation as her priestess."

Nidaba lifted her head slowly. "He will never believe it."

"His belief will be my concern, Nidaba," the king said, his voice deep and none too steady. "Yours is only to compose the message."

A guard took Nidaba's arm, led her to a waiting chair, and drew a small table before her. Upon it was a moist clay tablet and a selection of stylus reeds. Apparently there had never been any doubt that she would comply with the king's wishes.

"Have I no other choice?" Nidaba asked, looking around the room as tears began to pool in her eyes again.

"None," the king told her. "But you will have compensation, Nidaba. You will be richly rewarded for your loyalty to my son."

"Your rewards don't interest me in the least. Nor does compensation from a king who would threaten a priestess to bring about his own ends."

"Be very careful with your words, girl."

Nidaba held his gaze for one long moment, then sat down and took up the stylus with a trembling hand. Then she put it down again. "No," she said. "I will do what you wish, but I will say my piece first. I may not yet be a priestess, but I have studied and learned, and I know the Goddess would not approve of these events. Conspiracies and threats, deceptions and cruelty. You are king. You rule by her favor. There was a time in this land when no one was more revered than a priestess of the Goddess. Now, we are treated as servants to the kings, rather than as his most valued advisers. Worse yet, we've become servants to the priests! Kings and soldiers talk of war and invasions and battles and conquests. Their concerns are of earthly power and might,

rather than spiritual enlightenment and wisdom. I have
studied our kingdom's history. I have seen the way these
things have changed over the past century. It is wrong.
And one day soon, mark my words, Inanna will have
her vengeance!"

With every word she spoke, the king grew more pale,
until he was on his feet and trembling with rage. He
lifted a hand, pointed a finger at her. "Silence!"

"I will never be silenced."

He was quiet, staring at her, his lips thin. Then he sat
down again, with a sigh as if of surrender. "So be it,"
he said. Then he glanced at the soldier who stood holding Lia's shoulder. "Kill the priestess."

The soldier's sword flashed in the torchlight as he
yanked it free, lifted it high. Lia cried out.

"No!" Nidaba shouted. "No, no, please!"

The king held up a hand, and the soldier paused with
his sword in the air. Looking at Nidaba, the sovereign
of Lagash lifted his brows. "Well?"

Blinking in shock at the heights of cruelty she had
never before perceived in the man, Nidaba sat down at
the small table and finally picked up the stylus again.
"I'll do as you wish," she said. But she told herself that
this would not be all there was. She would speak to
Natum herself. Privately, away from these authoritarian
eyes. She would go to him just the moment she was out
of their sight. She would explain to him that she had
done this only to save the life of her priestess. She would
give him one last chance to tell her that it was all a lie.
That it was she he wanted. Not Puabi. No matter what
his father said.

She *had* to do that much.

Bending over the clay, Nidaba pressed the symbols
into its face, writing exactly what the king had told her
to write, rather than risk any further trauma to poor Lia,

who was shaking so hard now she could not even get up from her kneeling position on the floor. There was wetness spreading on the stone floor beneath the terrified priestess's knees and staining her robes, Nidaba realized, her heart wrenching in her chest.

Swallowing hard, she finished the message. Lastly, she removed the pendant from her neck—the small bit of onyx with the name "Nidaba" inscribed on its face. She rolled it gently over the clay, impressing the symbols there.

Then sitting up, she replaced the pendant at her throat. "It is done," she whispered. But she felt empty inside.

"Lathor," the king said.

At his word, the High Priest came to the table, turned the tablet around, and perused the symbols Nidaba had made upon it. When he finished, he nodded. "It is good," he said to the king.

Nidaba got to her feet, though her legs were shaking so hard with tightly leashed rage she could barely walk upright. Her back straight, furious tears leaking through despite the battle she waged against them, she wished only to flee to the haven of her chamber and let loose the torrent while she gave them time to go their way. And then she would slip out and find a way to see Eannatum—even if it meant scaling the palace wall to his chamber window. Unsteadily, she moved toward the doors.

But suddenly the king's soldiers were at her sides, gripping her arms and stopping her progress. She bit back a cry, and looked up with narrowed eyes from one to the other of them, then glared at the king. "What more do you wish of me?" she asked, as he rose and came forward. "I have done as you commanded! Why do your men treat me as if I am a criminal now?"

"Silence, Nidaba. You have served your king, your

prince, and your kingdom well this day, despite your insolence. And you will be rewarded, for I am a man of my word. But you've shown me clearly that you are every bit as headstrong and stubborn as Lathor warned me you were. I need to do what is best for my kingdom."

"I don't under—" But even before she finished speaking, one of the soldiers was pulling her hands behind her back and binding them tightly while another wrapped a strip of cotton around her mouth so that she could not speak or cry out.

Nidaba struggled, casting her panicked eyes at the others in the room. The king kept his head lowered, his hand on his forehead, covering his eyes. The High Priest Lathor stood tall, watching, his lips pulling at the corners as though he battled a smile. Lia remained on her knees sobbing as she cried out, "Forgive me, Nidaba! Please, forgive me!"

Denial raced through Nidaba as the soldiers tugged her toward the back of the room, where another armed guard waited to open a small rear door. Beyond it she saw the camels waiting, packs dangling from their sides as if in preparation for a long journey. And she knew then that they were having her taken far away.

Fury welled up in her, and she felt the floor beneath her feet begin to vibrate, to tremble. The golden chalices and goblets teetered, and the king lifted his head to stare at her, his eyes wide, his face paling visibly.

"What's this?" he demanded.

Lia sent a desperate glance at Nidaba, and Nidaba saw and read it clearly. If she revealed the powers she had never understood, she would be more than banished. She would be killed. And so might Lia.

She fought to control the violence rising within her. The tremors eased and finally died.

"Perhaps, my king," Lia said, her voice choked and

hoarse, "the girl was correct. Perhaps the Goddess is angered by this night's work."

The king looked toward the heavens, his face twisted in fear, and then Nidaba was hauled through the door, pushed and lifted onto the back of a camel. A soldier mounted right behind her, and held her in a cruel grasp as he urged the animal forward.

It began to run, its long legs and bouncing, bone-jarring gait soon putting miles between Nidaba and the lush city-state of Lagash, carrying her deeper and deeper into the desert night. Farther and farther away from her prince. Her Eannatum.

She vowed in silence that she would never love another the way she had loved him. And she would find him again—somehow she would tell him the truth of all of this.

She *would!*

5

Nathan forced his tired eyes open, stirred to awareness by some sound or movement. He started when he realized he had fallen asleep.

And he knew something was wrong.

Nidaba's head twisted from side to side on the pillows, her face contorted, her breaths coming in short, sharp little bursts while her hands curled into fists and clutched at the covers.

Nathan shot to his feet and leaned over her, pressing a hand to her cheek. "It's all right," he said, and he tried to make his voice soothing and low, but feared that it came out hoarse with worry. "It's all right, Nidaba. I'm right here. You're safe. No one can hurt you here."

She only thrashed harder, and small sounds of anguish seemed torn from her chest now as she became more and more agitated. He put his hands on her shoulders, tried to still her frantic movements. "Nidaba, it's all right. Calm down now, it's all right. You're safe, do you hear me?"

Her legs began to twitch, her hands to swing in the

air, and it was all he could do to hold her. She was strong, even in this state.

"Dammit, Nidaba, it's me! It's Eannatum!"

It was, he realized, the wrong thing to say.

Her thrashing ceased all at once. And her eyes flew open. Wide, wider than any eyes had a right to be, with tiny pinprick pupils drawn tight and irises like blue-black ice. Anger seethed in those eyes, so potent it hit him like a physical blow. The bed began to shake, to tremble and rock, as did the lamp on the nightstand and the floor under his feet. It shocked him so much that he drew back from her. His second big mistake of the night.

She swung her arms forward, her upper body rising from the bed even as she closed her hands around his throat. The force of the attack sent him reeling. He fell backward into the chair where he'd been sleeping, and Nidaba came with him, landing half sprawled atop him, her hands still clutching his throat with crushing force. The lamp on the bedside table crashed to the floor. He couldn't breathe.

But only for a moment. He quickly grabbed her hands to try to pry them away. But then Nidaba's death grip eased suddenly, and her body relaxed atop his. The violent shaking around him stopped. Her face fell to his chest, tangled hair veiling it from him.

He drew a ragged breath, then another as he carefully moved her limp hands away from his neck. Then he pushed her hair aside, cupped her face between his hands, and tipped it up to see that those fiery eyes had fallen closed once more.

"What the hell was that about?" he whispered to her unresponsive face. "By the Gods, Nidaba, was that hatred really directed at me? Or was it just mindless fury?"

No reply came. No clue whether he'd just been given a glimpse of the drug-induced madness possessing her or of the cold, harsh reality that lurked beneath it. He sighed and leaned forward to press his lips to her cool forehead. She couldn't possibly harbor that kind of hatred for him, could she? And why, for the love of the Gods? Then again, he thought slowly, she had attacked only when she'd heard him say his name. As if. . . . as if just hearing it was enough to reach past the drugs still polluting her blood to the rage those drugs were supposed to suppress.

Rage against him.

But why?

The door flew open, and Sheila rushed into the room, then stopped and stared. And no wonder. He must have made quite the picture, lying across the chair with an unconscious woman draped over him. Behind Sheila that stray dog lingered in the hall like a shadow. Gorgeous beast it was, now that it was dry and clean. Its mouth wasn't drawn into a threatening snarl, but relaxed, almost smiling. If a dog *could* smile. Its hair wasn't bristled in warning, but instead, its tail wagged briskly. Nathan almost smiled at his earlier warning to George. This dog was anything but vicious. It almost bounced with friendliness.

"Nathan, what in the name of—"

He held up one hand, shook his head. "It's all right, Sheila. Nidaba just . . . it was some kind of a reflex." He gently closed his arms around Nidaba's waist, lifting her so he could get himself upright, and then scooped her up more carefully. "Get the covers, will you?"

Sheila came forward, straightened the mess of tangled covers, and pulled them back. "What in the world was that rumbling I felt, Nathan?" she asked, her voice tight. "Like an earthquake, it was."

"Must have been that thunder clap, just now. It . . . rattled the windows."

Sheila frowned, tilting her head sideways. "I didn't hear any thunder clap."

"No?"

Sheila's sharp eyes were raking the room, taking in the broken lamp, and then Nathan himself as he bent to lay Nidaba down.

"She attacked you," Sheila said. "And don't bother lying to me. She tried to throttle you, didn't she?"

He glanced sideways at her as she spoke, saw the way her gaze was riveted to his neck, and reached up to touch the sorest places. His fingertips came away bloody.

Clucking her tongue, Sheila hurried into the adjoining bathroom, and he heard water running. He tucked Nidaba in, shaking his head as the dog came padding into the room and stretched itself out near the foot of the bed, as if intent on staying. "The drugs are starting to wear off," he said. "Enough to let her break through momentarily, at least."

"Oh, yes, enough so she can try to kill you, Nathan. No doubt you think it's a good sign." Sheila came out of the bathroom with a wet cloth and handed it to him.

"I *do* think it's a good sign, actually," he insisted. He thought he did, at least. "It didn't mean anything, Sheila. It was just some kind of . . . misfiring in her mind as the chemicals wear off. It was like a spasm—a reflex." He paced away from the bed, pressing the cool cloth to the scratches on his neck. It soothed away some of the sting.

"You can't be sure of that, and you know it," Sheila said.

"I'm as sure as I need to be."

"She was in that hospital for a reason, you know," she pressed on. "She jumped off a roof, for God's sake!"

"Or fell, or was pushed." He couldn't tell Sheila that even if she had jumped, it hadn't been an attempt at suicide. A forty-story plunge wouldn't leave so much as a lasting bruise on an immortal as old as Nidaba.

"She attacked a paramedic."

"Yes," he said, suddenly feeling a bit better about things. "Yes, she did, didn't she?" He even smiled a little. "That proves it was only a reflex, doesn't it? It wasn't me. She would probably attack anyone right now." He turned, taking the cloth away from his neck, and gazed at Nidaba, who had returned to a deep sleep.

"You sound glad about that," Sheila said. "She's violent, Nathan. This is not a reason for celebration."

He disagreed, but didn't say so.

"She needs a nurse here, someone familiar with mental illness, who would know what to do for her. You're doing her no favors by refusing to hire qualified caretakers for her, you know."

"If anyone finds out she's here—" he began.

"Listen to me. I'm your friend, Nathan. So for once, just listen to me."

Sighing, he turned to face Sheila, and forced himself to at least look as if he were listening.

"I know people," she said. "People . . . who can keep a secret." She came closer and put a hand on Nathan's arm. "Trust me, Nathan. I won't put you or your lady at risk."

He met Sheila's eyes steadily. "Exactly what are you suggesting, Sheila?"

"I have a friend. She was a mental health nurse Down Under. We came here on the same ticket, Nathan. She's the only friend I have from back home, and she can be trusted. I swear it. I've known her all my life. She wouldn't betray her best friend." She shrugged. "And even if I wasn't her best friend, she wouldn't betray me. I know enough of her secrets that she wouldn't dare tell one of my own. Let me call her. Let me ask her to come here and help us out for a few days. Please, Nathan?"

He glanced down at Nidaba, then up at Sheila again. Nidaba needed constant care. Sheila was right about that. She needed food, liquids—she was thin as a rail, pale, weak. "All right," he finally agreed. "All right, we can get her here. But be careful, Sheila. Please, don't take any chances."

"I won't." She reached out and gave him a hug. "It'll be all right now, you'll see."

Sheila left the room, but paused in the hallway when Nathan called to her, saying, "You'd better take the dog with you. I don't want anything around that might startle Nidaba if . . . when she finally comes around again."

The dog looked up at him, big eyes narrowing on Nathan's face as if in some intelligent contemplation of his words.

"You heard the man. Come along, Queenie."

"Queenie?"

Sheila shrugged, holding the door as the big Rottweiler trotted happily through. "George has already named her, love. I'm afraid you're not the only one with a penchant for bringin' home strays."

Nathan rolled his eyes, muttering, "That's all we need."

Choosing to ignore him, Sheila closed the door. Nathan returned to his vigil beside Nidaba's bed.

The dog padded down the stairs behind Sheila, curled up by the fireplace, and lay there relaxing and soaking up the heat as Sheila telephoned a friend she called Lisette.

The conversation was exceedingly dull, until Lisette, it seemed, tried to refuse Sheila's request for assistance.

"Don't you forget, girl, what you owe me," Sheila said, her voice lowering. "You'd be rottin' in a cell in

Queensland if not for my help. I'm callin' in the favor, and you'd do well to honor the debt."

It was obvious by the way Sheila's face eased that the woman had become more agreeable. "Right away, and not for more than a week. She may be well by then, or she may not, but a week is all I'll ask of you, either way. You'll be well paid, Lisette. Well paid. Nathan is a generous man." There was a pause. "That's fine. I can come pick you up, then. Noon tomorrow. No later. Good. Good. Thank you, Lisette."

Sheila hung up the phone. She sat back in the easy chair, looked at the telephone for a long moment, and then, pursing her lips, nodded. "It will be for the best," she told herself. "No better nurse on the planet than Lisette. Never was. Never will be." Nodding firmly as if to affirm that it was true, Sheila rose and walked back up the stairs.

The dog sighed and settled into sleep.

Morning came. And with it, another change. As the sun rose and slanted in through the bedroom windows, painting Nidaba's face with soft golden light, Nathan saw that her eyes were wide open. Dazed-looking, extremely unfocused, but wide open.

He got out of his chair and went to her, sitting on the edge of the bed. Taking her hand in his, he felt the jolting awareness shooting through his hand at the contact. "Nidaba? Can you hear me?"

She didn't respond. Didn't blink.

"Can you hear me at all, Nidaba?" He patted her hand gently. Still, no response or reaction . . . until her fingers moved just a little.

"You're coming back to us, aren't you? Bit by bit, the drugs are wearing off and you're coming back to us."

The bedroom door opened, and Nathan smelled the mingled scents of ham and eggs, and his favorite morning tea, ginseng and peppermint. "Mmm, that smells wonderful, Sheila," he said, not taking his eyes off Nidaba. Had her nostrils flared just now? Or had he imagined it?

"It's not Sheila," a voice said. Nathan turned his head as George came into the room with a tray in his hand. "She asked me to bring this up to you," he explained. "And to tell you that she would be back early this afternoon. By two, she said."

"Where did she go?" Nathan got up, took the tray from George, and put it on a table beside the bed. The dog at George's side kept looking from Nathan, to Nidaba, to George, almost as if it was taking in the conversation, and maybe hoping for a scrap.

"She has a friend who's coming to help us take care of the lady," George explained. "She's gone to get her."

Nathan felt his lips thin, his gut tighten. Nidaba's stomach growled noisily, and the dog's ears perked up at the noise.

"George, that dog probably shouldn't be in the bedroom," Nathan said.

"She's a *nice* dog, she really is." As he spoke, George stroked the dog's head. The dog sent George an adoring look and wagged her tail.

George grinned from ear to ear.

Nathan sighed. "There's a fenced-in area off the garage," he said. "If you truly want to keep the dog, she's going to have to stay there. We'll rig up some kind of dog door so she can get in and out of the garage. It's heated, so she'll be warm and dry."

"But she likes to be in the house," George said. "With me."

Nathan shook his head. "She's too big, and too new

to us just now, George. Give us some time to get used to her, and her to us, and then . . . well, we'll see."

George's lower lip thrust out, but he would obey. He turned and moped slowly out of the room, the dog going with him only after he called her several times.

Nathan adjusted the bedside table, pulling it closer to the bed. Then he sat down on the bed again, reaching for the stainless-steel cover on the plate of food, but paused when he saw the morning paper there. Picking it up, he flipped through it and finally found what he was looking for. A small story about the escape of an unidentified mental patient during the confusion of a brief power outage and false fire alarm at Brooker Hospital.

Escape. Not abduction.

Good.

He put the paper down and lifted the cover from the plate, eyeing the food. The ham would never do. But the eggs were scrambled, soft and fluffy. There was oatmeal, made extra thin. And the juice—well, that would be the test, wouldn't it? If she couldn't swallow liquids all bets were off. He took the small glass of orange juice from the tray and lifted Nidaba's head with the other hand. Those wide black eyes stared unblinkingly into space. But her nostrils flared at the scent of the juice, he saw it clearly this time.

"That's right, Nidaba. It's juice. I'm going to tip the glass up now. Try to sip. Just a little. All right?"

No reaction. He hoped to God he wasn't about to choke her to death. He tipped the glass up, just until the juice moistened her parched lips. Then a bit more, so some of the liquid slid between them, into her mouth. A small amount trickled down her chin.

And it happened. She swallowed.

Nathan lowered the glass and grabbed a napkin to dab her mouth clean again. "That was very good. Very good.

Do you want to try something a little more solid?"

Nothing. He dipped up a spoonful of the oatmeal and carried it to her lips. Her mouth worked, accepting the food, moving convulsively to take it, grind it, swallow it. Oatmeal dribbled down her chin. It didn't matter. She needed nourishment.

This was not lucidity. Swallowing was a reflexive action. Her body was hungry, and her brain knew how to accept food. But it was progress. She was reacting, in physical ways, if not mental ones. It was progress.

By the time the bowl was empty, Nathan thought there was as much oatmeal on the outside of Nidaba as on the inside. It stuck in the long tangles of her hair, and coated the front of the hospital gown.

It was high time he get her out of that thing anyway. He'd done some shopping in preparation for her visit. The closet was well stocked. He set the rest of the food aside and hurried into the bathroom to insert the stopper and turn on the faucets of the claw-footed bathtub. The water flowed, covering the bottom and slowly climbing up the sides.

There was no one here to help him with this, he thought, knowing full well that Sheila would probably disapprove. George certainly couldn't deal with the task. No matter, though. It wouldn't be the first time he had bathed Nidaba. Only the first time in . . . forty-some-odd centuries.

Besides, maybe it would help pull her back to reality. Something had to. Because he damned well wasn't going to lose her again. Even now, the memory of the first time he suffered such a loss brought him close to despair.

6

The message had been brought to his chamber early in the day by a temple servant. Eannatum had read the still moist clay tablet inscribed in Nidaba's unmistakable hand, signed by her own seal, which she wore around her neck. But he didn't believe it. He couldn't believe it. She loved him. She'd told him so, and by the heavens, he would make her tell him so again.

He threw his robes on haphazardly and ran through the halls of the palace to the rear doors, and through those to the worn roadways of the city. He didn't stop, not until he stood outside the temple doors, hands braced on his knees, panting for breath, his heart pounding like a *lilis* drum.

He caught his breath and stiffened his spine. She would see reason. He would only need to kiss her once to make her admit the truth. Tugging the doors open, he strode inside, only to be met in the entry corridor by the priestess Lia. She was as pale as a demoness, dark circles beneath her eyes, her skin drawn and taut. She rose from the chair in which she had been sitting, and said, "I have been expecting you, my prince."

"Where is Nidaba?" he demanded.

Lia's head lowered and her eyes never met his. "I am sorry. She is gone, Eannatum."

"Where?" She said nothing, until he gripped her arms and held them hard. "Tell me where she is, by the Gods!"

"I cannot. She refused to tell us where she would go, only that she would serve the Goddess as priestess in another temple, far from here. She took with her a tablet, with the mark of the High Priest Lathor, attesting to her rights to take the final initiation as a priestess of Inanna. And that is what she intends to do, my prince."

"No." He let go of the woman's frail arms and turned slowly away from her. "This is wrong. How could she leave Lagash on her own? I don't believe it. She couldn't have struck out on foot, into the desert, alone!"

"There was a caravan passing last night, my prince. She took a mule and rode out to join them."

He had not wanted the explanation to be so simple. Drawing a breath, closing his eyes, he asked, "Which way was this caravan moving?" His voice was softer now.

"East," Lia said, after a slight hesitation.

He looked over his shoulder at the woman and wondered if she was lying. And if so, why? "She will not leave me," he stated. "I will find her, and it matters not how far she has gone. I will have her with me again. And I vow, I will marry none other."

"I fear it is too late for that, my prince. I only wish it could be as you say."

"It can be," he said. "It *must* be."

But it wasn't. Oh, he tried. He ordered soldiers and

messengers to every corner of Sumer in search of Nidaba. But to no avail.

He could barely tolerate food. Refused to take part in any revelry of any kind. Rarely slept. All he truly did was train for battle, and that simply because it was his only means of exhausting himself to the point where he was too tired to feel the pain. He trained with a sword until he could best every man in his father's army. He trained until his body looked like that of the mighty one of old, Gilgamesh, who some claimed was half god. And still the pain of losing Nidaba ate at his gut.

One day a trusted soldier, just back from yet another fruitless search, saluted Eannatum with his fist to his palm, bowed his head, and said, "I am sorry, my prince, but this journey, as all the others, has yielded no word of the woman you seek."

Natum frowned as suspicion tickled at the back of his mind. It had been weeks. *Weeks.* "How is it," he asked slowly, "that the most powerful army in all of Sumer can expend so much time and energy in such an extensive seach . . . only to find nothing?"

"Prince Eannatum, I—"

"No, no. Look up at me, face me as you speak," Natum commanded.

The soldier, Garon, was his own age. They'd attended *edubba* school together. Garon had been one of the few boys who'd tried to be Eannatum's friend when the others had shunned him. He knew this man well.

"I do not know how to answer your question," Garon replied. But when he said it, he looked away, just a quick flicker of his eyes toward the expanse of room behind him, and the doorway at its end.

He feared someone was listening! Eannatum realized it with sudden, startling clarity. And he would fear only one man above his prince.

His king. Eannatum's own father.

Realizing the danger to Garon should he press him here and now, Eannatum nodded slowly. "I am only frustrated at being thwarted. I know you and your men are doing your best. Go, Garon. Go on home to your pretty wife and your children."

Garon's lips pressed together tightly, and he couldn't seem to look Eannatum directly in the eye as he nodded, saluted again, and turned to leave.

An hour later, when Garon stepped out of his small white house with a water pail in hand, Eannatum was waiting. He stepped out of the shadows near the well, directly into Garon's path.

The soldier's head came up fast, and he sucked in a breath.

Eannatum held up a hand. "It's all right. We are alone now, my friend. No one listening at any doors, or lurking in secret palace passageways. You may speak freely."

Slowly Garon closed his eyes. "I am sworn to your father, Eannatum. I cannot betray him."

Eannatum shook his head. "I believe it is my father who has betrayed me," he said softly. "I believe he conspired to have Nidaba sent away, so that he could more easily convince me to play along with his ambitious plans. All of this is clear to me, Garon. The only thing unclear is where he has sent her."

Garon licked his lips, glancing from side to side nervously.

"If I were to lead a troop myself, Garon, which way would I lead them?"

Nothing. Silence.

Eannatum impaled the man with his eyes. "I have trusted you above others, Garon. I'll be king soon. And I'll need to know who of my men I can trust so fully. I believe you are one of the few. Prove to me that my faith has not been misplaced."

The soldier bowed his head, expelled his breath in a rush. And finally he spoke. "I have always heard tell that the city of Mari, far to the north, is a sight to behold, my prince. If I were to travel, I believe that would be my destination."

Nodding heavily, Eannatum closed his eyes. Mari. The temple of Mari was one of the most heavily guarded in all of Sumer. It housed great treasures, riches beyond compare. And it was a favored target of Sumer's enemies.

"Thank you, Garon." He clapped a hand to the man's shoulder. "No one will ever know of this meeting. You have my word."

"They may very well know already, my friend. For I've no doubt you were followed from the palace."

"You give me too little credit. I wouldn't risk you that way."

"Not even for her?" Garon asked, looking up. But then he smiled bitterly and lowered his head again. "By Enlil's wings, Natum, I can't even blame you. I'd have done the same."

That he'd slid into the old habit of addressing Eannatum by his casual name seemed to signal a shift in the conversation. A dropping of the pretenses and formalities of solidier and sovereign, a return to the conventions of two young friends.

"I promise that you'll be rewarded Garon, for your loyalty to me," Natum told him. "Tell me what you wish, and I'll see that it's granted."

Garon sighed as he looked Natum in the eye. "Fool that I am, I've but one wish, my friend. Take me with you on this journey north. Let me bring my regiment. You'll need us if you hope to return alive."

Eannatum tipped his head to one side. "Things are that bad in the north?"

"That bad and worse. Ummamite hordes have been gathering for months, just beyond the borders. They prepare for something momentous, Natum. And in the meantime, they amuse themselves with midnight raids on defenseless villages. Mari has had to become a veritable fortress to keep them at bay. The outlying areas have not been as fortunate."

Eannatum frowned. "Nidaba is not safe there."

"For a prince, your vision is narrow, Eannatum. *No one* in Sumer is safe just now."

Was this soldier chastising his future king? No, Eannatum thought slowly. No. This old friend was advising his comrade. And he was right. "My father has told me these things, but I thought he exaggerated the danger . . . better to persuade me to fall in with his plans."

Garon nodded. "I can see why you would mistrust him after all he's done, Natum. But while he's guilty of a great deal, on this score at least he gave you the truth. The situation is dire."

"We'll find a way to eliminate the threat of the Ummamites. Just as soon as I've found Nidaba and brought her back to Lagash."

Garon pursed his lips, as if he had more to say, but refused to say it. "As you wish, my prince."

Eannatum turned and left him there, his thoughts on his woman, not his country. Not invading hordes and not the security of his people. He was glad Garon had held his tongue, because he didn't want to hear what the man had to say. Deep down, he knew it full well.

The regiment, some fifty soldiers strong, marched northward with the dawn, much to the consternation of the king. For days they journeyed, marching on foot, a few mounted on the domesticated camels that were becoming an increasingly valuable mode of transportation, though they were still extremely rare in Sumer. Eannatum rode a camel. Garon rode beside him.

The journey was dusty, dry, hot. They crossed vast expanses of barren desert, too far from the shores of the blessed twin rivers to enjoy the life-giving kiss of their waters. By the time they neared Mari, Eannatum's dark skin had burned, even through the robes he wore. His lips were as parched as dried dates, and each time he blinked he felt sand scratch his eyes. And even then, he smiled when he saw the gleaming walls of Mari rise up in the distance.

"It is late, Eannatum," Garon said. "The men are tired, and the city gates will not open until dawn. Let us make camp here. There is a small village nearby. That means water, and perhaps even a meal of something besides hard bread and dried meat."

He stared at the walls ahead. So close. He wanted to ride to that city, to climb those walls and go to her. And yet fear gnawed at his belly. What if she really had left of her own volition? What if she really didn't want him?

He swallowed hard, refusing to believe it. Gods; it had been so long since he'd tasted her lips. He could almost taste them now.

"Eannatum?" Garon said.

Natum licked his parched lips. "We'll do as you suggest. It's a good plan."

Garon angled his camel toward a stand of *hashur* trees, where a spring bubbled with life. Then he held up a hand and shouted an order. The parade of men came to a halt, and the weary soldiers began to make camp.

It was near midnight, and the men's bellies were full, their thirsts sated, their tired limbs resting at last, when Eannatum *felt* something. He wasn't certain at first just what it was. Not a sound. The only sounds were those of the desert night. A jackal, yipping incessantly. A night bird's cry. The all but silent flapping of a pair of giant wings. The squeal of a bat. The bubbling of the spring. It wasn't a sound that woke him, made him sit bolt upright, frowning. It was something else.

A sense.

Then a vague vibration of the ground. As if a great thundering herd of cattle were pounding over it some distance away. He nudged Garon with his foot, and the soldier was on his feet instantly.

Only then did the sounds come. Shouts, battle cries, screams. Flickering torches took form in the distance, some arching through the night as they were flung.

"The village!" Natum shouted. "It's under attack!"

Garon's men came awake at once, as Garon shouted orders, and as one they rushed to defend the village. Of that battle, Eannatum remembered very little. He armed himself with a massive spear, a heavy shield, a club, and he surged into the fray. He recalled darkness, dust, smoke, fire. He recalled a wall of men, Ummamites, too many of them to number. And he recalled the blow to his head that rendered him useless.

He woke to the dawn.

Blinking his vision into focus, he managed to take stock. He was on his back on the ground, with the desert sunrise searing his eyes in their sockets. He was assailed by the scent of blood, of death. He looked around, and saw them, villagers, soldiers, women, children—bodies were scattered in every direction. The village was gone, except for smoldering remnants of what had been serene homes.

He heard sobbing, wailing, saw an old woman holding the lifeless body of a child to her breast.

"Eannatum, you're alive!"

He turned toward the sound of Garon's choked voice.

The man limped toward him, his face black with soot and smeared with blood. "I seem to be," Natum said, as Garon grasped his hand and pulled him to his feet. "And I'm glad to see you are as well. But this . . ." He looked around again at the horror surrounding them. The anguish of the few survivors was heavy—a sodden blanket weighing him down, thickening the very air. They were his people, and their pain, his pain.

"This is happening daily up and down the northeastern borders of Sumer," Garon said, his voice grim.

More voices reached him now, and Eannatum saw a group of people approaching from Mari. Men, women, priests and priestesses. They fanned out among the dead and wounded to help the survivors. And at last, he saw the face he'd dreamed of nightly for so long—the beautiful, sculpted features of Nidaba, as she broke away from the others and ran toward the old woman who cradled the dead child. He heard her cry out. Heard the pain in her voice clearly, and felt it even more vividly in his heart.

His eyes burned as he watched her embrace the old woman and gently take the child from her arms. "See to your wounded, Garon," Natum said softly. And he moved forward until he stood behind Nidaba.

She lay the child down on the ground, her back to him, and she gently reached up to smooth a lock of dark hair away from the girl's still elfin face. "She did no wrong, this child! She did no wrong." Kneeling, Nidaba tipped her face skyward and opened her arms to the heavens. "Go in peace, child. Go into the bosom of Inanna, and there find healing and love. Go now. Linger in this pit of death no longer."

He couldn't remain silent. He put his hands on her shoulders and felt the tingling jolt of that contact. Nidaba lowered her arms. "Natum?" she whispered.

"Yes."

She rose slowly, turned to face him, and then suddenly, desperately, she flung herself into his arms and sobbed as if her heart had been smashed to bits. He held her hard, kissed her face, her neck, her hair. The ice encasing his heart seemed to melt at her very touch. "Gods, Nidaba, how I've longed to hold you again."

"And I, you," she told him.

He found her mouth, kissed her with everything in him, tasted the salt of her tears on his lips, and finally stared into her eyes. "Cry no more, my love. I've come to take you back with me. We won't be kept apart any longer. I promise you that."

Her expression changed. Her eyes widened just a bit, and her grip on him eased. Slowly she unwrapped her arms from around him and took a single step backward, out of his fierce embrace. "Eannatum, though I love you, surely you see now why we can never be."

He frowned. "I see nothing but an enemy to be defeated. I'll send my armies, and it will be done. It has nothing to do with us, Nidaba."

"It has everything to do with us!" She closed her eyes, bit her lip. When she opened them again, she seemed calmer. She took his arm. "Come with me."

They walked. Away from the scene of the battle, and all that carnage, far away, and up a hillside outside the city of Mari. Higher and higher they climbed, and though he plied her with questions, she never spoke a word until they reached the summit. Then, turning toward Umma, she pointed. "There."

He looked. And his heart seemed to freeze in his chest. Beyond the borders, just inside the land of Umma, he saw hordes—more soldiers than he had ever seen in one place before. Thousands of them, camp after camp, as far as the eye could see.

"Your armies cannot hope to stand against those masses. Within months, Eannatum, Sumer will fall to the Ummamites. And more innocent children will die at their hands. More young women will be enslaved by their soldiers."

"I'll find a way," he said, gripping her shoulders, staring into her eyes.

"Your father has already found a way." She lowered her eyes. "I didn't want to believe it either, but since coming here, I've begun to see the way things really are. Eannatum, Sumer will fall unless you can unite its cities. And you can do that only by marrying the princess of Ur and assuming the kingship of all Sumer. Then, and only then, will you have a chance to drive the Ummamites back and defeat them so soundly that they will not dare take up arms against Sumer again."

He shook his head in denial, even knowing her words were true. "It's you I love, Nidaba. How can I marry another when it's you I love?"

"You have no choice," she whispered, her voice growing hoarse. "I realized that after the third of these midnight raids that I witnessed. That's why I took the initiation. I am a priestess now, Eannatum. And you are a prince. We could not be together even if you were free. I serve the temple. You, your kingdom."

He swallowed hard. "We cannot wed. But we could be together. As king, it's my right to have any woman I desire. It's the law."

"An arcane law. No king enforces it anymore, Eannatum."

"This king will."

She closed her eyes, shook her head. "You love your people," she said softly. "I know you, Eannatum. I know you'll do the right thing. If you didn't, you wouldn't be the Natum I love so very much."

He closed his eyes. In a moment he felt her lips on his, light as a breeze. "Good-bye, Natum. Do not forget me."

And then she was gone. When he opened his eyes again, he saw her, running away down the hill, her white robes flowing behind her. It was a blade straight through his heart. But he knew she was right. He had his duty, and she had hers, and if they failed to play their parts, the blood of thousands would stain their hands.

Damn fate and all its cruel twists. Damn him, for falling so deeply in love with a woman he could never have. Damn the world, and everyone in it.

7

The tub was full, and Nathan turned the water off, went back to the bedroom, and slowly peeled the blankets away from Nidaba. She lay still, unresponsive, her face sticky. She didn't look like a holy woman or a High Priestess, much less an immortal High Witch, just now. She didn't look like the queen she should have been. She looked like a messy little girl trapped inside a woman's body.

He knew better, though. He'd watched her grow from a child into a young woman right before his eyes. And what a woman she had become. He had seen her again, after she had left him on that bitter hillside. He had seen her on the day of his coronation.

He would never forget . . .

Nathan closed his eyes against the memories that burned in his mind and told himself to focus on the present, not the distant past. When he opened his eyes again, he forced himself to see not the sensual priestess he remembered, but the helpless, frail-looking woman lying on the bed, staring at nothing with eyes that seemed afraid.

"Forgive me, Nidaba. Even now, the memory of you burns in me as if it were fresh and new." He ran a hand across his forehead, reconsidered what he was about to do, then laughed at himself. There was no shyness in Nidaba. No humble, blushing virgin in her. There never had been.

He rolled her up onto her side, untied the hospital gown in the back, then laid her flat again. His hands at the sleeves, he pulled the garment off her.

Gods, she was so thin. The drugs in her system must be slowing everything down, including the restorative powers of their kind. He could see her ribs, and her belly was concave. The bones of her hips and her collarbones jutted sharply against skin that seemed to have thinned. He peeled away the white underpants, tossed them aside, and slid his arms beneath her.

His palms slid over soft skin, and his body came alive, not just with the jolt of immortal touching immortal, but with longing. A hunger that should have died long ago. And the craving wasn't in his body alone, but in his heart.

She was helpless right now. But she wouldn't be for long. Not Nidaba. When she was herself again, she would be fully capable of destroying him utterly. And if he didn't get his feelings under control, he would end up letting her.

He drew away from her, tugged the covers back over her, and contented himself with bringing a warm cloth from the bathroom and washing her face. Sheila would return with help. For once he was glad of her bossy ways and take-charge attitude. Sometimes, he admitted with a sigh, he needed to be protected from himself.

•   •   •

"Nathan! Nathan! Oh, Nathan, she's gone!"

George's frantic cries accompanied his feet clomping up the stairs at top speed several hours later. Nathan had been sitting with Nidaba, watching over her, reading aloud, talking to her about times long past, about his life today. Anything to pass the time. He'd made use of her bath himself, leaving the door open wide in case she should cry out or become afraid. It had been a quick bath. Exhaustion, mental as well as physical, had tempted him to linger in the hot water, to relax into its soothing embrace. His back and shoulders ached from the hours spent in the chair beside her bed. But he didn't dare linger He bathed, dried himself, put on fresh clothes. He didn't even take time to shave, because there was no line of sight from the sink to the bed where Nidaba lay, and he was sure something would happen if he took his eyes off her for too long.

There had been no significant change in her condition all morning, however.

It was after two when the door opened and George stood there, breathless and wide-eyed wearing a bright green pullover with a white tab collar and a chartreuse clip-on bow tie attached. "Nathan, she's gone!" he said again.

"Who's gone?" George was in pain. Nathan's empathic tendencies brought that pain and worry to him as sharply as if it were his own.

"My dog! My Queenie, she's gone! I took her to the fenced-in place, just like you said. And I put food and water out there, and I stayed with her for a long time. Then I thought she was getting bored. So I went up to my room to get her a ball to play with, and when I came back, she was just gone! Where could she be, Nathan?" As he spoke, George battled tears without much success.

Nathan was out of his chair and across the room before George finished speaking. He held George's big shoulders, felt like hugging the man, who was more childlike right now than he'd ever been. "She's all right, I'm sure of it, George. She's all right, wherever she is."

"But . . . but . . ." George's eyes filled with shimmering pools that would flood at any moment.

"Come on, sit down." Nathan led George to a chair near the window, settled him into it, pushed the heavy damask drapes open and looped the gold braided tie-backs around them. "Look outside, George. It's a beautiful day. That dog is probably running around, chasing rabbits, having fun. There's nothing out there that could hurt her. Is there?"

George looked out the window, his gaze intent. "Well . . . I don't *see* anything that could hurt her."

Nathan felt the big guy's worry easing just a little, and he pressed on. "There *isn't* anything. She's a big dog, George, a strong animal. Besides, I know you may not want to think about this, but you have to consider for a minute that she might have belonged to someone else. Maybe she went back to her home."

Innocent eyes searched Nathan's. "Do you think so?"

"Well, she was a purebred Rottweiler, George. A beautiful animal. It's hard to believe a dog like that didn't belong to someone."

Blinking, George pondered that for a moment. "She wasn't wearing any collar. No tags."

"No. Some dogs are pretty clever about wriggling out of their collars, though."

"They are?"

"Oh, yes. I've seen them do it. Listen, you take my advice and don't worry about her. Later on, when Sheila gets back with her friend, I'll ask her to drive you around looking for Queenie. And we can put an ad in the local newspaper if you want."

"We can?"

"Sure we can! Someone will have seen her. And even if she does belong to someone else, at least you'll know. And maybe you can visit her. And if she doesn't have a home, then we'll find her and bring her back here. Either way, there's no cause for you to be so upset. She's a smart, strong, healthy dog, romping around somewhere having the time of her life. I promise. She's fine."

George sighed, his shoulders slumping in obvious relief. "Thanks, Nathan. I feel better." He looked at the floor. "You always make me feel better."

"I'm glad." Nathan's throat felt inexplicably tight.

"I think I'll walk around outside for a while, see if I can find her."

"Just don't go too far, George. And stay out of the woods."

"I will," he promised. He got to his feet, glanced at the bed, then at Nathan again. "How is the lady doing?"

"Not much different than this morning, I'm afraid."

"She'll get better, Nathan," George said, and he patted Nathan's shoulder. "You'll see."

"Thank you, George. I'm sure she will."

George smiled. "Did I make you feel better?"

Looking up, Nathan saw the hope in his big, innocent eyes, and he forced a smile. "Yes, you did, George. Thank you."

"You're welcome, Nathan."

The sound of a car pulling into the driveway made them both turn to the window again. Nathan said, "There's Sheila now, with her friend." He almost sighed in relief. Gods knew, he needed the help. Just enough time to slip away for a shave and a bite to eat, knowing that someone was there with Nidaba, would be a blessed relief. Something moved in the woods alongside the

driveway, and it caught Nathan's eye. His first thought
was that he'd spotted George's precious stray running
through the underbrush. But the shadowy form vanished.
He watched, eyes narrow and searching, and caught one
more glimpse of . . . something. But this time it looked
like a person moving amid the trees, and then there was
nothing at all.

A little shiver raced up Nathan's spine. He gave his
head a shake, told himself he was overtired, his eyes
were playing tricks on him. Still, he couldn't quite shake
the ominous feeling.

"I swear, I don't know what's keeping Lisette," Sheila
said, pacing the room once more. She'd spent the past
hour telling Nathan about her friend Lisette's qualifica-
tions. She was an RN with experience in caring for the
mentally ill, and she owed Sheila a favor. Apparently a
very big favor, because Sheila was convinced she could
trust the woman to keep quiet about Nidaba's presence
here.

"Give her some time to get her bearings," Nathan advised. "She's probably unpacking, getting settled in. Besides, your word is good enough for me, Sheila. If she's
willing to do the job, and you trust her, then she's hired.
I'll pay her whatever she wants. Just so long as she does
a good job." He glanced into the bathroom, where he'd
started running another bath for Nidaba. "Tub's full."
Walking in, he shut the water off.

"She's not the kind to dawdle, Nathan. I promise you
that." Sheila frowned. "I'd best go and check on her."

"No need," a woman's harsh, raspy voice said as the
bedroom door swung inward. "I'm right here."

Sheila's startled frown made Nathan wonder what was
going on. He studied the woman standing in the doorway. She was small, slender, with silver hair in a swept-

up style, and incredible skin for a woman of her age. Her eyes were vivid blue, and penetrating.

"Whatever has happened to your voice?" Sheila asked.

"I'm sure I don't know," she whispered. "It got this way only minutes after I arrived. I suppose I'm allergic to something in this house."

"Until this morning we had a dog running around the place. Could it have been that?" Nathan asked.

"Ahh . . . that's it," she rasped. "Dogs'll get me every time." Nathan smiled as the woman held out her hand. "You must be Nathan King." He had to strain to hear her. "Sheila has told me so much about you."

He reached for her hand, but she drew it back, looked at it, and shook her head. "Best not. If it's not from the dog, then this thing could be catching," she said, pointing at her throat.

"It's very good to meet you, Ms . . . ?"

She smiled and said, "Call me Lisette."

"Lisette, then. I want to thank you for coming on such short notice. You're doing me a great favor by taking this on."

She shrugged, and he frowned. "But if you think you might be contagious, perhaps—"

"No worries," she whispered. "I'll use antibacterial soap and gloves with the patient. She'll be in no danger."

Nathan nodded, glancing again at Sheila only to see her still frowning at her friend in what looked like confusion. He wondered at that, but the woman was already moving forward, looking at Nidaba in the bed, glancing into the adjoining bathroom.

"I see you've got a bath run for her."

"Yes, she's in need of it. That is, if you don't mind getting started right away."

"Of course I don't mind." That sandpapery rasp scraped his nerve endings.

"I realize we haven't discussed terms yet. I'll pay you triple the going rate. All I ask is that you treat this patient with extreme kindness, be gentle with her, and see to it she has whatever she needs."

The nurse's eyes narrowed on Nidaba. "You care for the woman a great deal, then?"

For some reason, the question bothered him. "She's . . . an old friend. A very dear old friend."

"Don't worry, Mr. King. I'll take *very good* care of her."

He nodded as Lisette went to the bed, tugged at the covers, and then looked at him sharply. "Who undressed her?" she asked.

"She . . . dribbled oatmeal all over herself this morning," he replied.

The woman frowned. "Highly inappropriate, Mr. King," she said, and pulled the covers back around Nidaba. She rushed into the bathroom and returned with a large towel, then she yanked the covers down again, and proceeded to wrap it around Nidaba, rolling her up onto her side to do so. When Lisette touched her, Nidaba jerked, and her eyes widened.

Nathan jumped, but Lisette held up a hand. "It's all right. She'll need to get used to me if I'm to help her. Now she's ready. Carry her into the bathroom, Mr. King, and put her in the tub, towel and all. I'll see to the rest myself."

Sheila cocked her head to one side as Nathan scooped Nidaba up from the bed. She walked beside Lisette as they followed him into the bathroom. "I vow, Lisette," she said, "you're like a different woman when you're working. If I didn't know your face so well I don't think I'd recognize you at all."

From the corner of his eye, Nathan saw Lisette send her friend a smile. "I care very deeply about my work . . . but you know that, now, don't you?"

"Yes. Yes, that I do. But . . ."

"Hush, my friend. We'll talk later on, when the work is done. Save your worries, won't you?"

"Sure. Later on. And I'll brew you up something soothin' for that throat."

Lisette squeezed Sheila's hand and sent her a warm smile.

Nathan stopped beside the bathtub, staring down at Nidaba's wide, unfocused eyes. "Now, I'm going to put you into the bathtub, Nidaba. There's water. Warm, but not too warm. It's going to feel good to you, do you understand? There is no reason to be afraid, to be startled by this. No reason at all. This is good for you."

He continued speaking softly, telling her how good the water would feel, as he lowered her carefully into the tub. She started, just once, when the warm water touched her skin, but then she returned to oblivion again and lay back in the water.

Nathan knelt beside the tub, one hand always on her, to keep her from slipping. He had everything ready and within reach so Lisette wouldn't have to leave her alone for an instant and risk her drowning herself.

Where he touched Nidaba's shoulders he could feel the sharpness of her bones beneath her skin. And her thighs looked so thin, so slight, below the towel. Had they even fed her in that place?

Anger stirred in his gut.

"Go on now," Lisette said in that odd voice. "I'll take care of her from here."

He looked at the woman. Then he sought out Sheila's eyes.

"She's right, Nathan. Go on, have a shave, get some

lunch. I saw the breakfast I made for you this morning, sitting cold and untouched on the plate. You need to keep yourself well or you'll never be able to care for this one. You know that."

"I . . ." He couldn't say it. He didn't want to insult Lisette or hurt Sheila, but he just couldn't bring himself to leave Nidaba alone with this strange woman. He barely knew her, after all.

"I'll stay," Sheila said, reading him so clearly it almost made him dizzy. "I'll be right here. I'll not let her out of my sight, Nathan, and if she needs you for anything, I'll call for you. All right?"

Meeting Sheila's eyes, seeing she wasn't angry with him for mistrusting her friend, he nodded. "I don't know what I'd do without you, Sheila."

"Oh, curl up in a corner and die, no doubt. Now go on. Out with you. This is woman's work."

Feeling slightly better, he left the room. But he didn't go far. He went into his own bedroom, just off Nidaba's, where his bed remained untouched, unslept in. He dug out a shaving kit he kept in the top drawer and stepped into the hallway to head to the guest bathroom, since his own was currently being used by the women.

He got only about ten steps when he heard the ear-splitting shriek and the crash. Choking on his own heart, he spun and raced back along the hall, through his bedroom, tossing his kit onto the bed on the way to Nidaba's room, and finally to the bathroom beyond.

Sheila was dripping wet, standing back and looking surprised, while Lisette gripped Nidaba's frail shoulders, attempting to hold her still while she thrashed and splashed and fought.

Nathan ran forward. "Let go—let go of her!"

Lisette did, and Nidaba instantly stilled. She sat stiffly in the tub, eyes wide, breaths rushing in and out of her parted lips in short panicky bursts. She was shaking. Visibly trembling.

Nathan knelt in the puddle beside the tub, but didn't touch her. "It's all right. I'm here, Nidaba. It's all right." He watched her, wishing to the Gods he knew what sort of nightmares went on inside her mind where she was trapped. "What happened in here?" He asked without taking his eyes from her. Her collarbones poked up so sharply it seemed they'd pierce the thin layer of skin that covered them. Her small breasts rose and fell in time with her breaths.

"I'm not sure," Lisette said.

"Not sure, eh? Well, I am," Sheila cut in. "She started to get antsy as soon as you left the room, Nathan. Stiff, and jittery-like. Let me take the towel off, all right, and even wash her up a bit. But as soon as Lisette poured a bit of water on that hair of hers she went crazy on us. Thrashed about like a wild woman, she did."

Nathan nodded, his gaze slipping only briefly away from Nidaba. "I heard a scream."

"That was her, all right," Sheila said with a sharp nod.

"So you can speak after all, hmm?" He looked hard into those black eyes and they stared back, wide, but clearer than they had been before, he thought. Then he told himself that might be an illusion. Wishful thinking.

"I'm sure it was only the water on her head that set her off." Lisette was on her feet and beside the tub now. "Some mentally ill patients go into a panic when water touches their faces."

"And I think it was the fact that Nathan left the room," Sheila said.

"That's nonsense."

"Is it now, do you think?"

"I'm the one who's experienced with mental patients, Sheila," Lisette said in a harsh mutter that was closer to speaking in a normal tone than anything Nathan had heard her say thus far.

"Lisette's right," Nathan put in. "Besides, she didn't react right away, when I left her. You said yourself she let you wash her up a bit, didn't you, Sheila?"

Sheila's gaze narrowed. "That's right. Maybe it's you she dislikes, Lisette." She said it teasingly, the way a friend would to another friend, with a nudge of the elbow or a wink. But Lisette's scowl led Nathan to think she didn't take the comment in the same manner.

He hated to see tension brewing between Sheila and her long-time friend, so he stepped in. "Let's put it to the test, then, okay?" He looked around, not getting up from his knees, and spotted the small plastic pitcher Sheila had been using. Then he filled it and touched Nidaba's hair.

"Your hair is all tangled and dirty," he said slowly. "I'm going to wash it for you. All right?"

She didn't respond, just stared straight ahead. Nathan tipped her head back a little, to keep the water out of her eyes, and slowly poured. She didn't fight, didn't panic at all. So he dipped another pitcher full and poured that as well, and she tipped her head back farther. Her eyes fell closed.

He almost smiled. She liked this. He continued dipping and pouring until her long hair was thoroughly soaked. Then he applied a generous amount of baby shampoo and worked up a lather. He massaged her scalp with his fingertips, scrubbed gently and thoroughly, for a long time. Her hair, masses of it, tangled around his fingers as she lay back, relaxing more as he rubbed, eyes remaining closed. Her breaths came deep and slowly. He watched her chest rise and fall with it. And finally he began rinsing, pitcher by pitcher.

"You're very good at this," Sheila whispered, leaning

close. "You must have the touch." She pressed another bottle into Nathan's hand. Conditioner. Guaranteed to remove all the tangles, so combing wouldn't be such a chore. He poured a quarter of the bottle over her head, and worked it in, rubbing it down to her scalp and out to the ends of her hair.

His patient was almost limp, she was so relaxed now. So he kept it up a little longer. She liked this. He hadn't thought Nidaba was capable of feeling anything . . . particularly pleasure. But she was doing precisely that, and he would keep it up just as long as it pleased her.

"I imagine the water is getting cold by now, Mr. King," Lisette said. And her tone, raspy, but louder still, made her disapproval very clear.

Too bad.

"It *is* beginning to cool down a bit." Nathan reached up and cranked on the hot water tap, then sent Lisette an innocent smile. "Easily remedied." And then he went back to massaging Nidaba's scalp while she reclined like a queen, relishing it, he thought. He made small circles with his fingertips, massaged her temples, and her neck just behind her ears, and then her nape, at the base of her skull. She let her head fall forward when he did that. And all her breath rushed out of her. When he eased her back again, he thought her face looked more placid than he had seen it in centuries.

Eventually, he rinsed the conditioner away. But she didn't sit up or move when he finished. A soft sound came from her throat, and if it meant anything at all, he thought, it meant that she wanted more of this. Fine, then. He would continue.

He reached for the sponge Sheila had put in here for him, the one he'd never bothered to use, and the scented body wash that he'd borrowed from the guest bathroom when preparing for Nidaba's arrival. Vanilla. Very slowly, he lathered one long, slender arm, lifted it, and rinsed it clean. Slow, soothing strokes up her outer arm, and then around to the more sensitive inner part. The well opposite her elbow. The hollow underneath. Her hand, her palm, and one by one each and every finger. When he finished with both arms, he washed her chest. He lathered and rubbed her small breasts, and her sunken belly.

Her eyes opened. Fixed on his hands. Darkened.

No. That couldn't be what it looked like.

Nathan rinsed the lather away, and pulled her forward just a bit, to soap and scrub her back and shoulders. And she seemed to like that so much that he continued far longer than was necessary. She acted as if the muscles of her back ached though he could barely see how they could. There seemed to be no muscle there to ache. There was nothing to her but skin and bone.

Sighing her displeasure, Lisette paced back and forth on the side of the room nearest the door. Sheila kept herself busy—she was wielding a mop over the spilled water right now. She seemed perfectly content to let Nathan perform this entire bathing duty.

When Nidaba finally leaned back again, Nathan moved along to the bottom of the tub, clasped one of her tiny ankles in his hand, and lifted it. Then he ran his hand and the soapy sponge over her leg, beginning at her foot, and moving slowly up over her calf, and down her shin. And then higher. He began to soap her thigh. And he watched her face, watched it intently. Her gaze seemed to heat as his hand neared the crux of her legs. And it was *not* his imagination. He was sure of it this time.

"You're in there, aren't you?" he murmured. "You're alive and kicking in there. Why won't you speak to me? Hmm?"

His hand edged closer to her center, but he moved
past it and began working the other leg. Down the thigh,
over the calf, to the foot. "Talk to me, Nidaba," he
urged, massaging the small of her foot briskly. "Talk to
me. Fight the grip of this darkness that holds you."

She didn't. But she was, in a way, responding to him
more than she had since he'd found her in that hospital.
Responding, Nathan realized, to his touch. He sponged
a path back up the thigh, intending to bathe every inch
of her . . . to *touch* every inch of her, if that was what it
would take to draw a real response.

Dammit, he wished he'd gone with his initial instinct
and bathed her himself when he could have been completely alone with her. But he hadn't expected this.

"Sheila, why don't you and Lisette go and get some
clean clothes out of the closet for our guest?" His hand
inched higher on Nidaba's thigh. He watched her eyes
heat, felt her legs move just the slightest bit farther apart.
That part of her hadn't shut down, then, had it? The
sexual part. The hungry part. It was there he could reach
her.

"Whatever you say, Nathan," Sheila chirped, merrily
turning away. "I see you've got things under control
here." She walked past Lisette on her way, and Nathan
hoped the woman would have the good sense to follow
her out of the room.

"I'm not leaving this room," the nurse said. "It's inappropriate."

"You think I'm going to pull her out of the tub and
rape her?" Nathan asked, his voice quiet, his eyes on
Nidaba's. Hers, alive, feeling, wanting . . . but still staring off into the distance.

"It wouldn't be the first time a man had taken advantage of a mentally ill woman, Mr. King. But you can

bet it's not going to happen on my watch. I'd be shirking
my duty if I left you alone with her."

Nathan sighed, but his hand was still on Nidaba's inner thigh, and she was still sitting there, head tipped
back, eyes burning. And Lisette was standing halfway
across the room, too far to see what Nathan might be
doing with his hands beneath the soapy water.

"I'll remind you who's paying your salary, Lisette,"
he said. "If you doubt my integrity so much, maybe I
should look for someone else to—"

"I didn't mean to insult you, Mr. King."

He nodded. "If you insist on staying, fine. But could
you at least get me some dry towels? They're in the
small linen closet just down the hall."

With a muttered agreement, Lisette turned her back.

Watching Nidaba's eyes—her remarkably *clear* eyes—
Nathan moved the soapy sponge higher, brushed it gently between her legs. Her lips parted and a breath sighed
out of her. He rubbed again, up and down, soaping her,
caressing her with the loofah. "Look at me," he whispered. "Look at me, Nidaba."

Her gaze faltered, shifted slightly, and her thighs
parted further. She pressed against the sponge, and he
rubbed a little harder.

"Look at me."

Suddenly, her gaze snapped to his, and locked on.
Fire. Heat. Fury. Rage. So many passions boiled in that
gaze. But it was clear, and it was focused on him.

Was this wrong, what he was doing? Probably. But
suppose he could reach her, pull her out of the grip of
her mind? Then wasn't it to her benefit that he do so,
any way he could?

She arched her hips against the sponge he held, and
he pressed, and moved it over her. Lisette would return

soon, damn her to hell. Nathan dropped the sponge, moved his hand away.

Quick as lightning, Nidaba's hand closed over his and pulled it to her, pressed it against her, rocking her hips. Her eyes flared wider and held his with a fierce gaze.

Nathan swallowed hard against something that felt a lot like fear. But it couldn't be that. It made no sense to be afraid of her, despite the ferocity and the feral hunger in that gaze. And yet it made all the sense in the world. He was so close, so close to reaching her, yet not knowing what he would find when he did. But he was near, he could feel it.

Lisette's footsteps were coming back down the hall. Only seconds and his chance would be missed. All right, then, right or wrong . . .

Nathan moved his fingers against the woman, parted her folds, stroked her just a little. "Talk to me, Nidaba. Come on. Tell me your name," he whispered. He flicked his fingers over the core of her need. "Tell me."

Lisette's steps got louder, coming through the bedroom now.

"Come on, say it. Say your name." He rubbed her harder, faster.

She parted her lips, closed her eyes and whispered "Nidaba" on a trembling sigh.

Lisette went still just beyond the doorway.

Nathan smiled, and stroked her once more, pressed her between his thumb and forefinger, and she gasped in pleasure. He rolled that tiny nub of need, pinched and pressed and kneaded it. Lisette was coming into the room now. Three more steps and she would be through the door, and able to see where his hand was, what he was doing. He pinched her harder, rubbing the swollen kernel faster between his thumb and forefinger, and he leaned low, and whispered very close to her ear, "Let it go, Nidaba. Let it go for me."

Her body arched, and she cried out loud, going stiff in the water for a moment suspended in time. Lisette stopped walking, her frown dark and probing. Then Nidaba relaxed her shuddering body back into the bathwater, squeezed her thighs together around his hand, as if to keep it there.

He drew in a quaking breath, shivering with a desire that burned deep in his gut. "Good girl," he whispered, before he took his hand away. "That's my good girl."

He stopped touching her, and she stopped responding. Slowly, the veil he'd seen before took its place over her eyes. Her focus faded. She'd retreated again.

8

"You'd best come down a moment, Nathan," Sheila
said, as he sat his lonely vigil beside the bed once again,
waiting for Nidaba to give some sign of being ready to
come out of this catatonia. Her eyes remained open. He
supposed that was a good sign.

Lisette lingered about the bedroom almost constantly.
And while he had expected to be relieved at having some
assistance, he wasn't. The woman made the hairs on the
back of his neck prickle. He felt uneasy, but for no apparent reason.

"What is it, Sheila?" he asked as she stood in the
doorway.

"There's a lady at the door." Sheila hesitated, shifting
her stance uneasily. "Says she's looking for a relative of
hers who spent some time recently at a New Jersey psy-
chiatric hospital."

Nathan's head came around swiftly and he saw the
nervousness in Sheila's face, and her stance. He glanced
at Lisette, who was listening with apparent interest, and
schooled his features to reveal nothing. "Odd that she'd

think we would know anything about it. What did you tell her?"

"That we knew nothing about it, of course. But she refuses to leave until she's spoken to you directly." She pressed her lips together tightly. "I tried my best, Nathan."

"I don't doubt it." He rose, started for the door, then glanced back at Nidaba uneasily. "Stay here, Sheila. If she wakes, she could be more than Lisette can handle, and I don't want anyone getting hurt."

"All right, then." Sheila took the seat Nathan had been using.

He left the three women alone, hating to do it, but knowing he could not remain at Nidaba's side constantly. He just wished he could shake the constant feeling of impending disaster. His senses were too well honed to be mistaken—something was wrong. Nidaba was not safe, but he couldn't pinpoint the source of the threat. His disquiet about every stranger to enter the house, right down to that poor dog of George's, were irrational. He needed to find a focus for the feelings, isolate the danger, pinpoint its true source. Until he did, he couldn't banish this mistrust of every newcomer.

He walked down the stairs into the front parlor, and found a very slight woman perched uneasily on the edge of the settee. Her hair was cropped short, golden blond, and her eyes were huge and lustrous.

"I'm Nathan King," he said, and she was on her feet before he finished speaking, her big gaze turned on him, one hand flexing near her side.

She eyed him somewhat warily. "My name is Arianna Sinclair-Lachlan," she said. She didn't offer her hand, so he didn't offer his. But the fact that she didn't touch him put him on guard. Immortals rarely offered a hand to strangers—for fear of giving themselves away should

the stranger turn out to be an immortal as well. Was she
the threat he'd been sensing?

"I'm sorry to intrude, but this is a matter of some
urgency. I'm looking for a dear friend."

"A relative—or so Sheila told me." He watched her,
testing her.

"She's family to me." Her reply was not really any
kind of answer at all.

"I'm afraid I'm not going to be of any help to you,
either way." He sighed as if he truly regretted it and
hoped he was convincing. "I sincerely wish I could."

"Mr. King, I know you went to see Nidaba at the
Brooker Hospital the day before her disappearance."

He kept his eyes hooded, his tone flat. "And how do
you know that?"

"Every car that enters the parking lot is caught on
videotape, Mr. King. I got the tapes from that day, got
your plate number, and had a friend trace your name
through the department of motor vehicles."

He lifted his brows. "Are you some kind of detec-
tive?" he asked.

She didn't answer that question. "Your car came in
only minutes before a male visitor signed in to see Nidaba. And while he signed himself in as John Smith,"
she said with a smirk, "the nurse on duty gave an ex-
cellent description, which you fit to a tee. And, as it turns
out, you may very well have been the last person to see
her before she was taken."

"Taken?" He tipped his head to one side. "The news-
papers called it an escape."

Her slender brows rose. "Then you've been following
the story?"

"Is that so surprising?"

"If she had simply escaped, I'd have heard from her

by now," she said, her eyes narrowing on him. "I believe she was taken."

Nathan shook his head as if the woman made no sense to him. "Suppose she simply wanted to be alone? Honestly, I see no reason to jump to conclusions here, Miss . . ."

"Ms.," she said. "Sinclair-Lachlan."

"Yes, of course. Look, I'll explain myself to you if it will help ease your mind. I went to see your . . . *friend* because of the photo in the paper. She looked familiar to me. But when I actually saw her, face to face, I realized she was not who I thought she was, and I came home. End of story," he finished. He opened his mind, tried to reach out with the rusty tendrils of his empathy to see if she was swallowing a word of his story. But he was so out of practice. For too long he'd blocked out everyone. Other than Sheila and George, he had trouble picking up on anyone these days.

The woman paced across the room slowly. Nathan looked past her, and felt his heart leap in his chest. In the living room, just beyond the arching doorway at her back, the fireplace was clearly visible—along with the portrait above the mantel. The portrait he'd painted of Nidaba, in the flowing white robes of a Sumerian High Priestess, with the golden circlet and its crescent bow upon her head. All the woman need do was turn and look . . .

"Come, let's go sit in the library. I'll pour you a drink and—"

"Are you aware that a doctor was killed that day, right outside Nidaba's room, shortly after your visit?"

He shook his head. "No. No I wasn't," he lied. But it wasn't lost on him that she'd said "killed." Not "attacked." So Dr. Sterling hadn't made it after all.

"I have reason to believe the person who killed her was after Nidaba," the woman said.

Right. And she probably knew that because she *was* that person.

"Another man was seen in the hospital the night Nidaba disappeared," the woman went on. "And according to the nurse who saw him, he also matches your description."

"So do several million other men in the world, I would imagine."

"Somehow I doubt that," she said.

He blinked, unsure whether he'd just been insulted or paid a compliment.

"Why did you go to see her?" she barked out without warning.

She was good. Sharp and quick. What she suspected him of, he could only wonder. What she wanted of Nidaba—well he had only two guesses for that. Either she was a friend, as she claimed, or she was a hunter, in search of an immortal heart more powerful than nearly any still beating. With the exception, perhaps, of his own.

If she were to succeed, this Arianna would have power beyond compare, because she would have to take his if she hoped to take Nidaba's. And with both, she would be nearly invincible.

"I'm trying to be patient with you, Miss, but you're pushing my limits here. I've told you already. I saw the photo in the newspaper, and it reminded me of someone I used to know. I went to see her. And once I did, I realized she wasn't the person I had thought she might be, and I left. I came back here that afternoon, and have remained here ever since. There are several people who can verify that for you, if you insist on it."

She watched him as he spoke. Watched him the way

a critic watches a film. Narrow-eyed and probing, constantly searching for flaws in the storyline, or the acting.

It made him uneasy, that probing gaze of hers. He broke the lengthening silence. "Tell me, what was she doing in the mental hospital, this friend of yours?"

It had the desired effect. The woman blinked and looked away from him. "Nidaba has had . . . a lot of trauma in her life. I think it finally got to be too much for her."

"What kind of trauma?" he asked, far too quickly.

Arianna stiffened, that sharp gaze shooting right back to him. "Why do you want to know? Why are you so interested, anyway?"

Shrugging in a careless manner, he shifted his eyes away from her. "Just curious, I suppose. I did visit her, and I couldn't help but feel pity. I am human, after all."

"Are you?"

He snapped his gaze to hers. She looked away.

"Believe me, Mr. King," she said, "if we had known where she was, we would never have left her there." She sounded slightly defensive now. "But by the time that article was brought to our attention, she was gone."

"*Our* attention? There are more than one of you?" He strode to the front door and looked outside.

"The others don't know I've come," she said. "They aren't as . . . reasonable as I am."

"You call this reasonable? You come to my home and practically accuse me of kidnapping a mental patient, and that's reasonable?"

"For me?" She seemed to battle a smile for just a moment. "A year ago I'd have kicked the door in, beat you senseless, and searched the place for myself, Mr. King. Some of my friends still would. You wouldn't believe how lucky you are that I've grown . . . calmer than I used to be. But I'm warning you, the others will follow the same trail I did, and it will lead them to your door. If they find out you've harmed Nidaba—"

"Harmed her?" He feigned deep offense. "What kind of man do you think I am?"

She just stared at him. So he went on with the right-eous indignation routine. "I think maybe you'd better leave now, Ms. Lachlan-Sinclair." She felt guilty. He picked up on it, and thought his rusty skills might be freeing themselves up at last.

"Sinclair-Lachlan," she corrected, but her voice was softer now. "And I'm sorry. I didn't mean to come here and offend you. Especially if you really are . . . innocent in all this." Then her eyes narrowed. "But if you're not, I'll find out. And may God help you then."

Either she was sincerely worried about Nidaba, or she was a very good actress, he thought. And from every-thing he could sense in her, it was the former, not the latter.

Then she drew a breath, swallowed. "What . . . what condition was she in . . . when you saw her?"

He mulled that one over. How much to reveal? In the end, just to see her reaction, he said, "Catatonic."

Moisture sprang into the woman's eyes. A flash of her pain hit him—so much so that his resolve started to waver. "Oh, no," she whispered. "Even at her worst, she was never quite that far gone."

"Then, she's had these sorts of episodes before?"

"I thought she was over it. I thought . . ." She clamped her mouth closed, looking up at him sharply. "I've al-ready said too much. You've made it quite clear that this is no concern of yours."

"The suffering of another human being is always of concern to me," he countered.

"That's a very pretty speech."

"But not a convincing one?" He shook his head,

walked through the foyer, and yanked open the front
door, praying she wouldn't look through the doorway
and glimpse that portrait. "I wish you luck in finding
your friend," he said. "But I have things to do."

"Don't think I won't be back," she warned. "If I get
even an inkling you've been lying to me—"

"I haven't been. Good-bye."

"Hmmph." She stepped through the door, but before
he could close it she said, "Wait." She dug in her pocket
and pulled out a card and a pen. "This is my hotel . . .
and the room number is on the back." She scrawled it
as she spoke. "If you remember anything, or . . . whatever . . . call me."

Nodding slowly, he said, "All right. I will." He
reached for the card. She didn't give it to him. Instead
she set it down on the stand just inside the door, then
turned and walked away.

Nathan picked the card up, looked it over as he closed
the door, then carried it idly with him back into the
living room, and put it into a drawer for safekeeping.

He stood still for a moment, wondering who in hell
this Arianna really was and what she truly wanted from
Nidaba. Immortal, she had to be. She had deliberately
avoided touching him. She said Nidaba had suffered
trauma. What trauma? Could this woman have known
about his past with her? Or had there been something
more?

And what kind of fool question was that, anyway? Of
course there had been more. Centuries had passed since
the anguish he'd rained down on Nidaba's head and she
on his. Surely there had been more.

Footsteps on the stairs alerted him, and he turned to
see Sheila coming down. His senses jumped. "Sheila,
what are you doing down here?"

She looked at him with a frown. "Lisette asked that I

bring up some broth for the patient," she said. "Whatever is the matter with—Nathan?"

But he was sprinting past her, taking the stairs two at a time. He raced down the hall, threw the door open, and saw the nurse leaning over Nidaba, her back to him so he couldn't see what she was doing.

"Lisette!"

She went stiff and still for just a moment. Then she straightened and turned slowly. The only thing in her hand, he saw, was a hairbrush. Even as Nathan blew a relieved sigh and called himself an idiot, Lisette pressed a palm to her chest, as if to calm her racing heart.

"My goodness, but you scared me half to death! What's wrong?" she asked him.

Swallowing his nervousness and feeling like a fool, Nathan said, "Sorry. Nothing. Nothing at all." He was going to have to stop being so irrational. The woman was a nurse, for God's sake.

Lisette sighed and resumed brushing Nidaba's hair. Nidaba lay stiff, jerking her head with each stroke.

"Why don't you let me do that?" Nathan asked.

"Oh, now, what did you hire me for, if you're going to do everything yourself?"

He didn't take no for an answer, though. "It's not you," he said. "I just like taking care of her." He stepped forward, took the brush away from the nurse, and waited for her to step aside. When she did he said, "Go now. Take a break. Get some dinner and rest. I'll handle her myself for a while."

"But—"

"Go."

With a sigh, she finally did.

Nathan watched her until she closed the door behind her. Then he turned to Nidaba, smoothed her hair with his hand, and whispered, "I'm here. It's okay, she's gone." He pulled his chair up and began running the brush through her ebony hair in long, slow strokes. And he thought she relaxed just a little bit. "You don't like Lisette at all, do you, Nidaba?"

Naturally, there was no reply.

"You're as bad as I am, then. I don't like her either. But I wonder why," he murmured softly. "I honestly do wonder why."

The woman who called herself Lisette lingered in the hall, pacing nervously and wringing her hands as she hoped to the Gods that Nathan King would not discover the drug-filled hypodermic needle she had shoved underneath the mattress when he'd burst in on her.

Dammit, she'd barely hidden the weapon in time.

Then she slowed her pace, calmed herself. A slow, knowing smile spread across her face. So what if he *did* find it? It wouldn't change anything. She would simply have to find another way to do what she had to do— what she should have finished centuries ago!

And she would.

She always found a way to do what must be done. And this time there would be no question, no deception, no mistakes. This time Nidaba would die by Puabi's own hand. As it should have been on that hotel rooftop. As it should have been over four thousand years ago.

9

He fell asleep brushing Nidaba's hair, and he dreamed. Memories he'd locked deep inside long ago resurfaced now, to torment him again, as fresh as if they were new.

Eannatum sat at his father's bedside, clasping the old king's withered hand in his own younger, stronger one. "I am here, Father," he whispered.

The king lay still, swathed in coverings of the finest fabrics. Sacred incense burned, and tendrils of its smoke lingered in the air, like spectral dancers. The powerful smell of the smouldering herbs laced each labored breath his father took, but Eannatum knew the herbs would not save his father. Nor would the incessant chanting of the priest who sat on the chamber floor. Nor the prayers and supplications of the entire kingdom. Death hovered, waiting to take the once mighty king away. Natum could almost hear the Dark Goddess's raspy voice, whispering from the dim corners, from the hidden realms, from the underworld . . .

I am the Darkness behind and beneath the shadows . . .

I am the absence of air that awaits at the bottom of every breath . . .

"Silence!"

Eannatum's shout caused the priest to stop his chanting. "No, I . . . didn't mean you," Eannatum said, but it didn't matter. The young man got to his feet, bowed deeply, and left the room.

But Eannatum sensed he was not alone with his father, even then. The Dark Goddess was there, lurking, waiting. He could feel her cold breath on his nape, and smell her foul stench in the air. Ereshkigal.

I am the decay that fertilizes the living . . . the bottomless pit . . .

"Shut up, Crone. Let him live!"

"My son." The voice, weak but real, came from his father. And Eannatum bowed over the old man, tightening his grip on his father's hand. "Do not speak so to the Dark Goddess. For it is into her embrace I go, and she alone will see me to the other side."

"Father, you mustn't say such things. You'll be well. I've sent for more herbs, more priests—"

Sadly, the old man shook his head. "It is over, my son. I am dying. My time in this world is done. It is as it should be."

"But—"

"Be still, Eannatum." The voice strengthened just a bit. "A dying old man I may be, but I am still your king and your sire."

"Speaking will only tire you."

"There are things that must be said."

Swallowing his objections, Eannatum nodded. He reached for a drinking vessel and held it to his father's lips, lifting the old man's head. When the king finished drinking, he lay back and stared at his son.

"Upon my death, you will receive my crown, Eannatum. The kingship of Lagash will be yours. But because of your impending marriage to Puabi, daughter of Ur, you will be called King of Kish, Ruler of all Sumer. You will take your throne on the first New Year's Day after your marriage, by sacred tradition."

"I do not wish—"

"I have no care for what you may or may not wish. I am your king. I am your father, and you will do as I command. For the good of your country, Eannatum. For the sake of peace. Already you have seen the power of Ur and Lagash joined as one. From the day word went forth that you intended to make Puabi your queen, the Ummamites began to cower. When our armies, united, began to patrol the borders, those raiders scurried like scarab beetles in full sunlight. If you don't go through with your promise now, they will fall on Sumer and rip it apart. Tell me you will keep your word. Tell me you will marry Puabi upon my death."

Inclining his head, Natum sighed. It was as close as he could come to showing his consent.

"Puabi will remain in her father's palace in Ur until after your coronation. This is wise, and best for her sake as well as your own. But as soon as you are crowned king, she will join you here in Lagash, and you will take her as your wife and your queen."

"Yes." The word was wrenched from him against his will.

"Good. It is good." For a moment, the king rested, caught his breath, before he gathered his waning strength and continued. "On New Year's Day, Inanna herself will anoint you as her chosen ruler, through the ritual we call the Sacred Marriage Rite. You know what this entails."

He nodded. He knew.

His father went on as if he did not. "The High Priestess of the temple will be cleansed and purified. She will call the Goddess to come to her, to inhabit her body. And then she will mate with you, so that you will become part God yourself. Her servant always. Her consort in human form, ruling her people of Sumer by divine right. You understand?"

He nodded slowly. "It shall be as you wish it." The High Priestess . . . Lia had been elevated to that station right after Nidaba's abandonment five years ago. It would seem sinful to copulate with the woman who had been his teacher, and Nidaba's. Almost a mother to her, in fact. It would seem wrong.

"There is no time to waste, my son. Your power must be established at once. The new year is but a quarter moon from today."

A frown bent Eannatum's brow. "I assumed you referred to the next new year, my father."

Weakly, the old man smiled. "Optimist. I've not a year left in me. No, it must be now."

"But . . . Father, you yet live. I can't very well claim the crown while you . . ." He frowned, a heaviness forming in his stomach.

Closing his eyes wearily, the king said, "This night is my last."

"No . . ." Eannatum leaned closer, touched his father's face, and the old eyes opened again. "Father, how can you know this? You might live for many weeks, months, even."

"My time ends tonight, my son. Your time is come."

"You cannot know that!"

"I know. Give your solemn vow to me that all shall be as I have told you, that I might go in peace to the underworld."

"Father—"

"Give it to me!" his father demanded, his eyes flaring wider as he came off his pillows.

"I vow it. I shall do all you ask of me. But Father—"

"Good," his father said. "Good. Now, give to me the rest of my wine, and I will sleep."

Eannatum took the chalice, held his father's head up, and put the rim to the dry, parched lips. His father drank and drank, and when Eannatum tried to take the cup away, the king pressed a hand to it to keep it there, tipping it higher, draining it.

He breathed when he finished, then lay back on the pillows, and muttered, "It is done. For the good of Sumer, it is done."

Blinking, Eannatum looked from his father's face to the cup he still held, and realization flashed blindingly through his mind. He sniffed at the contents, then tasted the remaining droplets, only to draw back and grimace at its bitterness. "No!" he cried, hurling the baked clay goblet away from him. The cup hit the wall and shattered to bits. "Father, what have you done?" He bent over his father, whose face had gone lax now. Gripping the front of his robes, Eannatum shook him. "Wake! Wake, curse you! Why have you done this? How *dare* you do such a thing! Father! Father!"

The door was flung open, and then someone was pulling at his shoulders. That young priest, Eannatum saw when he whirled on the offender.

"*You* gave it to him! Didn't you, priest? *Didn't you?*" he demanded, shaking the pale, frightened man until his teeth rattled.

"*I* gave it to him," a deep voice said.

Natum released the priest, who fell into a quivering heap on the floor, and looked up to see Lathor, the detestable High Priest who was unworthy of the title, standing in the doorway. "You?"

"Yes. I. It was his final wish, and as his most trusted

friend, and spiritual counsel, I had no choice but to obey."

"You murdered your king! Traitor!"

"If you go shouting that about the palace, my prince, it will be you who will be called traitor. For you will destroy what your father gave his life to protect. This kingdom. And your throne."

Eannatum stopped halfway to throttling the bastard. He was right. Damn him, he was right. But grief and fury raged in him, and he shuddered with the very effort of restraining himself. The need for vengeance warred with the knowledge of what was best for his kingdom.

His kingdom.

Turning to the bed, he dropped to his knees and folded himself over his father's prone form. He lay his head on the silent chest, and allowed the tears to come. . . .

Time passed. Hours perhaps. The two priests had left him, for how long, he did not know. His father was dead. He was to rule. To take the throne and then to marry Puabi. He lifted his head, rubbed at his eyes, and stared at his father's still, white face with blurred vision.

"Have you had enough of mourning, then?"

He turned slowly, and saw the High Priestess, Lia, standing just behind him. Swallowing hard, he let his chin fall. "I will never have enough of mourning, it seems."

"I am sorry for your loss, my prince," she said softly. "But I have come to offer words that may be of some comfort."

"What words could comfort me now?"

"Only these. I will not serve as your *lukur*, the vessel of the Goddess, for the Sacred Marriage Rite."

"How can you . . . ?"

"I have charge of the temple. And of the spiritual guidance of Lagash now that Lathor has fled."

"Fled?" Eannatum shook his head. "But he was here . . ."

"Two days ago, my prince. You have been closeted with your father's body for two full days."

Eannatum could only blink, looking around the room in confusion. He ran a hand over his chin, felt the growth of whiskers that proved the priestess's words to be true.

"Therefore, I am the highest-ranking official of Inanna's temple in all of Lagash. And I have decreed that I am unable to fulfill this role and have also set forth the solution."

Frowning, Eannatum looked at the priestess, searching her face, unable to make much sense of her words.

"The High Priestess of every temple in all of Sumer will journey here in time for the New Year's celebration. And they will dance for you, their king. They will dance the sacred Dance of the Seven Veils, in remembrance of Inanna's descent to the underworld. And when they finish dancing, my prince, you will choose the one you wish to serve as your *lukur*."

If her words were meant to offer comfort, they fell far short. "Fine," he said. "So be it."

She nodded, some secret hiding behind her eyes. But her hands on his shoulders were soft. "Come, my prince. You need to be attended. You are tired, hungry, and grieving. Let me care for you."

He turned back toward the bed. "But my father . . ."

"I have twenty priestesses waiting to attend your father, Eannatum. With tenderness, love, and deep respect. They will take care of him, I vow it to you on my honor."

He nodded slowly, knowing it needed doing, and he let the gentle High Priestess lead him from the room.

The burial passed in a blur of grief. All Eannatum wished for was Nidaba, to feel the comfort of her arms around him. And yet if she had remained here, as a priestess serving in the temple, she might have been compelled to join in the most grim portion of the burial rites. And then he would have lost not only his father, but Nidaba as well.

Bitter irony that he *had* already lost her, and yet still couldn't quite wrap his mind around the concept, much less accept it as final. Nidaba lived. So long as she did, he would never accept it as final.

He drank too much of the barley brew and paid little heed to the events of the next several days. And yet, as the only son of the king, it was required that he be there, overseeing it all. A great pit was dug, some thirty feet deep, outside the city. A two-room stone crypt was erected in the bottom, but only one of the rooms was given a ceiling. That was the room where his father's body was interred. Eannatum had to choose his father's finest robes, his favorite sword and shield. Only a few of the king's belongings could be placed with him in the small burial chamber. It was a dire task, and one Natum could perform only when he'd nearly numbed himself with brew.

A priest took his father's most precious possessions and placed them into the burial chamber beside the king. The wall dividing that room from the other was then sealed off with baked bricks as Natum stood nearby, battling his grief and a newfound sense of his own mortality.

And not only his own, but the mortality of those around him. His father had told him that death was an accepted part of life, more a change in form than an ending. But his father was a stiff corpse now, and many of the warm bodies surrounding him soon would be. He wanted to rage against the foolishness of it all. The uselessness of it. And yet it was the way of things. It had been for many generations and would be for many more.

The second room, the one beside the burial vault, was larger, and a stone ramp had been built from the sandy surface of the ground down into it. Its only ceiling was the sky, and its only contents a large pottery urn filled with poison-laced wine and fifty unadorned golden chalices that stood in a gleaming sunlit circle on the dirt floor. As soon as the burial vault's wall was sealed, the closest advisers of the king, his friends and courtiers, and several of his most devoted young priests and priestesses marched down that tiny ramp. They strummed stringed instruments, lyres and harps, they beat drums and shook rattles in rhythm with their singing. They wore their finest garments, and one by one, smiling, they walked into the pit, picked up a chalice, and dipped wine from the urn. When they all stood with glasses filled, the singing and music grew louder, faster, the drums and rattles beat an urgent tattoo, and then all at once it stopped. Silence. And every last one of them drained the golden goblets.

Then, still smiling, they lay themselves down in perfect symmetry, all save one or two who picked up their harp and lyre and began again to play music of unearthly beauty.

A shadow crossed the wall. Eannatum swore he saw her—the Dark Goddess, dancing her dance of death, sweeping her cloak of night around Her willing children. Their chalices beside them, the poison still wet on their lips, they lay there with their eyes closed, and one by one they died. The harpist fell sideways, her fingers plucking one last lingering note. The lyre fell from limp hands to the ground. And it was done.

Lathor should have been among them, Natum thought grimly. But like a coward, he'd fled. Natum doubted that any of the innocents in the pit had deserved death as much as Lathor did. Though, perhaps, Inanna's dark sister had a less honorable method in mind for that one's demise.

As Natum turned to walk away and the sun began to sink low on the horizon, eunuchs came forward and began to cover the bodies with a layer of earth. Tomorrow another room would be built atop the corpses and packed full of the king's most prized possessions. His weapons, his armor, his favorite robes, and jewels. Then that, too, would be sealed and buried, and a single marker placed atop it all.

More than fifty people followed Natum's father to the netherworld.

It was supposed to be a great honor to his father that so many wished to serve him even beyond this lifetime. But it left Eannatum with a dull feeling of sadness, and a sense of waste. Such a great, great waste.

When he died, he hoped he would have time to plan as his father had. He hoped he would sense the Dark Goddess coming for him. Because if he did, he would strip himself of his royal robes and any clue as to his identity. He would wander into the desert, alone, and lie down in a private place where no one would find him for many days. His flesh he would give, as a welcome feast for the jackals and for the crows. And by the time a mortal man set eyes upon his corpse, he hoped there would be nothing left but bones, bleached white by the sun.

He would journey alone to Ereshkigal's underworld realm.

Better than this madness, he thought. Far better.

Wakefulness crept closer, inexorably closer to Nidaba, but she fought it. It was not easy. She became more and more aware of her body. The way it ached, its stiffness.

Her hunger. The pounding in her head and the dryness in her throat. The bed beneath her. The warmth surrounding her. The voice constantly speaking in her ear.

Eannatum's voice.

But it couldn't be that, for he was long dead.

Fighting still harder, knowing she could not do so for much longer, she clung to her dreams . . . her memories.

She'd been serving as High Priestess in the temple of Mari, far away in the lush and verdant northlands. But she had been summoned by the king, and his own soldiers—acting, they said, under orders of his spiritual counsel—had arrived to escort her back to Lagash.

She had never intended to set eyes on Eannatum again. They had made their painful choices long ago. The security of an entire kingdom obviously had to come before the foolish yearnings of a young prince and a young priestess in love. He had agreed to wed the spoiled and beautiful princess of Ur. And as soon as word of that impending union spread, the nighttime raids of the Ummamites came less and less frequently. When the joined armies of Lagash and Ur began patrolling the borders, those raids ceased entirely. Peace reigned in Sumer. But it was a fragile peace. The entire world, it seemed, held its breath—waiting to see if the prince would honor his word to his kingdom.

She had no idea now why she was being summoned back to Sumer. Peace had hung precariously for two years, and during that time, she had been elevated to the rank of High Priestess. But the Ummamites were growing restless. Soon they would test Sumer's unity and the king's resolve. Times were volatile. Danger and tension were everywhere.

Nidaba's journey southward was long, and never once was she told why she had been summoned. Upon her arrival in Lagash, she peered at her beloved city from

the windows of the ornate sand sled in which she rode.
But there was barely time to notice all the changes. She
was taken quickly to the ziggurat tower, led up the outer
stairs by the king's own guards, and placed in a small
chamber.

For a time she paced, furious, unable to so much as
look outside in this enclosed, windowless room. But finally a tap sounded at the door, and then it opened, and
she saw her onetime friend Lia standing there, wearing
the golden headband of a High Priestess herself.

"Lia . . ." Tears sprang into Nidaba's eyes at the sight
of her beloved teacher, and she hurried forward, embraced the woman warmly, and kissed her face. She bore
no ill will toward Lia. She knew the woman had done
only what she had to. She'd done the same herself, so
how could she blame the woman? "Lia, what is happening? Why have I been brought here?"

Lia stood back, brushed a lock of hair from Nidaba's
forehead, and smiled weakly. "To serve your king, of
course. Eannatum is in need of—"

"Eannatum?" Nidaba asked quickly.

"Oh, yes. Had you not heard? His father has passed,
Nidaba. Eannatum is king of Lagash now, and before
this New Year's Day ends, he will be crowned Ruler of
all Sumer."

Nidaba lowered her gaze. "So . . . he has married her,
then? Puabi?"

"No, child. He will wed her only after he takes the
throne. But he cannot take the throne at all without the
sacred rite."

Very, very slowly, Nidaba raised her head. "With you
as his *lukur?* The vessel of the Goddess? *You,* Lia?"

"No, child. You will be your king's *lukur*, not I."

Eyes widening, Nidaba pressed her hands to her
cheeks. "Never!"

"Nonsense. I have gone to great trouble to arrange this. I am convinced it is as the Queen of Heaven wishes it. You and the other High Priestesses I have summoned here will be properly prepared, and will dance before the king. The Dance of the Seven Veils, in remembrance of Inanna's descent to the underworld. King Eannatum alone will choose the one to serve as his *lukur*. And he will choose you, Nidaba."

Nidaba shook her head, backing away from her once trusted friend. "I will leave here," she whispered. "I will leave *Sumer*."

"You will do your duty as a High Priestess of the Queen of Heaven." Lia clapped her hands twice, and a dozen young men, eunuchs all, surged into the room. They came to Nidaba, even as she turned first one way, then another in sudden panic. But before she had a chance to flee, as every part of her was screaming to do, they were gripping her, holding her still, urging her with their soft voices to be quiet, to be calm, even as they began stripping away her robes and her gown.

"You will be gentle with her," Lia ordered, her voice deeper, firmer than Nidaba could remember it ever having been before. "But you will see to it that she complies. She is to be prepared in the manner I have told you. And time is of the essence. See to it."

"Wait!" Nidaba cried.

Lia was turning to go, but she paused at the doorway, stepping aside to let four more eunuchs enter, carrying a huge tub that brimmed with steaming, scented water.

"I have warned them, Nidaba, that you have a way of . . . making the earth appear to tremble when you are angered. They are not going to flee in terror if you do so. But they *will* likely carry tales of such an event beyond these walls. Simply let them carry out their orders.

This is to your benefit." Her face and her voice softened. "And my way of righting an old wrong."

"I know you were forced to do what you did, Lia. Just as I was."

Lia nodded. "They'd have done far worse to you, I fear, had I not obeyed."

"I know. And I knew they would harm you if I fought them as well."

With a deep sigh, Lia said, "There was a time when a priestess wielded more power than any man, even the king himself. But that time is long past, Nidaba. Men think of battles and wealth ahead of procreation and peace these days. And the might of woman wanes."

"Like the moon, Lia, it will wax again."

"Someday, perhaps. For now, we do what we must." She nodded at the men. "Go on, do your duties."

Nidaba shook her head. "I do not want this, Lia."

But it didn't matter. Within a few moments she stood naked, her arms and legs gripped by soft hands. She was lifted off her feet, and lowered into the tub of water. Some of the men held her gently, while others ran soft brushes over her body, up and down her legs, and between them. Over her back, and her arms and her breasts. She didn't fight the attendants. It wasn't their fault, after all, and it was her duty as a priestess to comply with the request of her king. But it was Natum. It wouldn't be an act of duty—not with him.

A hand cupped her chin, lifted her face, and Nidaba blinked back her impatience to see Lia staring down at her. "I am doing this for you, Nidaba," she whispered. "Don't you see? It is the only way you will ever be able to know him."

"I do not *want* to know him," Nidaba said softly.

"Oh, but you do," Lia said. "You want it with everything in you. You know you do. You always have."

"We said good-bye," she whispered. "I can't bear to go through it all over again."

Shaking her head slowly, Lia said no more. She only backed out of the room and left Nidaba to the ministrations of the eunuchs.

They finished washing her, and she was lifted from the tub and stood on her feet, dripping. Then yet another eunuch came in, bringing a tray filled with elaborate containers of sacred oils and perfumes and pots of body paint. She tugged at the hands that still gripped her arms.

"Please, Holy Lady," the newcomer asked softly in a voice that had never deepened with maturity. "This is no fault of ours. We do only as we have been ordered to do. If we fail, it will be our heads."

Nidaba stopped struggling and eyed the young man. He was slender as a *shushima* reed, his hair long and pale, for a Sumerian. A golden-brown color that marked him as a foreigner. His eyes, too, were tawny gold, and gentle.

"All right," she finally told him. "Do what you must."

"Thank you, *Nin*-Nidaba." She saw genuine relief in his eyes, and he quickly backed away, setting the tray upon the floor, and turned to fetch a robe of purest white from a peg in the wall. "Release her," he told the others, and when they did, backing away warily, he came to her and draped the robe around her. Then he gestured toward a stack of silken pillows, nodded for her to sit upon them, and she did.

"What is your name?" she asked him.

"I am called Aahron."

Lifting her hand, she said, "Thank you for your kindness to me, Aahron." And as she spoke she lowered her hand to his shoulder.

A jolt of awareness sizzled through her hand and up into her arm. It was much like the way she felt when

she touched Eannatum. She had thought it to be a reaction that could occur only with him.

Aahron's eyes widened. "By the wings of the Gods,"
he whispered, so softly that she was certain only she
could hear him, and his gaze fell to her legs. He clasped
the robe where it came together, tugging it to the side
and baring her left flank.

She yanked it back again. "What is it you seek, eunuch?" And if her voice suggested she ran short of patience, then it was good he know it now, in time to save
himself from her wrath.

"I . . . was told you bore a mark of some . . . unique-
ness . . . upon your left hip," he stammered.

She shook her head slowly. "You were told incor-
rectly," she said, and she saw him sigh—whether in relief or disappointment, she could not guess. "The mark
I bear is on the right." Nidaba quickly flipped the robe
the other way, giving him the merest glimpse of the
berry-colored crescent moon.

He was still for a long moment. Then suddenly, he
turned to the others in the room. "The rest of you may
go," he said with a tone of command. "Nin-Nidaba
wishes that I alone attend her."

There was muttering, a shaking of heads, until Nidaba
herself spoke. "I am a High Priestess, and a powerful
one," she told them. "Do not make me demonstrate the
proper method of calling down a curse!"

Within seconds, they scurried toward the door, and an
instant later she and the golden-haired young man were
alone. Facing her, he said, "I, too, bear the mark of the
crescent upon my right hip."

Nidaba stared at him in shock. "But . . . what does it
mean?"

"You do not know?"

She shook her head slowly. Closing his eyes, he

sighed. "A great deal, Nidaba. A great deal. But above all, it means that you are a sister of mine. Not of the flesh, but of the soul. If you wish to escape this place . . . I will help you."

Facing Aahron, she saw courage and determination—amazing in one so young—he couldn't have seen more than 17 years. Despite her desire to escape, she felt a certain protectiveness toward him. She liked him. "They would kill you," she said.

"Not an easy task, I assure you."

"You are brave . . . but foolish. No. Perhaps it is good that I see Eannatum one more time. I have . . . I have words for him."

"He hurt you once, did he not?" Aahron asked.

"He hurt me. Yes. But through no fault of his own. We . . . we hurt each other."

"He was a fool to choose Puabi when he could have had you."

She felt her face heat, and cast it downward. "Perhaps tonight he will know just once, how it could have been, had the fates smiled on the two of us." Then, lifting her chin, she glanced at the tray of pots and vessels still sitting on the floor. "Make me beautiful, Aahron. That is the task with which you've been charged, is it not?"

Aahron smiled gently. "The Gods completed that task long before I came to be in this temple, Lady." But he did fetch the tray, and bringing it back, he sat down and placed it on the floor in between them. "But I will do my best to gild an already perfect lily."

"Then do so."

Aahron brushed her hair and pinned it up in intricate loops and twists. He anointed her with holy oils that smelled of exotic fruits and herbs. He lined her eyes in kohl that extended outward from the outer corners, and painted their lids and then added a series of dots just

above her brows that followed their curve. He darkened
her lashes and painted her lips, and drew sacred symbols
upon her breasts and her belly. Then he reached for the
final pot, and she knew what it held before he said, "The
honeyed wine."

Swallowing hard, she nodded. "Apply it."

Aahron knelt before her, taking the soft brush from
the jar. A thick, glistening mixture of wine and honey
dripped from the end of the brush. Carefully, Aahron
painted her breasts with it, coating them lightly, more
heavily at the tips. Then he sat back on his heels. "If
you wish to do the rest yourself . . ."

"It is the custom that this be applied by a eunuch,"
she whispered, her voice nearly gone now. She forced
her legs to part. Aahron closed his eyes respectfully as
he dipped the brush again and brought it out, dripping,
to stroke a path in her most private places. Three times
he dipped the brush and painted her with it. And finally
he said, "It is done."

Nidaba opened her eyes, felt her face burning, and
was glad to see that Aahron had turned away from her.
Good of him to think of doing so. He fussed with the
jars on the tray, capping and righting them. And then he
went to the corner, where a wooden chest sat alone, and
he drew it closer, opened its lid, and said, "The costume
of the sacred dance of Inanna."

She nodded, knowing the contents. She had studied
the tale of Inanna's descent. She had learned the dance.
As a priestess it was a part of her duties to know these
things. He pawed through the box's contents as the honeyed wine that coated her slowly dried to shining hard-
ness.

Finally, Aahron held out a hand. "Come."

She took the hand he offered and let him draw her to
her feet. And when she was standing he took the items

out of the chest one at a time. The crown of the Goddess, a ring of gold with elaborate stones affixed to its face, he placed upon her head. A necklace of lapis lazuli stones he tied around her throat. He encircled her waist with the girdle of purity, which was little more than a golden belt with chains of precious stones dangling from it, shorter at the outside, longer at the center—just long enough to hide her honeyed woman's charms from view. And finally, the twin *nunuz* stones. These were small oval stones, luminous and multicolored, each suspended from a tiny chain, at the end of which was a small, spring-controlled metal clasp.

Aahron looked at her wide eyes, and she saw sympathy in his. He squeezed the clasp so that it opened its tiny teeth, then placed it on his own fingertip and released it, letting it bite down. Holding his finger up, the clasp attached, the chain and *nunuz* stone dangling from it, he said, "It pinches only a little, and the weight of the stone is not so very much."

She nodded and closing her eyes held her arms out to her sides. "Affix them as you must, Aahron."

He cleared his throat and stood very close to her. She could feel him there. And then the teeth of the tiny clasp closed on her breast, right at the nipple. They bit into her enough to make her gasp, though not in real pain. But when he took his hand away, the weight of the stone tugged at her nipple, and she could only bite her lip in bittersweet anguish as he affixed the second stone in the same manner.

As she tried to accustom herself to the sudden throbbing awareness and constant tugging at the tips of her breasts, there was a voice at the door. "Time is short!" Lia called. "The others are at the palace already."

"We are nearly finished," Aahron called. "Only a moment more."

Nidaba trembled, and every movement set the stones to dancing and pulling at her. But Aahron's gentle smile soothed her. He reached into the chest to begin pulling out the multicolored veils, all silken, which he began to drape artfully about her body. "There is much I need to tell you, Nidaba. Much you do not know about yourself. What and who you truly are."

"What can you know of me that I do not know of myself?"

He arranged the first veil about her face, covering her nose and mouth. The next two he draped 'round her shoulders, to cover her breasts. "I know that you are immortal, my lady."

She blinked down at him as he bent to suspend two more veils from the girdle of purity in the back to shield her buttocks, and another in front. The final veil was knotted at her wrist and hanging freely from it. Its use would come later, should the king desire to bind her as the Goddess had been bound during her time in the Underworld.

"Immortal? There is no such thing! What foolishness."

"It's true," he whispered. "You cannot die—well, not easily, at least."

Nidaba shivered even though she laughed at his far-fetched tales. There was something about his words that touched a chord in her, and reverberated deeply. But then the door opened, and Lia stepped into the room. "It is time," the priestess said.

Nidaba hesitated, glancing at Aahron.

"It will be all right," he told her. "And we will talk again . . . later."

10

"Nidaba. Come on, now, it's all right. Calm down." Nathan watched her thrash in the bed, her head twisting from side to side on the pillows as her fists clenched the blanket and sheets and her feet kicked at the covers.

He leaned close to her and put his hand on her cheek to keep her head still, but he was careful, remembering what had happened the last time she'd become this agitated. He could see the rapid movement behind her closed eyelids, and he sensed her need to escape from the dreams that plagued her.

"Nidaba. Come on, stop fighting it. It's time to wake up."

The restless movements stilled all at once.

"Open your eyes," he whispered. "Come on, Nidaba. Open them."

The long lashes shielding her eyes fluttered, then fluttered again, and finally, slowly, they lifted. Her eyes were blank. She stared past him at some invisible spot in space.

"Look at me."

She didn't so much as blink.

"Nidaba, look at me." He held up his finger, trying to put it in the spot at which she stared so intently. Then slowly he brought his hand to his face, and amazingly, Nidaba's huge blue-black eyes followed it. She stared at him, and the dazed, unfocused quality faded as that gaze sharpened. Her brows drew together, and her lips moved, but barely a sound came out.

"It's all right," he said, and quickly filled a glass with water from the pitcher on the nightstand. He held it to her lips as he lifted her head from the pillows. She drank. And drank some more. When he took the glass away, she came off the pillows, placing a hand over his to pull the water back to her, and drank still more. Water dribbled down her chin, wet the front of her nightdress, and still she drank. She drained the glass, and only then did she release his hand, staring down at it as she did, no doubt aware of the tingle of energy that had jumped and crackled between them when they had touched.

He reached for a tissue to dry her face. But she was already wiping it dry with the sleeve of her nightgown. She sat up in the bed, looking around the room, examining every corner, every piece of furniture, every lamp and drapery and square foot of carpet, all in dead silence.

The tension stretched tighter, and finally he could take it no more. "Do you know who you are?" he asked her softly.

Her head turned, her dark gaze coming back to him. "Yes," she said at last.

"Good, good. Tell me your name."

Those eyes narrowed. "You know my name," she said in a voice so deep he thought it sounded like an echo from beyond the grave. She looked away once more, scanning the room.

"Yes, that's right. I do. I just want to be certain you do. So . . . please, tell me, who are you?"

Her head snapped back again, eyes narrow and fierce. "I am the woman you lied to. The woman you betrayed. The woman you tried to murder, Eannatum. I am the woman who will make you pay for your past sins if it is the last thing I ever do."

He recoiled instinctively, backing away as if she'd struck him. Then he stood still, not believing the power of the hatred he saw blazing from her eyes. "Then you *do* remember—my name, at least. Nidaba, I don't know what you think I did to you, but—"

"Think? What I *think?*" She flung back the covers, swung her legs out of the bed, and surged to her feet, only to sink floorward fast.

Nathan lunged forward, gathering her to him before she could hit the floor. He held her close, and she leaned into him, hands pressed to the front of his shoulders, face lying weakly on his chest.

"What have you done to me, Natum? Why am I so weak? My knees feel like water, my head . . . swimming."

His throat went dry. "You think *I* did this to you?"

Her head lifted, eyes meeting his, searching them, mistrusting him. "Is it poison?"

His hands tightened around hers. "For the love of the Gods! Of *course* it isn't poison. Nidaba, I found you in a hospital. You'd been drugged, your doctor attacked. Killed. Perhaps by someone who was after you. I broke the law to take you away from that place, and I brought you here to protect you and to try to make you well again."

In silence she contemplated all he had said before replying at last. "You're a liar."

She said it flatly, no expression on her face, no in-

flection in her tone. As if it were a simple fact, and one
that caused no reaction at all in her. As if it were something she had accepted long ago.

He sighed in disgust and eased her into the chair
where he had been sitting only moments before. "Fine.
Believe what you will. Whether you like it or not, Nidaba, you're stuck here with me for the moment. Once
you get your strength back, you can do what you want.
But until then, you're dependent on me."

She raised her chin, her eyes narrowed to mere slits
and shifted rapidly as they scanned his face. "I *always*
do what I want, Natum. And I've never been dependent
on anyone. Nor will I."

"I hope you're not expecting me to argue with you.
You're in no shape to fight with me right now." And
besides, he thought, fights with Nidaba were seldom
won. He turned away from her, tugged back the covers
of the bed and looked at the damp sheets. Damp with
her sweat and her tears. His jaw tight, he began peeling
them off the bed.

She watched him the way a cat watches a mouse as
he tossed the sheets aside. They landed in a white heap
near the door. Then he walked into the bathroom, feeling
her eyes on his back all the way. He took a clean set of
linens from the closet and brought them back into the
bedroom. Still her gaze burned into him. Ignoring it, he
began remaking the bed.

"Do you think," she asked very slowly, "that all of
this will absolve you of your guilt? Nothing can do that."

"You have no clue about the state of my conscience,
Nidaba, so don't pretend to."

"Are you saying you *feel* no guilt? That what you did
to me was not a crime worthy of hell's hottest fires?"

He looked up from the smoothly tucked sheets. "I
don't believe in hell. You know that. Neither do you."

He jerked the blankets roughly back into place.

"Oh, I believe in hell, Eannatum. I've *been* there."

Her froze at her words, then slowly, he turned to face her, searching her eyes. "What . . . happened to you, Nidaba?"

Her eyes were cold. Colder than he had ever seen them. "It has been over four millennia, Natum. A great deal has happened to me. But none of it more terrible than the crimes you yourself perpetrated."

"You are wrong. Whatever you think I did to you, Nidaba, you're misinformed . . . or confused."

She skewered him with her gaze. "I know what I know, *Your Highness*. I am not insane."

"I thought you were dead," he whispered. "Do you realize that? All this time, I thought you were dead."

"And I *hoped* you were. But you live." She lowered her eyes. "I had heard you were murdered in your bed, but of course, not whether the killer had taken your heart."

"She tried."

"She?" Nidaba asked, looking up at him again. Then slowly, a smile spread across her face. "Do not tell me your bitch-queen was a Dark High Witch all along?"

"No. She only aspired to be." He stared at her in silence for a long moment, seeing a surprised expression cross her face. "Nidaba . . . the Gods know we have a great deal to talk about, you and I. Four thousand years have passed, but even before, there were things you didn't know. Many, many things. Give me the benefit of the doubt, will you?"

She snapped her head away. "Never."

"You loved me once," he said, his voice soft. "And I . . . Look, I only brought you here to protect you. If I had wanted to harm you, I would have done it by now.

God, when I saw you in that place where they had you locked up, I—"

She held up both her hands, and he went silent. "You are right, Natum. The past is dead. What has been done cannot be undone by telling a revised version of the tale. So let us discuss it no more. I am dizzy with hunger. I need food. This penance you seem so determined to pay, does it extend to feeding me?"

"It's not a penance," he said. "But of course I'll feed you. I'll get you something right away. But first, Nidaba, I want to know what has happened to you."

She blinked rapidly at him, brows up, a sarcastic mannerism of hers he had always found enchanting. "I will starve to *death* in the time it would take to tell you what has happened to me in the past four millennia."

"That's not what I meant." He sighed, pushing a hand through his hair. "They said you jumped from a rooftop in Manhattan, Nidaba. You revived in an ambulance, broke an attendant's arm. They sedated you, and you, naturally, became catatonic, so they transferred you to a mental hospital and kept you there, tranquilized into a state of nothingness."

Her sarcasm vanished. Her face paled. "Drugs . . . have an exaggerated effect on our kind."

"I know."

"They had me . . . imprisoned, you say?"

He bent lower to try to see her face, which was turned downward. "You were in a locked room and a strait-jacket."

Her jaw tensed, and she raised her eyes. "Then I am glad I was drugged. Being held captive for the amusement of my captors has never been my favorite pastime."

"You say that as if you speak from experience."

She only stared at him, and an icy rage shivered through him as he thought of who might have held her, harmed her. He was going to have to find out exactly what had happened to her, and who was responsible. And then he was going to have to kill them. Slowly.

It felt odd, the rise of that murderous taste for blood. It was totally at odds with the man he thought he had become. Or was that simply the man he had been pretending to be? Because truly, his time without this woman in his life seemed less than genuine somehow. Like one long act, a way to kill time until she reappeared to turn his world inside out again.

Her stomach growled.

"I'll get that food," he said, and when he left the room, she didn't say a thing to stop him.

He felt as if he were escaping some new, cruel form of torture as he stepped into the hall. To see her alive, awake, alert—and to see the hatred in her eyes, and hear her accusations—it was almost more than he could bear. And there was still the question of her mental state. She seemed perfectly lucid now. Perfectly sane, despite her wild accusations. But the young blonde woman who had come looking for her had mentioned insanity. Was Nidaba truly sane? Did she really believe the things she'd accused him of or was it part of some delusion?

"You look like the very living dead, Mr. King. Has there been some change in the patient?"

He sighed wearily as Lisette walked toward him through the hall. "She's awake, and alert," he said slowly. "I'm going to find Sheila and see about getting her something to eat, and—"

His words were cut off by an ear splitting shriek from somewhere far below. Nathan's head came up fast and his heart jumped. "Gods, that was Sheila!"

He told himself as he raced down the stairs that Sheila had in all likelihood spotted a mouse in the basement. But he knew better. Sheila didn't panic at the sight of mice. And he could feel something emanating from her. Something horrible and dark.

He ran down the stairs, hit the bottom and raced through the house toward the back. The kitchen was back there, along with the nearest entrance to the basement, from whence Sheila's cry seemed to have come. There was only one other, a hatchway door outside.

He reached the kitchen, and his blood went cold because Sheila screamed again, and he felt the horror, the despair in that sound, felt it down deep in his bones. Something was wrong. Horribly wrong.

And every cell in his body told him that whatever it was . . . it was only the beginning.

11

Eannatum was alive. And here, in this house—so close and so real and so vibrant that the very sight of him had caused her heart to pound and ache and yearn. It had been all she could do to keep from crying—from flinging herself into his arms and kissing his face. She had touched him, felt his heat. She had heard his voice, and seen the light of life in his eyes. Felt his breath on her hair, and his arms around her . . . again.

Why was it so difficult to despise him? And why had her feelings for him not died a thousand deaths by now? All this time! By the Gods, seeing him again, even now, even knowing what she knew of him . . . it was as if the years in between had never even been.

She was just as torn now as she had been before. Torn between surrender to an all-consuming, insanely passionate hunger for him and surrender to the equally insane need to crush his corded neck between her slender hands.

Nidaba sat in the chair beside her sickbed, barely able to hold her head up. Strength in an immortal never waned this low, except as a result of some foreign substance flowing through the veins. Eannatum had told the truth about one thing, at least. She *had* been drugged.

So she'd been drugged. But by whom? That remained to be seen. She tried to recall what had happened to her, how she had come to be here, or in some hospital, if he were indeed telling the truth about that as well. But for the life of her, she couldn't remember anything other than . . . than returning to Scotland on the four hundred eighty-eighth anniversary of her son's death—his *second* death— and finding his burial site defiled, his body gone. Taken.

But that had been a full year ago. How she knew that was unclear, but she did know it. Was certain of it. And yet the time in between remained fogged, and fragmented into hazy bits that made no sense.

It hurt to see Eannatum again. It stirred to life old memories of innocent love, freely given. Of burning passion, eagerly sated. Of dark betrayal too vile to believe. He had taken everything from her once. Her love, her life, her soul . . .

Her son . . .

Yes, her son. Nicky's first death, when he'd been a small, sloe-eyed boy—that rested squarely on Eannatum's broad shoulders. And for that, she would never forgive him.

The bedroom door opened, and Nidaba had no more time to contemplate these things. A woman stood there in the doorway.

The woman was small, her smooth skin at odds with her silver hair. Her eyes seemed too sharp and clear to need the glasses she wore. And Nidaba frowned as she stared into those eyes. Because there was something about them—something familiar. They did not belong in that face, those eyes.

The woman smiled, but it was false. She carried a

stack of towels in her hands and came further into the room.

Nidaba got to her feet slowly, in a smooth motion she hoped did not betray the swamping dizziness and weakness she felt. "I prefer to be left alone for now," she said in the strongest, firmest tone she could manage.

The woman halted in mid-stride, brows arching in surprise. "Have your strength back, do you?"

"Every bit of it," Nidaba lied. Every one of her nerve endings quivered with warning, and the hairs on her nape bristled. She did not like this strange woman.

"Well, now, I'm the expert, you know. Perhaps you ought to let me be the judge of that, hmm?" The woman came closer, and Nidaba suddenly knew that her smile was false, but the hatred in her eyes . . . that was real.

And deadly.

Nathan ran through the large kitchen, nearly colliding with George as he rounded a corner.

Pale and wide-eyed, George stood staring through the open cellar door and down the stairs, obviously torn between his longtime fear of the dark and his love for the woman he'd heard crying out. "It's Sheila," George said, fists clenched, almost bouncing on his feet in his agitation. "Somethin's wrong with Sheila!"

Nathan flicked the light switch at the top of the stairs. Nothing happened. "It's all right, George," Nathan said, pushing past him and starting down the stairs. "Stay right where you are. I'll take care of this." He took the stairs two at a time, reached the bottom, tried the light switch there. Again, nothing happened.

"Sheila?" he called.

Then he listened. Soft sounds reached him through the damp darkness—ragged broken breaths, as if she were crying. "Sheila, love, what is it? What's wrong?" Step-

ping forward, Nathan fumbled in his pocket for a match,
a lighter, anything. But he found nothing. Then he saw
the small beam of a flashlight, lying cockeyed on the
cellar floor, illuminating only a few bricks in the wall.
Sheila must have dropped it.

Nathan picked up the pace, bent to snatch up the light,
and began moving its beam around. "Sheila, sweetheart,
talk to me. Where are you? Are you hurt?"

Then the beam of light found her, and Nathan halted.
He thought his heart stopped beating. Sheila sat on the
basement floor, cradling a body—an obviously *dead*
body, already stiff with rigor mortis. It was a woman,
clad only in her underclothes. Nathan swore and moved
closer, kneeling down near Sheila, aiming the beam of
light on the woman's face.

And then his head spun, and his chest contracted. "My
God, that's . . . *Lisette!*"

"I don't understand it, Nathan!" Sheila was sobbing,
rocking the body in her arms. "I was only just talking
to her . . . but she's dead. She's dead, Nathan, my best
friend, my mate Lisette, she's dead!"

The woman in Nidaba's room flung her stack of towels
aside. In her hand a dagger gleamed. A dagger with a
jewel-bedecked hilt.

Nidaba's hand shot to her thigh automatically, but her
own blade was not there. And the woman who she knew
must be a Dark Witch, lifted hers and charged. Nidaba
reacted with the instincts of a seasoned warrior. She
ducked the blade and grabbed up the nearest weapon she
could get her hands on. A water pitcher. Damn! Nearly
useless. The blade hissed past as Nidaba lunged to the
side. Then she swung the half-filled pitcher as hard as
she could, and it slammed into the woman's head. Water
sloshed and splashed everywhere. But neither it nor the

force of the blow seemed to faze her attacker, and within seconds Nidaba found her back pressed to the mattress by the weight of the Dark Witch.

Nidaba held the woman's wrists, fighting to keep the blade away from her own flesh. But she was so weak, and this other—an old immortal, obviously—so strong. Nidaba let go of the woman's left hand, using both of hers to grip the right one, the one that wielded the blade. The only result was that the evil one's left hand was free now, to pound and punish. It clawed, it struck, it bruised. And yet Nidaba bore it, focused only on holding the knife's razor edge away from her body. Her *heart!*

Her face split and bleeding, her body racked with pain, Nidaba broke out in a cold sweat as she lay there, locked in an endless standoff with the woman. The muscles in her arms quivered and burned with exhaustion as she held fast. Her elbows gave, and she shot them straight again. They weakened, and she forced them firm. They fell . . . and the blade came down . . .

"Noooooooo!"

The sound was a long, drawn-out bellow, like the blast of an infuriated, charging bull. And the next thing Nidaba knew, her attacker was knocked off of her by another body.

Eannatum's body.

The impact launched the Dark Witch through a nearby window. Glass shattered, and Nidaba jerked her head around. But all she saw was the demolished window. Then her view was blocked by Eannatum's strong back as he looked outside, down at the ground far below.

"Is she . . . ?"

He turned, breathless, staring at her. "Gone. Dammit, she's long gone, whoever she was!"

Nidaba lay still, her entire body shaking with shock, adrenaline, pain, and this damned debilitating weakness.

"Is this how you plan to hasten my recovery, Natum? By placing me in the care of Dark Witches intent on carving out my heart?"

He came to her, and she could see the damage of her own face reflected clearly in the grimace of his. "You're bleeding." He hurried into the bathroom and returned seconds later with a basin of water and a cloth. Settling himself on the bed beside her, he gently cleansed each cut, bathed each bruise.

He did not seem at all like the man she knew him to be. The man who had tried to have her killed. Who had ordered the execution of his own son in order to protect his precious throne, his precious kingdom.

Even then she'd doubted he was capable of such an atrocity. Even then. And those doubts had plagued her all this time. The murderers had been *his* soldiers, *his* men—men who wouldn't *dare* to go against his orders. And yet those doubts lingered.

She turned her head to the side to avoid his ministrations. "It will heal soon enough. Don't forget what I am."

"I know full well what you are, Nidaba," he said, dropping the cloth into the basin and setting both aside. "But the regeneration process has been slowed in you. Probably because of the tranquilizers you were given, and your weakened state."

"All of which would pass quite quickly if you would stop fussing and simply *feed me.*"

He thinned his lips. "Come downstairs, then. I don't dare leave you alone again . . . and I have a . . . situation to deal with."

"With a Dark Witch in your house, I would imagine you do."

He held out a hand, and she merely stared at it.

"In case you haven't noticed, Nidaba, someone is trying to kill you. Now until you're back in fighting condition, you're going to have to trust someone."

"Someone, perhaps. But you?"

"I just saved your life," he pointed out. He was still holding out his hand, staring into her eyes.

With a sigh, she took it and let him help her to her feet. "Don't think that saving my life just now even begins to make things right between us, Eannatum."

"I am called Nathan King now," he said, pulling her to her feet.

"Why?"

He lifted his brows. "It's more in keeping with the times. No one here knows what I am, Nidaba. I would like to keep it that way."

She sniffed. "No doubt. I would be ashamed too, in your place." She started toward the door, but when she would have pulled her hand free of his, he tightened his grasp.

"I am not ashamed."

She glanced back at him, at his blazing eyes as proud as if he were still a mighty king. "You should be." Then she tossed her head, even though the act made her dizzy. "As for me, I am a Witch. My name is Nidaba. I will not change it, nor will I pretend to be something else, as you do. I am no ordinary mortal, Eannatum. Don't dare expect me to act like one."

"Why would I expect that, Nidaba? You didn't *act* like one when you *were* one."

She looked at him quickly, in search of the smile she heard in his tone. But it was evident only in the slight sparkle of his eyes.

"Do you mock me, Natum?"

He shook his head slowly. "No, Nidaba. I'm just glad to see you haven't changed all that much."

"Haven't I?"

He shrugged. "You still seem to believe you're as much goddess as woman." Reaching out, he tucked a lock of hair behind her ear. "It was always one of the things I loved best about you."

She averted her eyes abruptly, and her voice became choked and hoarse. "Please . . . don't use that word when referring to me."

"What word?" he asked.

She didn't answer. Instead she moved carefully into the hallway. Her legs buckled, though, causing her to sway and grip the doorjamb. Eannatum slid his arms around her, beneath her, and swept her up off her feet.

"I can walk," she protested.

"Not unless you're strong enough to make me put you down," he said.

She knew she wasn't, so she let him carry her through the hall and down the stairs, and she tried not to notice how very protective his strong arms felt around her, or how warm and solid his chest was beneath her, or how deep his eyes were when she looked into them from this close.

But she noticed all of that anyway.

He set her down gently in a rocking chair in what seemed to be a library, and called out to someone. Soon enough a giant of a man, wearing a bright orange necktie over a yellow knit sweater came thumping into the room.

"George, this is Nidaba," Natum said.

George looked at her and his eyes widened. "You're the lady!"

She felt her brows go up.

"You got better! I knew you would. I told you she would, didn't I, Nathan? And she did! See?"

"Yes, George, you were right."

George eyed her steadily. "I'm a nice person," he said.

"My name is George. Nathan is my friend. Are you going to break my arm?"

Nidaba blinked, tilting her head to one side, and studying him with a hint of amusement. "Of course I'm not going to break your arm," she said. "Are you going to break mine?"

George shook his head emphatically from side to side. "No way. I promise."

"Well, then, I suppose we should get along."

"George," Nathan said, "did you take Sheila up to her room as I told you?"

"Yeah, I did. But she's not right, Nathan. She's all curled up on her bed, and she's crying something awful. I tried to make her stop, but nothing I said made her feel any better. I never seen Sheila cry before."

"Neither have I." Natum pinched the bridge of his nose as if to pinch away some nagging worry.

"I don't like it, Nathan. I want you to make her stop. What happened in the cellar that would make Sheila cry like that?"

Natum clasped George's arm, squeezed, and Nidaba saw that the big man was quite like a child. She also saw clearly Natum's affection for him. "I'm going to explain all of that later, George. For right now, I want you to stay here with Nidaba. I don't want you to let anyone come near her. You understand?"

"Not even Lisette?" George asked.

"Especially not Lisette."

"Okay, Nathan."

Nidaba sighed, about to argue that she needed no protection, but then decided it would carry no weight, since she couldn't even get down the stairs under her own power. And Natum sent her a glance that was almost . . . kind. Warm. "I won't be long."

She simply nodded and watched him go.

"So," she said to George, who had taken a seat beside her, and was staring at her oddly, "who is this ... Sheila?"

George smiled. "She's Nathan's friend, just like me. She lives here, does the cooking, and takes care of the flowers, and things like that. She's an awfully good cook, you know."

"Is she?" So some woman lived here with Natum. Nidaba wondered what that signified, and then wondered why she cared. "I am starving nearly to death. I would love to sample some of her cooking."

George looked at the floor. "We could ... go to the kitchen and get some ... but the cellar door is still open, and I don't know what happened down there."

Nidaba frowned. "Something happened in the cellar?"

Nodding, George cast a nervous glance toward the closed library door. "Sheila was down there screaming. And the lights wouldn't work. And then Nathan went down to see what was wrong. And then he came running back up, pulling Sheila behind him, and he told me to get her to her room, and then he ran up the stairs again. I don't know what happened. But something sure scared Sheila pretty bad."

"It scared you too, didn't it, George?"

He bit his lip and picked at his sweater.

"Maybe we don't need to go to the kitchen," Nidaba said, feeling sorry for him. Feeling almost ... protective of him, if that wasn't the strangest thing in the world. It wasn't like her to go soft over mortals. But this one ... well, he'd touched something inside her. "Isn't there any food any where else in this house?"

George's looked up and smiled. "There's a fruit bowl in the living room!"

"Then let's go to the living room," she suggested.

Still grinning, George swooped down on her like the

world's clumsiest hawk, awkwardly lifting her up into the air. When she protested, he said, "Nathan said for you to stay off your feet." Then he carried her right out of the library, through a formal dining room, and into a wide parlor with a fireplace on one side and exquisite antique furnishings all around.

None of that caught her eye, though. What caught her attention was the painting—larger than life—above the mantel. An image of a woman in the unmistakable white gown and headpiece of a Sumerian High Priestess of Inanna. She stood in the desert, amid ruins of once great towers, with her arms extended up toward the giant moon. Crescent-shaped moonbeams reflected from her black eyes, and a nimbus of light surrounded her. As if she truly were some sort of divine being. "It's . . . me," she whispered.

"Yeah. I thought so too, but Nathan wouldn't admit it," George said, plunking her down into an armchair. He reached out for a bowl of fruit and set it in her lap.

Narrowing her eyes, Nidaba tried to make out the signature that was barely visible in the left corner, hidden within the swirling strands of long black hair. Eventually she saw it. But it was made up of lines in the shape of the old cuneiform script, rather than any modern alphabet, and appeared to the casual observer to be no more than swirls in the blowing sand. But she was no casual observer. The symbols stood for his name: Eannatum.

A scratching sound drew her head around. George leapt to his feet, his face lighting up as he lumbered unevenly toward the closed door.

"George, don't—" Nidaba began, but even before she could finish the sentence, George was opening the door.

Nidaba tensed . . . then relaxed as a beautiful, sleek-coated dog dove through the door, leaping on George, and licking his hands. George fell to his knees, hugging and petting the animal. "Oh, Queenie, I'm so glad you came home!" he said, laughing.

Nidaba couldn't help but smile at the two of them as she bit into a gleaming red apple. "You mean she's been missing?"

"I was so afraid she wouldn't come back!" George said in between laughter, hugging the animal, rolling on the floor with the dog.

Like a little boy and his long lost pup, she thought as she watched them.

Nathan watched her eat.

And he thought that a few days ago he had been leading a placid, calm, even respectable mortal life and had been perfectly content with it. And then, with no more than a glimpse of that face in a blurry newspaper photo, everything had changed. He had broken-and-entered, kidnapped a mental patient, fled the police, and at this moment there was a dead body lying in his basement.

He didn't know what the hell he was going to do about poor Lisette. Right now, Sheila was upstairs resting, with the help of a double dose of sleeping pills. And George was confused, frightened by all the turmoil, but thankfully distracted from it by the reappearance of his stray. The dog lay underneath the dining table at George's feet, eagerly but delicately devouring the bits of food George offered.

Nidaba, in stark contrast, wolfed her own meal as if she hadn't been fed in a month. She didn't even seem to notice that it consisted of prepackaged frozen foods he'd dug out of the freezer and heated in the microwave, with dehydrated side dishes. The stuff must have been buried in there since his pre-Sheila days. Pseudo fried chicken, instant mashed potatoes, heat-and-serve gravy. He was not untalented in the culinary arts, but he'd been in a hurry. The meal had all the flavor of cardboard, but flavor wasn't what Nidaba needed. Protein and carbohydrates were. Calories, for energy and the strength to restore her. There were plenty in the food he served her.

As she ate, he could already see the changes taking place: the color, slowly creeping more deeply into her skin; her hair, losing that limp dullness, and coming alive, thickening, shining. The changes were so gradual mortal eyes would likely never notice—not until later, when they might well look twice and wonder when she'd improved so drastically. But his eyes were not mortal. And they saw everything. The way her cheeks began to plump and fill out, the slow fading of the dark circles beneath her eyes, and of the bruises that had just begun to form on her face. The mending of her split lip and the cut in her cheek.

George, thankfully, was oblivious to all of it.

Finally Nidaba seemed to have sated her hunger. She drank two full glasses of water, leaned back in her chair, and looked at him, looking at her. Her arms no longer resembled twigs beneath the white nightgown. Her collarbones no longer protruded so sharply. He let his gaze slide lower, to where her breasts pushed at the buttons on the soft white cotton nightgown as they had not done before, making the fabric pull tight and gape slightly in between. He knew she was aware of his gaze, because of the way those breasts reacted to it—peaks stiffening as if his stare were a physical touch. And he could not help remembering the first time he'd seen them full and healthy, and aroused. For just a moment, he allowed himself the pleasure of exploring that memory. He couldn't have resisted it even had he wanted to.

Eannatum sat upon the satin pillows in the throne room, which was filled with honored guests come to attend his coronation. Platters of food were heaped on every table. Chalices were filled to overflowing, and the pleasant, excited hum of conversation filled the room. But he was hearing none of it. He had only one thing on his mind.

Nidaba. He had finally made sense of the priestess Lia's words to him just after his father's death. She had arranged it so that every High Priestess in the kingdom would come here—so that he would be allowed to choose from among them which one would serve as his *lukur*. And Nidaba, according to Natum's dying father, had been elevated to High Priestess status in the faraway land of Mari. By royal command, she had to be here.

She had left him long ago, chosen to serve her Goddess, made him realize he must serve his country. She had broken his heart, and he knew he had broken hers. But he was not the same heartsick boy now. Two years of training with his father's armies, battling in skirmishes with the Ummamites to prove the new united Sumer equal to the task, had changed him. And now . . . now he was her king. And tonight she would serve *him,* as custom and the law decreed. He could not but help come alive at the prospect. He wouldn't have been human to do otherwise. He was burning inside. Tomorrow he would marry another, but tonight . . . tonight he would know the woman he'd wanted for what seemed like his entire life. Tonight, Nidaba would be his.

He had waited as long as he could. All propriety had been observed. He clapped his hands twice, and the din turned to silence. "Begin the dance," he commanded.

Immediately the musicians began to play. The *algar* and harp players plucked at their strings in a harmonious and sensual melody while the others kept time with the jangling cadence of the *ala* and the beat of the drums. One by one, the High Priestesses entered the chamber, cloaked by veils of colorful silk that floated and swirled as they moved. Eannatum's eyes searched for Nidaba's among the women who twirled before him. But they were covered well . . . and they kept their eyes respectfully lowered.

Lia retold the tale as the woman danced and twirled.

"Long ago the Queen of Heaven turned her eyes to the Great Below. The Queen of the Great Above did turn her eyes to the Great Below. And so she journeyed there. Inanna, unafraid, peered into the darkness that so frightens us all. Bravely, she journeyed there. And at each of the seven gates, she was stopped by the guardians of the netherworld. Seven times she was stopped by the netherworld gatekeepers. And at each gate, as was the custom, she had to give over one of her garments before she was allowed to pass. For no one carries earthly costumes, nor masks, nor jewels, nor riches, nor titles with them into the land of the dead. The darkness must be entered into naked. With no pretense, no pride. Only the true self. This is what makes visiting there so frightening."

At Lia's nod, Natum clapped his hands once, and the first of the seven veils fell away from each woman. The one that had covered their hair. Narrowing his eyes, Natum got to his feet and moved among the dancers, eyeing each one closely. There were twenty women dancing for him. Twenty dropping a second veil, and a third. Twenty hoping to be chosen as the king's sacred *lukur*. But only one he wanted.

"Naked, Inanna was brought before her Dark Sister, Ereshkigal. Naked, she had to face her own Dark Sister. Her own dark side. Just as we must each face the darkness within us. But Inanna emerged from the darkness— proving that we can do the same. Meet, embrace, accept, understand, and in the end gain mastery over our own shadow side."

Natum clapped his hands again, and the fourth veil
fell away. Twenty beautiful copper-skinned bodies gy-
rated for his pleasure. Round, delectable buttocks swung
from side to side as he passed. Golden breasts bounced
for him, *nunuz* stones weighing down their swollen tips.
Soft bellies, dark eyes . . .

Nidaba's dark eyes.

He stilled when he saw her, and kept his gaze locked
only to hers. She didn't look away, but held his eyes.
Her hips rolled toward him, and away, and only three
veils remained on her. The one that covered her nose
and mouth from his view, the one knotted at her wrist,
and the one that hung from the chain of gold at her
waist, draping down to cover her center. He didn't clap
his hands. Instead he reached out, and took that veil
away from the chain at her waist. Then he held up his
hand, and the music and dancing stopped.

The chains of precious stone that dangled from her
waist concealed very little of her. Her small waist and
large breasts pleased him immensely, as did the unusual
length and grace of her arms, and her endless legs. He'd
never seen her unclothed before. But he'd known she
would be exquisite, and he was not disappointed. And
with a flick of his wrist, he tugged the delicate scarf
away from her face so he could watch her every expression.

"Turn around," he told her.

Her eyes widened ever so slightly. But she knew she
had no choice here, and she did as her king commanded.
She turned.

And he took his time. He let his eyes feast on the long
curve of her spine, and the swell of her rounded buttocks, and the slight crease at the base where they met
her thighs. He would press his lips to that crease tonight.
He saw with some surprise the birthmark she bore. The

crescent moon blazed on her thigh. Perhaps it was a sign of divine approval, for he bore the same mark himself.

"Face me," he told her.

Again, she did as he told her, her eyes defiant but full of fire. And he knew beyond any doubt she was as aroused right now as he was. Though she might have denied it, he could see it there in her eyes. Her chin was high, her stance proud. But her eyes blazed with secret longings, denied desires. He reached up to touch the *nunuz* stone that dangled from her breast, fingered the stone slowly. Each time it moved he saw the reaction in her eyes, until finally he gave the stone the slightest tug, and heard her suck her breath through her teeth. "This one," he said at last, catching the veil that was tied to her wrist and pulling her out of the group of priestesses. "This is the priestess who shall be my *lukur*. Take her to the sacred bedchamber to await the arrival of her king."

At his nod, his men-at-arms came forward and flanked Nidaba, ready to lead her away. How times had changed, he thought vaguely. Only a generation ago, it would have been the High Priestess doing the choosing. She would have had final say over whether the son of a king was worthy of the throne, and if he fell short of her standards, she would have chosen his replacement.

Now, the reality of the old ways was rapidly fading into symbolic acts with far less meaning, played out to reinforce the image of the king as supreme commander of all within his reach—even the High Priestesses of Inanna.

"Do not forget, my king," Nidaba said softly, shocking everyone in the throne room by speaking to him without permission at such a formal event. "It will be the Goddess you embrace this night. Not me. Inanna will use my body as her sacred vessel. I myself will have no part to play. But if you displease her, she may very well strike you down."

He leaned in close, and whispered in her ear, "Do you really believe that is the way it will be, Nidaba?" His cheek brushed over hers. "I do not. But we shall see. Either way, I have no intention of displeasing . . . the woman I will be with tonight."

Straightening, he commanded his men. "Go. And remember this is the body of the Goddess you have in your charge. Treat her as such. She is to have anything she desires."

She turned away from him and marched toward the door like a martyr to the pyre.

"Inanna is an impatient Goddess," someone said. "Already she lives in this priestess! See how proudly she moves!"

"Fool, don't you recognize her? She's the priestess who is half goddess already!"

"They say she has strange powers. . . ."

"Left on the doorstep of the temple by the Goddess Herself . . ."

The murmuring spread. Nidaba stopped walking and turned to watch, as several bowed their heads in respect when she passed. A look of confusion crossed her features as she met Eannatum's eyes once more. He placed his right fist in the palm of his left hand and bowed his head. A gesture of deep respect, which he gave willingly, and meant sincerely.

Then everyone in the room followed his example, saluting her, bowing their heads. A frown creased her brow as she turned to go.

"You are staring," Nidaba said in her deep, rich voice, like honey on his senses.

Nathan blinked and shook himself out of the past. "I

was . . . remembering. The coronation." He glanced sideways at George, expecting to see the man there, looking
puzzled, but George had gone into the front parlor with
his dog, and the two were relaxing near the fire. "When
you danced for me," he said, finally.

Nidaba's thick lashes came down to veil her gaze. "I
was confused when they all began to treat me as if I
were the Goddess herself. As if she had already de-
scended into my body."

He smiled very slowly. "But she had, Nidaba."

"No. She never did. She turned her face away from
me that night. Abandoned me because I did not serve
her well."

"You're wrong. How have you managed to live so
long, and not yet come to understand your own nature?
A woman like you, Nidaba, is the Goddess personified.
She didn't need to take over your body. She already
lived in you, from the day you were born."

That same tiny frown he'd seen in the past, marred
her brow. He would have said more, but Sheila's voice,
groggy and thick, interrupted him.

"Nathan, what are we goin' to do about poor Lisette?"

He stalled for a response even as he hurried to help
her to the table. "Come, Sheila. Sit. Are you all right?"

"I slept some," she said, sniffling, and shuffled her
feet as he led her to a chair. Then she sank into it as if
boneless.

"Nidaba, this is Sheila. She's my most trusted friend."

Nidaba studied the woman, and Nathan thought she
looked first relieved at the sight of Sheila and then concerned as she perused Sheila's wet, red eyes and puffy
face. Nidaba glanced at Nathan then, a question in her
eyes. "Is she one of—?"

"No." He said it quickly, not giving her time complete
the question.

Nidaba looked doubtful. "That's what you thought about the other one, you'll recall."

"Sheila's been with me for years. The other one . . . only a day or two."

Nidaba sniffed, but eyeing the woman again, seemed to accept his word that Sheila was not a Dark Witch on the hunt.

"It's good to see you up and around, miss," Sheila said. "I only wish it had been under better circumst'nces. Not with death itself breathing down our very necks." And she shivered as she said it.

"Death?" Nidaba looked from Nathan to Sheila and back again.

"Sheila's best friend, Lisette, was a nurse," Nathan explained. "We hired her to come here, to help us care for you."

Nidaba lifted one brow in regal sarcasm. "Oh? Was she the one who tried to murder me a short while ago?"

"Tried to *murder* you? I'd like to know how she managed it when she's been lyin' dead in the basement all the afternoon!" Sheila cried, her voice breaking near the end.

"Please," Nathan said, before Nidaba could respond yet again. "If the two of you will let me speak." They both fell silent. "Good. Sheila . . . Dammit, I don't know how to say this gently."

"Say it straight, Nathan. I'm no frail flower, as you know very well by now. Or ought to."

Drawing a breath, Nathan sighed. "Your friend Lisette has been lying in that basement far longer than you realize. In fact, I suspect she was put there within a few hours of her arrival here."

"Well, now, don't be daft, Nathan! She's been right up here with us, helping to care for your ladyfriend. We've both seen her, spoken to her . . ." Sheila stopped herself when he held up a hand.

"The woman who's been walking around here with us was an impostor. Someone who killed Lisette and then made herself look just like her in order to fool us."

"Impossible!" Sheila said. Nidaba, though, remained silent.

"Remember how she lost her voice right after she got here?" Nathan asked. "So she wouldn't speak above that odd, hoarse whisper? That was because she couldn't change her voice. Only her appearance, Sheila. If you had heard her speak at full volume, you would have known it wasn't your friend's voice."

Sheila blinked. "But . . . but . . . how? She looked—it was no disguise, Nathan. She looked exactly like Lisette. Even a makeup artist couldn't have done such a convincing job of disguising herself."

"A glamourie," Nidaba murmured. "By the Gods, she must be good."

"A glam . . . what?" Sheila rubbed her forehead with two fingers. "I don't understand any of this! Even if someone *could* make themselves look that much like Lisette, why would they bother? Why would anyone want to murder her and then impersonate her? It just makes no sense!"

"To try to get to me," Nidaba said very quietly. "I'm very sorry your friend got caught up in all of this, Sheila. It seems I've brought this upon you, and for that . . . I am deeply sorry."

Sheila, though, was still shaking her head. "It makes no sense," she said again. "She looked . . . she looked exactly . . . How could anyone be that convincing?"

Nidaba's eyes met Nathan's. Only an immortal High Witch, and a very old one at that, would be likely to have mastered such an art, and Nidaba knew that as well as Nathan did himself. He could see the knowledge

there. This enemy they faced could be more powerful
than they had first believed.

"What are we going to do with her, Nathan? I . . . I
just . . . if we call the police . . ."

"If we call the police, I'll be arrested for kidnapping
Nidaba, she'll probably end up back in the mental ward,
a sitting duck for this killer, and you'll in all likelihood
get yourself deported. We could both easily end up as
suspects in Lisette's murder, as well. I don't think that's
what she would want. Do you, Sheila?"

"Well . . . well, no. I think she would want the person
who did this to her caught, and . . . and punished."

"I'll see to it that they are. I give you my word on
that," he said. "But not if we get the police involved."
Nathan got to his feet, came around the table, and took
Sheila's hands in his. "Did she have any family, Sheila?"

Sheila shook her head. "She was alone. Oh, there may
have been a cousin or two, back in Queensland, but aside
from that . . . no. No one." She met his eyes, and he
could see that she understood. Slowly, she nodded. "I
want her buried proper, Nathan. Not tossed into a swamp
somewhere. She deserves respect. Words said over her.
A decent resting place."

"I'll see to it," he promised, lowering his head as a
heavy ache settled in his chest. "Trust me."

12

Nidaba stood on the cliffs above the sea, with George on her right and Sheila on her left. The ever present Rottweiler, Queenie, sat at George's feet, her gaze focused on the tiny boat, just as everyone else's was. The small craft bobbed and bounded on the waves as Natum rowed further and further out into the sea. The sky beyond him settled to a darker shade of gray, and moments later the little boat was barely visible.

"I can't see him anymore," George said, sounding scared to death. And no wonder, with the wind, the darkness, and the knowledge that a killer lurked somewhere near.

Nidaba had realized almost from the first words she had exchanged with the big man that he was a child in a man's body. Part of him—that innocent part—reminded her painfully of the son she'd had once, long ago. Her Nicodimus.

She automatically closed her hand around George's larger one and squeezed. "Don't be afraid, George. He'll light the lamp in a moment, you'll see."

"And we should light ours, as well." At Nidaba's other side, Sheila bent down to do just that, then stood, lifting the kerosene lantern so its soft golden glow spilled all around them.

The wind blew in off the sea, and Nidaba's hair snapped and danced in time with the lantern's flame. She wore a long black dress she had found in the closet. Eannatum had, Sheila told her, stocked it himself, choosing each item for her personally. This gown, a simple one of some clingy modern fabric, had a scooped neckline and long sleeves that fit her arms snugly. It hugged her body the same way, all the way to her hips. From there it flowed freely to puddle around her feet. A braided cord of silver, gold, and black served as a sash, tied loosely about her waist, the knot dipping lower in front, forming a vee. It was very much like the clothing she had worn of old, except in color. And she felt the tug, the calling of the High Priestess she had been and still was, deep inside. One of her duties had been to comfort the bereaved on occasions such as this one. She had, she realized dully, fallen into her old role with barely a pause.

Finally, in the distance, an answering light appeared on the sea. It rose, ghostlike, then moved slowly from side to side in wide arcs.

"It's time," Nidaba said.

Sheila lowered her head in silent prayer, her free hand closing around Nidaba's, though she may not even have been aware of it. She was not an immortal. Natum had assured her of as much, but Nidaba knew it for certain by her touch. And by her trembling, she knew the woman was in pain.

"Good-bye, dear friend," Sheila whispered at last.

"Not good-bye," Nidaba said softly. "She goes into the arms of the Goddess, where she will find comfort and perfect love as she adjusts to her new form. No longer physical as we are, but every bit as alive, every bit as real. Your friend is still with you, Sheila. She lives on. And she's all right. She truly is."

Blinking, Sheila turned to Nidaba. "You really believe that?"

"I do. Speak to her, if you need evidence of it. Ask her for a sign."

Sheila's face puckered with her frown. But she didn't speak. She only turned to stare out at the sea as the wind made the lamp flicker.

Nidaba closed her eyes, focused her energies, silently called on the departed soul to send comfort to her friend. As she opened her eyes again, the clouds parted, and the lopsided gibbous moon shone down on the waves for just a moment. Something arched up out of the water, moving gracefully, its skin slick and shining in the moonlight. Then it splashed down again, vanishing beneath the waves.

"Was that . . . ?" Sheila began.

The creature jumped again, and with a final slap of its tail, submerged.

"It was . . . a dolphin," Sheila said. "But it shouldn't have been. Not this far north, this late in the season."

She looked at Nidaba. "What does it mean?"

Nidaba smiled. "You tell me."

Blinking, Sheila bit her lip, but it didn't stop the tears. "When we were girls together, in Townsville, in Queensland, we used to go to Halifax Bay and spend hours just watching the dolphins." She dashed away tears. "When we were sixteen, we bought matchin' pendants." She touched the necklace at her throat, lifting it. And in the glow of the lantern, Nidaba saw the pendant, a tiny silver dolphin with a gleaming topaz eye.

"You've had your sign," Nidaba murmured. "Speak to her, if you wish. She'll hear you."

Swallowing hard, Sheila closed her hand around the pendant, and shut her eyes. "I loved you, Lisette, my friend. Like my own sister you were, and are. I'll cherish your memory always, love."

"Go in peace," Nidaba intoned.

She could not see Nathan sliding the lifeless, lovingly wrapped body into the sea. But she sensed it happening. Nathan knew the ocean here. Knew the tides. He hadn't weighted the dead woman's body, but instead had placed her into the loving embrace of an outgoing current that would sweep her quickly out into the sea's forgiving depths.

Sheila sniffled. Nidaba felt a true tug at her heart. These two people who flanked her were, she sensed, very dear to Nathan. It was not difficult to see why. Looking sideways at the woman's tear-filled eyes, she was moved to speak. No longer in the role of comforting High Priestess, however, but in that of avenging angel. "I promise you, Sheila, the person who killed your friend will pay. I will see to it."

Looking back at her, Sheila studied her for a long moment, then nodded once. "I do believe you will," she whispered.

Glancing out to sea, Nidaba saw the tiny golden light of Nathan's lantern moving slowly, steadily, back toward shore. It was done.

Still holding their hands, Nidaba led the other two away from the shore and back to the house. It would take time for Natum to make his way back to them. Sheila was exhausted, emotionally drained. And George had dealt with far more excitement today than he was used to. They entered the house through the rear door, which led into the kitchen. Nidaba released their hands and went to the stove, rummaging around in search of a pot, and teabags.

"You needn't do that, now," Sheila was saying. "You're the one who's been so . . . so ill. I ought to be fixin' tea for you."

Nidaba offered a smile. "Nonsense. You've been waiting on me hand and foot while I've been lying like a lump in that bedroom upstairs. But I'm fine now. Better every moment, in fact."

She saw the doubt in Sheila's eyes, even as the woman slumped into a kitchen chair. "It truly is amazin', how fast you seem to be recovering," she said.

Nidaba knew she was likely making conversation only to keep from thinking too much about her loss. It was natural, and she was glad to play along. "It was a re-action to the drug they gave me that made me so ill," Nidaba explained, knowing the woman might still have some lingering doubts about her mental state.

Sheila frowned. "Like . . . an allergy, Nathan said."

"Exactly like that." Locating the kettle, Nidaba filled it and set it on the burner to heat. "I was given a tran-quilizer, and when I reacted the way I did, it was mis-taken for a mental breakdown of some kind, and treated with more drugs, which only worsened the reaction."

Nodding, Sheila sighed. "And that's why they had you locked up in that hospital. I vow, it must have been horrible for you."

Nidaba found cups, lined three of them up on the counter, and began opening cupboards in search of tea-bags. "I don't remember much about it, to be honest. I wasn't even certain I believed Ean . . . er . . . Nathan when he told me that part."

"Oh, I can vouch for him on that. I was with him when he first glimpsed your picture in the paper. I thought he was goin' to faint dead away, by the look on his face. And I was with him again, the night he took you out of there."

"You were?"

Sheila rose and came across the room to open yet another cupboard, from which she took a sugar bowl and a canister brimming with assorted teas. "Yes. I was driving the car. I could scarcely believe it was our dear Nathan committing a crime like that in the dead of night, running from the police."

"I helped too!" George said from the table where he sat.

Cocking her head to one side, Nidaba studied them both. "It seems I am more deeply indebted to you two than I even suspected."

"Oh, no," Sheila said quickly, setting the sugar and the tea canister onto a silver tray. "We'd do anything for Nathan. And by the looks of it, he'd do anything for you."

"Do you really think so?"

Sheila shrugged, turned to the refrigerator and took out the cream. "Well, isn't it obvious? He's never had so much as a parking ticket, missy. Not in all the time I've known him. He takes great pains not to draw attention to himself and keeps his life so quiet and mundane that it—well, it's almost tedious. And yet, along you come. Out of the blue. And he turns everything upside down. For the love of heaven, Nidaba, have you not even noticed what he's out there *doin'* this night? Disposin' of a body, of all things!"

Nidaba paused in placing the cups on the tray. "I suppose that's true. He's putting himself and his . . . his mundane lifestyle at great risk by all of this, isn't he?"

"Ah, now, I didn't mean to make you feel badly for it." Sheila patted Nidaba's hand in a motherly fashion. "It's what he wants to do. There's no talkin' to Nathan when he sets his mind to something he wants. And I, for one, think he's doin' the right thing. It's you I'm concerned about."

"Why?" Nidaba picked up the whistling teapot and poured the three cups full of steaming water. Then she lifted the tray and carried it to the table. Sheila followed, taking a seat and helping herself to a cup.

"Well, now, do you remember what happened to cause them to give you the tranquilizer in the first place?"

Nidaba thought back, but only fuzzy bits came. "No. I guess—I think there was an ambulance, but . . ." She shrugged. "Nathan said something about a fall from a building."

"They claimed you'd jumped from a rooftop," Sheila said, dipping her teabag slowly. "Called it a suicide attempt."

"Um-hmm," George said, taking a cup himself and adding massive amounts of cream and sugar. "I remember that. Your picture was in the newspaper, and as soon as Nathan saw it, he got all quiet . . . sad, like." George stirred his tea rapidly, whipping it with the spoon as if it were pudding, then lifting the spoon out to lick the clinging bits of sugar from it. When he finished he had a wide-eyed look on his face as he said, "Hey, you won't go jumping off our roof, will you? 'Cause that might upset the birds."

"The birds?" Nidaba asked, looking from one of them to the other.

"I keep pigeons up there," Sheila explained.

"You should go up and see them, Nidaba," George began, but then he bit his lip. "But not if you think you might want to jump again."

"Don't worry, George," Nidaba said. "I promise you,

I won't do that. I didn't try to commit suicide before either."

"You didn't?" George asked.

"No. I don't remember what did happen, but I know better than to think that."

"I'll wager you had some help off that rooftop, missy," Sheila exclaimed, her voice deep and angry. "This evil visitor we've had—some black-hearted murderess who wants to harm you badly enough to kill my Lisette in order to do it—who's to say this was the first time she's tried?"

"Indeed," Nidaba said. "I only wish I knew for sure." Small pieces of memory came back to her. A confrontation. Yes. A battle. Her dagger had been in her hand. There had certainly been another immortal on that rooftop with her.

"Bah. How many people have more than one enemy out to do them in?" Sheila asked. "It's rare enough to have one in a lifetime. Much less two."

Nidaba sipped her tea. Sheila couldn't know how far off base she was. Nidaba had lived far more than one lifetime, and she'd crossed blades with countless Dark Witches whose only goal had been to do her in. No matter how many she killed, she knew there were always more to come.

Always.

She sighed, truly tired of the violence of her existence. And for a moment she almost understood why Natum had chosen to live a lie, pretending to be an ordinary mortal. Perhaps the endless violence had been too much for him.

Oh, but what he'd given up to be rid of it. His identity. His nature. His freedom.

"You and Nathan . . . you've known each other before. In the past. Haven't you, Nidaba?" Sheila asked.

Meeting her eyes, Nidaba nodded. "Yes. A long time ago."

"I could tell. It's a rare kind of thing I see when he looks at you. I've seen it in him only once before. One night when I couldn't sleep, I got up and came wanderin' down the stairs. He stood there, all alone in the dark, nothin' but the moonlight flooding through the windows. He stood there, just staring up at the portrait that hangs above the hearth, and the way the moon lit it from above. And I vow, there were tears on his cheeks."

Nidaba opened her mouth but couldn't speak.

"I thought that might be something you ought to know," Sheila said with a sigh. "I'm goin' on up to bed now, love. Thank you for helpin' me through this difficult night." She patted Nidaba's hand. "And you truly did help, you know. You truly did."

"It was true, what I told you out there at the cliffs," she assured the older woman. "Your friend is still alive, just in a different way."

She nodded. "I believe it. I do."

"Take a sleeping pill," Nidaba advised, but her voice was choked and barely audible. "The rest will do you good."

Sheila nodded, leaving the room, and Nidaba turned to George. "You may as well go to bed too," she said. "You can barely keep your eyes open."

"I'll wait for Nathan," he said. "I don't want to leave you alone. What if that bad lady comes back?"

Nidaba looked around, spotted the dog lying at George's feet. "You can leave your dog—what do you call her?"

"Queenie," George said proudly.

"Well, you can leave Queenie here to protect me. She certainly looks up to the job."

"Oh, she is! She's the best," George said. He got out

of his chair and crouched near the dog's head, stroking
her muzzle. "You hear that, Queenie? You have to stay
here and watch out for Miss Nidaba. Okay?"

The dog didn't *quite* nod, but it was close.

"Good girl," George praised. Then he drank the last
of his tea, which was, Nidaba guessed, two-thirds cream
and sugar. He set the cup down again. "Good night,
Nidaba."

"Good night, George," she said. She watched him go,
sipping her tea and trying hard not to hear Sheila's
words about Natum echoing in her mind. But they echoed anyway.

To distract herself, Nidaba stared at the dog, who
stared right back at her. It really was a beautiful creature,
with broad shoulders, and a wide powerful chest. Feet
like a bear, and a wide, untapered muzzle. She weighed
close to a hundred pounds, or a bit less, and Nidaba
imagined that if she turned on an intruder, she'd tear
him to shreds in minutes. If she were so inclined.

The dog rose and walked toward Nidaba, her eyes
piercing. The hair on the back of her neck bristled upward, and a low, menacing growl came from deep in the
beast's massive chest.

Nidaba blinked, and got to her feet, taking a step
backward. "What is it, Queenie? What's wrong with
you?"

The growl got louder as the dog crept closer, half
crouching now as if she would spring.

"There, now," Nidaba said, backing further away,
edging toward the door behind her. "Don't you remember me? I thought we were going to be friends . . ."

The door opened before she ever reached it. The
growling ceased, and the dog eased her stance instantly.
She looked up even as Nidaba turned around. And when
the dog saw Nathan standing there, she seemed to relax.

Then she turned and trotted away in the direction George had gone.

Nidaba still had one hand pressed to her chest. "By the Gods, I thought the beast was going to eat me alive."

Frowning, Nathan came forward, shrugging off his peacoat on the way. "Are you all right?"

"Yes." She sighed, feeling a bit sheepish. "George told the dog to guard me. I guess the beast understands far more than I realized. She must have heard you coming before I did. She got all wrought up."

"Really?" He seemed surprised, staring after the dog. "She's never acted at all menacing before."

"Well, she certainly did just now." Nidaba shrugged. "Maybe she senses the danger in the air. That's the only explanation I can think of. Once she saw it was only you at the door, she was fine again."

Nathan rubbed a hand over his chin. "Might not be such a bad idea to have a dog like that around the place."

"No, I suppose not."

He came closer and placed his hands on her shoulders, his eyes searching her face. "It frightened you, though. You've had a hellish day, haven't you?"

Lowering her gaze from the probing power of his, she said, "I've had worse."

"I know you have."

Drawing a breath, he released her. He fetched down another cup and poured himself some tea. "I think it's time we talked, you and I. Don't you?"

"I suppose it's inevitable that we do so sooner or later."

"Come on. We'll go out onto the veranda where no prying ears will hear too much." He took her arm and led her back through the dining room, into the front parlor, toward the library off to one side. But she stopped him and turning, stared up at the portrait above the mantel.

"Do you like it?" he asked her.

She couldn't quite manage to look at him as she asked, "Why did you paint it, Natum?"

He stood motionless. "I was afraid I might . . . forget you. Your face. Your eyes. I was wrong, of course, but . . ."

She finally turned to him, but he shrugged and looked away.

The veranda was through a set of French doors in the library. It was simply a cement pad, rounded and extending from the edge of the house. A railing surrounded it, and it sported a glass-topped umbrella-shaded table at its center and benches on its sides. Natum walked past the table, stopping beside the bench farthest from the house. He stood until she sat. Then he sat down beside her.

He stared at her for a long moment, and finally said, "I hardly know where to begin. At the beginning?"

"Begin at the end," she said. "The beginning is too long ago to be important to us now."

"Not for me, Nidaba. The beginning was long ago, yes. And it's painful as hell to revisit. But to me, it's very important. Maybe . . . the most important part of my life."

She turned her head away.

"Nidaba, we have to talk about what happened between us back then," he said, touching her face, turning her to face him again. "Please."

Her eyes burned with unshed tears. "If you pound a nail into the heart of a sapling tree, it bleeds. It hurts, and it bleeds, but it survives. It lives and it grows. Layer upon layer, year upon year, until that nail is so deeply buried that it's invisible. Oh, the tree knows it's there.

It's still piercing the heart, after all. It's still painful. But to remove it after so much time—don't you see? It's not possible. Not without cutting the tree down. Not without killing it."

"No. You're wrong—"

"You put this nail in my heart long ago, Eannatum. It has healed over. Don't try to pull it out, because you'll only start the bleeding anew. Leave it. Just leave it."

"*You* are the one who left *me*."

"*You* are the one who married *her*."

He clenched his jaw. "I had no choice. You were the one who made me realize that."

"I know," she said, about to argue that he did have a choice. He could have chosen her over his throne. A secret part of her had wanted him to do just that. To throw it all away just to be with her. Foolish, foolish notion. But why rake over these old ashes again? She sighed, met his eyes. "It would never have worked between us, at any rate, Natum. You obviously see things far differently from the way I do. I cherish my freedom, relish my immortality, and live fully within it. While you confine yourself, hide what you are, live as mortal."

"I'm as free as any man. I live this way because I choose to."

She shook her head. "You're a prisoner, Natum. And this house is your prison, and this persona you've created, this Nathan King, is your jailer. It's the same as before, don't you see? Only then the prison cell was a gilded palace, a royal throne. Duty was your jailer then."

"I don't see it that way, Nidaba."

"No, of course you don't."

"If you'd let me explain . . ."

"I do not care. It doesn't matter now, Eannatum. In fact, all that matters just now is the enemy who has found me here. The one who is trying to kill me."

Nathan drew a deep breath. "I think I know who it is," he said at length.

"Do you?"

"Yes. There was a woman here, looking for you. An immortal—I never touched her, but I sensed it. She claimed to be a friend."

"I have no friends."

"I thought as much. She said her name was Arianna. Arianna Sinclair-Lachlan."

Nidaba's head came up quickly. In her mind's eye, she saw her son. Nicodimus . . . and the young woman Nidaba had long blamed for his death. Her memory of the past year seemed to clarify all at once, flashing into place so brightly it was nearly blinding. Suddenly everything made perfect sense.

She had lost her son—twice—but a year ago, she had found him again. Alive, immortal, wonderful . . .

"Nicodimus," she whispered, her heart quaking at his name, tears brimming. How could she have forgotten? He wasn't dead. He lived!

"Nidaba? Is something wrong?"

She looked up at him quickly, confusion making her hesitate. Nicodimus was this man's son. Eannatum's son. And yet . . . did she dare tell Natum that he lived? He'd had the boy killed once before . . .

He couldn't have!

But what if he did? And even if he didn't, she couldn't risk Nicky's being dragged into this situation with her. Not now. Not yet. She could end up losing him yet again, to the blade of this Dark Witch, whoever the hell she might be.

If Natum knew his son was alive, he might not be willing to wait to contact him. And if he knew Arianna was a friend—Nidaba's daughter-in-law, in fact—he might contact her as well. No. She must wait. Bide her time. Make very, very sure it was the right thing to do before she confessed any of this to Natum.

Her heart doubted he had ever done anything to deliberately harm his own child. But her mind wasn't as certain. Not even for Natum would she place Nicodimus in harm's way.

A hand brushed her face. "Are you all right?"

Staring into his eyes, she nodded. "Yes. Please, go on."

"All right. Nidaba . . . for any Dark Witch to be this gifted at casting a glamour, she must be very old. Very powerful."

Nidaba lifted her chin, shaking off the remnants of her overwhelming emotions. She felt stronger now that she had remembered finding her beloved son again. "So am I," she said.

"But you're in a weakened state."

She waved a hand dismissively. "A good night's sleep, another solid meal, and I'll be back to one hundred percent. I'm nearly there now."

"Still . . ."

"Eannatum, I need a dagger. They must have taken mine from me at that hospital. And I do not wish to face this bitch alone unarmed again."

For the first time in their entire conversation, Natum smiled slightly. "Changing the subject, Nidaba?"

"No." Sitting straighter, lifting her chin, she said, "I do want to talk to you about the past. About . . . all of it." More than that, she wanted him to tell her he was totally innocent in the attack on her and her son. And she wanted to believe him when he did. "But don't you think we need to focus first on keeping our hearts in our chests where they belong? We'll talk, Natum. Soon. And I will listen to what you have to say to me. I promise you that. But right now, I need . . ."

"Some time?" he asked.

She frowned at him. "A blade," she told him.

He blew a sigh, shook his head. "You always have had a one-track mind."

"A blade, dammit."

"All right, all right. Come on, come with me." He held out his hand, and Nidaba took it. Then Natum looked down, and she did too, at his large, strong hand enveloping her smaller one. He closed his eyes briefly, as if touching her were almost painfully sweet.

There were so many things he wanted to ask her. He knew she'd borne a child—but he had never been sure if that child had been his, or what had truly become of the boy. And he never knew exactly what had happened the night Nidaba and her son had allegedly perished in a terrible fire.

Not in all these years.

But the pain that came into her eyes at the merest mention of that time was too much for him to bear. So he told himself he could wait to learn all of those things. He could wait. Until she was ready to speak of them.

He put her into his car and drove into Boston, to his gallery, which he hadn't opened since she'd returned to his life.

"What is this place?" she asked when he unlocked the door and took her inside.

"It's my business, Nidaba. I buy and sell antiquities. And, um . . . my most private collection is here. Though I never display it. I keep it here because the security is far superior to that at home. Come." He led her through the gallery, with its swords and shields from various eras displayed on the walls. Pottery and statues lined every shelf. Tapestries and cloaks were arranged on the walls.

Glass cases held chalices and spears and golden coins from civilizations long dead.

In the private display area, the small alcove he'd created for his eyes alone, were cylinder seals from the land of Sumer—one of them the very seal of the once great king, Eannatum.

His eyes stung a bit each time he visited this area, and more so this time, for Nidaba pulled him to a stop. "By the Gods, Natum," she whispered. Her fingers dragged across the face of the glass case, where slabs of cuneiform tablets stood on display stands, where headdresses and jewelry from days long forgotten decorated lifeless mannequin heads.

"It's . . . just memories. That's all," he whispered.

"But . . . but Eannatum, the *lilis* drum. It's one that was played in your own palace! And the headdress . . ."

He watched her eyes widen. "Is the one you wore when you danced for me. And the lapis lazuli necklace as well. Yours, Nidaba. I preserved them as perfectly as I could. And if you . . . *when* you leave here, you may take them with you."

Were those tears brimming in her eyes?

"You kept them—all this time . . ."

"They were all I had left of you. They and . . . and this." Reaching into his pocket, he pulled out the small bit of stone, worn with age, into which she'd carved his name, and hers, and the symbol for eternity.

Nidaba looked at it. Then at him. "This is the piece I made for you, to celebrate your initiation."

He nodded. "You gave it to me when we did the rite by the river, and filled the Euphrates with fish. My first act of magick, Nidaba. A time—and a friend—I could never forget."

Blinking, she averted her eyes. "I can't believe you've kept it all this time."

"Come." He replaced the stone in his pocket, closed his hand around hers, and led her to his office in the back, unlocking the door, and flicking on a light. Then he turned yet another key. This lock was hidden within the woodwork of a wall-sized bookcase. Only it wasn't really a bookcase at all. It was a sliding door that concealed another glass case, this one with his collection of daggers mounted inside. Dozens of them. It covered one entire wall of his office.

"Where did you get them all?" Nidaba breathed.

"Immortals. Light Witches who were murdered. Dark Witches I had to kill. I suppose "immortal" isn't exactly the word we ought to use to describe ourselves, is it? Not when every dagger in this case represents one who has died."

"Not died," she muttered. "Only moved on. Even mortals are immortal, Natum." She walked along in front of the case, examining the blades. Double-edged, single-edged, serrated and curved. Long and short. Handles of wood, bone, iron. All decorated with jewels. Sapphires, diamonds, rubies, emeralds, every stone imaginable in every possible combination and arrangement.

"Take whichever one pleases you. Hell, take several if you want them."

"I couldn't—"

"You know perfectly well you could. And you will." He watched her face as she tried very hard to conceal her delight. "You don't fool me, you know," he said. "You've always loved beautiful things. Jewels. Baubles. Enjoy this. Let me enjoy giving you pleasure, just this once."

She met his eyes, and hers were smoky and dark. "Giving me pleasure would take far more than a glittery gift, Eannatum."

His blood heated at the double meaning of her remark,

the teasing warmth in her eyes. She was a heartless tease, just as she had always been. "We'll get to that," he promised her, leaning close. And when she didn't push him away, he brushed his mouth lightly over hers, lips apart, his breath fanning her.

Her breath stuttered, stopped, and her eyes fell closed expectantly. So he wrapped his arms around her waist, pulled her to him, and closed his mouth more completely over hers. He felt her lips part in invitation, and he slid his tongue between them in reply. He tasted her. Gods, he hadn't tasted her in so long!

Fire blazed between them, as it always had. The physical response when they touched, when they kissed had always been explosive, and that hadn't changed. His blood rushed and his heart pounded. Her hips arched against him, rubbing his erection to a state of painful need. His hands closed on her buttocks, tugging her harder to him, and he thrust his tongue deeper, drinking from her mouth the way he wanted to drink from every part of her.

Finally, he lifted his head, and stared down into her sparkling eyes.

And she blinked, then closed them, and turned away. "What in the names of the Gods am I doing?"

"Nidaba?"

"How could I?" She faced him again, tears brimming in her eyes. "I will not love you, Eannatum. I swear I will not love you again."

Gods, that she could still hate him this much simply because he had married another. "What I did, I did for my country, Nidaba. For Lagash. For all of Sumer."

Her face went stony and cold. "Then you admit it?"

"What is there to admit? I did it. You know I did it. And it was a sin against my own heart, Nidaba, and against you—one I have paid for ever since." Frustrated,

Nathan sighed and paced away. "Choose a dagger," he told her. "You need to be armed."

"If you gift me with one of these blades, Eannatum, I'll likely use it to cut out your heart."

Spinning to face her again, he said, "All of this venom! All of this hatred, simply because I wed another woman to avoid a war that would have destroyed us all?"

She frowned fiercely. "No! For the love of the Gods, Eannatum, marrying Puabi has nothing to do with my anger at you! Are you so blind you do not realize that?"

"Well, what, then? What, tell me, am I guilty of doing to so wrong you that you would continue to hate me after four millennia?"

She stared at him in disbelief. "Eannatum, your soldiers hunted me down. Under your orders, they hounded me for years, until they finally caught up to me."

"I sent them after you because I couldn't bear to live without you, Nidaba! I wanted them to bring you back to me."

She shook her head very slowly. "And I was gullible enough and deeply enough in love to believe that, Natum. Until they finally caught up to me. Attacked me. They tried to murder me, Eanntuam. And they *did* murder my son."

She lifted her head, met his eyes. "*Our* son."

13

He stood there staring at her, struck motionless by what she had said. "*Our son?*"

Swallowing hard, she nodded.

"And for this, you held me responsible?"

She turned away from him.

He caught her shoulders and turned her back. "Tell me. Tell me you honestly believe I could have ordered such a thing."

She couldn't even seem to look him in the eye. "I don't know what I believed. You chose Puabi over me. Your kingdom over me. Even when the threat had ended, you remained with her. I thought I knew the power of your love for me, Natum. I thought it was more powerful than anything in the world. And I knew that if you would give me up for the sake of your kingdom, there could not be many other things you wouldn't do for its sake as well."

Stunned, he released her, cut to the bone.

"An illegitimate son with a claim to the throne would have been a far greater threat to the well-being of Sumer than an affair with a temple priestess ever could have been," she said, driving the blade of her words straight through his heart.

He couldn't speak to her. He was so angry he was trembling with it.

She looked into his eyes, and when she did, she went pale.

He opened his mouth, then closed it, almost too furious to think. "I don't even know what to say to you."

Her face changed, regret swimming in her eyes, but he held up a hand, saying nothing. Instead, he reached into the glass case, drew out a gold-handled Sumerian dagger and its leather sheath. He handed it to her, closed and locked the case, and strode back through the building, out the front to his car, vaguely aware that she followed. He drove her back to the house, all without uttering a word.

He didn't dare speak. He'd have cursed her, he'd have lashed out and cut her to the quick the way she had cut him. Only when they returned to the house and he'd battled his fury into some semblance of submission did he dare to speak at all. He stopped her on the way inside. "Wait. We need to finish this."

But then the front door was flung open, and George stood there, waving his hands. "Nathan! Nathan, come, please! Sheila's crying in her sleep and I can't make her wake up!"

"Dammit, George, not now." Nathan gripped Nidaba's shoulders, but she shook her head, and her face remained stony.

"Go. See to Sheila." She strode into the house ahead of him.

He followed on her heels, having to push past George to do so. "The hell I will! Damn you, Nidaba. I'm angry as hell at you right now. You've got no right to accuse

me of something that vile. All I ever did was love you,
and I think you know that. Whatever you think happened—no, by the Gods no. You *can't* believe any of
that. You *can't*. You don't."

A crash came from upstairs, causing them both to look
up sharply. Nathan sighed. Sheila was no doubt thrashing in the grip of some nightmare. She'd stopped having
them six months after coming to live with him and
George, but apparently they'd come back full force. No
wonder, considering recent events in this house.

"Go," Nidaba said, her voice deep, her tone firm.
"This discussion has waited a long time. It can wait a
bit longer."

"Not a hell of a lot longer, it can't. And it won't." He
had to go. But dammit, he didn't want to. "Come along,
then," he said to Nidaba. "I'm not leaving you down
here alone with this maniac on the loose."

"I won't argue with you." She preceded him and
George and the lumbering, ever attentive dog through
the house and up the stairs. But she stopped at the master
suite's door and said, "I need to get some rest if I'm to
be fully recovered any time soon. If there is anything I
can do for Sheila, don't hesitate to come for me. Otherwise, though, I . . . would prefer not to be disturbed
tonight."

She didn't wait for his argument, though she had to
know it was coming. Instead she just went inside and
closed the door on the dog that tried to follow.

Nathan grated his teeth and stalked along the hall to
Sheila's room.

Nidaba closed the bedroom door behind her, leaned back
against it, and covered her face with her hands. She
knew, deep down in her heart, what the truth was. She
had always known. But Gods, the pain had been so

much easier to bear when she'd had someone to hate.
Someone to blame.

He'd scorned her, chosen another woman and his
royal duty over her. She had no one to blame for that
but herself—she knew that. She was the one who'd convinced Natum what his duty was. But she couldn't accept that, and so she had punished him by pretending to
believe him capable of the most vile crime imaginable.
She may even have fooled herself into thinking she truly
did believe that of him. But she knew now that she never
had. She never had.

Natum had seemed truly shocked by her revelation,
that her child, her Nicodimus, had been his own son.
Perhaps he hadn't even known that much for certain.
And yet his soldiers had hunted her endlessly, tirelessly,
for years on end. And when they had finally found
her . . .

She didn't want to go back to believing Eannatum's
love had been real. Not when it had hurt her so to trust
him with her heart, only to have it broken time and time
again!

She heaved a sigh, swiped angrily at her eyes. She
was too tired to contemplate it right now. Her body, still
weakened, needed sleep to heal. Nidaba couldn't have
fought it had she tried.

No more than she could fight the dream . . . the memory, so vivid and fresh.

She waited in the sacred bedchamber—a special room
on the uppermost level of the palace. Small it was, but
lined with silk pillows and spreads in rich jewel tones.
Deep green and scarlet and midnight blue. Censers
burned with sacred herbs, and a hundred candle flames
danced, lighting the room with a soft illumination that
was alive and ever-changing. As she picked her way
between the pillows and spreads, it seemed she walked

among a dozen living shadows that danced around her in celebration. She breathed the incense smoke, and tasted the other fragrances. Fruit and flowers. The table on the far of end of the room had no room for anything more. The most prized fruits in all of Sumer filled golden bowls to overflowing. Wine jugs and jeweled chalices stood at the ready. And blossoms littered every bit of space in between.

At the very center of the table stood a small stone image of the Goddess Inanna. She who would come to inhabit Nidaba's body this night. It was good, Nidaba thought. She would likely not even remember what transpired. She would likely not even feel it, or be aware of his touch . . . his kiss . . .

Something clenched tight in her belly.

She had no one to ask. The previous king's *lukur* was an elderwoman, an honored crone, living in a palace all her own in the mountains to the north. There had been no time to travel there, to consult with her. And no other woman alive had experienced this rite.

Kneeling before the image of the Goddess, Nidaba breathed deeply, slowly, filling her lungs with the sacred smoke and emptying her mind. Softly, she began to chant. *"Inanna me en, Inanna me en, Inanna me en. Uta am i i ki."*

Over and over she spoke the words until they became a litany in her mind, running together, and making no sense. She lifted her arms to her sides, and upward, tipped her head back, and closed her eyes. She waited for the Goddess to fill her.

"Nidaba," Eannatum said softly.

Her eyes opened. Slowly she lowered her arms and turned her head to see him standing there. The door was closed tightly behind him. His dark eyes gleamed in the candlelight. He came closer, and she wanted to tell him to stop. To warn him that she was not yet ready, that she was still Nidaba—not miraculously transformed into the Queen of Heaven. And yet to do that would be to admit that she had failed.

And even had she been willing to confess it to him, she couldn't. She couldn't form a word to save her life. His gaze moved freely over her barely clothed body, and she burned with wanting him as she had wanted him for most of her life.

She loved this man.

He came to her, standing while she knelt, and slowly stroked his hands over her hair. "So long, Nidaba. So long I have waited for this."

She shut her eyes at his touch, wondered why if he wanted her so badly, he had not come for her, even though it would have spelled disaster for everyone else in Sumer.

But it didn't matter. Suddenly none of that mattered. He was hers tonight, not Puabi's. He was hers. And she was utterly his. She leaned forward, and pressed her lips to the hard bulge between his legs, with only the royal robes between his flesh and hers. "My king," she whispered.

His fingers clenched in her hair, and he closed his eyes.

Nidaba rose slowly to her feet and stood before him. "The dance," she said softly. "Was it pleasing to you?"

"*You* were pleasing to me. I saw no others." His eyes opened, skimming her from head to toe. "This . . ." He lifted a hand, ran his fingers over her belly and the chain wrapped around her waist, with its dangling curtain of precious stones. "Is it heavy? Uncomfortable?"

"The metal is cold . . . or perhaps it is my flesh that is warm."

He lifted his gaze to lock with hers. His hands,

though, remained at her waist, and he fumbled with the clasp, found its release, opened it. Then he slowly took the girdle of stones away, letting it fall with a jangling sound into the nest of pillows on the floor. "Better?"

"Yes. Better."

His eyes roamed down her body, all but naked to his hungry gaze. Everywhere he let that gaze linger, her skin seemed to heat, and tingle. "Yes," he said. "Much better." He reached out to the *nunuz* stones that dangled from the tips of her breasts, stroked them slowly, then set them to swinging with a flick of his fingers. "And these? Are they unpleasant?"

The tiny clamps bit into her nipples with minimal pressure . . . but the weight of the stones tugged with every swing, every touch. "They pinch only a little. And their weight pulls somewhat. Though it is not . . . unpleasant, exactly."

"No. Not exactly." His smile was slight. He reached up and gently removed the stones from her breasts, but he didn't toss them aside as he had done with the girdle. Instead he tucked the clamps into some hidden place within his royal robes.

Sensation rushed into her nipples, where before the flow of blood had been pinched off. They throbbed and burned. He kept his eyes focused on her there, and she saw the blatant desire in them. Lifting his hands again, he cupped her breasts, running his calloused thumbs over her nipples repeatedly. The flicking motion over those sensitized peaks made her bite her lip to keep from crying out loud.

Frowning, Eannatum took his hands away. "You feel . . . sticky."

"It was part of the preparation," she said. "I was painted with honeyed wine for you."

His gaze snapped to hers, widening, blazing. "Well, now . . ."

Hands closing on her waist he lifted her, setting her on the edge of the table, knocking bowls of fruit aside. Flower petals were her cushion. Standing back, examining her at his leisure, Eannatum lowered his head, and she knew what he would do even before his tongue snaked out to taste her breast. "Mmm," he said, and then licked again. He caught the peak in his lips and suckled her. He took her nipple into his mouth and drew hard on it, flicking his tongue over the very tip as he sucked hungrily at her. He licked her breast clean, and continued even then, nipping with his teeth and pulling at her as if he would devour her whole.

Nidaba felt sensations she had never felt before. A sharp pleasure such as she had never imagined tingled through her. It bordered on pain and intensified unbearably when he bit down. Then he moved to the other breast, and devoured it even more frantically. And while he fed at it, he caught the other in his hand, drew his fingers together at the tip and pinched her deliciously. She braced her hands on the table behind her, let her head fall backward as her body clenched and tightened and liquified low in her belly. She arched her back and whimpered and he responded by exerting still more pressure with his fingers and his teeth.

Eannatum drew his head away then, looking into her eyes. He leaned down, kissed her long and deeply, thrusting his tongue into her mouth and lapping it as if it tasted as sweet to him as her honeyed nipples had done. She could taste the honey and wine on his tongue.

Then he straightened away and his hands crept up to her breasts again. She sucked in a breath of surprise when she felt the bite of the clamps closing once more on her nipples. The teeth felt sharper than before, their grip tighter now that those tender crests were stiff and throbbing. A cry was wrung from her.

And Eannatum whispered, "Trust me, Nidaba." Then he knelt, his hands pressing to her thighs, shoving them wide, and exposing her very center to his probing eyes. With his fingers, he parted her folds. Then he touched her, fondled her there in her most private places. He even thrust his long finger inside her, then drew it slowly out again. He brought it to his lips, tasted it. "Mmm, just as I thought. More honey."

Before she could know what he intended, he pressed her thighs wider, and buried his face between her legs. His lips, then his tongue, swept over her, flicking, licking, stroking. He licked up inside her, seeking every drop of the honeyed wine with which she'd been coated. And he laved her in places where the eunuch's brush had never dared touch.

Nidaba fell backward on the table, tipping fruit bowls over and sending their contents helter-skelter. She twisted and writhed while he fed at her. And then he found the tiny kernel of her most frenzied need and sucked at it, stabbed at it with his tongue, bit at it with his teeth. And she felt as if her body would shake itself to pieces. His hands came up then, caught the *nunuz* stones, and as his mouth worked her even more hungrily, he tugged on them. The clamps pulled painfully at her nipples, stretching them, biting deeply, and his teeth closed on that pulsing nub at her center. And her body shattered in screaming, trembling release. She cried his name, shuddered uncontrollably, and finally pushed him away from her, panting and sweating.

Natum gathered her into his arms, though, and carried her to the cushions on the floor. He lowered her into them and again took the stones from her breasts, tossing them aside this time. As she lay there, shaking, breathless, shattered, he removed his robes.

And she saw him, looking more God than man, and more king then he had in his crown and royal vestments. "Eannatum," she whispered, "what is this magic between us?"

"This is what is meant to be," he told her. "What will be, from now on. I'll not let you leave me again, Nidaba. Not ever. Not now." He knelt over her, cupping her face in his hands. "I love you."

"I am a High Priestess," she whispered.

"And I am a king. But I love you, Nidaba." He lowered himself atop her, and she opened to him in an instinct born of nature. When he nudged himself inside her, he did so slowly, gently, kissing her face, and her neck and shoulders, whispering love words to her the entire time. She felt stretched as her body accepted his, then pain flared through her when he pressed past her maiden's barrier. She bit her lip, but it was brief, that stab of pain. And then he was moving gently, slowly, in a rhythm that made her body respond. That made her hips begin to move in answer to his call. That made the fire in her belly flare up anew. And soon she was clutching him to her while he fed at her mouth. She moved to a faster pace, and he followed. His hands slid beneath her then, closing on her buttocks and holding her to him as he thrust deeper inside her than before. And finally, his powerful movements sent her again into spasms of ecstasy. Only this time, she did not go alone. This time she felt the answering tremors racking his muscled frame. She heard that pained pleasure in his low moaning of her name. He filled her . . . and she embraced him. And then he relaxed bit by bit, slowly rolling to the side and folding her into his strong arms.

He held her for a long time, and finally, his voice still

hoarse, he asked her, "Nidaba, why did you leave me in the dead of night the way you did?"

She frowned, lifting her head from his chest, and staring into his black, moist eyes. "Why does it matter? It was what was necessary. We both came to realize it, didn't we?"

He didn't reply to that. Perhaps he'd changed his mind, then? Hope flared in her breast, but she went on. "They told me you wished to marry Puabi, and do your duty as king. They told me you regretted your promise to me, but were too noble to break your vow. That you would wed me, only because you could not hurt me by refusing to do so, but that it was not what you wanted. And they made it clear I had no choice but to leave Lagash, to give you a way out. They even implied that Lia would pay the price should I disobey."

As she spoke he sat up, staring down at her in horror. "Who told you these things?"

She lowered her eyes. "Your father, Eannatum. The king told me. And Lathor. And even Lia." She felt her heart break again, and tears surged into her eyes. "I'd have doubted the others, but Lia—I knew she would not lie to me—or not unless her very life depended on it."

"By the eyes of the Gods," he said softly. "They *did* lie to you, Nidaba. And to me as well. I knew nothing of any of it. I told my father I would wed you and none other. And the next day you were gone, and I had only a stone tablet, its markings in your hand, telling me you had decided to serve your Goddess rather than your heart."

She blinked up at him. "You mean . . . you didn't want me to go?"

"I wanted you to be my queen." He pulled her to him, cradled her in his powerful arms as if he would never let her go. "And by the time I found you, you'd already

taken your initiation as a priestess. Sworn to remain un-
wed. To break such a vow . . ."

"It would be death, Eannatum," she told him. "I
would be stoned for such an offense." She kissed his
strong neck, and wrapped her arms around his waist.
"But it doesn't matter. We did what we did for the good
of Sumer. Even if we were tricked into it, at first, we
soon saw that it was the only way. And now, you . . .
you are about to wed another. You have your queen."

"A woman I barely know!" he snapped.

"Oh, come now, Eannatum. You journeyed to Ur, you
met the woman. The arrangements have been made. I
have heard of the passionate Princess Puabi. Do not tell
me her embrace left you cold."

"Her embrace only left me wishing it were yours," he
told her fiercely, his voice coarse with passion.

"On the morrow," Nidaba whispered, "your queen
will arrive at her new home. You will speak your vows
to her. It will be her bed you share. Her face you see in
the morning. . . . There is no place for me in your life
now, Eannatum."

"I won't let you go," he said. "Nidaba, please, please
don't do this. Don't leave me again. I cannot live if you
do."

Sitting back from him, she searched his face. "What
would you have me do?"

"Stay. I'll make you High Priestess of the temple here.
And send Lia to take your place in the temple at Mari."

Shaking her head sadly, she sighed. "I would have to
see you with your new bride every day if I stayed here,
Natum. It would surely kill me."

"No. No, it will not kill you, Nidaba, because you are
strong and fierce. And you will know it's you I love,
not Puabi. You will know that every moment I spend
with her, I wish for you. And you will know that every

night, under the cover of darkness, I will come to your arms, not hers. In our secret places, we will be together. I know it is not enough. I know you deserve a great deal more. But it is all we have."

She closed her eyes. "And what of Puabi? Would her heart not be wounded by this?"

"Puabi knows I'll never love her. Our marriage is a treaty. A pact between city-states and every bit as cold as one."

Nidaba said, "You'll need to produce an heir with her."

"Perhaps. In time." He caught her face between his palms. "The king of Sumer may have any woman he desires. By law and divine right! It has always been so. Puabi knows this, and she knows too that I love another. She agreed to this arrangement with the truth presented to her. Fidelity was not a part of our agreement. And you know full well it is not forbidden for a priestess to love, only to marry. Nidaba, I thought I could live without you for the good of Sumer. I've found that I cannot. It's not possible. Please, stay with me."

She bit her lip, searching his eyes. "I may not be as strong as you think I am, Eannatum. But I do love you. More than my own heart, or my own soul."

"Then . . . then you'll stay?"

"I will try. That's all I can promise. To try. And we must be discreet. Legal or not, acceptable or not, nature is nature, Natum. I'll not be the cause of another woman's pain."

He pulled her securely against him, kissed her gently. "We'll find our happiness, Nidaba. I promise you we will."

But she knew even then that she would find only misery in being his mistress. His concubine. Only misery.

She couldn't have guessed, though, just how much.

• • •

It was no less than an hour before Sheila talked herself out, took another pill, and fell back into a troubled, restless sleep. After tucking her in, Nathan finally dragged himself back to the master suite, walked into his bedroom, and saw the door to the adjoining room closed tightly. He knew before he even tried the knob that the door would be locked. And he was right. Sighing, he rested his forehead on the cool wooden door. Dammit, he needed to talk to Nidaba, to get all of this out in the open once and for all.

She was lashing out at him. Hurting him, or trying to, because of the way she had been hurt by him. He didn't understand fully just why, but he knew one thing. She did not believe he had killed his own son. Nidaba knew him far better than that.

Or at least . . . he hoped she did.

Without bothering to turn on the light, he tugged at the buttons of his shirt and moved toward the bed, feet dragging. There was no denying it, he was exhausted. Unused to so much excitement and intrigue, he was wearing himself down emotionally, mentally . . . perhaps even spiritually. Dammit, he'd just dumped a body into the sea. How much lower would he have to sink before all of this played itself out?

Maybe this was just the price he had to pay for all these years of solitude and relative contentment. Living like an ordinary mortal man when he was anything but. He was a pretender. And now the world was extracting payment for his make believe existence.

He peeled the shirt from his body, dropped it onto the floor, heeled off his shoes and kicked them aside. His hands went to the snap and button of his jeans, freeing them, sliding the zipper down. Finally, naked, he crawled into his bed and sank almost at once into blessed sleep.

He didn't know how long he slumbered. A breath on the nape of his neck woke him, though, from the very depths of sleep.

He rolled over, groggy and puzzled, blinking in the darkness.

Nidaba lay in his bed, naked except for the sheet that came up only to the narrowest part of her waist. Her breasts swelled full and inviting, round silhouettes in the darkness.

"Nidaba," he murmured, "what are you . . ."

"Sssssssh." She held a finger to her lips and, reaching out, caught his head and tugged him forward. He started with surprise when she kissed him voraciously. And he responded at once, kissing her back. He felt himself growing hard with arousal, hungry with need . . . and yet something tickled up his nape and coiled in his belly.

"We need to talk, Nidaba," he said, breaking off the kiss, but it came out gruff. She dragged her nails over his nipples, and he lost the ability to speak at all. Then she leaned down, and replaced her nails with her lips, and her tongue. Her hand stroked a sensuous path down his abdomen. "God, Nidaba," he moaned, thoughts of discussion fleeing.

The bedroom door burst open, and Nidaba stood there, wide-eyed, staring at him and at the woman feeding on him like some succubus.

Like a dash of cold water, it hit him all at once.

He shoved the impostor away from him, and she landed on the floor. Her face rippled for a moment as the glamour she'd cast faltered, but she rolled and lunged out of the bedroom almost on all fours.

"Stand and fight if you want me, bitch!" Nidaba surged after her, and Nathan saw the glint of the dagger in her fist. He shot to his feet, tripping on his jeans, and pausing to tug them on again. Then he ran into the hall behind her, terrified that she'd be killed.

But in the hallway he saw no one other than Nidaba. Nothing. Still, she charged from room to room, flinging open doors. "Where are you? You damnable coward, face me if you dare!"

"Nidaba, stop!" He caught her from behind, closed his hands on her shoulders. "It's no use. Dammit, she could be anywhere. She could be any*one*, for that matter."

Nidaba lowered her head, her shoulders shaking. "Oh, she's not anyone, Natum. Don't you know who she is? *Don't* you?"

He frowned, shaking his head. "I—no, I—"

"How could you?" she asked, her voice laced with bitterness. "How could you do it to me yet again, Natum?"

"Nidaba, I thought it was you."

Chin lifting, her eyes locked with his. "You thought it was me? Did you not recognize her? Her voice? The feel of her lips on you? Her scent, Natum? Because I did. I did. I saw through her glamourie when it faltered for just an instant, even if you were too blinded by lust to see anything. She was your precious bride, the one you chose over me so long ago. Your queen. The bitch was Puabi."

The truth hit him like a mallet between the eyes. "Puabi," he whispered. "She lives!"

"You must have known she was immortal!" Nidaba accused.

Nathan lowered his head and, sighing, took Nidaba's arm and led her along the hall to George's room. Peering inside, seeing George sound asleep, and no one else except the dog in sight, he turned the lock from the inside and pulled the door closed. He did the same at Sheila's room, to be certain they would both be safe for the night. Then finally he led Nidaba back down the hall toward his room. "She was no immortal when I knew her," he told her. "But . . ."

"But?"

A muscle clenched in his jaw. "She knew about immortality. She sought to gain it."

"And you never warned me?"

"Hell, Nidaba, how could I? You forget, you fled Sumer long before either you or I knew what we were, or that such beings even existed at all!" He pushed a hand through his hair, shook his head in frustration. "Come. Just come with me, dammit. We're far too vulnerable to attack standing out here in the dark like this."

She stopped fighting him and let him lead her back to the bedroom, where he closed the door, locked it, and then finished fastening his jeans. The jeans had a belt in them, and a sheath hung from that belt, with his dagger inside.

Lifting the skirt of her nightgown, Nidaba sheathed her own blade, which she'd been carrying at the ready the entire time. The sheath Nathan had given her was fastened around her thigh with a red garter she must have found among the things he'd bought for her.

"It's not safe for me here," Nidaba said. "Short of killing anyone who comes close to me, I have no way to defend myself."

"You're right."

She looked up at him sharply. "I didn't expect you to agree."

"Well, I do." He looked at the bed where he'd so recently been lying naked with Puabi, and he almost gagged in revulsion. An icy chill worked its way into his bones. He turned away and went into the adjoining bedroom, holding the door open until Nidaba joined him there, and then closing it, turning the locks. "I'm sorry . . . about what you saw."

She said nothing, simply crossed the room with her nightgown flowing like ghostly tails and poured a glass of water from the pitcher beside the bed. Then she paused, glancing down at the water. "Sheila," she said softly. "Even with all that's happened, she came in here and replaced the water pitcher." She shook her head slowly. "And the broken glass . . . ?"

"I cleaned it up earlier."

She nodded, and then drank the water down before she faced him again.

"When did you find out what Puabi was?"

Pacing the room, Nathan parted the curtain and looked out the window. Seeing nothing there, he checked the closet, the bathroom, and looked underneath the bed. "Just now," he said. "I told you, I didn't know. I know she once sought it, but I had no reason to believe she'd been successful, Nidaba. Heaven knows, if she had, I'd have expected to have crossed paths with her before now."

"Perhaps you have," Nidaba replied. "Perhaps once she perfected the glamourie, she crossed your path as often as she liked, with you never the wiser."

He nodded thoughtfully. "That could very well be. Much as I hate to admit it. But I didn't know. She wasn't immortal when she came to Lagash to live in the palace as my queen," he said, speaking slowly. "But you already know that part."

"Tell me anyway. Perhaps, Natum, it's time for us to relive the hell of our past together and come at last to the truth."

He settled into a chair. "You're right. It's long past time we do that, in fact. And the way I see it . . ." he glanced at the clock, then at the darkness beyond the glassless window. He'd had to put the removable screen in to keep the insects out. The night breeze was light, but filled with the pungence of autumn. "The way I see it, we're better off staying right here until dawn. So what better time? But mark me well, Nidaba, you're going to hear the truth this time. All of it. And so am I."

14

As he spoke, Nathan saw the past unfurling in his memory, clearly, vividly.

He could almost feel the heat of the desert sun beating mercilessly down on the lush oasis city. He could nearly smell the fishy aroma of the nearby Euphrates and feel the roughness of the bleached white stone that made waist-high walls on either side of the broad palace steps.

His bride of a little over a week, Puabi, stepped down from the litter that bore her, aided by two men-at-arms. Eannatum had known she would arrive in style, but he had not expected quite so much pomp. They'd wed in a formal ceremony only a day before, but tonight would be their first one living together as man and wife. She'd had affairs to get in order, belongings to pack and bring along to Lagash. As he stood at the bottom of the palace steps to greet her, massive stone lions on either side of him, he battled a grimace of distaste at her antics. She stepped from the litter onto a silken pillow, hastily placed beneath her feet by a young slave girl who seemed afraid to get too close. Two others, looking equally cowed, raced ahead, unrolling a carpet between them that lined the walk, then up the steps, all the way to the palace doors at the top. Eannatum had to step aside to get out of their way.

Two soldiers walked two steps behind Puabi as she started forward. The slave girls knelt and bowed. The woman—his queen—certainly looked the part. Her headdress was the most elaborate he had ever seen, made of enough gold and lapis to please a Goddess. Tiny bits of round hammered gold, like coins, layered around and around the piece, and they moved, shimmering, each time she took a step. Her gown, too, was golden, gleaming as brightly as the sun. It was made of some fabric that shimmered and shone almost as if it were metallic. Great amounts of paint enhanced her eyes—kohl lined them, and colored powders had been applied in a rainbow of stripes that covered the entire area below the brow, while tiny jewels dangled above it from the headpiece.

Behind her no less than twenty men and women awaited her word. They had all walked, while she rode upon the litter, borne by four of her strongest slaves. Across the desert they had borne her. She had refused to come by boat, as she claimed she suffered illness upon the waves. Water had to be hauled along on the journey, and she had portioned it by cruelly small amounts. Eannatum had reports that three of her slaves had not survived the journey. And he liked his new queen less than he ever had.

She reached Eannatum on the steps, inclined her head toward him, the husband she barely knew. And he bowed respectfully to her in return.

"Welcome to Lagash, Queen Puabi," he said.

"I am glad to finally be here." Smiling very slightly, she turned to face her entourage, and they all genuflected

so automatically it was like a wave moving over them.
"These are my people. My soldiers, slaves, and advisers.
I trust accommodations can be found for all of them?"

"Of course. Had I known you would be bringing so
many, I'd have had rooms prepared. They'll need rest,
and a solid meal after such an arduous journey." He
nodded to one of his own generals, his old friend Galor,
who had been told in advance to see to it that the trav-
elers were taken into the coolness of a nearby storage
building and given plenty of fresh water to drink, beds
of reeds upon which to rest, a solid meal when they were
ready, and anything else they needed. Galor immediately
stepped into the crowd and began speaking quietly to
the exhausted men and women.

Puabi shrugged. "The soldiers are to serve alongside
your own, and they will keep their rank. Except for these
two—" she indicated the large men flanking her—"who
are my personal guards. I want them housed in the palace."

"As you wish," Eannatum said, already disliking the
thought of soldiers he did not know serving alongside
his own trusted troops, much less taking up residence
under his own roof.

"My astrologers, diviners, and soothsayers must be
housed near the palace. I need them close to me, and
they are to be given free access to my quarters as well."

Eannatum lifted a brow. "And what use have you of
magicians, my queen?"

She shot him a narrow glance. "I am Queen of all of
Sumer," she said. "They are my advisers."

It did not truly answer his question, but he didn't press
it just then. "And the others?"

She looked down quickly, dismissively. "The slaves,
you mean? Put them where you will. I've no care where,

except that they be able to come quickly when I send for them."

He drew a breath, exhaled deeply. "During his reign, my father outlawed slavery within Lagash," he told her.

Her nostrils flared just a bit. "I do not come from Lagash."

"But you're here now."

Her gaze clashed with his, and Eannatum decided to let the matter rest. He would not embarrass her publicly, but her slaves *would* be freed, either to remain as paid servants or to return to their homeland with whatever compensation he could give them. He would make that clear to his arrogant new bride—later—in private.

"Let me introduce you to my closest advisers," he said at length. "My general, who is even now seeing to the comfort of your people, is Galor. The man on my right hand is my first soldier, Ris. And the woman on my left is the High Priestess of the temple, Nidaba."

Puabi nodded politely at Ris, the large soldier who was already sizing up her own men-at-arms. But when her gaze touched Nidaba's, Eannatum could almost feel the tension that crackled between them. The two women stared at each other for a long moment.

"I've heard of you," Puabi said, her face almost a sneer. "Part woman, part goddess, they claim." She blew air through her nostrils. "You look less goddess-like than my lowest slave girl." Then Puabi looked at Eannatum again, having exchanged not one further word with Nidaba. "I would go inside now," she said in a very low voice. And without waiting for him, she moved forward, up the steps to the palace doors. As he turned to follow, he saw her leaning close to one of her soldiers, speaking near his ear, even as she slanted a backward glance at Nidaba. A cold feeling crept through Eannatum when he saw that look, and when he quickly glanced Nidaba's way, he knew she had felt it too.

A full moon cycle later, as Eannatum lay in the darkness of the desert, wrapped in blankets and in his beautiful priestess's arms, Nidaba whispered, "She knows about us, Natum."

"No. I've taken care, Nidaba. I never slip away until she is asleep. I've not once been followed. I don't have to do these things. I have every right to be with you, as king. I take these precautions only because you ask it of me. But I do take them. She does not know."

The stars sparkled overhead in a canopy wider than any in the world. And they sparkled in Nidaba's dark eyes. Gods, how he loved her. He hated that she insisted they see each other only in the dead of night, that they hide their love from everyone in the kingdom. She deserved so much more.

"You have not been followed," she whispered, leaning on his chest, staring into his eyes. "But I have."

His frown was swift and deep, and he quickly looked around them, scanning the dunes for prying eyes but seeing only swirls of sand, nothing more.

"Not here, love," Nidaba assured him quickly. "No one has managed to stay on my heels through the secret passages of the temple. But those men of hers . . . they appear wherever I go. I look up from a table of cloths in the market square, or after blessing a boat before it journeys on with its load of fruits or sacred herbs, and they are there. Always. Just . . . watching me. Following me. Listening to my every word, and often talking to the people with whom I have had conversations."

He searched her face, knowing her too well to think she would imagine such things as these. "Then she must suspect something. But she cannot know about us, Nidaba."

Nidaba rolled off him, sitting up and drawing her knees to her chest, pulling the blanket more closely around her shoulders. "Those necromancers of hers, they frighten me more than her guards, Natum."

He sat up beside her, startled. "What have they done to you?"

"Done? Nothing. But they—there is a darkness about them. They've been speaking to every priestess in the temple, asking questions about me. And to the villagers as well. It's as if your queen has set out to learn all there is to know of me . . . of us. Our past. What we have been to each other, and what we are to each other now."

Eannatum felt his jaw go tight. "I'll put a stop to it. Puabi has no right—"

"No, Natum. You are wrong. As your bride, your queen, she has every right."

He looked at her sharply.

"She is your wife."

"A political alliance and nothing more. She knew that from the start."

"Nonetheless, you wed her."

"I do not lie with her, Nidaba. Or kiss those cold lips of hers. I feel nothing for her. It's you I love."

Lifting her hands to his cheeks and pressing her palms there, she stared into his eyes in the desert night. "I know, Natum. And I love you as well. But . . . but it's wrong, what we are doing."

He frowned in utter confusion. "It is my right as king! It is the way of our very culture, Nidaba. It is only you who sees a need to keep it secret."

"It's wrong because it is hurtful. I serve the Goddess, Natum, I know what I feel, and that is what I feel. I fear the price we pay will be higher than either of us can bear."

"I won't give you up, Nidaba."

She nodded slowly, then challenged him with her eyes. "Then give up the throne. Come away with me. We'll run away to some foreign land. The lost paradise of Dilmun, perhaps. Where the rivers run with honey."

"That's not real."

"It could be, for us. If you were with me, free to be with me . . . any place we were would be paradise, Natum."

He gently pulled free of her hands, stared upward at the starry sky. "Are you saying I have to choose? Is that what this is, Nidaba? Are you forcing me to choose between the woman I love and the kingdom I rule? Between you and thousands of my subjects? Between you and the promise I made to my dying father, to my Goddess, to myself?"

She lowered her head, licked her lips. "Yes."

"Even when it was you who made me see that I had to make this sacrifice for the good of Sumer?"

"Yes," she said softly. "Even so. Circumstances have . . . changed. The Ummamites have backed down."

"They'll begin again the moment they sense weakness!"

She lifted her gaze to his. "If it were only for me, I would never ask it, Eannatum. But it has become necessary now that I think of more than just myself. I must consider the greater good. And for me to remain here, playing the part of royal harlot, is no longer acceptable."

"You know that is not how I think of you!" He shot to his feet, pacing away from her as his bare feet sank in the sand.

"It is how all of Lagash is coming to think of me, Eannatum." She got to her feet as well and came to him, placing a hand on his shoulder. "Or do you still insist that no one knows about us? Because they do, you know. It's obvious to any who care to wonder. When

you look at me, Eannatum, there is fire in your eyes.
When you speak to me, your voice deepens, softens.
When you touch me . . ."

He spun around to face her. "I *cannot* choose. Do not
ask me to do this, Nidaba. I cannot."

Her lashes lowered, and he thought they were damp.
"All right, then, my love. I will not ask it of you again."

He sighed in profound relief, pulling her close to him.
"She will tire of Lagash soon enough," he promised.
"You'll see. She'll return home to Ur to take up residence there in her homeland, in her palace. And I'll remain here. It will be better then."

"Yes," she whispered. "Yes, I believe you."

Tears threatened as she listened to Natum retelling the
tale of their last night together, but she blinked them
away when she realized he was staring hard into her
eyes.

"But you didn't believe me, did you, Nidaba? Instead,
you ran away. That very night."

Nidaba sniffled. "There were . . . things you didn't
know, Eannatum. Things . . . that made it impossible for
me to stay."

He looked so pained, so hurt, even after all this time.
"What things?" he asked gently.

"Puabi, for one." Her face grew hard at the memory.
"She had come to me earlier that evening. In the temple.
Dressed in her full royal splendor, right to the headdress,
she came to me. I was in the *cella*, burning incense and
praying for guidance, for I was very troubled, about so
many things. There was a young eunuch, a servant of
the temple, an immortal, like me. He kept trying to tell
me about the nature of what I was, but I thought him
insane. And yet his words troubled me on some level I
could not understand. I finally sent him away to

serve at the palace to be rid of his constant far-fetched tales. And I felt horribly guilty about that. I sensed I had done something very wrong.

"So that was one of the things that troubled me. But there was another, an even greater worry on my mind that evening. So I went to the *cella* to pray. When I heard footsteps in the rushes, I turned and saw her there. Queen Puabi, her gold baubles gleaming in the torch-light. It was just after sundown. The room was alive with shadows that danced over her face, over the walls. The way the torchlight gleamed in the lapis eyes of the stone gods, I almost felt they had all come to life—and had gathered there to judge me for my sins.

" 'I know what you are,' she told me. 'My necroman-cers, my occultists, they have told me your vile secret.'

"I caught my breath, and felt my heart pounding in my chest. I was certain she meant that she knew about us, about our secret meetings, our lovemaking. But that wasn't it at all.

" 'Daughter of the Goddess, indeed,' Puabi all but spat, striding closer to me, kicking the fresh rushes aside without a care. 'Daughter of demons, more likely. You're no more divine than I am, Nidaba. You are a sorceress. A Witch!'

"When I heard the accusation, I nearly laughed, such was my relief.

" 'Do you deny it?' the queen demanded. She stood very close to me now, and I rose, for I had still been kneeling. Standing upright, I was a good deal taller than she, and for a moment it gave me confidence.

" 'Of course I deny it! I am a High Priestess of the Goddess!'

" 'You are a priestess of darkness, born of demons. No human parents ever claimed you. No. You were left on the steps of the temple by the forces of evil, who placed you there knowing you would take over one day. Taking the name of a Goddess! Learning the sacred script when it was forbidden to women! Can you deny any of those things?'

"I stared in shock, stunned that she could know so much about me. 'No one knows who left me on the temple steps. But I can assure you, they were perfectly human.'

" 'Were they? And what of your powers? Hmm? Do you deny them, as well?'

" 'What powers?' Shaking my head, I took a step backward.

" 'I know about them!' she cried. 'How you can make the earth seem to tremble and quake when you grow angry. How your rites and charms cause far greater effects than those of any other priestess in all of Sumer! And this!' She reached out, striking with the speed of a viper, her clawlike hand clutching at my white ritual gown and tearing it down the right side.

"Gasping, jumping back, I fought my anger. If it got the best of me, if I lost control, I would reveal the powers she accused me of possessing. And that was something that Lia—and later the eunuch with all his wild tales—had warned me never to do.

"But Puabi pointed now, at my right flank. 'There,' she said. 'It is just as my spiritualists said. You bear the mark on your thigh—the crescent moon! Demon! *Asakku!*'

" 'No! I'm not!' I cried, backing away from her. But it shook me to the core, because Aahron, the eunuch, had told me of the mark's significance, and I had not believed him.

" 'Yes,' she said. 'You are, and the mark is proof. If I choose to reveal your secret it will mean certain death, Nidaba.'

"I stood a little straighter, sure of myself. For I knew that my king, her own husband, bore the same mark I did. Yet something warned me not to mention that. If she had not learned of it on her own . . . I had no wish to imply that you, too, were the demon she believed me to be. 'You would not be believed!' I told her instead. 'You are a foreigner, and I, a High Priestess!'

" 'I am a queen, and you an enchantress. One who has bewitched the king, stolen his seed, and even now carries her demon spawn who could well lay claim to the throne of all Sumer!'

"I fell silent, my blood rushing from my head so quickly I grew dizzy with it. 'How. . . . how could you know such a thing?'

" 'My diviners, I have told you. They are not pretenders like you, Nidaba. They see the truth in the bowels of birds and the livers of beasts. And even were there doubts about my claims in the minds of the people, do you truly think they would risk it? A child is not something you can hide, Nidaba. Not for long, that is. They would never risk Eannatum's leaving the throne of Sumer to the son of the *Asakku* demon.'

"I had never believed in the divinatory powers of self-proclaimed occultists . . . but I had no choice but to believe then, for it was the truth. I was carrying your child."

Natum had sat in silence, listening to her speak until that point. But now, Nidaba stopped speaking, and looked at his face—the face she had so loved, once.

"You were pregnant. And you knew it. You were pregnant with my child."

"Yes, Natum. Your son."

He closed his eyes, and she could see his pain growing ever deeper. "I . . . I guess I knew, deep down. I just . . ."

"Puabi said she would see to it that my child was murdered at birth, unless I agreed to her terms."

Natum knelt at her feet, gathering her hands in his, his head bowed. "What did she demand of you?"

"That I see you only once more—to tell you goodbye. To end what was between us firmly, and finally. That I go into hiding, in a place of her choosing, and remain there, under her guard, until the day I gave birth. And that I then surrender the child to her."

Natum lifted his head slowly, staring into Nidaba's eyes.

"She wanted, I believe, to claim our son as her own."

"Damn her!" he spat. "I had only been with her once up to that point—to consummate the vows."

"Once . . . up to that point?" Nidaba asked, wondering if that meant he had been with the woman again later.

But Natum ignored her question and rose to pace away from her. "She likely felt that if she hadn't conceived my child that night, she might never do so." He pounded a fist onto a table. "But why? Why would she want to pretend to have borne my child?"

"She wanted a son. She wanted your love," Nidaba said, deciding that perhaps she did not want to know the rest. "And perhaps more than either of those things, she wanted to secure her hold on the throne of Sumer. With her son as heir, her own power would have been irreversible."

He nodded. "She craved power more than anything else. I knew that about her from the start." He returned to where Nidaba sat. Lifting his hands, he stroked her hair, her cheek. "So that was why you asked me to run away with you that night? To choose between you and my throne?"

"Yes."

"And when I couldn't choose . . ."

"I fled, by dead of night. I knew Puabi meant to kill me in the end, and I knew I wanted no child of mine being raised by that cold, evil woman. So I fled, to raise my son alone. You issued a proclamation far and wide that I was to be found and returned to Lagash. You sent your armies to pursue me into the wilderness."

"Because I loved you. I didn't think I could go on without you, and even if I could, I didn't want to."

"That was what I believed at first. That you sought me out of love. They hounded my every step, your soldiers. For years, my child and I knew no peace, settled in no home. And still I believed in you, in your honor, your love for me. Until they caught up to us at last."

Natum stood perfectly still. "What happened that night, Nidaba?"

Rising to her feet, she strode to the window, and gazed out, unable to face him and recall the most horrible moments of her entire existence. "They placed us under house arrest, surrounded the small hut where we had been living, far in the northlands. They stood guard all the night through, telling us not to fear. That we would be escorted back to Lagash, but were in no danger of harm. That they were under strict orders to care for us as they would for the king himself." She smiled a little bitterly as she let the curtain fall back in place. "And we believed them, my Nicky and I."

"It was the truth. Those were the orders I issued to my men."

She turned, facing him squarely. His hand was braced on the chair where she had been before. "Three of your soldiers crept into the house in the night, Eannatum. Assassins. Trained to kill and sent to do murder. Nothing less. Your son . . . oh, you'd have been proud if you could have seen him. So brave. He stepped in front of me, tried to protect me. And they ran him through."

Eannatum made a strangled sound, half cry, half shout, and dropped to his knees in front of that empty chair.

"And when I fell to the floor to cradle my dying child in my arms, they ran me through as well."

Natum's head fell forward, his eyes closed and yet a tear escaped to roll slowly down his cheek. "You . . . were immortal, though you couldn't have known it then."

She nodded. "Yes. I still didn't believe in the tales the eunuch Aahron had told me. But I would soon have all the proof I could ever need that they were true. I was immortal. But my boy was not."

"Gods, Nidaba—" Natum got to his feet, came toward her, but she held up a hand to stop him.

"You said you wished to hear all of it. There is more."

He stiffened. "Go on."

"When I revived, the hut was engulfed in flames. I knew nothing about immortality, about High Witches, Dark or Light. I could not understand why my son lay dead, his precious body already cooling, while I lived. My wound miraculously, it seemed, had healed. But his remained. Somehow I managed to escape the flames. And all the while the eunuch's tales were echoing in my mind. He had told me that the only way I could die, other than having my heart cut still beating from my chest, was by fire. And he had told me it was the most horrible death imaginable for an immortal—that the heart itself would burst into flames and burn within the body, blistering and searing the flesh from within. And even then, it was not by any sane method of calculation that I escaped. I merely stumbled out, blind and numb with grief, and half mad, I suppose. But not so mad that I was not aware that an illegitimate son would have been a threat to the throne of Sumer. Or that you finally had made that choice I had asked of you a decade before. Between me and your throne. And that you had chosen the throne."

He did come to her then, striding forward and gripping her shoulders. "My men were under orders to care for you as they would a Goddess and to bring you back to me. Nothing more." He shook her slightly. "Nidaba, by the Gods, you must believe me!"

Her own tears flowed now, slowly, like old, deep rivers. Not a ripple of a sob or a sound accompanied them. "I don't *want* to believe you, can't you see that? It nearly killed me, losing my precious Nicky. And when I finally made my way through the hell of that, there was another waiting. The knowledge of your betrayal. Because I believed in you so deeply. But I survived, Eannatum. I survived. It would be very foolish of me, don't you think, to believe in you again? To give you the same weapon that I gave you before? One that would surely kill me this time, should you turn it on me once again?"

His hands dug into her shoulders, and the expression in his eyes was fierce. "You know I'm telling you the truth, Nidaba. Deny it all you want, but you already do believe me. You know me. You know I couldn't harm my own son."

She averted her face from his probing black eyes. One finger came up to her chin and lifted it, though, so she couldn't look away and he stared deeply into her soul. "I should hate you for even pretending to believe such a thing of me. But . . . I can't hate you, Nidaba. I never could."

Then he kissed her. Long, and tenderly . . . so tenderly that her tears flowed anew. And when he lifted his head away, she knew she wanted to believe in him again more than she had ever wanted anything. And even more certainly, she knew that she already did. And always had.

But she didn't say so. Instead, she looked past him, through her veil of tears, to the orange glow painting the sky beyond the window screen, and she murmured, "It is dawn."

"I don't care."

"Yes, you do. You care about your friends. And you know as well as I do that they are not safe in this house. We need to get Sheila and George and Queenie away from here. Someplace safe, Eannatum. And we need to do it now."

15

Reluctantly, Nathan agreed. "This conversation is far from over."

She only looked at him sadly as she got to her feet. "It's beyond over, Natum. It's long dead."

"You know that's a lie." Taking her hand, he led her through the bedroom, into the hallway, and down it to Sheila's room. Unlocking the door, he led Nidaba into the room where Sheila lay sleeping, but as he stared at her, relieved that she remained where he'd left her, Nidaba nudged him with her elbow.

"Don't be a fool, Natum. The real Sheila could be lying dead in the basement right now for all you know. Go over there . . . touch her. Make sure she isn't . . ."

He hated to admit that she could be right, but there was no denying it. Slowly, he moved to the bedside, reached out a hand, and touched Sheila's where it lay atop the sheets.

The older woman started and opened her eyes. Then she smiled at him. "Whatever are you doin' in my bedroom, Nathan?" But her smile died slowly, as memories of the day before, the night before, returned to her eyes. "What's wrong? Has something else happened?"

"No. Everything's fine. Nidaba and I simply feel it would be far safer if we took you and George . . . away for a time."

"Away? To where?"

"I'd rather not say just now."

"Rather not say what?" George said from the hallway. When Nathan turned he saw George standing there in his big checkered bathrobe, his hair tousled and feathery, sticking up in places.

"Where you and Sheila are going to go and stay for a few days."

"Oh," George said. Then he frowned. "Oh! But what about Queenie? I mean, can she come too?" As he spoke he lowered a hand as if to scratch the dog's head. But she wasn't at his side as usual, and he glanced back down the hall with a frown.

"I thought about that, but no. It won't work. You're going to be traveling, George. The dog's going to have to stay here, but I promise, I won't let anything happen to her," Nathan said.

"But . . . but . . ."

"It will only be for a couple of days, George. You know I'll take very good care of her while you're gone. Don't you?"

"Well, I . . . I guess."

"This will be like a vacation," Nathan put in. "You're going to have fun. I promise. All right?"

George smiled uncertainly. "All right."

"Good. Now the only catch is, we have to stay together, all four of us, every minute, until we get out of this house. Okay?"

George's smile died. "You think the killer's gonna get us. Don't you, Nathan?"

"I'm not going to let the killer get you," Nathan said firmly. He slanted a glance toward Nidaba, who stood silently beside him. "Not any of you. And that's why we're going to stay together while we pack and get ready to leave. Understand?"

"I guess," George said.

"It's not necessary for all four of us to remain together," Nidaba offered. "Remaining in pairs would do just as well, Natum, and speed may very well be of the essence here."

He held her gaze, nodded slowly, and knew she must be feeling the same shivers up her spine that he was. A foreboding. A threat, lingering, looming. Clapping his hands together and forcing a smile he was far from feeling, Nathan said, "Great idea. Nidaba, you can help Sheila get her things together, and I'll go with George and help him get packed. All right?"

George clapped his hands in exactly the same way. "All right. Let's go, then!"

The bags packed, Nidaba and Sheila waited in the driveway for George and Natum to go and pull the car around. It gave Nidaba time to think. To wonder. This ability of Puabi's, this astounding talent she had, just how advanced was it? What if, for example, Puabi tried to take on Natum's form? How would Nidaba know?

And yet, she thought, she *would* know. She was certain of it, in fact. Surely Puabi couldn't be *that* clever.

The question lingered though, what if she could?

Never. I know Eannatum far better than his so-called wife ever did, Nidaba thought coldly. *She couldn't fool me. Not for a moment.*

Which begged another question—how had the clever Puabi managed to fool Natum last night into believing *she* was Nidaba? Surely he knew Nidaba far better than Puabi ever had.

Then again, he likely hadn't been thinking with his mind just then.

It angered her. Infuriated her.

It shouldn't.

Gods, she still loved the man.

He pulled the car around and got out, opened the trunk and came to take the suitcases that sat at Sheila's feet.

"Do you suppose it's safe now, to discuss where we'll be going?" Sheila asked at length.

Already, Nidaba could feel the easing of the tension that had settled over them back inside the house. The gloom. The pall of death, holding them all in its grip. The tension between her and Natum, however, was still as powerful as ever. She didn't want him to know what she felt for him. It made her far too vulnerable to him to feel this way. Gods forbid he should realize it.

"There's nothing to discuss. Just get in the car and go. Don't tell me where. Don't even decide where, until you're out of here," Nathan ordered. "When you get somewhere safe, call me at home. Let me know you're all right. I won't ask you where you are, or a number where you can be reached. If I do, don't give it to me. You understand?"

"But . . . how will you know how to reach us, Nathan?" Sheila asked.

"Jot a phone number on a postcard and send it to the gallery address. Don't sign it, don't put a return address on it, and mail it from some other place or send it to someone else and have them forward it for you. I'll know what it is, and I'll call you as soon as it's safe to come home. Understand?"

"My heavens, Nathan, do you really think all this is necessary?" Sheila asked, her eyes widening.

It was Nidaba who answered the question. "You of all people, Sheila, should know that it is. This woman, this murderer, is smart. She'll use anything she can to get to Nathan and me. Including you."

Shutting her eyes, Sheila nodded. Then she opened them again and glanced at George. Nidaba did too. He looked so frightened, so pitiful. Smiling brokenly, Sheila stood on tiptoe and whispered something in his ear. His face split in an instant smile. "Can we? Can we really go *there*?" he asked, all but bouncing.

"Yes. Just remember, it's a secret." To Nathan she said, "We'll call you by six this evening. No later. I don't want you hanging about this house any longer than necessary waiting for us to call."

It seemed very odd to Nidaba that she should feel like hugging the two of them before they got into the car. Even more odd to feel tears threatening at the thought of them leaving.

And yet that was exactly what happened. She hugged Sheila tight, and the woman patted her back and squeezed her in return. "Please be careful," Sheila told her. "And don't forget . . ." Then leaning closer, she whispered into Nidaba's ear, "He *loves* you."

Nidaba had to fight back tears as she kissed the woman's cheek. Then she found herself wrapped in a powerful bear hug and picked up right off her feet. George swung her from side to side, squeezing her tight. Then he put her down and grinned at her. "Don't cry, Nidaba. We'll be back soon. Won't we, Sheila?"

"Yes, we will," she told him.

"You'll take extra good care of my dog, won't you, Nidaba?"

"You know I will," she promised, sniffling, wondering vaguely where the lumbering beast had wandered this time.

It was worse yet when she had to watch George's eyes tear up as he hugged Natum. "Please don't make us stay away too long," he said.

"I couldn't get along without you for very long, my friend," Natum replied, his voice tight.

Then Sheila hugged him, and Nidaba saw, even through her misty eyes, that she whispered something in Natum's ear, too. She wondered if it was the same thing the woman had whispered to her.

Natum looked up, caught Nidaba's eye, and said to Sheila, "Once, maybe that was true."

"Once true, always true. Some things don't die, Nathan. You remember that." Sheila kissed Nathan's cheek, and then she took George's hand and led him to the passenger side.

Nathan turned away from the car as they got in and pulled away. He lowered his head and pressed his forefingers to his temples, rubbing small circles there as if his head ached.

"You'll miss them terribly," Nidaba murmured.

"They're my family."

"I know." She lifted a hand, tentative, hesitant, and finally touched him. She stroked his hair, caressed the back of his neck in an effort to rub his pain away. "It's going to be okay. We'll make it safe for them, and then they'll come back."

He met her eyes, nodded twice, but didn't look convinced that what she said was the truth. "Let's go. We've got to pack our own things, close up the house, and collect that damned dog."

"If we can find her," Nidaba said, glancing to the left and right. "She's nowhere around at the moment."

"We'd *better* find her," Natum said grimly. "George will never forgive us if we don't."

•   •   •

When Nidaba came down the stairs with her few possessions packed in the carpetbag Nathan had given her, he was sitting in a claw-legged armchair, staring into the burgeoning flames of a newly built fire. In one hand he held a crystal tumbler half filled with amber liquid that turned red in the firelight.

"I thought we were leaving."

He didn't look up. "I know."

"Have you changed your mind?"

Drawing a breath, he seemed to gather himself. He turned his head slowly, faced her. The firelight painted one side of his face in orange and yellow, leaving the other side in dark shadow, so he looked like some demon prince sitting there. "I've been thinking."

She sighed, set her bag on the floor, and came closer. "Thinking about what, Eannatum?"

His gave her a thoughtful, penetrating look. "It's been so long since anyone has called me that. It almost feels like someone else's name now."

"I apologize if it makes you uncomfortable. It's who you are to me. Who you'll always be. To me, 'Nathan' is a stranger."

"Nathan is the man I wanted to be. The man I've been pretending to be for years now. I'm comfortable being him. It's safe. Peaceful. Predictable."

"And fraudulent. You're a ruler, a warrior, and an immortal High Witch, Eannatum. Not a gallery owner or an antique dealer. You're no quaint New Englander, but a Sumerian king." She drew a deep breath, sighed. "But you know all of that. Natum, you said we would stay here only long enough to gather a few things and George's precious stray, and then we'd be off again. Go someplace safe."

"I haven't found the dog yet," he said.

"Nor do you seem to be looking for her. Natum, you told me—"

"I know what I told you. It was a lie. What I told you was not what I intended to do. And it's not what you intended either. Is it, Nidaba?"

He stared at her, brows raised, eyes so piercing that she finally had to look away. "I don't know what you're talking about."

"Of course you do. You were going to go along with my plan, and slip away from me at the first opportunity, to come back here and wait for Puabi. To take her on by yourself."

She made a face. "You think you know me so well, do you?"

He shrugged. "It's what I was planning to do. We've always had certain things in common, Nidaba. Bull-headedness being one of them."

Slowly she lifted her eyes to his. "You were planning to come back here without me?"

He nodded.

"Why? She could as easily kill you as the other way around."

He smiled, very slightly, just one side of his mouth pulling upward. "Why were *you* going to do it?"

Nidaba narrowed her eyes. "I owe the bitch. Besides, I'm a warrior. It's what I do."

"I owe her as well, you know," he said softly.

"Ahh, but *you're* an ordinary antique dealer. Mild-mannered, model citizen. Boring as milk toast and content to remain that way."

His eyes seared hers with a flash of anger before he banked it again and drew a calming breath. "Sit down, Nidaba. I think it's time we finished our talk."

"I've no wish to discuss the past any further."

"You don't need to do anything but listen. Sit down."

Blinking in surprise, for he sounded just then more like the king she remembered than he had since she had seen him again, Nidaba met his eyes, searched them. "All right." She took the rocking chair and pushed it closer to the fire, closer to him, then stepped around it and sat down. "I'm listening."

He nodded, his face tight. "It pains me to think that you believe what you do of me."

"And what is that?"

He looked at her. Just looked at her. His eyes, as dark as ever they had been, and so, so intense. She could see all the way into his soul, she thought, in the power of that look. And it was obvious that he could see clear to the core of her own. She couldn't look away. Her heart seemed to shudder beneath the force of that gaze. To crack and split apart.

"You tell me," he said, his tone deep, commanding, uncompromising.

"No."

"Tell me, Nidaba. Say it."

"Don't do this to me," she whispered.

"The hell I won't. Nidaba, you *know*. You've always known. I need to hear you say it."

She jumped to her feet, turning away, but he was up in a heartbeat, gripping her shoulders, forcing her to face him. "I didn't know you were pregnant when you left Lagash, Nidaba. I didn't know you'd had my son."

"Stop."

"But even so, I turned over every rock in Sumer, and beyond, searching for you. Trying to find you."

Tears flowed down her face now. "To have me killed. To protect your throne," she whispered, her throat so tight she could barely force the lies through it.

"To bring you back to me. Because I didn't want to live without you. Because I loved you, Nidaba."

"No!" She pulled free, turned her back, and fought not to break down in front of him. But the racking sobs tore at her, straining to escape.

"Is it easier to believe it was me, Nidaba? Is it easier somehow if you can blame me, hate me? Did that make all those years of loneliness go by any faster? Did it?"

"You ordered the death of my son," she rasped. "It was your soldiers who killed him."

"No. It was Puabi who did that. I've only now come to realize that. It's the only way it could have happened, and I think you know it."

Nidaba went stiff. It was not with surprise, because he was only telling her what she'd finally begun to surmise—but refused to admit, even to herself.

"It all fits," he said. "She brought soldiers with her when she came to live in the palace. She had loyal men placed in the ranks with mine. And no doubt she ordered them to kill you both on sight. To burn your bodies in order to cover up the crime. No doubt she knew what you were, even though I did not. She knew the heat of a fire would cause your heart to explode in flames within you, destroying you utterly."

"No," Nidaba denied. "If Puabi had known what I was, she'd have wished to take my heart for herself. It's obvious now—that was her goal all along. To make herself immortal, a Dark High Witch. She needed to take the heart of a Light One to do it. So why not mine?"

"You were too far away. You'd have revived before she could have got to you."

"Then she'd have had me bound and brought to her as a captive." She'd been over all of this in her mind already. She knew all the arguments. She'd waged them with herself.

"I had dozens of soldiers there under orders to protect you with their very lives if need be," Natum said. And then he tossed in an argument she'd never thought of in all the times she had imagined this discussion. "I told my men they would pay with their lives if any harm came to you while under their care. They knew I meant it, Nidaba. So much so that over half the troop fled Sumer after that fire that supposedly killed you, rather than returning to Lagash to face my wrath. Puabi had only two or three of her own men among the troop that finally found you. It would have been impossible for them to bring you back to Puabi as a captive when my men so outnumbered them. Don't you see, Nidaba? It was Puabi, not me. I could never harm you . . . much less my own son. Never."

His hands curled around her upper arms, warming them. "Please, Nidaba, if you ever cared for me at all, tell me you know I didn't do this thing." His voice broke on the final two words.

The shield of stone she had constructed around her heart crumbled and fell to bits. And she whispered, "I know."

"Do you?"

Turning slowly, she stared up into his eyes. "I've always known, Natum. I never truly believed . . ." Fresh, hot tears flooded her eyes. "I'm so sorry. No matter what pain we've caused each other, I had no right to say what I did. I knew in my heart it wasn't you. I . . ."

He closed his eyes, pulled her close, held her to his chest and stroked her hair.

Sobs wracked her body as so much anguish finally spilled free. Her hatred released at last, there remained only pain. And her words tumbled from her lips without pause or forethought. She wasn't even sure they made sense. "I had to hate you. Because if I stopped there was nothing left but to love you, to miss you, to accept that you loved your country more than you did me. And all of that . . . was just too painful. It was easier to hate you, Natum. So I tried to do that. But I never did. Not really."

He sighed his relief, and she felt his body quiver with it. He cupped the back of her head with his hand, and she rested her head on his shoulder, her body shuddering with the emotions she'd kept pent up for so long.

"I needed you," she whispered. "Gods, I needed you so desperately. But you were with her. You were with her, and I . . ."

"I'm here now, Nidaba." His palm cradling her cheek, he turned her face until her mouth slid over his, and clung to his lips. He kissed her. Fully, deeply, passionately, he kissed her. And she kissed him back, with every bit of heartache and anguish, every bit of grief and agony she had felt for centuries spilling out and into the kiss.

His hips moved against hers, his hands curling over her buttocks to hold her tight to him. She didn't think, not now. She only felt. And what she felt was fire, the same white-hot fire that had always raged and burned between them. She tugged his shirt free of his trousers, pushed her hands up underneath it to the skin of his back, and higher, to his shoulders. His skin was warm to the touch, firm beneath her palms. She'd always loved running her hands over his hard body. He tugged at the skirt she wore, and she heard the fabric rip, but she didn't care.

Still feeding at her mouth, he pushed the skirt off her, and it fell to the floor. He shoved one hand inside her panties now, touching her, burning her, invading her the way only he would dare to do. When she moved her feet apart, they tangled in the fabric, and she stumbled backward. Her hip hit a table, and a lamp crashed to the floor. And then Eannatum was tearing her panties away, lifting her off her feet, anchoring her legs around his waist. She locked her ankles behind his back and felt his hot erection forced inside her, all the way. Her back pressed to a wall, he thrust hard against her. She clung to his shoulders as he rocked into her, over and over.

He took his mouth from hers, and muttered, "the blouse . . ."

His hands were busy, holding her backside captive, keeping her pinioned tight to him to accept every one of his powerful thrusts. With her hands, she gripped her blouse in front, and pulled it open, tearing buttons free. It didn't matter. He mattered. He wanted the blouse gone, spoke a command, and she obeyed because he sounded for once like the king she had known. Her king, for whom she would do anything. And she, his Goddess incarnate, for whom he would gladly die.

It was a powerful illusion. Even if it was only temporary.

Her breasts spilled free, and he jammed himself deep inside her and said, "Feed me, woman." Her hands rose, cupping her own breasts, lifting them to his mouth, holding them for him to suckle and bite and torment.

Then his hands closed on her waist, and he lifted and lowered her in time with his thrusts, lifted and lowered her, forced her down harder, bit down on her sensitive nipple with his sharp white teeth.

When she came, it was a searing explosion that blinded her, deafened her, so she couldn't even hear the sound of his name on her own tortured cry.

He held her close, and she felt the pulsing heat of his seed spilling into her. And then he sank slowly to his knees, cradling her in his arms as if she were a small child.

Tears. She felt them, wet on her face, but surely they couldn't be hers. She never wept. What had just happened between them meant nothing, she knew that. It was comfort, and an outpouring of long-held emotions. It was needed. It was cleansing. It was blessed release.

"Why, Natum? Why did she have to kill my Nicky, when it was me she hated?"

Eannatum stroked her hair. Gently he righted her blouse, fastening what buttons remained until she was decently covered. He reached out for her skirt, on the floor, drew it around her. When he finished, she looked as if she'd been through a battle. But she was dressed. He set her gently into an easy chair near the fire. Then he righted his own trousers and rebuttoned his own shirt.

"She was mad with jealousy, Nidaba. After you fled Lagash, your name took on the same mystique as that of Gilgamesh. You were spoken of in awed tones—as half goddess, half mortal. Rumors grew, and many spoke of the love between you and me, as well. Puabi wanted your fame, your mystery. And she wanted my love. I just couldn't give it to her."

She heard something in his voice, and swiping at her eyes, she looked up at him. "There is more," she said, her tone flat, her eyes moving rapidly over his face. "What aren't you telling me, Natum?"

He shifted away from her. "You always see the truth in my eyes, don't you? How do you do that, Nidaba?"

"Tell me," she whispered.

Sighing, he forced his gaze level with hers. "There was . . . a child."

Nidaba's heart lurched. "Yours? With . . . with *her?*"

"Though I couldn't love her, Nidaba, I was human. A man. And a king. I didn't know you'd borne my son, and I needed to provide my country with an heir."

In a pained whisper, Nidaba said, "*You* made a child with *her?*"

He nodded. "You had been gone for five years. I had little hope of ever finding you again, and I had finally come to believe that you honestly did not want to be with me anymore. It crushed me, Nidaba. But it infuriated me as well. I turned to my duty, because I had nothing else. And part of my duty was to know my queen and to produce an heir."

He pushed a hand through his tousled hair. "And maybe it was a way of . . . striking back at you for running away from me the way you did. Maybe, deep down, I wanted to hurt you back."

"You certainly succeeded, Natum. In a thousand ways you hurt me. And had I known of this, it would have hurt me still more. But I never knew."

"That's because the infant was stillborn," he said and sighed deeply. "Puabi . . . she lost whatever sanity she had at that point. Ordered the servants out of her chambers, bolted the doors and decreed that anyone coming inside would pay with his life. She locked herself in her room with that dead child for days."

"Days?"

He nodded. "I was away." He looked at her steadily. "Out looking for you, actually. On one of my endless quests, following yet another fantastical report that you'd been seen in some remote and unlikely locale. But I returned the moment word of the tragedy reached me. I had the doors broken down, the child taken from her, had it buried." He shook his head slowly. "I thought it would kill her. I honestly did. She hated me for it, and I knew she always would." He drew a breath. "It was only a short while later we began to hear rumors that you had been seen far in the north, and that you had with you a fine and healthy son some five summers old. I think that must have been what pushed her completely over the edge. She had to know your child was mine, even though when I heard the rumors I was unsure. Mostly I believed they were fantasies—so many had already been spun around your disappearance . . ." He shook his head slowly. "But Puabi believed it. And I think it was more than her grief-crippled mind could bear."

Nidaba lifted her gaze, speared him with her eyes. "I hope you're not trying to excuse what she did, Natum. A mother who knows the pain of losing a child should be damned to eternal torment for inflicting the same pain on another!"

He stared down at her. "I wasn't trying to excuse her. Your child . . . he was my son, too, you know. And I didn't even get the chance to know him."

Nidaba rose slowly, lifted a trembling hand, touched Natum's cheek. "No. You didn't." Her own words, those she had just spoken, played again through her mind. *A mother who knows the pain of losing a child should be damned to eternal torment for inflicting the same pain on another.* Wasn't that exactly what she was doing by not telling Eannatum the truth about their son?

"I made the wrong choice when I chose my kingdom over you, Nidaba. And I made the wrong choice when I married a woman I didn't love, much less slept with her while you yet lived—it was a sin against our love. One I know you can probably never forgive. And it was my own army that tracked you down, enabling Puabi's assassins to kill our son. For that—for that I can't even ask your forgiveness. Just know, Nidaba, that I have suffered too. At least you got to know him, to be with him, for a little while. But I never did. And while our feelings for each other have . . . have changed after all this time, the love a parent feels for a child never can."

She blinked as a sudden pain struck her in the chest. His feelings for her had changed? Well. Of course they had. It had been four millennia. They couldn't have done otherwise, could they? But . . . they had made love, and it seemed as if they'd never been apart.

And yet she knew that meant very little. Physically, there would always be this explosive passion between them. But emotionally—

Besides, even if their feelings were the same, it could never be good between them. They were too different.

"I wish to Gods I had known him," he said, not even noticing her pain in the face of his own, she was certain.

"You will," she whispered.

Startled, he lifted his head, searched her face.

"For those . . . bad choices of yours, Natum, I will try to forgive you. I cannot yet say that I have, but I know that I should. What difference do they make now, anyway? As you said . . ." She swallowed, unable to repeat his words back to him. "But as for your son . . . our son . . ." She raised her chin, met his eyes. "He died trying to protect his mother from the blade, Eannatum. You *do* know what that means."

Slowly, Eannatum turned in a circle, searching his mind, it seemed. "It means he would come into his next incarnation with the gift of immortality. But Nidaba, we'd have no way of knowing him. Of finding him."

She let her lips pull into a very sad, very slight smile. "I am a High Priestess of Inanna. I was legend in my own time, as much Goddess as woman. I am a Witch, Eannatum. Do you really think that I would not know my own son?"

He stopped turning, and stood facing her, his hands closing on her shoulders. "Do not torment me, Nidaba. Tell me straight out. My son . . . he lives? Now, today?"

As if on cue, the dog they had been searching for all afternoon, came wandering into the room, along with a cool draft, as if somewhere a door or window had been left ajar. The dog stopped walking when she stood beside them. Her head came up, ears perking as if she sensed the importance of the conversation.

"He lives," Nidaba said. "His name is Nicodimus, and he does indeed live. He's magnificent, Natum. You will be so proud."

"By the wings of angels!" Natum cried. He enfolded her in a fierce embrace, and she could feel the emotions surging in him. His entire body trembled with feeling. "Why didn't you tell me before now, Nidaba? For the love of Inanna, why?"

Sniffling, she clung to his shoulders, stared up into his face, and saw the wetness, damp and gleaming on his cheeks. "I don't know. At first my memory was so skewed that even I didn't realize I had found him again. And when I did . . . I told myself I was protecting him—from you, from this situation, from Puabi. But I knew you wouldn't risk his life any more than I would, Natum. I hope you can forgive me for waiting until now to tell you the truth."

"Of course I can forgive you. Just . . . Gods, just tell me, where is he? Is he near?"

She pulled free of him, turning away. It was too painful to have him hold her so fiercely now, when he'd only moments ago admitted that his feelings for her were no longer what they had been once. "I don't know for sure. But . . . that woman, Arianna, who came here looking for me, she is his wife. So if she is near, he must be as well. When you first mentioned her name, I was still disoriented. Confused by the drugs that were still polluting my blood and my mind. It was only much later, when I was clear headed that I remembered the rest. I didn't tell you and I should have, Natum. I just—I don't want them brought into this situation. I don't want that bitch Puabi to have another chance to take my son from me."

"She'd have to kill me first," he muttered.

Nidaba stared up at him, and a flutter of doubt skittered through her mind. What if she was wrong? No. She wasn't wrong. Eannatum would not let her down again. He would not harm her, or harm his son. Not deliberately, at any rate.

But he could still manage to break her heart. Because it was completely in his power to do so, all over again. She had been a fool then, hadn't she? She had done such a thorough job of convincing herself that she hated him, that she had forgotten to stop loving him. And now that the hatred she'd tried to make real had fallen away—as any false notion had to do in time—all that remained was the love. The desperate, hopeless love of a woman who had vowed never to feel its power again.

The problem was, she had never stopped. Not really. She had become a woman of stone. Granite-hearted and cold. Fierce and frightening. She had nearly killed poor Arianna when she perceived the woman as a threat to her son. Because her Nicodimus was the only person Nidaba had allowed herself to love. And the only part of Eannatum she had left.

But Eannatum was here, alive and within her reach. She loved him in spite of her determination not to, and in spite of her certainty that they could never make it work. Her, with her love of freedom and her need to relish her immortality to the hilt. Him, with his need to hide what he was and live a make believe life as a make believe mortal.

She had never been more afraid in her life.

The dog stretched slowly, pushing her forepaws out in front and arching her back in a luxuriant manner. Then she turned and padded almost happily out of the room.

Sighing, Nathan looked at the portrait that hung above the mantel. "Four thousand years' worth of secrets and revelations," he said. "All in the space of the past few days. Gods, but I think it's a bit much even for a once great king to deal with."

"I feel we've been weathering a storm, Natum. A fury. And this is only the eye. I fear there's far worse ahead."

"This time," he promised, "whatever comes, we'll face it together. Openly and honestly. If nothing else, Nidaba, we owe each other that. Agreed?"

She nodded. "Agreed."

"Good." Then he glanced down at his watch and frowned. "Sheila should have called by now."

16

"How did the dog get in here?" Natum asked a few minutes later.

Lifting her brows and her shoulders at once, Nidaba shivered. "She just . . . walked in before." She smiled at the great beast, who had bounded back into the room and was dozing now near the hearth. She looked none the worse for wear.

"Or someone let her in." Bending down to the animal, Natum scratched her head. "Who was it, girl? Hmm? Was someone here?" The dog opened her eyes, and appeared to arch the brown spots above them quizzically.

"Natum, really. If there had been anyone around, this beast would have torn out their throat. I didn't hear so much as a growl."

"Do you feel that?"

Blinking, Nidaba lifted her head, forced herself to be mindful of her senses, instead of just her emotions. "There's . . . a draft."

"Dammit," Natum said, shooting to his feet. "Someone's been here!" He grabbed Nidaba's arm with one hand, drew his dagger with the other.

Nidaba yanked her torn skirt aside, and pulled her own dagger from its sheath with a deadly hiss.

"Stay behind me," Natum said softly.

Together, they moved through the ground floor of the large house. It seemed utterly empty. Utterly silent. More empty and silent than it ever had, Nidaba thought. It was a heavy silence, a living one. Like a shroud, invisible, but weighty and covering the entire place.

They walked through the dining room, stepping lightly, searching every corner, every shadow as they moved into the kitchen beyond. Nidaba sent a nervous glance toward the cellar door, recalling what had happened there so recently. But it was closed tight. Not gaping wide as it had been before.

As she turned and started forward again, though, she saw that the back door, which led outside, stood wide open. The cool autumn breeze blew in, bringing scents of the ocean, of decaying leaves on its crisp biting air.

Pulling her behind him, Natum stepped into that open doorway and looked outside. And then he went still.

"Please," he whispered. "Not this . . ."

His words jolted her, and she peered past him . . . and saw Sheila, lying on the walkway just beyond the door, a spiderweb of blood on her forehead.

"Sheila!" Nidaba shouldered past Natum, racing forward, falling to her knees beside the woman. Gently, she lifted Sheila's head and stared down at her face.

"Damn you, Puabi!" Natum roared behind her. "Damn you to hell! First my son, now my friends! What the hell do you want from me!" He was shouting at the sky, fists clenched until his knuckles were white. "I'll kill you for this, by the Gods, you know I will!" The wind picked up, and gnarled, dark cloud fingers reached in to claw at the face of the moon.

"Natum—"

"How could she have found them, Nidaba?" he shouted, slamming one of his fists into the side of his house so hard that the brick he hit crumbled with the force of the blow. "How could she have found them?"

"Natum."

"And George! Jesus, Nidaba, where the hell is George?"

"Natum!"

He looked down at her, his face tortured.

"She's alive, Natum. We need to get her to a hospital. The rest—we can figure the rest out on the way."

Natum scrambled down the steps, leaned over Sheila, and pressed his fingers to her throat, sighing in relief first at the warmth of her skin and then at the thrumming beat he felt beneath it.

Her eyes fluttered open. "Sheila," Natum whispered, his voice tight and hoarse. "Sheila? Can you hear me?"

"She . . . she . . . she . . ."

"All right, all right." He held her shoulders gently as Sheila struggled to sit up. "Be still now. Just relax and take a breath. Where are you hurt? Can you tell me that?"

Blinking him into focus, Sheila stared up at him. "Nathan?"

"Yes. It's me. You're safe now. Just tell me—"

"Put me . . . into the sea, Nathan," she whispered, a tear squeezing from the corner of her eye, "with Lisette."

"Sheila, no. Don't talk like that. Come on, you're going to be fine, I promise you," Natum said desperately. "Just tell me where you're hurt. And . . . and where is George?"

Sheila's eyes widened, and she sucked in a sharp, painful breath. "George! Oh, God, *George!*"

"Calm down. It's all right. Just—"

Sheila's hand closed tight around Natum's, and she pulled herself up a few inches from the concrete walk. "She . . . went after . . . George!" She managed to force the words out, each one seeming to cost her dearly. Then she let go, fell back again, exhausted.

Nidaba pressed her palm to her mouth to stop herself from crying out. Gods, not that! Not George in the hands of that horrible, cruel woman! A child. He was only a little boy, no matter what he looked like. A mere child.

And Nidaba knew how little regard Puabi had for the innocence of a child.

"*Save him.*" Sheila's words came on a long, slow breath. Her eyes fell closed, and she didn't draw another.

"Sheila? *Sheila?*" Natum's voice broke. He felt for her pulse again, searched her neck, then her wrist, then lowered his head to her chest to listen there, but the look on his face told Nidaba he heard no answering beat. "Sheila, dammit, no!" Lifting her, he held her gently to his chest, bowing over her, rocking her in his arms.

Nidaba closed her hand on his shoulder. "There's no time for this now, Natum." Her own voice was thick with tears. "She's gone. She's gone now. Let her go."

Sheila's hand had fallen open, and a slip of paper lay within it. Nidaba picked it up, and read the line written there.

"Everything you love," was all it said.

But she understood.

She crumpled the note in her fist, imagining it was Puabi's heart she was crushing.

Running back up the steps and into the house, Nidaba searched the kitchen and finally spied Sheila's old raincoat hanging from a peg near the back door. She took it, and walked outside. Natum was just as he had been before. Sitting on the walkway, holding Sheila in his arms, rocking her.

"Lay her down, Natum. We must take care of her. We don't want George to come upon her here, like this."

Nodding, Natum got to his feet, lifting Sheila's body up with him. Nidaba gently covered her with the rain-coat. And side by side, they began walking, each of them knowing instinctively where they were going.

Sheila was an illegal alien with no family. Questions would be asked. It would be best for all concerned if they simply honored her final request. And that was what they did.

Her body between them in the small boat, they rowed out among the gentle swells of the sea. "Just a sheila from Down Under," Natum muttered, leaning down, kissing her cheek. "Born in the bush, and raised with the joeys."

Nidaba pressed her knuckle to her lips, but the sob escaped all the same. "You were so good, Sheila. Such a rare, and precious person. Go now, to the light. Find your peace, your friend, your purpose."

Each of them at one end, they lifted the woman's body, and lowered it gently into the water. They let go, and Sheila sank slowly out of sight.

Natum reached out, wrapped his arms tightly around Nidaba, and held her hard. She cried unashamedly, silent tears that fell softly for the sake of his pain, and for the loss of a woman she'd cared for in spite of herself. She felt Eannatum's shoulders shuddering with emotion. He held her so hard she thought if she were an ordinary woman, he would have crushed her bones.

Then he let her go, all at once, and turning, rowed rapidly back to shore. She'd never seen him look so angry. No tears. He was too furious to shed them, she thought. Perhaps they would come later. But now there was only rage. And she pitied Puabi if Natum could get his hands on her now. Because he wasn't the quaint mortal New Englander Nathan King anymore. He was King Eannatum at his most dangerous.

He held her hand as they climbed out of the boat, and even as they started toward the house, he began calling for George.

Nidaba raced along beside him, determined not to leave his side even for an instant. She wouldn't give Puabi the chance to murder him as well.

"Everything you love," the note had said.

It could have been directed at Natum. But Nidaba didn't think so. Puabi must have been watching them, somehow, when they put George and Sheila into the car, and then she followed them, just waiting for her chance. She must have seen the affection between Nidaba and Sheila when they'd exchanged that emotional good-bye. And she wanted to destroy everything Nidaba cared about.

Everything.

She intended to take away everything Nidaba loved. And she had only begun.

Something brushed Nidaba's skirt as she tramped through the woods beside Natum, and she looked down to see the big dog, loping along and looking almost concerned, if a dog could manage such a thing. Nidaba bent down and rubbed her head. The dog whined softly and nudged Nidaba's hand.

"Find George," Nidaba whispered. "I know you can do it. You find him, Queenie. Go on. Find George!"

With a soft "woof" the dog ran ahead.

Midnight.

Nathan was exhausted, filthy, damp with sweat, and chilled to the bone. His legs were scratched and bleeding, and Nidaba was in worse shape than he was. And yet they'd found no sign of George.

The dog paced the house, inconsolable, it seemed. She kept wandering from room to room as if looking for her beloved friend but unable to find him. Whining in a deep, plaintive tone, she would look from Nathan to Nidaba, as if asking what they planned to do about this. It was heartbreaking. The Rottweiler finally lay down near the fire, likely as exhausted as Nidaba and Nathan were.

"There's nothing more we can do," Nidaba told him for the tenth time. "Nothing mundane, at least. By the Gods, Natum, have you nothing in this house that we can use for divining? No cards, no board, no crystal balls?"

"No." He said it softly. "I never was much for scrying or . . . divination."

"Sorry excuse for a Witch then, aren't you?" She tried to make her tone teasing, light, he knew, but there was no lightening his mood. He sat in a chair by the fire, slumped and miserable. "If she had intended to kill him, Natum, we would have stumbled upon his body by now. Or found it awaiting us at the door. She is attacking us, trying to cause us as much pain as she possibly can. She would have made sure we knew it if George were dead."

He nodded slowly. "Exactly. And she knows that hurting him, making him suffer, will cause us even more pain."

"No. She's using him, Natum. She wants something. And all we can do is wait for her to tell us what it is."

"I dislike waiting."

"You always did."

He looked at her and realized he was being an ass. She had come to love George too, in the short time she'd known him. And Sheila as well. He stretched out a hand to touch her cheek where a long, curving scratch marred its perfection. "I'm sorry."

"Don't be, Natum. This is not your fault. It's me she wants."

But it *was* his fault, and he knew that with sudden clarity. Nidaba was right, and had been all along. He couldn't live a lie, pretend to be a mortal to escape the violence of his existence. It didn't work that way. What he was . . . followed him. And brought its violence to those he loved.

"We should shower," Nidaba said. "Clean up. Eat a solid meal. We can't sleep. It wouldn't be safe, not even one at a time. But we need to be strong. To be ready. And we need to keep busy if we're to stay awake."

"I agree."

"Then?"

He nodded and got to his feet. Taking her hand, he led her up the stairs.

There was no time for passion, nor could he think of pleasure when George was out there somewhere. Alone and probably terrified. He stood watch while Nidaba washed the briars and thistles from her hair. Then she got dressed while he took his turn in the shower. The door remained open the entire time, neither of them willing to risk the other being out of sight for a moment.

By the time they finished, their many scrapes and wounds were nearly all healed. The natural regenerative processes that were a part of their immortality had done their work. Nathan looked at the fading scratches on his arm, the one on Nidaba's cheek, now only a pale pink streak, and shook his head. "It never stops amazing me, though I should be long used to it by now."

"Being used to it doesn't make it any less amazing," she said softly as he toweled off and began to dress. "You never told me, though. How did you first discover the truth . . . of what we are?"

He hesitated for a moment. He'd pulled on a clean

pair of jeans and was in the process of sliding his belt, with the dagger and sheath attached, through the loops. Nidaba had curled catlike on the foot of his bed, and a distant sadness shadowed her eyes.

"It was Puabi."

"Of course it was."

"You must understand, she was not an immortal. But she had learned about our existence." He finished lacing the belt and reached for a shirt.

"Even when we ourselves didn't know what we were," Nidaba muttered, shaking her head.

"Yes, even then. It all came out a year after your . . . your death—" He closed his eyes briefly, experiencing a stab of pain even now at the memory. "After your death was reported to me," he said, completing the sentence this time. "I had been angry at you for leaving me. I'd thrown myself into my rule, my duty, almost lashing out at you in the process. But this was different. Believing you dead was a far, far different thing."

She nodded. "You hated me for a time, or tried to. Just as I tried to hate you."

"Yes, I guess I did. But when they told me you'd burned in that fire . . . I fell into a deep melancholia. Instead of eating the meals that were served me I stared at them and felt ill. Instead of sleeping, I haunted the palace halls at night. Sometimes I would even slip away from the palace, without guards or escorts, and go to our secret oasis on the far side of the river and just sit in silence for hours."

He tucked his shirt in, fastened his jeans, buckled his belt.

She turned halfway, her face in profile, moonlit on one side and shadowed on the other. "I'm sorry you suffered because of me."

"I didn't suffer a tenth what you did, Nidaba. But I did

suffer. I knew you'd had a boy with you, that he had been killed as well. And though I couldn't be certain, I suspected he was my own son. I . . . I wanted him to be. And I spent all my waking hours dreaming of how things might have been had I married you instead of Puabi. How the palace's grim halls would have been filled with the laughter of my son and my beautiful wife."

She lowered her face. To hide a rush of tears, he thought.

Reaching for her hand, he pulled her to her feet. She'd put on the black dress again. She liked the old ways, he thought. Maybe he did too. Maybe he wished he could go back in time and live it all again. Gods, but he would do things so differently this time.

Side by side, they walked into the hall and down the stairs. "When Puabi lost her child, years before, part of me . . ." He lowered his head, shaking it slowly. "Part of me was riddled with guilt—because I hadn't fully wanted the child. I wanted a son with you, not with Puabi."

She nodded slowly, her cheek brushing against his shoulder because she walked so closely beside him. If he thought for a moment that there was a chance she could ever forgive him for all his mistakes—mistakes that had cost her everything—But no. That was foolish thinking.

They stopped in the kitchen, both of them avoiding the back door. The memory of what they'd found out there, too fresh and too recent.

"It's an honest emotion, Natum," Nidaba said. "Your being less than thrilled about Puabi's child had nothing to do with its death."

"I know that. But knowing it did nothing to ease the guilt I felt." Sighing, he went on, even as he pulled out a chair, and guided Nidaba into it. "Later, when they told me you were dead, I didn't even want to live. I was glad I didn't have a child to look after, to be responsible for. I was devastated when I learned that you'd had a son, and that he had died so young, and I tormented myself with wondering if he had been my own. And even then, I didn't know it was murder. I was told it was an accidental fire."

"It is good, perhaps, that you didn't know the truth, then," Nidaba said, staring into space now, her face grim.

Turning his head, he kept his eyes fixed on Nidaba's face. "I'd have killed her if I had known. I swear to you, Nidaba, she would have paid with her life."

She cast her eyes downward, neither accepting his words nor arguing with them.

"Puabi knew how I mourned you. She couldn't help but know it. And she knew I mourned your son in a way I had never mourned hers. She thought, I suppose, that once you were gone, I would stop searching for you, stop longing for you. Perhaps turn to her, in your place. But losing you only made me realize the gravity of my mistakes. And I regretted having married her more than I ever had before. She tried to come to me, to make me love her. But I couldn't. I couldn't do it. And she hated me for that."

"Being rejected by her own husband would not have set well with that one," Nidaba said.

"No. No, it didn't. But she struck back." He reached into the refrigerator, and pulled out a covered dish, swallowing hard. "Chicken stew," he said. "Left over from the last meal Sheila cooked us."

"She's at peace, Natum."

"I know." He turned to the counter, filled two dishes with the stew, then popped them into the microwave and pressed a button.

"You said Puabi struck back at you," Nidaba said. "How did she do that?"

He watched the bowls revolve. "She began to speculate that I was cursed, under an enchantment. She whispered suggestions of black magick. Said these things even beyond the walls of the palace, and whispered accusations of all kinds against me. She thought to discredit me. But her plan reversed upon itself. The people began to talk, as people will do. But rather than condemning me, they compared my state to the madness of Gilgamesh, the legendary hero, after his best friend Enkidu was killed. I was loved more than ever before. The people said I ruled by the blessing of a real and true goddess who had for a time walked among them. They said that the mysterious High Priestess Nidaba wasn't just named for a goddess, but actually had been one. One who blessed and favored their king. But that she had died horribly, and they feared that I would soon follow, wasting away in mourning for her, unless I could be shaken free of my heartache. Gifts were piled upon the palace steps, public prayers for me uttered in the city square, musicians played outside my chamber windows. And a statue was erected in the temple in your likeness, Nidaba . . . in an effort to comfort me."

"I did not know."

"You were a true legend," he said. "And when rumors persisted that you had been seen in foreign lands, long after your supposed 'death,' the people became even more convinced of your divinity."

A look crossed her face, as if this tale pained her somehow. "Please, continue."

He closed his eyes, shook his head, took the two steaming bowls of stew from the microwave and placed them on the table, along with utensils, bread and butter, and salt. Then, sitting down, he let himself fall into the memory as he told the tale of the night his queen had killed him.

17

Eannatum paced in his royal bedchamber. Just beyond the window, several of his most longtime advisers stood watching while a band of musicians played the lyre and harp and drums, and sang songs of the greatness of their king and the glory of the High Priestess Nidaba, who had rejoined her mother, the Goddess, and even now reigned from a heavenly throne and smiled down upon the people of Sumer.

It did nothing except etch the pain ever more deeply on his soul. Bad enough to have believed she had left him, bad enough to live without her . . . but this . . . this was surely more punishment than any man deserved to bear. Knowing he would never see her again, never touch her, knowing she had a son who might have been his own—dead, just as she was. Dead.

He threw a goblet at the wall, and the sound rang in the hollowness of the room. It was followed by another sound. That of the large oak door creaking open, of the footfalls of small slippered feet. And then of the voice of the woman he'd been forced, by circumstances and vicious fate, to wed.

"It has been over a year, Eannatum," Puabi said, her tone impatient and tinged by disgust. "Can you not let go of this mourning even now?"

He turned to look at her. She was beautiful, truly. Small and slight, with delicate features, a tiny waist, and round eyes of vivid lapis blue. Those eyes looked weary now. Nearly as weary as he felt. And yet they remained haughty, proud, and cruel.

"My mourning is no concern of yours."

"To think I hoped you might turn to me, now that your whore is finally gone," she said, bitterness overshadowing her beauty—making her seem ugly instead. "To think I had any hope at all you might do the honorable thing. The right thing for your country."

He grated his teeth and clenched his hands into fists at his sides. "You are a political ally, Puabi. You knew that from the start. It is not my fault if it pains you, now, to see me mourning another woman."

"Pains me? You think you have the power to hurt *me*, Puabi, Queen of all Sumer?" She tossed her head, stalking away from him in quick, angry strides. "It is not pain I feel, Eannatum, but humiliation. You may as well strip me naked, roll me in camel dung, and parade me through the streets. You're making a fool of me before the entire kingdom! And a bigger fool of yourself. All over some nothing little priestess who's dead and gone."

He spun on her. "That little priestess was twice the woman you'll ever be, Puabi. Speak ill of her again, and you'll regret it, I vow."

She sniffed indignantly. "Act like the king you are," she cried. "Stop wallowing in your sorrow before all the world."

He glared at her. "Perhaps you should consider returning to Ur, ruling from your palace there."

"I am queen of Sumer, not merely of Ur. Lagash is the chief city of Sumer—thanks to our marriage. It is my right to sit on its throne, and you will *not* move me from it!"

They locked gazes, hatred flashing in her eyes more brightly than he'd yet seen it. A tap came at the chamber door, and she banked the emotion, turned and flung the door open. A servant stood there, bearing a tray with wine and chalices. Puabi took the tray and then turned back again.

"What's this?" Eannatum asked, his tone sarcastic.

"Ah, but don't you see it, your highness? This is your devoted wife, playing the role you asked her to play. Ordering up wine to soothe her husband's misery." She slammed the tray down onto a nearby stand, poured wine from the jug so clumsily that it slopped over her hand, then spun and held the chalice out to him. "Take it," she snapped. "Accept a bit of comfort from the wife you never wanted. And choke on it, you bastard."

He snatched the chalice from her, sneering at her as he did, and slugged back its contents in one long draft. Then he dragged the back of his hand across his mouth and let the chalice fall from his hand to the floor. "Happy?"

Her expression changed. It darkened. She smiled very slowly. "Yes. More than I have been since I agreed to this loathsome arrangement."

No sooner did she say the words than dizziness struck Eannatum. He pressed a hand to his head. But the dizziness only grew worse. He blinked as her face swam before his eyes. "What is this, Puabi? What have you . . . ?" He tried to lunge toward the door, but stumbled instead, and found himself sitting on his own bed.

Suddenly Puabi shoved him backward, so he was lying down, and she straddled him. She tore open his robe. And he stared up at her, shivering, ill, too weak to even ask what she was doing. He couldn't fight her. The room seemed to spin around him. His hands, his arms, refused to obey his mind's commands to move, to push her off. He couldn't convince his voice to shout for help.

"I know what you are," Puabi said, her voice almost a growl. "My sages and sorcerers have told me about your kind. But you don't deserve immortality, Eannatum. You waste it, grieving over what you've lost instead of relishing what you have!" She drew a dagger from a sheath. "You don't deserve eternal life," she said. "But I do! I do!"

Eannatum blinked in shock, realizing she meant to kill him. He forced himself to move, lifted his arms weakly to fend off her attack, but his struggles were useless. "You . . . what are you . . . No!"

Puabi lifted the blade high, and drove it into his chest. It was like fire and ice all at once, splitting him. He felt the searing pain of his flesh being sliced wide, felt the blood bubbling forth like a hot scarlet geyser, and a cry was forced at last from his lips.

A cry that was heard, for even as he lay there, pain screaming through his mind, blood bubbling out of his body, the chamber door burst open, and two of Eannatum's men lunged into the room. Galor was one of them, and it was he who tore Puabi off him, disarmed her, dragged her away. But it was too late, Natum thought as he lay there. He could feel the life ebbing from his body. He was dying.

"Take her to the dungeons," Galor shouted.

"No!" Puabi cried. "He's a demon, your king. Cursed by that demoness who pretended to be a priestess. He's not human, I tell you! Mark me, you'll see! You'll see!"

Her voice faded. There was nothing more. Eannatum lay there, in a pool of his own royal blood . . . and he died.

It took a long time for him to revive. And later, much later, when he would learn about such things, he would wonder why that was. Perhaps because of the damage Puabi's blade had done to his body, his heart, or perhaps because of the sleeping powder she had put into his wine. But he truly thought that it was more likely because he had no will to live at that point. He'd been like a walking corpse ever since he'd been told of Nidaba's death. So there was no vitality in him, no life. And he suspected that was the reason he remained in the throes of death for so many hours.

When he felt that first rush of breath splitting his lungs, arching his body, jolting him wide awake, he thought he was feeling Puabi's blade driving into his heart all over again. But the pain, the shock, faded fast, and he blinked his vision clear and looked around him.

At first he saw only the earthen walls rising high on three sides, and the solid brick one at the fourth, completely finished. But he took little notice of the odd room, thinking instead of the mortal wound in his chest. He pressed his hand there, quickly, and sat up, looking down.

But there was no wound, no blood. He was dressed in his finest robes, his crown, his sword, and his dagger lying all around him. Quickly he tugged at the collar of his garment and looked inside at his chest. It was dark in this small room, but he could see, and he found that odd, disorienting. And even odder, there was no mark on his skin. No wound.

Had it been some kind of dream? A nightmare?

An aroma wafted toward his nose. He sniffed and realized it was the familiar smell of censers filled with burning herbs. Then he heard muffled chanting coming from beyond the solid brick wall.

All at once it hit him where he was, what had happened to him.

He was sealed in his own tomb, and even as he sat there, trying to understand, to make sense of what seemed impossible, he realized what was going on in the outer chamber.

Someone played a lyre. Others hummed or chanted or sang. Drummers beat a slow rhythm, a death beat. "Gods, no!"

He raced to the brick wall as the drumbeat and the chanting grew faster, louder, more and more frantic. He pounded on the bricks, clawed and kicked at them, cried out over and over, but it was all lost in the pounding beat. And when that drumming reached its crescendo, only to go silent all at once, he knew they were all out there, his advisers, his courtiers, priests and priestesses, and loyal followers . . . all of them, lifting the golden chalices to their lips, and sipping the sacred Elixir of the Dead.

"The poisoned wine," he whispered. "No! Stop, I'm not dead!"

He pounded and kicked at the wall even harder. Then he snatched the dagger from where it lay, and began attacking the mortar with its blade, fighting to loosen just one brick. Anything to get to them, to stop them in time.

Finally, he scraped and pried enough to loosen a brick. Freeing it, he managed to kick several others loose until there was a hole big enough for him to crawl through. But the moment his head emerged on the other side, he knew he was too late.

He dragged his body through the opening, but his pace was no longer rushed or frantic. Then he stood in

the midst of them all, and death surrounded him. His
friends, and soldiers, his priests and priestesses, and the
very musicians who'd been playing outside his chamber
windows such a short time ago. They lay there, all of
them. Dead. Dying. Reclining on the dirt floor, looking
peaceful, beautiful, serene. Some were still breathing,
barely. Silver ribbons were twined in the hair of the
young women. One priestess still clutched the lyre.
Those golden goblets lay beside them. Toppled and
empty.

God, one of the dead men was Galor!

He wanted to scream, to cry out loud and rail against
the meaninglessness of it all. His attendants, his first
soldier, Ris . . . all of them had died, believing they were
journeying with their king, to serve him in the other-
world. Never had he known such a heavy silence. Such
a weight of sadness.

But it would not last. At any moment, he knew, the
procession would arrive from the temple, and they
would begin throwing the first layer of earth into the pit,
to cover the bodies. He had to force himself to move.

Weakly, he ran up the sloping earthen ramp that his
loved ones had so recently used to walk into their own
mass grave, and when he reached the surface, some
thirty feet above, he ran through the night, away from
the city. He vowed he would never look back.

Eannatum got to his feet, pacing the kitchen. His bowl
of stew was barely touched. He filled a glass with water
and sipped it slowly. "I heard what happened next only
by rumor. But it seems that one of the priests, when he
returned to begin covering the grave, noticed the missing
bricks. And upon checking further, he realized that my
body was gone. He declared that Puabi had been telling
the truth when she claimed I was some kind of nether-

world demon. She was restored to the throne at once."

"What became of your bitch-queen then, Natum?"

He looked down at her bowl. "Eat your stew."

"I have no appetite."

"Eat. Be strong. Better to kill her when she comes, Nidaba."

With a fierce look, Nidaba spooned some of the stew into her mouth.

Natum did as well. When he had swallowed it, he went on with his tale.

"I was confused. I did not know what it could mean, that I had somehow revived from death. I thought of going after her—had I known then that she was responsible for the attack on you and our son, I would have. But for my own personal vengeance . . . it just wasn't worth the effort. I'd had my fill of ruling as a king. I was still in mourning for you. I went away. Far, far away, to try to find the answers to what I was, what my existence meant. Shortly afterward, Puabi returned to Ur. And that was where she ruled for many years to come. She had our marriage record stricken, had every mention of any alliance between the two of us erased. Stone tablets were crushed and new ones engraved. History was changed. I was remembered as a king of Lagash and onetime ruler of all Sumer, she as the mystical Queen Puabi of Ur. But never was there mention of the two of us having so much as met. And there never will be. No tablet with our true history will ever be found."

He paused, sipped his water.

"She took the heart of another immortal, made herself immortal for as long as its power lasted," Nidaba said slowly. Then she gasped, and widened her eyes. "By the Gods, Natum, there was only one other High Witch in Lagash—Aahron! That sweet young man who tried to tell me what I was. But I wouldn't believe him. I sent

him to serve in the palace." She drew a trembling hand
to her lips. "I sent him to his death."

He could feel the grief that rose up in her at the
thought. He couldn't bear to see her hurting so deeply.
"You can't know it was Aahron's heart she took, Nidaba."

"But he was the only—"

Nathan caught her hand in his, drew it toward him,
and brushed his lips over her knuckles. "He was the only
High Witch you knew of, in Lagash. There could've
been others. How would you have known, then? You
knew nothing of our kind."

She lowered her head. "I pray it wasn't Aahron." Nathan squeezed her hand and wished he could assure her
it hadn't been her young friend who'd fallen victim to
Puabi's blade. But he feared that if he did, he'd be lying.
"Regardless of whose heart she stole," Nidaba went on,
"she killed in order to preserve her own life. And when
the heart of her victim weakened, she took another, and
another, and another. Do you know how many innocents
she must have murdered to keep her evil alive for over
four thousand years, Natum?"

"I can only imagine," he said. "But it will end. Because she will come here, in search of us. And I will
kill her."

"Unless she kills you."

"That won't happen, Nidaba."

"She is clever. She even made you believe she was
me."

He winced, remembering what had happened, regret-
ting it to his very soul. There was pain in her voice when
she spoke of it. Pain he'd caused, this time. "It hurt you
deeply, when you saw me with her."

She shrugged, averting her eyes. "I only wonder how

a man who claims to have loved me so completely could
be so easily fooled."

"Because when one sees something he wants so badly
to see, he tends to overlook minor details, Nidaba."

Blinking her eyes, she examined his face. "What you
wanted to see . . . ?"

"Nidaba . . . when I looked at her, I saw only you. I
saw your hands on me, felt your lips on me. I was helpless to resist."

"Why?" she whispered.

He smiled just a little. "Why? Because I crave you
still, Nidaba. You must know that, after what happened
between us earlier tonight. Neither of us can deny it,
now, can we? Between us, Nidaba, the fire still burns."

Her tongue darted out to moisten her lips. "Even if
the love does not. That's what you mean to say, isn't
it?"

He drew his brows together. So she wanted to make
sure he understood that this was no more than physical?
The knowledge dug deep, confirming what he had already known. Hell, how could he have thought her love
for him would survive so many lifetimes? So much
pain?

"Nidaba, it's all right. Don't feel badly over that."

She returned her attention to her stew, cleaning the
bowl and dropping the spoon inside. "What makes you
think I feel badly? What happened between us earlier
was only an explosion. An outburst of feelings held in
check for far too long. And not just feelings of desire,
Natum. But feelings of anger, hurt, betrayal . . . all of
them."

He almost got angry. Almost. Would have, if not for
the hurt he saw in her eyes and the slightest trembling
of her lower lip, that suggested maybe she was being
less than honest here. By the Gods, could it be? Might

she still harbor some kernel of love for him? Was he a
fool to even imagine such a thing were possible?

He moved back to the table, turned her chair around,
then leaned over it, and braced one hand on the table on
either side of her. "Then . . . what about now?"

"What do you mean?" She looked nervous. Why, he
wondered.

"We've released all those pent up feelings, Nidaba. If
that's all it was, between us, that must mean it's over—
that you no longer feel desire for me at all."

She closed her eyes. "I burn for you, Natum. You
know I do," she whispered.

He nearly closed his eyes, such was his rapture. Oh,
it wasn't a confession of love. But it was a start. "Thank
the Gods for that, woman, because I need to feel you
tonight." He leaned closer, kissed her deeply, hungrily.
She responded without reserve, her lips parting eagerly
to welcome his invasion. When he finally lifted his head
away, he said, "Sex without love, Nidaba? Is that all this
will be?"

"Sex has many more facets to it than those of the
heart, Eannatum."

She looked at him as if meeting his challenge, answering his dare. When, dammit, she was the one who
had just denied having feelings for him. Other than desire, at least. But he wanted her. He was hard already,
just from kissing her. And in his mind's eye, he remembered the night she had danced for him.

So many things had hit them both tonight. They'd
been under attack, and the only shelter they had from
the horror, the anguish, the pain . . . was each other.
Maybe, for right now, that was enough.

"She may have looked like me," Nidaba whispered,
"But you must admit Puabi could never give you the
same pleasure I can, Eannatum."

"In four thousand years, no woman ever has."

"I would hate to think you couldn't tell the difference between her touch and mine."

"Remind me of the difference then. For just a little while, Nidaba, take me away from this nightmare we've fallen into. And I'll take you away from it too. Just for a little while . . ."

She closed her hands in his hair, and pulled his face her for a blatantly carnal kiss. She nipped his bottom lip in her teeth before she drew away slightly to soothe the sting with her tongue. "Oh, I will," she promised in a husky voice. Rising slowly from the chair, she pressed her hands to his chest, and licked his lips, pushing him backward until he was against the wall. Then she flattened her body against his, continuing to sample his mouth, and she slid her hands along his arms, from his shoulders, upward, until her fingers laced with his, and his arms stretched above his head.

One of her hands darted downward, and her dagger appeared in it. She stabbed it through his shirt sleeve, and into the wall beyond. He gave an experimental tug to test his delicious restraints, and the dagger held. Anticipation made his blood pulse hotly. His erection hardened painfully, and he bit back a groan.

Smiling wickedly she sank to her knees in front of him, and opened his jeans. She freed his erection, her very touch making him shudder. Looking up at him, staring straight into his eyes, she licked her lips, and moved them closer to him. When that succulent mouth finally touched him, it was only lightly, teasingly as she rubbed her wet lips back and forth over the swollen head. Nathan arched his hips toward her, an unspoken plea. But still she tormented him, flicking her tongue over him until he was panting with need.

Finally, she took him into her mouth. Nathan shud-

dered as her lips slid over him, moved up and down the
length of him, and her tongue swirled and lapped at him.
She used her teeth on him, making him gasp and moan.
He arched his hips toward her as she suckled and teased.
He wanted to tangle his hands into her hair and hold her
captive, so he could thrust into her mouth, but he didn't
do that. He could have torn his arms free and done just
that. But he didn't. He let her play just to see how long
he could bear the succulent torture. She tormented him
and pleasured him with her mouth and her tongue for a
long while, never letting him find release, working him
into a frenzy, only to deny him the ultimate goal, over
and over, until his mind spun out of control. He was
quivering, sweating, moaning her name.

And finally, when he could bear no more of it, he
gave a deep growl and tore his arms free, ripping the
fabric of the shirt in the process. He grabbed her shoulders, and pulled her to her feet, and ravaged her mouth,
thrusting his tongue into her almost viciously. He tasted
her and tangled with her tongue, licking the inside of
her mouth. Savagely, he peeled her dress up her body
and tossed it aside. Then, lowering her to the kitchen
floor, he spread her thighs wide, and knelt between them.

She moved in supplication, arching her hips off the
floor, but he didn't take her. Not yet. Instead he gathered
her wrists in one hand, pinning them to the floor above
her head. "My turn," he whispered, determined to give
as good as he got.

Using his free hand, he touched her. He slid his fingertips slowly over her chin, her neck, down her ster-
num. He dragged them lightly over her breasts, pausing
to press her nipples just a little. A tiny pinch, only
enough so she whimpered for more. Then he moved on.
His finger made spirals over her belly, slid downward,
over her abdomen, and then teased her center so softly

she rocked her hips in search of a firmer touch. He flicked lightly, over and over until he saw the sweat break out on her forehead.

Smiling, he touched her more firmly, and then still more, sliding his fingers into her slick passage, and moving them slowly while she squirmed.

"Damn you, Natum," she whispered. "Take me now."

"Oh, I don't think so. Not just yet." He hooked his arms under her legs, lifting them, anchoring them over his shoulders. And then he bent his head, and licked a hot path over her juicy center. Using his fingers to spread her open wide, he lapped at her there. He loved her taste. He thrust his tongue inside, drew it out again, stabbed at her, sucked at her until she was writhing and screaming in ecstasy. And then he held her down, and licked some more.

"Please, Natum, please . . ."

He rose and looked down at her. Her body was flushed, her nipples hard, her face, rapturous. God he loved seeing her like this.

He caught her hands, and rolled onto his back, pulling her with him, so she was atop him. She sat up slowly, her eyes glistening, hooded, fiery. Bracing her hands on his chest, she positioned her legs outside his, and lowered her body. He felt her shudder as he slid inside her like a dagger into its sheath, and Nidaba closed her eyes and moved. She rode him, slowly at first, then faster and harder, her head tipping back, her eyes falling closed. He caught her breasts in his hands, and tormented her nipples, holding them captive in a sweet, firm pinch so that when she moved, they pulled against his fingers. She rocked even more fiercely, took him even more deeply, until his mind and body exploded in wave upon wave of unimaginable pleasure. She ground her hips against him, her body squeezing him, milking dry as she climaxed with him, murmuring his name and raking her fingernails across his chest.

Then she went limp, slumping down atop him in a boneless sprawl. He wrapped his arms tight around her waist, she nuzzled his neck with her lips. "Sated yet, Priestess?" he teased her gently.

He felt her lips smile against his skin. "I've not been with a king in over four thousand years."

"I've not been with a goddess in just that long."

"Then we've much time to make up for."

"I was hoping you'd say that." He sat up, gathered her into his arms, then snatched up her dress and her dagger. He carried her up the stairs to the bedroom, wryly amazed that he was ready for her again so soon. But it had always been this way with her. The more he had Nidaba, the more he needed her, craved her. And he knew it wasn't just sex with her, no matter what she might think or want to believe or be willing to admit. For him, it was more. Far more.

He laid her on the bed and made love to her again— Gently, this time. Leisurely. Tenderly. He kissed her, caressed her, spoke to her in soft whispers that emerged in the old tongue, as if they'd gone back in time. He tried to memorize every part of her, the way she felt against his hands, the way she tasted, the way she smelled, the way she sounded and moved and breathed in his arms. And for that short span of time, he found heaven.

Afterward, they lay sated and exhausted. Natum had opened the window to let the sea breeze in. It smelled like the ocean, like autumn, and like a looming rainstorm. Every once in a while distant thunder rumbled ominously.

Beyond the window, the ocean danced in the fall wind's touch. The scents of the sea and the fall leaves

and the impending storm lingering on the air were in-
toxicating. And the dog, which had wandered into the
room to lie down on the floor beside the window,
seemed to fit the scene perfectly. "You really do love
this life you've built here, don't you, Eannatum?"

He glanced at Nidaba's face and smiled. "It's been . . .
a haven."

"It is a beautiful home."

"It's not just the house. Or the gallery in Boston. Or
George and Sheila." He paused there, swallowing hard
at the mention of Sheila's name. "It's . . . it's more than
that."

"I know," she said softly. "It's a mortal's life you're
living, Natum. The Dark Ones . . . they don't even seem
to know you exist."

"Except for one," he said. "And who knows how
many others Puabi has told about me by now? No, Nidaba, my peaceful little life has ended." He sat up in the
bed, began slowly to put his clothes back on.

Nidaba shook her head, sitting up as well, and the
breeze caught her hair, mussing it more than Natum had
done. "I know the way that woman thinks," she told him.
"She hasn't told any others. She wouldn't. She always
wanted you all to herself—even now that she apparently
wants you dead."

He lifted a brow. He'd pulled on his jeans, but nothing
else, and he propped his shoulder against the window as
he watched her with interest.

"Chances are, once we rid ourselves of her forever—
you'll be able to continue on with your life just the way
you have been," she said, sitting up in the bed, allowing
the sheet to fall to her waist.

Even now, he wanted her. "And what about you?" he
asked, his gaze taking full advantage of her nakedness.

She shook her head, got to her feet, wrapping the

sheet around her sarong-style, and moved until she was beside him at the window. Turning her face into the wind, she gazed out at the whitecaps dancing on the sea. "My notoriety now is almost as widespread as it was in Lagash," she said.

"A legend yet again?"

"Among the dark ones, yes. Although it's not the kind of fame one would wish for."

"They hunt you." He caressed her jaw with a fingertip. "What has it been like for you, Nidaba?"

"Not so bad."

"No. Tell me the truth now. There's no more reason for lies between us. Not after all this." He reached for her nightgown, hanging over the chair's back, and she stood still while he pulled her sheet away, and gently dressed her in it. Then he put his own shirt back on. "Let's walk outside. You can talk to me."

Nidaba let him pull her with him into the hall, down the stairs, right at the bottom, rather than left into the living room. He took her through the library and out through the French doors onto the veranda.

She noticed the walkway, lined on both sides with late blooming flowers, that led around the house. "What's back there?"

He followed her gaze. "More flower beds, garden plots, and the stairs up to the roof." The dog got up and trotted happily at their side. "But you're changing the subject. I asked what it's been like for you."

"What is it you want to know?" She pretended great interest in the cobblestone lined flower beds that surrounded his great old house above the sea.

"You . . . said once that you had been held captive. And that woman, your—our—daughter-in-law . . . she seemed concerned about your mental state."

She shrugged as if none of it mattered. "What's on the roof?" she asked.

"Pigeons. Sheila keeps—kept—them up there. Listen, you can probably hear them."

Nidaba remembered George mentioning that there were pigeons on the roof, and she could indeed hear their gentle cooing sounds if she listened closely. "It's not natural to keep them caged. That doesn't seem like something Sheila would do."

"You're right about that. They were never caged, not really," he explained. "Sheila always left the pens open by day. They just always come back at night."

Frowning, Nidaba tilted her head to one side. "I guess they're like you. They don't mind living in captivity. Even . . . like it."

"I don't live in captivity," he insisted. He sat down on the stone wall that encircled the veranda. "What makes it seem that way to you?"

She shrugged again, and pacing to the veranda's edge, stood there with the sea wind whipping her nightgown around her legs, and blowing her hair behind her like a flag. "You aren't free to be what you are. You keep it secret, afraid to let it show. You pretend to be just another mortal. You live like one. It seems like captivity to me."

"And you . . . how do you live?"

Tipping her face up to the kiss of the wind, she closed her eyes. "Wild. Free. I travel the world. I amass fortunes and spend them at will. I *live*. I relish it." Taking a deep breath, she continued. "A long time ago, there was a man by the name of Nathanial Dearborne. He was a Dark High Witch and something of a scientist. He made a habit of taking Light Ones alive when he could and keeping them captive. Killing them in one way or another, and then watching them revive. Studying which manner of death would last longer. He even began taking their hearts . . . and then returning them to see if they would revivify."

Natum's next breath came from very close, and warmth rushed over her nape. His hands curled around her shoulders as he stood behind her. "I had heard such a thing was possible, but I never believed it."

"Believe it. It's true. I suppose that in a way I owe Dearborne a debt of gratitude. His experiments, the notes he left in his journals—they were what enabled Arianna to restore life to our son after his heart was taken." She turned and looked at Natum's startled eyes. "He laid in a grave for three hundred years. She found his heart, returned it to him, brought him back. So perhaps the torture was . . . in some twisted way . . . worth bearing."

"You were one of this Dearborne's captives?" His face seemed to pale.

She nodded. "You said you wanted to know."

"By the Gods . . ."

"Don't. It's in the past. Over. Dearborne is long dead. Nicodimus has been restored. And I . . . well, I learned how very much I value my freedom, and my life." She swallowed a lump in her throat. "Immortality is a gift, Eannatum. Why would anyone wish to ignore it—to live as if they were just like everyone else?"

"They hunt you," he said flatly. "You're forced to kill or be killed, over and over again. I lived like that, Nidaba, and I hated it."

She lowered her head. "Freedom comes with risk." She glanced up toward the roof. "I guess for some the security of domestication is worth the sacrifice." Then she stared out at the sea, spotted a gull swooping and diving. "And for others, freedom is far more important. I'd rather fight and die free, Natum, than live forever in a cage."

He looked back at his house. "This is hardly a cage."

"Yes, it is. No matter how gilded, it still has its bars."

He nodded. "We've grown very different in all this time, haven't we, Nidaba?"

"More than I ever would have guessed," she said. And she understood now why he couldn't love her anymore. He wouldn't give up the kingdom he'd built to run away with her now any more than he had been able to that night in the desert so long ago. And if he brought her into it with him—assuming that she could bring herself to live that way—she would bring battle, strife, chaos with her. And his kingdom would fall. Crumble into the sea.

It was impossible, then, wasn't it?

She met his eyes, and saw that he knew it too. And a new despair settled over her. "I used to think that a person could only live so long and remain sane. That eventually the body of an immortal would outlive the mind."

"And why did you think that?"

She shrugged. "I suppose I saw my own mind as the best example. I went a bit insane after I lost my son for the second time, in the sixteenth century when a Dark Witch took his heart. But I survived. Eventually I returned to myself. I sought vengeance on the Dark Witch who had murdered my son, but it was I who was trapped, captured, tortured. I only escaped three years ago—both my mind, and my body were broken for a long time."

"But again, you recovered." He stroked her hair, fingertips gentle on her temples. "Perhaps the mind of an immortal heals itself just the way the body does."

"Perhaps. I recovered slowly, and only when I found my son again."

"Loss . . . has a profound effect on us, Nidaba."

Then how, she wondered, was she going to bear losing her Eannatum when this was over?

"This is a pointless discussion."

"No. I needed to know these things," he said softly.

"I can't imagine why. They have no relevance to the threat facing us now."

"Everything about you has relevance for me, Nidaba." He paused. "What happened on that hotel rooftop?"

She stared into his eyes, so filled with concern, for her. "It wasn't another bout with insanity, if that's what you've been thinking. No. It was far simpler, Natum. A simple attack by one of the Dark Ones. Something that has become routine in my life, I'm afraid. However this Dark Witch had hedged her bets. When it looked as if I would defeat her in a fair fight, she pulled a weapon—a gun. I had to either let her shoot me and carve out my heart while I waited to revive—or jump and hope to revive before the ambulance arrived. I happen to think I made the sane decision." She pursed her lips in thought. "Though had I known what would follow, I think I'd have taken my chances with the gun."

"Gods, when I think what you've been through . . ." He leaned closer, kissed her cheek. "You're getting cold. We should go back inside." One arm around her, he urged her through the French doors.

She shivered, realizing only now how chilled she was, and started toward the living room, moving ahead of him. She was eager for the warmth of the fire. Natum followed her, then headed back into the library. "I'll be out in a moment," he called.

Nidaba kept walking, rubbing her chilled arms and thinking about how differently they saw things now. She touched the long, thin nightgown she wore, and it reminded her vaguely of the sacred white gown she used to wear in the temple. She wasn't wearing anything else, except, of course for the dagger at her thigh.

It hurt, very deeply, to know that he felt only desire for her. That the love he had professed of old had not been as immortal as they both were. But he had made love to her as if nothing had changed. And for now she would have to be content simply to pretend. It was painfully obvious they could never go back to the way things had once been.

Nidaba stopped short when she stepped into the living room and saw the dagger that pinned a scrap of parchment to the wall beside the mantel like a butterfly's wing.

"Eannatum!" she cried.

He appeared a moment later, a blanket in his hands, which he draped over her shoulders. "Right here," he said. "I just wanted to grab this throw out of the library for you to . . . Nidaba? What's wrong?"

Lifting a finger, she pointed.

Natum followed her gaze. She heard the hiss of his dagger sliding free of its sheath. "Stay close to me," he whispered, moving around her, clasping her hand behind him.

Nidaba drew her own dagger, its golden hilt cool in her palm. Slowly they moved across the room, looking all around them, listening, every sense alert. Even the dog looked uneasy as she lifted her head and looked around.

Natum reached up, yanked the note from the dagger's blade, leaving the blade where it was. And then he read it aloud.

"A trade," he read. "George for your son."

18

"How could she know? How?" Nidaba sank into a chair, the blanket around her shoulders, her head in her hands. The skin around her eyes was already stinging from the drying salt of so many tears. But she was angry now. Frightened for George and furious for his suffering, and for Sheila. But this was more. This was her son.

Natum's face was cold and grim. "She . . . must have overheard us talking when you told me he was still alive, that you knew where he was," he said. "I just don't understand how. There was no one here, but us, and the dog and—wait a minute. Wait a minute, that's it! The dog."

Nidaba shook her head even as Natum started looking for the dog. "No, it's not her, Natum. I've touched her. I would have known."

"Wait, here she comes," he warned. "Come on, Queenie. Here, girl."

The big Rottweiler trotted up to him, and when he reached out to stroke her head, she turned it and licked his hand. No sparks. Damn.

The dog went to the door then and scratched it with a forepaw.

Absently, Natum opened it and let her out. "I was so sure."

"She can't take my son from me again, Natum. I won't allow it."

"Of course you won't. Nor will I!"

"But George—she has George," Nidaba muttered.

Natum stopped pacing, looked slowly from the note to Nidaba. "What if she doesn't?"

"What do you mean? Her note says—"

"Never mind what her note says. She's evil, Nidaba, she'd certainly have no compunction about lying to get what she wants. All we have is her word that she has George."

"And Sheila's," Nidaba reminded him.

"No. No, Sheila said, 'She went after George.'" He turned to the windows, pushing the curtains back, staring out into the ever thickening darkness. The storm was rolling closer now. The thunder was closer, louder, and Nidaba could feel the static in the air.

"What if George saw her attack Sheila and ran away?" Natum said.

Nidaba sat up straighter in her chair. "Then Puabi would have gone after him."

"She'd never have found him. Not if he made it to the woods before she caught up."

Sighing softly, Nidaba got to her feet. She went to where he stood and put a hand on his shoulder. The familiar tingling jolted through her hand at the contact, then faded to warmth. "Natum, I know you love him, and you want to believe he's all right. But Puabi is a High Witch over four thousand years old. George is just a simple mortal. Besides, we searched the woods. There was no sign of him anywhere."

He nodded slowly. "I know. George loves those woods. He used to vanish for days at a time. And damned if I know where he hid, but wherever it was, he got there by way of the woods." He let the curtain fall, turned to face her. "I used to search—hell, the neighbors and the volunteer fire department even got involved one summer. We turned those woods inside out. But we never found him. He showed up safe and sound when he was ready. I got so worried I had to ask him not to go out there anymore. And when he saw how upset I was, he promised he wouldn't."

Nidaba blinked. "Do you really think there is a chance George could be so well hidden that even Puabi cannot find him?"

"I think there's a chance, yes." He closed his eyes. "Gods, please let there be a chance," he whispered, and she knew it was a prayer, heartfelt and potent.

"I don't think we should count on it, Natum."

Drawing a long breath, he expelled it quickly. "Maybe . . . it's time we call Nicodimus."

Nidaba's head came up sharply. "What do you mean?"

"We have the name of the hotel, the number. The woman, Arianna, left it with me. We should let our son know what's going on."

"Why?" Her brows bent deeply as she searched Natum's face in horror. "He would only come rushing out here to help us, Natum!"

"Which would force Puabi to show herself."

"You want to use my son as *bait*?" Nidaba's eyes narrowed on him, and she looked more closely. At his skin, its texture, his eyes, their color.

He held up a hand. "Just hear me out. You said yourself Nicodimus is a powerful immortal. A strong warrior. We'd never let him out of our sight, Nidaba, and when

Puabi came for him, she would have all three of us to contend with."

She shook her head in disbelief. "You would risk him that way? Your own son?" She backed a few steps away from him.

Natum frowned. "No. No, Nidaba, you're misunderstanding me. There would be no *risk* to it. Puabi would have to go through me to harm him, and that's not going to happen." He took a step toward Nidaba.

She took a step back.

Natum stared at her, his eyes widening. "Nidaba, don't look at me that way. If Nicodimus is half the man I think he is—I know he is—then he would want to make this decision for himself. He would want to be here to help me protect you from Puabi."

"My son died protecting me once. It will not happen again. And if you can even suggest what you just have, then you are not worthy of calling yourself his father."

The dog came wandering in from the kitchen then, halted halfway across the room, stared at Natum, and suddenly began to growl deep in her throat.

Nidaba shot a panicked look at the animal, then back at Eannatum again. "Oh Gods, no," she murmured.

He held up a hand. "No, Nidaba. Don't . . . don't think what you're thinking. It's not—"

"Stay away!" She took a step backward for every one he took forward and yanked her dagger from her thigh, holding it up between them.

"Don't do this, Nidaba."

"The dog knows you're not Eannatum," she whispered. Her breaths came faster, shorter. She told herself to lunge at him, to drive her blade into his chest, but for the life of her she couldn't do it. Even though she knew he must be Puabi. Otherwise, why would the dog behave that way? Growling at him, hairs bristling. He'd been

out of her sight when he got the blanket for her from
the library. Only for a moment, but still . . .

He just kept shaking his head, staring at her and shaking his head. "It's me, Nidaba. I only want to keep you
alive, protect you. I only want . . ." Then he reached out
for her, and in her panic she jabbed her dagger at him.
He swung one powerful arm, delivering a blow that sent
the dagger flying out of her hand. Left with no other
choice, Nidaba turned and ran from the house. And even
as she lunged into the night, and fled at top speed, he
gave chase.

"Stop! Dammit, Nidaba, wait!"

Thunder clapped loudy, and Nidaba turned to look
behind her as she raced around the house. She saw the
dog launch itself at Natum—or at the person who *looked*
like Natum—and send him face first to the ground. His
head connected with a rock. She saw blood, and he went
still, not moving again. Good. Then the dog raced onward, as afraid, Nidaba thought, as she was.

What the hell had that bitch done with the real Eannatum?

He couldn't be in the house. He'd have cried out. And
now that the stormclouds had rolled in, it was too dark
to see outside as well as she would have liked. Still, her
night vision was far better than that of a mortal. Dammit,
the storm was going to break any moment. Again thunder clapped, and this time the wind whipped with it.

She rounded the corner to the rear of the house and
saw the stairway there, hugging the back wall, angling
sharply upward to the flat roof. The dog raced ahead,
pausing on the bottom step. Even as the wind whipped
harder and the first few fat raindrops smacked her in the
face, Nidaba nodded. "Yes, the roof. I can see all around
from up there."

Mounting the steps, she started up them. The wind

whipped her hair, and her white gown snapped around her ankles. Bowing into it, she gripped the slender rail and made her way to the top, the dog right behind her.

Finally, she reached the flat, tar-coated rooftop and looked around in the darkness. The moon was blotted out now by dark clouds, and the sea in the distance roiled with whitecaps and froth. The wind was treacherous up so high, and getting worse by the minute. She staggered forward against it, squinting in the darkness to see the large square structure in the center. Cooing and scratching sounds told her what this was. The pigeons. Sheila's precious pigeons.

Lightning flashed, illuminating the night, and two things became visible, and invisible again, in that one blinding moment. The form of a large man, curled up, shivering and lying on his side next to the giant coop, and the body of the huge Rottweiler lying close beside him.

"George?" Nidaba cried out, and she started to move forward, but stopped in her tracks when the deep-throated growl came from behind her.

"Nidaba? Is that you?" George asked in a frightened voice.

Going utterly still, she swallowed hard and her mind raced. *But the dog was in front of me, lying beside George . . . so how is it behind me, snarling at me? Oh, Gods—two dogs. Two dogs. One, George's best friend . . . and the other . . .*

The beast behind her growled more loudly. Nidaba turned to face it, and she saw its eyes come alive, glowing with an unnatural yellow light.

"I always said you were a bitch, Puabi," Nidaba said. "But I didn't expect it to be literally true." Her hand touched the sheath at her thigh, but the blade was not in it, and her heart sank as she recalled that Natum had

knocked it out of her hand. Natum—lying down there
with his head split open, bleeding. The sky burst open
with an explosion of thunder. Icy rain fell in sheets as
the beast crouched and attacked. Teeth tore through
flesh, giant paws knocked her flat. George cried out, and
she heard the other dog—the real dog—snarling. The
dog-Puabi leapt onto her chest, and even as she clasped
its big head to hold the beast off, she knew she couldn't
win.

When the powerful jaws locked on her throat, and the
incisors ripped into her jugular, Nidaba knew it was
over.

But even as her blood pulsed out of her, and her life
force weakened, the lightning flashed. The killer beast
rose away from her. She saw the other dog, the real dog,
lunge at it, only to stop short and cower in fear. The
beast was changing, morphing, right before Nidaba's
eyes. And the shape it took this time was her own. A
Nidaba look-alike, white gown intact, throat unmarred,
Puabi knelt over her. And she lifted a blade, held it
poised above Nidaba's chest.

"Know before you die that I will take Natum and your
son next. Know it. Feel that pain. I want you to suffer
the way I have."

And then there was a deep menacing growl. Nidaba
turned her head weakly, and saw George's dog flying
forward, having overcome her fear in order to protect
Nidaba. Queenie's powerful paws hit Puabi squarely in
the chest, and the Dark Witch sailed right over the edge
of the roof.

Squinting through her fading vision, Nidaba turned
her head toward the place where George crouched with
his knees to his chest, rocking in abject terror. She tried
to call out to him, but her throat had been too torn apart
to allow speech.

The dog—the real dog—leaned over her, licking her face, as death swept her into its cold prison once more. She could only pray that the healing would take place in time to save Natum. And then there was darkness.

"Nathan? Oh, Nathan, are you all right?"

Nidaba had not once called him by his modern alias. Until now.

Nathan blinked the dizziness away, tried to shake off the pounding in his head, and managed to sit up. Nidaba leaned over him, cradling his head, speaking in an unnaturally hoarse voice.

"That dog—that damned dog—" Nathan began.

"It was no dog, Nathan. It was Puabi," Nidaba whispered, her voice far too soft. "I'm so sorry I doubted you, my love." She rubbed her throat and Nathan saw bruises there in the shape of hands.

"Are you all right?" he asked her. "What happened to you?"

"She attacked me. Choked me, and my vocal cords are slow in repairing themselves. But . . . it's all right, Nathan. I—I killed her. She's dead."

Nathan sighed and closed his eyes. Reaching out, he wrapped his arms around Nidaba, held her tight. "Thank the Gods. It's over. Finally, over. God, if only we could find George."

She nodded, sniffling and snuggling her head into the crook of his shoulder. "Well . . . for that we can get some more help. If . . . if you're up to it, Nathan, I think it's about time we made that call. You've waited far too long already . . . to meet your son. Don't you think?"

He brushed her hair away from her face, smiling at her. "Yes. Yes, I have. Go ahead, and call him, Nidaba. The number is in the drawer of that small table beside the fireplace," he told her softly. She looked toward the

house. "Go ahead," he told her. "I'll be along in a minute. My head is already on the mend." He lifted a hand
to rub at the spot on his skull and sent her a sheepish
grin. She returned the smile, and ran into the house to
search for the phone number.

Nathan managed to get to his feet, though his head
throbbed and dizziness swamped him. He drew his dagger and steeled himself against the gut-churning fear. He
didn't know where the hell Nidaba was . . . what the
bitch had done to her, or to George, but he knew one
thing without a doubt. *That* hadn't been Nidaba. Nidaba
had not once called him Nathan. And her touch had
never been cold, her voice soft, her demeanor hesitant.

He made his way to the front door, his dagger behind
his back. He walked quietly inside, step by step, closer
and closer to the woman who leaned over the small table
rummaging through the drawer. He brought the dagger
around, lifting it above his head.

Behind him someone screamed.

He whirled in time to see the blond woman, Arianna,
in the doorway, pointing at him and yelling, "I *knew* it!
I *knew* he was lying!"

And then a handsome, powerfully built man, with rus-
set hair and midnight eyes surged past her, landed a
blow that slammed Eannatum into the wall. His already
injured head cracked against the plaster, and exploded
in new pain.

"Nidaba! Gods, are you all right?" Arianna Sinclair-
Lachlan asked, rushing forward to spin the impostor
around and embrace her.

Eannatum fought to stay conscious, to keep from sliding to the floor, as the man strode up to him, gripped
the front of his shirt, and held him upright.

"Are you Nicodimus?" he managed to ask, before the
man could pummel him again.

The man nodded once and bared his teeth. "Yes, I am. And might I ask who the hell you are, before I put you into the ground for good?"

Nathan nodded weakly. Blood was running from his nose, and this man knew by now that he was an immortal from the shock at contact. Probably didn't know if Eannatum was Dark or Light, and even more probably didn't care.

"I'm Eannatum," he said. "I'm your father."

Nidaba dragged in her next breath, her *first* breath, the breath of life itself. It jolted through her, arching her back and filling her lungs to near bursting with storm laden air and rainwater. Someone leaned over her, patting her face.

She opened her eyes.

"George. Oh, George, you're really okay!"

"So are you," he said. Beside him his dog wagged her tail, and for a moment she went stiff with fear as memory surged.

The roof.

The pigeons.

Eannatum . . . the dog . . .

"Natum . . ." Her voice was raspy. She wondered why. And then she knew, even as she struggled to sit up, to stand. Still weak, not yet healed, she staggered to the edge of the rooftop, looked down over. The car in the driveway hadn't been there before. But it was a familiar model.

"Nicodimus! Oh, Gods, he's here."

Her hands went to her throat, and she felt the gaping wound. At least it was no longer bleeding as it slowly healed itself. But the damage within still made every breath a tortured wheeze. It hurt to breathe. Hurt more to call out. Yet she tried all the same. But the sound that resulted was barely as loud as the contented chuckling of the pigeons.

"It's okay, Nidaba. Come on, I'll help you down."

George pulled one of her arms around his shoulder and held her as she made her way toward the stairs. Stumbling, she fell to her knees once, but he pulled her right back up. He was not, she realized, in much better shape than she was—he was dripping wet, freezing, probably suffering from exposure, as well. He was cut and bruised and scared to death. "What happened after you and Sheila left here, George?" she asked as he slowly helped her down the stairs.

"The bad lady . . . she must have followed us. She ran us off the road and made us get into her car and come right back here. We never even got to go to the beach like Sheila said we could. And then . . . oh, it was bad. It was so bad, Nidaba. That lady, she said she was gonna take us into the house, so you and Nathan would know she meant business, and Sheila, she tried to get away."

"And Puabi killed her," Nidaba said. They had paused in the middle of the stairway.

"No. Sheila tripped, and she hit her head." His face contorted. "And then she just didn't get up anymore. Did she . . . did she . . . die?"

Nidaba pressed a hand to his cheek. "I'm so sorry, George. She did. She went to be with Lisette."

"I wanted her to stay with us," he said.

Beside him the dog whined softly, as if she too were mourning Sheila's death.

"I was scared," George said. "So I ran. I went and hid in the woods, and then I sneaked back here. Because I knew Sheila wouldn't be able to take care of her pigeons."

"So you came to take care of them for her."

He nodded and went back to helping her down the

stairs. "Then I was too scared to come down. But I thought the bad lady would never find me on the roof."

They finally reached the ground, and the doorway. She peered inside, and saw someone holding Natum against the wall by his shirt and pounding on his face. "George, the bad lady's in there, and she has made herself look just like me. You stay away from her."

"How will I know which one of you is which?"

"Code word," she told him. "I'll know our secret code word."

"What is our code word?" he asked, wide-eyed.

"Sheila. It's Sheila."

He smiled, nodded, and Nidaba threw open the door and rushed inside, pouring every bit of strength she had left into her attack. She reached out, grabbed Nicodimus by the back of his shirt, and yanked him off Eannatum with so much force that he lost his balance and fell on his backside. She looked down at her son and said, "Hello, Nicky. I see you've met your father."

He stared up at her in shock, then turned his head to look across the room. When she followed his gaze, she saw the impostor, looking just like her, with her arms around Arianna.

19

Nidaba stared at Nicodimus. Then at Natum, who was fighting to remain conscious as blood ran from his nose and split lip. He'd sunk to the floor, where he kept blinking, shaking his head.

But there was no time to help either of them, because Puabi was already in motion.

"Arianna, look out!" Nidaba shouted, but it was too late. Even as Arianna sent a confused look her way, the false Nidaba swung her clasped fists as one, clubbing Arianna on the head so hard she went down at once.

"What the hell!" Nicodimus leapt to his feet and lunged toward her, but Puabi was faster. She snatched up a paperweight and hurled it at him with deadly precision, and then he was on the floor too.

And it was down to the two of them. Nidaba and Puabi. Nidaba focused, knowing she could not match this woman alone, in her weakened state. She was still not fully recovered from Puabi's most recent attack. She needed help. And as a High Priestess of the Goddess, she knew where to get it. Nidaba focused her energy, drawing it up from the earth below and down from the sky above. Feeling the power pulsing in her body, she mentally contained it, directed it, forced it upward, to her eyes, and to the spot above them in the center of her forehead. "First sight, second sight, third eye, never lie."

She opened her eyes, and saw the vision, the glamour, begin to ripple. Like heat waves shimmering over the false face Puabi wore.

"You'll never make it work, Nidaba. I'm far more powerful than you will ever be," Puabi taunted.

"It's my face, you foolish sow," Nidaba whispered. "You might have been able to sustain any other form but this one. I know myself too well not to see the truth beyond the glamour."

"Then why are you still squinting so hard?"

Beyond the ripple, Puabi's hand swam higher, lifting a dagger. Nidaba was still unarmed. Her own dagger lay on the floor ten feet to her left. She took a step toward it, but Puabi moved into her path.

Nidaba eyed the woman coolly. "You cannot hope to defeat me, Puabi. Dagger or no. I am a High Priestess of Inanna!"

"Your Goddess turned her back on you long ago, when you betrayed her by falling in love with her chosen king, Nidaba. And you know that as well as I."

For a moment Nidaba's will weakened. And Puabi's glamour solidified again before her eyes. But then she glanced sideways at Eannatum, and his eyes met hers, though they were slitted with pain and he was barely conscious. She saw the love in his eyes, and she knew. She finally understood what he had been trying to tell her before. Her Goddess had never abandoned her. And neither had her Natum. Nidaba, had never done anything wrong. She and Eannatum were simply meant to be.

Nidaba lifted her hands and her head, closed her eyes,

trusting utterly. She heard Puabi rushing forward and yet she didn't move. She only chanted the sacred words she'd learned at Lia's feet so many years ago. *Inanna me en, Inanna me en, Inanna me en!* I am of Inanna, I am of the Goddess, and she is of me. We are one, and you cannot stand against us."

The blade came down. Nidaba heard it slicing the air close to her body. Calmly, guided by a force beyond her, she brought her hands down, palms outward, and opened her eyes to see the blade stop in mid-air. As if it had hit a brick wall. She saw Puabi as she truly was. Small, slight. Short dark hair framing her pixie-like face. Her round lapis blue eyes gleamed with hatred as she tried to force her blade to move, and looked stunned and confused when it wouldn't. Her fisted hand gripped the dagger more tightly, and her face contorted as she drew back and swung the blade again. But it was blocked by an invisible shield.

"Be gone!" Nidaba commanded, guided by a force that was beyond her. A bolt of pure energy burst from her palms, slamming into Puabi. She flew backward, airborne, her blade sailing harmlessly across the room. Her body crashed into the wall and she slid to the floor. But she scrambled to her feet almost immediately. Nidaba was so stunned by the power she had just channeled, that she was not ready for the second attack. She stood looking in awe at her hands, half expecting to see burn marks in her palms from the searing force that had burst from them.

Puabi bent low and charged, driving into Nidaba headfirst like a rampaging bull. The two rolled in a tangle of arms and hands and clothes. Furniture crashed to the floor, knickknacks shattered. Queenie raced around them, barking and growling.

They pounded, kicked, clawed, beat one another, until

finally, Nidaba landed a roundhouse blow that sent Puabi reeling. In the split second before she attacked again, Nidaba scrambled to grab a dagger from the floor, and sprang to her feet again, crouched and ready. She glanced down at the weapon in her hand. Puabi's jewel encrusted dagger.

Puabi, too, had used the opportunity to arm herself. She squared off, facing Nidaba, and in her hand, she held the gold-handled dagger that Eannatum had given to Nidaba.

The two faced each other, panting, breathless, daggers at the ready. A flash of movement caught Nidaba's eye, and she glimpsed Nicodimus, Arianna, and Eannatum standing together, staring at them. George cowered in a corner, apparently too afraid to watch. Nidaba realized that to their eyes, she and Puabi still looked exactly the same.

"My Goddess, what's going on here?" Arianna asked. She drew her dagger, eyeing the two women who circled each other amid the rubble of the room.

"Her name is Puabi," Eannatum explained slowly. "She was responsible for your first death, Nicodimus, some four thousand years ago. And she's come back now to try to kill you again."

"I can't imagine why she would want to," Nicodimus murmured, his gaze darting from one of the women to the other. "I don't even know her."

"Mostly, she just wants to hurt your mother," Natum told him grimly. "But she's also a Dark High Witch, so I suppose your heart would be an added bonus."

"So which one is she?" Arianna asked, looking from one woman to the other in bewilderment.

Eannatum frowned, his eyes sliding to the Nidaba on the left, as she sent him a pleading look, brimming with

love, begging him to recognize her. He then turned to
look at the Nidaba on the right. Her eyes met his only
briefly, and if looks could kill, he figured he would be
breathing his last about now.

Eannatum nodded toward her with a slight smile.
"That one's your mother. She's mad as hell because she
thinks I don't know which is which."

"Be gone," Nidaba said in an intense, resonant tone
that filled the entire room with an unnatural reverbera-
tion. She held her palm out toward her enemy, her dagger clasped in her other hand. "Be gone, Puabi."

Puabi shrieked and drove forward with her blade, but
again, it hit that unseen resistance. Eannatum blinked
and looked again, because for a moment it seemed there
was another woman in the room, larger than life, her
form like an aura around and above Nidaba's. Her eyes
were like winking bits of lapis, and the rest of her as
faint as a breeze. Her hand seemed to meld with Nidaba's as she held it out, palm facing her attacker.

There was a blinding flash of light that seemed to
emanate from Nidaba's palm, and Puabi flew backward
as if hit by a wrecking ball. Her blade flew from her
hand, and landed in the fireplace, burying itself amid the
coals. Puabi slammed into the wall with such force the
plaster crumbled as she sank into a broken heap on the
floor.

As her hold on the spell weakened, the glamour faltered, and Nathan saw Puabi for the first time in well
over four thousand years. Ever young, beautiful, selfish
and utterly ruthless.

Her dazed eyes met his for an instant. "I only wanted
your love," she whispered. "That's all . . . that's all . . ."
And then those vivid blue eyes fell closed.

Nathan turned away from her and sought Nidaba. She
was standing on the other side of the room, her body

nearly limp with exhaustion, bruised and bleeding. He rushed to her, caught her up in his arms, and held her tenderly against him when it seemed she could barely stand on her own.

"You were right," she muttered. "About the dog. There were two—part of the time, at least. George was on the roof, and I went up there. One dog attacked me . . . and the other . . . she saved me."

She sagged against him, stunned, he thought, at the events that had just transpired. Finally, though, she steeled herself, stood straighter, and looked up at him. "Tell me you knew which was really me?"

"I knew, Nidaba. From the very start. If you doubt me, you can ask your . . . our son." He offered a small smile, which died at Arianna's cry.

"Nicodimus!"

Nathan turned and for an endless moment, could only watch in horror. Puabi had roused unnoticed, and retrieved her blade from the coals of the hearth, where it had landed. Its blade glowed red-hot as she rose slowly, drew back her arm, and flung it at Nicodimus. It seemed to happen in slow motion, and yet too suddenly to prevent. Nic, hearing Arianna's cry, turned as the fire red blade whirled end over end toward him, and Nathan knew it would set his son's heart aflame if it pierced his chest—destroying him utterly.

Reaching out for his son, Nathan shoved Nicodimus away, stepping right into the path of that blade to do so.

It sank deeply into Nathan's chest, burning, searing him. He dropped to his knees as a cry of undiluted agony burst from his lungs. Flames leapt from the fabric of his shirt, from his skin. From inside him! Puabi's eyes widened. "No! No, not you, Eannatum! Not you!"

Arianna backhanded the woman, and her head connected with the hearthstone. Then she slumped into silence.

Nidaba jerked the knife from Nathan's chest, and tossed it aside. It hit the floor near the window, still glowing red. Ignoring it, Nidaba pressed her hands to the blazing wound, but the flames kept coming. And then a large, hulking form lifted Nathan away from her. She looked up. "George! No, George, you mustn't— George, wait!"

But George was hearing none of it. It looked bad, Nathan thought, as he clung to consciousness despite the screaming pain in his chest. His skin blistered and bubbled and he could smell the stench of his own burning flesh. George was scratched, bruised, his clothing torn, and soaked through. And he was limping even more badly than usual. But he shrugged off all the hands trying to hold him back, and loped toward the open door, and through it.

Nathan heard the others rushing out right behind them. George stood in the pouring rain, and lifted Nathan in his arms like an offering to the heavens, as the deluge came down.

Blessedly cool rainwater pummeled him, soothing the burning in his chest. Cooling the pain. Nathan opened his mouth to cry out in mingled anguish and relief. And the tongues of flame on his body hissed out their final breaths, and died. Nathan closed his eyes, certain he was about to do the same.

Nidaba raced forward, gasping at the sight of the thin spirals of smoke rising from her beloved Eannatum's chest. She stared aghast at his scorched shirt, the blistered skin and gaping wound with its blackened edges.

"Put him down, George. Right here in the rain."

"Did I . . . did I help him?" the big man asked, dropping to his knees to lay Natum down on the wet grass. He leaned over his friend, his face contorted with worry. Beside him the dog, Queenie, looked nearly as worried as George did.

"Yes. You helped him more than any of us could," Nidaba said. She knelt on Natum's other side and framed his face with her hands. "Live, Eannatum," she whispered. "Live. Damn you, you must. Do you hear me?"

"Nidaba . . . Mother . . . ?" Nicodimus knelt beside her, encircled her shoulders with his arm. "He saved my life."

"He only wanted a chance to know you. He's your father, Nicodimus. Or he was . . . in the lifetime before."

"I know. He . . . he told me."

"Live, Natum. Please, please, live. I can't bear this to be the end, do you understand me? I can't."

She pressed her hands to his chest, wishing with everything in her that she would feel his heart beating strong and steady. There was silence, utter stillness, but Nidaba then felt something else. That sensation of another person embracing her. Another hand, surrounding hers. Another force moving though her.

Her hand grew hot, and a soft white light came from her palm, suffusing the entire area of Nathan's wound in its glow. The heat intensified, grew, nearly scorched her, but she didn't move. She just let it happen.

And then the light faded, and her palm cooled . . . and she felt the beating of Natum's heart against her hand.

"Oh, my Goddess," she whispered as tears streamed down her face.

Exactly. The word echoed in her mind.

Eannatum's eyes opened. He stared up at her, lifted a hand, curled it around her nape and drew her face down to his. He kissed her, gently, softly.

"Oh, no, the house!" Arianna cried.

They all turned to look. The living room was fully engulfed in flames, and the fire was spreading rapidly, licking its way toward the roof.

"Puabi?" Natum asked.

"She was still inside." Nidaba spoke the words with a hint of regret, even though she knew Puabi probably deserved no sympathy, given all the harm she had done in her lifetime. She also knew that she and Eannatum were partly to blame for what the woman had ultimately become.

Natum closed his eyes, bowed his head. "I wish . . ."

"I know," Nidaba said softly. "I know." Drawing a breath, she looked up at her son. "Nicky, we need to get some help. The fire department. This is Natum's home, he loves this place. We have to—"

"No." Eannatum sat up slowly and reached up for a hand. Nicodimus closed his hand around his father's and helped him to his feet. For a moment, the two remained that way, standing there, face-to-face, hands clasped. Natum looked into Nicodimus's eyes, and his became moist. "Good to meet you . . . Nicodimus. At long last. You make a hell of a first impression, you know." As he said it, he rubbed his nose, which was already healing.

"So do you," Nicodimus said with a grin. "Saving my life, I mean."

"Natum . . . your house!" Nidaba tugged him around to face her, trying to get him to pay attention to his home. But he only looked at George, and smiled broadly.

"You okay, my friend?"

"I'll be okay, Nathan. I'm just glad I left the pigeon coop open." He looked up and pointed. The pigeons were already fleeing into the night, vanishing instantly, swallowed up by the darkness.

Natum turned to Nidaba. "We need to talk."

"But Natum, your house!"

He glanced toward Nicodimus. His son gave him a nod. "Hey, George, what do you say you come with Arianna and me? We'll fix up your scratches, get you something to eat, some dry clothes, okay?"

George looked down at the Rottweiler by his side. "Can Queenie come with us, too?"

"Sure."

"Just a minute," Nidaba said, and she moved forward, put a hand on the dog's head. No tingling jolt rushed through her. She nodded, satisfied this one was the real dog, and gave her a loving scratch between the ears. Then she nodded her assent. "It's okay. She's the real Queenie, not the impostor."

The imposter . . .

Nidaba glanced toward the flames and felt a heavy sadness for Puabi, in spite of herself. They'd had a lot in common, the two of them. Both willing to fight and die for the love of one man.

Natum gave George a nod and George walked with Nicodimus and Arianna toward the car the two had arrived in. Queenie ran along beside him. Nic called back, "There's an inn nearby. The Hampton. You know it?"

Natum nodded. "We'll be along. Later."

"Natum?" Nidaba whispered.

"I know, I know. My house. Come on, love. We still have not finished our conversation. I had no idea I had so much more to say to you, but I find that I do. Besides, we have a proper farewell to say. To Sheila."

"But the house . . ."

"Let the damned house burn. I don't need it anymore. What I need, Nidaba—*all* I need—is for you to come with me. Let me say what I need to say to you before you walk away from me again. I'm not going to let you go this time until you've heard everything I have to tell you. Everything I'm thinking and feeling. And until you've told me everything you are thinking and feeling in return. You understand?"

She nodded, looking into his eyes, and seeing a familiar gleam there. He radiated a familiar power. He was himself again, she thought. At last. She had located her long missing king.

As the dawn broke over the waves, Eannatum and Nidaba sat in the small boat, staring down at the still water. It was the same spot where they'd lowered Sheila's body, and while the currents had long since carried her away, they returned to this spot to honor her. Nidaba had chanted long prayers in Sumerian, and Eannatum had joined her. There hadn't been time before for more than a hurried farewell. So now they said their goodbyes, wished her soul well on its journey, shed their tears. Looking back at the shore, all Eannatum saw was a pile of smoldering wreckage, charred beams, refuse where his house, his haven, his make-believe world, had once stood.

"You were right, you know," he said very softly.

"Was I?"

He nodded. "I've been living a lie, Nidaba. I'm not an ordinary man. I'm not a quiet antique dealer from New England. I am Eannatum. Immortal High Witch. King of the greatest nation of its time."

She smiled. "You're more than that, you know. More than even I realized. We both are." She clasped his hands in hers and stared into his eyes. "We've been given this gift for a reason, Eannatum. Not just so we can live forever, grow more powerful, battle the Dark Ones. There's more to it. There has to be."

He hesitated for a moment. "I saw . . . something back

there at the house. A being . . . surrounding you like a nimbus."

"It was . . . something greater than any of us," she whispered. "A force beyond what I understood before. Beyond any God or Goddess I know by name . . . more like . . . All. Like All that ever was or ever will be, combined into one being that is you and is me and is . . . everything. Even Puabi."

He stared into her eyes. "And what does this being want from us?" he asked, his voice touched with wonder.

"I don't know. I only know . . . there's more to this than I have understood. We need to find out what, and set about the business of doing what we were put here to do."

"It has taken me four thousand years to understand one of the most important things I was put here to do, Nidaba. But I know it now. So perhaps we can start with that."

She nodded slightly. "Yes. Of course we can. What is it, Natum, that you believe you should be doing?"

He lifted a hand, cupped her cheek. "Loving you. Endlessly, deeply, passionately loving you, my beautiful priestess."

A joyful smile spread across her face and her eyes gleamed. "Eternity is a long time to love one woman."

"You are more like . . . like a collage of all womankind. Far beyond one woman. And I have already loved you for an eternity. If I couldn't stop in four thousand, five hundred years, even when I tried, why should I expect it to change from now until forever?"

"I cannot live as a mortal, Natum."

"And I cannot live without you, Nidaba." He smiled very slowly. "We should marry. The way we should have long ago. In fact, we should marry a hundred times, in every form of wedding rite that exists. We'll have a Christian ceremony, and a Buddhist one, a Wiccan handfasting, a Sumerian marriage rite, and everything else we can think of. Just . . . just tell me you still love me, Nidaba. Even if it's only a little bit. I know I've hurt you deeply, but I swear—"

"Shh." She pressed her lips to his and kissed him tenderly. When their lips finally parted, he was stunned to see tears in her eyes. "I have loved you for all my lifetimes, Eannatum. And for all those yet to come, I will love you still."

He looked at her beloved face, into her beautiful, dark eyes, and he knew she meant it. They were meant to be together, had been from the very first day they had met, a young prince and a precocious little priestess who wanted to learn to write her name. Chosen and placed on this planet for some purpose, yes, but one they could find, and understand, and ultimately accomplish only if they were together. This was their destiny.

"Gods, but we've wasted so much time," he said, pulling her close, savoring the miracle that was Nidaba.

"Yes, we have, my love. But we aren't going to waste any more."

Look for Puabi's return in "Immortality," a novella in *OUT OF THIS WORLD*, an anthology of stories by J. D. Robb, Laurell Hamilton, Susan Krinard, and Maggie Shayne, coming from Berkley in fall 2001!

Turn the page for an exciting preview of Puabi's story . . .

Prologue

For the first time in four thousand years, I was ready to die. And it looked as if I would get my wish. For the flames of Natum's home surrounded me, searing my flesh. Every breath I drew burned in my throat and lungs. And yet I could see him. Beyond the smoke and dancing tongues of ravenous fire, I could see him. My husband, the man I had loved, and his mistress wrapped up tight in his arms, safe outside, bathed in the cool night air while I roasted. I strained my eyes and watched them for a brief moment, through the melting window glass, beyond the flaming draperies and through the thickening smoke—and then the window exploded, and fire filled the opening. Even my preternatural eyesight couldn't pierce the wall of flames then.

It was over. He'd left me for dead, likely relieved to be rid of me.

I was tired, tired of living, tired of fighting to stay alive, and tired of hating. I told myself to just close my eyes. Just lie there, and let the hungry fire do its work. Natum would probably celebrate my demise.

The hell he would! I heard the words vaguely, from somewhere deep inside. Something, some part of me, rose up—fought back. Maybe it was the queen I had been. Or maybe it was some part of the immortal that just refused to die. Whatever it was, it made me struggle to my blistered feet. Insistent and irresistable, it forced me to drag myself through the inferno, toward what I sensed was the rear of the house. My dress caught fire. My hair smouldered and smoked, my skin blistered. I would have screamed in anguish had I a voice, or even a breath left in me. But I hadn't. If I'd been an ordinary woman, I'd have been dead. But I wasn't ordinary. I wasn't mortal. So I stumbled onward, a living torch, and I tasted the hell I'd never believed in. And finally, I fell, face down, unable to go any farther.

But it was cool, damp ground that greeted my fallen form. And a blessed soaking, icy rain pelted down on me from above. Life-giving rain.

Still that stubborn drive, that will to live, pushed me onward. I drew strength from the cool ground beneath me and from the rain, and called on it, to try to get to my feet. But I couldn't even rise as far as my knees. So I dragged myself forward. I clawed my fingers into the wet soil and I pulled myself along, inch by agonizing inch. I suppose I couldn't bear the thought of *them* coming upon me this way. Seeing me with my skin charred black, my hair burned away, my life force ebbing low. They would finish me off—if they found me.

Natum had taken everything from me. Everything. I wouldn't let his be the hand that took my life, as well. No, I would die in my own time, on my own terms.

And so I crawled . . . inched, toward the cliffs. "To hell with him," I whispered when at last I reached ahead of me to find there was no more ground to grasp. I opened my eyes, and saw yawning darkness and far, far below, the boiling white froth of the sea. "To hell with the both of them. And to hell with the world."

With one last effort, I, Queen Puabi, the darkest of the Dark Witches, pulled myself over the edge and into oblivion. And as I plummeted I wondered how many times I would drown and revive and drown again before my power ran out. And what would become of me then?

Could there be peace, for one as purely evil as I? Or would I remain trapped in some semblance of awareness even while the sea creatures fed on my flesh? I didn't know. I didn't care.

I didn't care.

Anything was better than the anguish I left behind.